Charles W. Tuttle

Capt. Francis Champernowne

The Dutch conquest of Acadie, and other historical papers

Charles W. Tuttle

Capt. Francis Champernowne
The Dutch conquest of Acadie, and other historical papers

ISBN/EAN: 9783337308223

Printed in Europe, USA, Canada, Australia, Japan

Cover: Foto ©Raphael Reischuk / pixelio.de

More available books at **www.hansebooks.com**

CAPT. FRANCIS CHAMPERNOWNE,

THE DUTCH CONQUEST OF ACADIE,

And Other Historical Papers.

BY

CHARLES WESLEY TUTTLE, ESQ., Ph.D.

EDITED BY

ALBERT HARRISON HOYT, A.M.,
WITH HISTORICAL NOTES.

WITH A MEMOIR OF THE AUTHOR,

By JOHN WARD DEAN, A.M.

BOSTON:
PRINTED BY JOHN WILSON AND SON,
University Press.
MDCCLXXXIX.

TABLE OF CONTENTS.

APPENDIX.

Table of Contents.

LIST OF ILLUSTRATIONS.

PREFACE.

CHARLES WESLEY TUTTLE was my intimate friend and companion, and his death is a source of abiding sorrow. By all who duly appreciated his character, ability, and attainments, his decease was greatly mourned. Speaking after the manner of men, he seems to have been cut off in the midst of his years, and before he had accomplished his most cherished purposes.

Mr. Tuttle contemplated an historical work of larger scope than anything he gave to the press, or anything he left in manuscript. His studies and many of his writings were but preliminary to this more elaborate undertaking. It will continue to be a matter of regret that this intent was not realized.

In his addresses and papers read before historical societies, in his contributions to the public press, and especially in his Life of Captain John Mason, the founder of New Hampshire, — a work completed and edited since the

author's death by John Ward Dean, A.M., with acknowledged ability and learning, — Mr. Tuttle gave ample evidence that he possessed in a large measure the qualifications
for writing authentic and authoritative history.

First of all, he was indefatigable and thorough in research, even to the minutest details. But, what is of the
highest importance, he estimated facts in their proper
relation and due proportion. To this it is to be added
that he was singularly free from the bias of place, of party,
and of early education. He had in a rare degree the
judicial faculty as applied to historical events and characters. Having reached his conclusions, he was fearless in
expression, — fearing nothing save the danger of falling
into error.

Born and bred in New England, and a life-long student of her history, he was proud of the stock from which
he grew, — a stock having its root in the civilization of Old
England, — the men and the women who colonized this
northern wilderness, and, under extraordinary hazards and
difficulties, laid the foundations for prosperous common-
wealths of self-governing peoples. A history of New
England colonization and of New England affairs in the
seventeenth century was suited to his trained faculties and
large information. Had he accomplished this, as he designed, the result could not have failed to be valuable.

Mr. Tuttle left a considerable number of papers on historical subjects which, it is evident, he intended to enlarge

and complete for publication in a durable form. These papers were carefully arranged and preserved by his widow and her father, the late Honorable John C. Park. Pursuant to the testamentary direction of Mrs. Tuttle, — as more fully appears on the fifty-eighth page of this volume, in the graceful sketch of her life by Mrs. Harriet Prescott Spofford, her intimate friend, — a selection from these papers has been made for the press. They constitute the chief portion of this collection of Historical Papers.

Having been asked to edit these Papers, I have endeavored to discharge the duty committed to me in such a manner as not to detract from the author's justly earned reputation. An effort has been made to verify every material statement by a careful reference to the authorities cited by the author and to other original sources of information. This has required much time and labor. Only such additions have been made as were necessary to complete the narrative of events, and only such corrections as were required in the light of facts discovered since the author's death. In no instance has any alteration been made which would in the slightest degree change his expressed opinions, judgments, or criticisms. These represent his deliberate conclusions, for which he was willing to be responsible.

Notes and other historical illustrations have been added by the editor where it seemed necessary or desirable. The most extended of these notes relate to Edward Randolph, and are intended to be illustrative of Mr. Tuttle's paper which precedes them. These notes contain much new matter pertaining to one of the most remarkable characters in the early history of New England.

The volume is enriched with portraits, views of historical scenes and places, and other illustrations. For the views of houses and scenes in Devonshire, the editor is indebted to the Reverend Richard Champernowne, M.A., the venerable Rector of Dartington, England, and to his nephew, the late Arthur Champernowne, Esquire, of Dartington Hall. To the Reverend Mr. Champernowne I am indebted also for the portrait of one of his most distinguished ancestors. He informs me that it is the portrait of Gawen Champernowne, grandfather of Captain Francis Champernowne. It is still preserved at the Hall, and bears the date of 1590. In the upper right-hand corner is the following inscription: " Il donne tout qui donne soi-même." This may properly be understood as referring to the valiant service in arms rendered by Gawen Champernowne to the Huguenots of France under one of their most eminent leaders, the Count Montgomery, whose daughter Gawen Champernowne married, as is related by Mr. Tuttle in the following pages.

The Appendix includes a considerable number of interesting papers and documents, obtained in part from foreign archives, and now for the first time printed. In the Paper (No. 1) entitled " Combinations for Local Government in New Hampshire," the editor has stated all that is known, as he believes, of the history and character of those early attempts at self-government.

Since Mr. Tuttle's death several of his most valued foreign correspondents have passed away. Among his English correspondents were the late Reverend Frederick Brown, M.A.; Arthur Champernowne, Esquire, already named; and Colonel Joseph L. Chester, D.C.L. Their warm interest in the author's researches entitles their names to this mention. Among the living, to whom the editor is much indebted, is Edmund Randolph, Esquire, of the Isle of Wight.

From John Ward Dean, A.M., the learned editor of the New England Historical and Genealogical Register, I have received valuable aid. The multitude of persons who for the space of twoscore years have profited by his remarkable knowledge of New England history will appreciate how serviceable that aid has been.

My acknowledgments are likewise due to John S. H. Fogg, M.D., of Boston, whose rich collection of original papers was always open to Mr. Tuttle, as it has been to the editor. I am also indebted to the Honorable Andrew M. Haines, of Galena, Illinois, not only for the use of his correspondence with Mr. Tuttle respecting the early history of Greenland, New Hampshire, but also for information on the same subject kindly communicated to me. Mention should also be made of assistance in my researches from the Honorable Charles Levi Woodbury, of Boston; from Mr. Edward F. Safford and Mrs. H. S. Hinman, both of Kittery, Maine; from J. Hamilton Shapley, Esquire, of Exeter, New Hampshire; from Mr. J. Clement Weeks and Charles W. Pickering, A.M., both of Greenland; and from Mr. Nathaniel J. Herrick, of Portland, Maine. My thanks are also due to Abner C. Goodell, Jr., Esquire, of Salem, for the generous loan of his copies of certain papers in the archives of the State. I should be remiss did I not acknowledge my obligations to the Honorable John J. Currier, of Newburyport, the executor of Mrs. Tuttle's Will, for his lively interest in the preparation of this volume, and for his wise counsel.

I gladly avail myself of this opportunity to return my thanks to Messrs. John Wilson & Son, University Press, Cambridge, and to their very excellent proof-readers and printers, who have so faithfully and successfully co-operated in the work of giving a fitting typographical dress to this volume. All here named have thus helped in various ways to carry into execution in a worthy manner the last Will and Testament of Mrs. Tuttle, in this final expression of her respect for the memory of her lamented husband.

A. H. H.

BOSTON, 16 MARLBOROUGH STREET,
20 September, 1889.

MEMOIR OF THE AUTHOR.

BY JOHN WARD DEAN.

MEMOIR.

CHARLES WESLEY TUTTLE was born in Newfield, Maine, Nov. 1, 1829. His father, Mr. Moses
Tuttle, was a descendant in the sixth generation from John
Tuttle, who settled at Dover, N. H., previous to 1640. His
mother, Mary, daughter of Lieut. Joseph Merrow, was the
fifth in descent from Dr. Samuel Merrow, or Merry, who
was an inhabitant of Dover as early as 1720. The subject
of this Memoir numbered among his ancestors many of the
early settlers of New Hampshire, and was allied by blood
to some of the most distinguished personages in the history
of that State.[1]

His boyhood was passed with his parents at Newfield,
and the rudiments of his education were obtained in the
schools there. From an early age he was an ardent admirer
of the works of Nature, and, having a keen eye and an
observing spirit, he soon became familiar with every flower,
tree, bird, and animal in his neighborhood. He delighted

---

[1] For Mr. Tuttle's paternal and maternal ancestry, see the New England
Historical and Genealogical Register,
vol. xxi. pp. 132–140; and the Hon.
John Wentworth's Wentworth Genealogy, Boston, 1878, vol. ii. p. 284.

in studying their peculiarities and habits. But his chief attraction was found in the sky above him. Night after night he watched with wonder and awe the myriad stars in the heavens, studying their motions when he had no help except that furnished him by a common almanac.

He availed himself of every source of information bearing upon his favorite study. When from twelve to fourteen years old, while attending the district school at Newfield, then taught by Mr. Eben Hurd, afterwards a physician, one of the scholars, Hannah Cranch Bond, some three or four years older than himself, had a copy of Elijah H. Burritt's book, The Geography of the Heavens, which she was studying. A schoolmate, Mrs. Hannah Drew Hutchings, now residing at Kittery Depot, Maine, who furnishes this information, writes to me that she remembers when Miss Bond, Charles, and herself were returning from spelling-schools in the evening, Miss Bond would often talk about astronomy, and point out the different stars and con- stellations; and she recollects that her schoolmate, at sub- sequent meetings, frequently expressed surprise at the judg- ment shown by Charles in his observations. Miss Bond was a niece of William Cranch Bond the astronomer, and a second cousin to Charles.

His mother died Aug. 23, 1845. Charles was the eldest child of the family which she left. Besides him there were four sons and one daughter,[1] all of whom are now dead, with the exception of three sons, — Freeman, residing at Cambridge, Mass.; Horace Parnell, attached to the Naval

[1] See Wentworth Genealogy, 1878, vol. ii. pp. 284-286, for their names and the events in their lives.

Observatory at Washington, a distinguished astronomer, the discoverer of Tuttle's Comet, and of two planets, Maia and Clytia; and Lieutenant Francis, of Oakland, Cal., an officer of the United States Revenue Marine.   Charles, who at the death of his mother was nearly sixteen years old, was placed in the family of his uncle, Mr. John W. Tuttle, of Dover, N. H.   Mr. Tuttle's wife was a sister, and he was a cousin, of Charles's father.   In religion they were Methodists, as were also — as might be inferred from the Christian names they gave to him, their eldest son — Charles's parents.   Under the influences of this denomination Charles was brought up.   Later in life his views inclined to Unitarianism, to which denomination his wife and her family belonged.   His father and uncle were Democrats in politics, and Charles acted with this party during his life.

At Dover, Charles attended the town schools, and made good progress in his studies.   An intimate friend of later years, the Rev. Alonzo H. Quint, D.D., who had charge temporarily of a school which he attended, has described him to me as a bright and studious scholar, and very quick of apprehension.   When the time arrived for him to select an occupation for life, he chose that of a printer, and pleaded hard that he might be apprenticed to it; but his uncle would not comply with his wishes, thinking it better that he should be taught his own trade, that of a carpenter. As an apprentice he was industrious and skilful, faithfully discharging all his duties.   The time not required for work, however, was devoted to study, and this was often protracted to the hour of midnight.   His passion for astronomy and mathematics continued, and books that taught him these subjects had a preference, though his reading made him familiar with belles-lettres, history, and general literature. He would sit with the household about him, with callers coming and going, and would know nothing of what occurred, so intent was he on the book before him. The neighbors made inquiries, too, as to who was at the Tuttles', for there was a light from one window all night long. His aunt, a sister of his father, sympathized with the lad, and to her he confided his plans of life. He said to her, "I mean to do something worth living for." This, it has been well said, was "the key-note of his single-minded and faithful spirit." His fondness for astronomy has been mentioned. "The sublime phenomena of the starry heavens made a deep impression on his youthful mind long before he could understand the science. The impressive phenomenon of an eclipse of the sun in 1836," when he was six years old, "forever fixed his interest in astronomy. The great comet of 1843, so grand and mysterious, also made a deep and lasting impression on him. While still a boy he constructed with his own hands the first telescope he ever saw, and was delighted to see in it all the wonderful celestial phenomena discovered by Galileo."[1]

This telescope is still preserved, and those who have seen it are surprised that so perfect a piece of mechanism should have been constructed, considering the disadvantages under which he labored. The telescope is now the property of Mr. James G. Shute, of Jamaica Plain, Mass., who was an apprentice in the same shop that Charles's uncle occu-

---

[1] Unpublished Memoir of Mr. Tuttle, author unknown.

pied when the telescope was constructed. Mr. Shute informs me that Charles could not wait to make a tripod on which to mount it before he tried it, but the two friends fastened it to a stake in a fence against a snow-drift, and took a look through it at the stars. It was on a very cold night, and Mr. Shute thinks it was in December. As neither of them had looked through a telescope before, they were both of course very much excited; but Mr Shute does not remember which looked through the telescope first. The friends had similar tastes, and Mr. Shute, who had a small library, loaned a number of books to his friend, among them Shakspeare's works, and a set of the writings of Thomas Dick, LL.D., whose books on astronomy were then very popular. It was the Practical Astronomy of Dr. Dick that suggested to the youth the construction of a telescope, and furnished directions for making it.

At one time Charles heard that Dr. Dick was coming to this country, and inquired about it of Dr. Robert Thompson, of Dover, a gentleman of literary and scientific tastes. Dr. Thompson was a native of Scotland and a graduate of the Royal College of Surgeons, and had recently settled at Dover. The conversation which followed, and the thirst for knowledge shown by the boy, caused the doctor, who had a large library, to say, "Charles, my library is always free to you." It is needless to state that the privilege was appreciated and gladly accepted. Young Tuttle found here many books on scientific as well as other subjects, the contents of which he eagerly devoured. Another place where he found food for his mind was the bookstore of Deacon Edmund J. Lane, who was often surprised by his inquiries for books that the veteran bookseller had never seen, and sometimes had never heard of.

He had heard of the Observatory, then recently established at Cambridge, and had an ardent desire to visit it. Availing himself of a holiday, he repaired to Cambridge. Without any introduction he presented himself at the Observatory and asked permission of Prof. William Cranch Bond, the Director, to examine the telescope. He was at first refused; but a remark which he made, as he was going away, struck Professor Bond with surprise, and he granted him permission. This was the first telescope, except the small one he had himself constructed, that he had ever seen.

In 1849 his father, who had the previous year married again, removed to Cambridge, Mass., and Charles went with him. It is said that Charles had some influence with his step-mother and his father in selecting Cambridge as their residence. Not long after their removal to that city Charles made the acquaintance of Truman Henry Safford, a youth of thirteen years, whose wonderful achievements in mathematics and astronomy were then astonishing the learned world. Young Safford, who was preparing to enter Harvard College, and was a frequent visitor at the Observatory, obtained the consent of Professor Bond to invite Mr. Tuttle to accompany him in his visits, — a privilege which was much guarded. The professor was struck with Mr. Tuttle's interest in and knowledge of astronomy. The result was that the latter was invited to accept a position there. Mr. Tuttle gladly availed himself of the opportunity. In July, 1850, three years after the Observatory had been established, he entered it as a student with a small stipend. Here he spent a few months in studying practical astronomy, and the use of astronomical instruments. The acquaintance with astronomy which he showed, — an acquaintance which he had derived solely from the study of books, and from sweeping the heavens nightly with his small telescope, — surprised Professor Bond.

Mr. Tuttle made such rapid progress in his astronomical studies, that in the following October he was elected by the College Corporation as Second Assistant Observer, and this election was unanimously confirmed by the Overseers, Feb. 7, 1851. He now had a larger salary, and entered with zeal upon his chosen profession, which he ardently hoped, and had good reason to believe, would be his life labor. His pursuit of astronomy, and particularly of practical astronomy, was rewarded with gratifying success.

Less than six months after he entered the Observatory as a student, and the month after his appointment as an observer, he was able to make an important addition to scientific knowledge. A series of observations on the planet Saturn and its rings had, since 1847, been made at the Observatory.[1] In one of these observations Professor Bond discovered new and interesting phenomena in connection with the rings of Saturn. On the 15th of November, 1850, Mr. Tuttle's observations led him to furnish a satisfactory scientific explanation of these phenomena by show-

[1] These observations were begun in the summer of 1847, and ended in the spring of 1857. An account of them is printed in the Annals of the Astronomical Observatory of Harvard College, vol. ii. pt. i., 1857, pp. 1–136.

ing the existence of a new interior ring, now known as the Dusky Ring of Saturn. Mr. Tuttle's record of his observations on that night is as follows: —

Saturn looks remarkably distinct, its belts are easily seen, and the division of the ring is quite conspicuous. I notice that dark penumbral light, on the inside of the interior ring at its greatest apparent elongation from the ball, which I have seen several times before on good nights. It resembles very much the unilluminated part of the disc of the moon just before and after conjunction with the sun. It is similar on either side of the planet. Its estimated width is about the same as that of the outer ring, or a little less. The greatest width of this dark ring is at a point on each side of the planet, in a line with the axis major of the other rings. From this point it diminishes as it passes behind and in front of the planet, where it appears as a dark line on the disc. Close to the inner edge of the interior ring, the inside of this dark ring is very sharply defined, but I cannot see that it is detached from it. A dark band of considerable width, the shadow of the ring on the disc of the planet, is seen below.[1]

Prof. William C. Bond appends the following note to the record as printed: —

On the evening of the 15th the idea was first suggested by Mr. Tuttle of explaining the penumbral light bordering the interior edge of the bright ring outside of the ball, as well as the dusky line crossing the disc on the side of the ring opposite to that where its shadow was projected on the ball, by referring both phenomena to the existence of an interior dusky ring. now first recognized as forming part of the system of Saturn. This explanation needed only to be proposed, to insure its immediate acceptance as the true and only satisfactory solution of the singular appearances which the view of

[1] Annals of the Astronomical Observatory, vol. ii. p. 48.

Saturn had presented during the past season, and which we had previously been unable to account for.[1]

In 1852 Mr. Tuttle, being worn out with long and uninterrupted application to his duties at the Harvard College Observatory, was advised to go into New Hampshire and there rest. " Upon this," he writes, " I resolved to visit the White Mountains, and satisfy a youthful longing and ambition. Taking a few scientific instruments for my amusement while absent, I set out for Dover, where I remained several weeks. While there I made an excursion to the Isles of Shoals, and stayed a few days at the Appledore House.[2] On my return to Dover I was so far recovered as to undertake my journey to the Mountains." He left Dover, July 13, and in two days reached Gibbs's hotel, and on the next morning, July 15, on horseback, began the ascent of Mt. Washington, reaching the summit at half-past twelve, after a ride from the hotel of three hours and forty minutes. His " chief purpose, a long cherished one, was to compare the lustre of the stars and planets, seen from that great height, with their lustre at the sea-level, and also to witness the sublime phenomena of a sunset and sunrise."

He found at the summit men engaged in building the first house erected on the top of that mountain. " It was a structure," he says, " whose walls were of rough stone, — quarried on the site, as I was informed, — one story high and of considerable length, with a wooden roof kept down to the walls by strong cables of rope thrown over the ridge

---

[1] Annals of the Astronomical Observatory, vol. ii. p. 48.

[2] A letter from him, dated July 7, 1852, from Appledore House, Isles of Shoals, was printed in the Dover Gazette about that time.

and fastened to rocks. Workmen were just finishing the southern gable, while others were employed inside." A straggling party of tourists followed him, but they returned about two o'clock in the afternoon. Mr. Tuttle asked permission to pass the night in the building, but was told that it was not ready. On explaining the object of his visit, he was told that he could stay if he would put up with their fare. Before sunset the summit of the mountain became enveloped in a thick cloud, shutting out the view of the heavens and the landscape on all sides. "A nightcap had been set," he writes, "on the head of Mt. Washington, and there remained till break of day, when it was silently and quietly withdrawn, to give me, what I much longed for, a sunrise, the most magnificent spectacle that I ever expect to witness. My disappointment in not seeing the stars and planets was much lessened on seeing the sun rise over so vast a region of territory. I did not cease to deplore my failure to see the midnight heavens. The workmen expressed their sympathy for me, but seemed to agree that I ought to be satisfied with having seen a sunrise, and with being the first traveller to sleep in a house on Mt. Washington."[1]

In the following autumn he took a voyage to Philadelphia, leaving Boston on the 25th of September, and arriving

---

[1] Three accounts of Mr. Tuttle's first ascent of Mt. Washington, in July, 1852, written by himself, have been printed. The first, a letter from Gibbs's Hotel, White Mountains, dated July 16, 1852, the day of his return from the summit, appeared soon after in the Dover Gazette. The second, a letter from Boston, dated Oct. 15, 1879, appeared in The State Press, Dover, N. H., on the 24th of that month. The third account, date unknown, was printed one year after his death, in Burt's Among the Clouds, — a newspaper printed on the summit of Mt. Washington, — July 14, 1882.

at Philadelphia on the morning of the 27th. A diary of this voyage is preserved among Mr. Tuttle's papers. He visited various places of interest in that historic city, and wrote two descriptive letters to the editor of the Dover Gazette, who printed them in his newspaper.[1]

On the evening of Thursday, March 8, 1853, at about nine o'clock, Mr. Tuttle discovered a telescopic comet in the constellation Eridanus, about five degrees south, preceding the bright star Rigel, and computed the elements of its orbit and an ephemeris of its course. This comet revolves around the sun in not less than sixteen hundred years. In a newspaper article by Mr. Tuttle, published in 1858, relating to fourteen comets which had then been discovered at the Harvard College Observatory, — nine by Mr. George P. Bond, one by himself, and four by his brother, Mr. Horace P. Tuttle, — the difficulties attending the discovery of telescopic comets are thus described : —

Few persons are aware of the patience and labor exercised by the astronomer in making discoveries of this kind. It requires several years' study and practice, to qualify one to discover a telescopic comet. It is undoubtedly very easy to look at a comet, already visible to the naked eye in the heavens ; but when it is required to discover an unknown one, wandering in its "long travel of a thousand years" in the profound abyss of space, the labor then becomes truly prodigious. The amount of physical suffering, occasioned by exposure to all kinds of temperature, the bending and twisting of the body when examining near the zenith, and the constant strain of the eye, cannot be fully understood and appreciated by one unacquainted with an astronomer's life.

[1] These letters bear date Sept. 29, and Oct. 1, 1852.

The astronomer with his telescope begins at the going down of the sun, and examines, in zones, with the utmost care and vigilance, the starry vault, and continues till the " circling hours " bring the sun to the eastern horizon, when star and comet fade from his view. It requires several nights to complete a thorough survey of the heavens ; and often these nights do not follow in succession, being interrupted by the full moon, by cloud and auroras, and by various other meteorological phenomena. He is frequently vexed by passing clouds fleeting through the midnight sky, and strong and chilly breezes of the night. His labors are continued throughout the year ; and his unwearied exertions do not slacken during the long wintry nights, when the frozen particles of snow and ice, driven before the northern blast, cause the stars to sparkle with unusual lustre, and his breath to congeal on the eye-piece of his telescope. It frequently happens that his labors are not crowned with a discovery until after several years' search.

It was with great satisfaction that Mr. Tuttle was able to announce to the scientific world, so early in his astronomical career, the discovery of a telescopic comet. Afterwards it was learned that the comet "had been seen two days earlier at Rome by Professor Secchi,"[1] but this discovery of course was unknown in this country.

It was not long before Mr. Tuttle became known among astronomers as a skilful observer and expert calculator. The archives of the Observatory show how diligently and extensively he explored the heavens while his health permitted him to do so. He and Prof. George P. Bond jointly made the observations of the fixed stars which form the first series of Zone Observations printed in the Annals of the Observatory.[2]

[1] Annals of the Astronomical Observatory, vol. i. p. clxxii.
[2] Annals, vol. i. pt. ii.

On Friday, the 26th of May, 1854, there was an annular eclipse of the sun; and preparations were made by Professor Bond to have it observed in New Hampshire from the top of Mt. Washington, and in its vicinity, points near the northern limit of the annular phase of the eclipse. In accordance with previous arrangements with Dr. Alexander Dallas Bache, the superintendent of the United States Coast Survey, three of Professor Bond's assistants, Mr. George P. Bond, Mr. Tuttle, and Mr. Richard F. Bond, were furnished with telescopes and time-keepers for this duty.[1] On the 17th of May they left Cambridge for the White Mountains. A diary of this expedition by Mr. Tuttle is preserved among his papers. After arriving at the White Mountains, Mr. Richard F. Bond proceeded to the Station House to take observations there, and Mr. George P. Bond and Mr. Tuttle, attended by guides, started for the summit of Mt. Washington, which they reached amid a drenching storm of rain and hail, on the afternoon of Thursday the 25th. "The storm raged fearfully, and the wind rushed around the summit with great velocity."[2] The rain continued on Friday, and as there was no appearance of its abating, at a quarter before 3 P.M. the party returned. After reaching the Glen House, there being indications that the clouds would clear away, the telescopes were adjusted for observations, but they were again doomed to disappointment.

The same month (May, 1854) Mr. Tuttle was obliged to resign his position at the Observatory, which he did with

[1] Annals of the Astronomical Observatory, vol. i. pt. i. p. clxxviii.
[2] Mr. Tuttle's Diary.

great reluctance.[1] " Too constant application to astronomical work brought on a serious difficulty with his eyesight, occasioned in part by the action of the intense light of celestial objects seen through the great refractor, and by reading the divisions on finely graduated instruments at night. A system of treatment failed to relieve him, and he was obliged to suspend observing altogether. After some delay, finding no relief for his eyes, he reluctantly resigned the position of Assistant Observer, a position which it had been the aim of his life to attain."[2] Professor Bond, in his annual report in 1854, thus refers to this event : —

During the year some changes have taken place in regard to the assistants at the Observatory. Mr. C. W. Tuttle found himself under the necessity of resigning his connection with the Observatory, in consequence of the failure of his eyesight, a circumstance much to be regretted, as he participated faithfully and ardently in our pursuits, and had proved an eminently capable assistant during the four years of his engagement. A journey to the West, afford-

[1] From an anonymous article published in the Evening Courier, Boston, June 7, 1865, I make these extracts : —
"The personnel of the Observatory has never been large ; and, in the order of events, those who first turned those magnificent instruments to the heavens are now no more. The lamented William Cranch Bond superintended the construction of the Observatory, and was its first Director. His son, the late George Phillips Bond, was appointed first assistant observer, and on the death of his father in 1859, became Director. Charles Wesley Tuttle was appointed an assistant observer in 1850, but his eyes proving unequal to the severe demands of astronomy, compelled him to resign after a few years' service. Truman Henry Safford, the eminent mathematician, who has won independent titles to distinction by important researches in theoretical astronomy, was then appointed assistant observer. These four embrace all who have had any official connection with the Observatory from its establishment in 1847.
"There are, however, three well-known scientific gentlemen who have been acting assistants at various times within the last ten years, — Major Sidney Coolidge, U.S.A., who fell in the great battle of Chickamauga, while gallantly leading his regiment to a charge ; Horace Parnell Tuttle, now in Europe, and attached to the United States Navy ; and Prof. Asaph Hall, now of the National Observatory at Washington."

[2] Anonymous Memoir before quoted.

ing relaxation from an undue exertion of his eyes, has so far arrested the progress of the malady, as to enable him partially to resume his duties as an assistant, while at the same time he has entered himself as a law student at Dane Hall. In July, Mr. T. H. Safford, of the graduating class of this year, was engaged as an observer and computer. More recently Mr. Sidney Coolidge has joined the Observatory.[1] .

Mr. Tuttle still kept up his interest in astronomy. "He not only made occasional telescopic observations, but he computed the parabolic elements of the comet of 1857, of the three that appeared in 1858, and in 1860 observed the occultation of Venus; and his several reports were published in the Astronomical Journal, printed in Boston, and edited by Dr. Benjamin Apthorp Gould."[2] He lectured on astronomical subjects, and contributed to the magazines and newspapers many articles on these subjects.

On leaving the Observatory he was undecided what profession to adopt. After much consideration he chose that of the law. On the 1st of September, 1854, he entered the Harvard Law School, where he remained till the 8th of August of the next year, attending the lectures, which gave him an opportunity to rest his eyes.

After the close of the academical year at the Law School, he went to England with one of the Chronometric Expeditions of the United States Coast Survey, for determining the difference of longitude between Liverpool, England, and Cambridge, Mass. Of this expedition Mr. Tuttle

[1] Annals of the Astronomical Observatory, vol. i. pt. i. p. clxxix.
[2] Memoir of C. W. Tuttle, Ph.D., by the Rev. Edmund F. Slafter, A.M., in Proceedings of the Massachusetts Historical Society, vol. xxi. p. 409.

had joint charge with his friend Mr. Sidney Coolidge. " In
this important undertaking about fifty chronometers were
transported across the Atlantic, a strict surveillance being
maintained over every circumstance which could affect their
performance.   It was a work demanding constant care, and
a great amount of labor and skill in conducting the astronomical observations, and in the treatment of the valuable
collection of instruments employed.   To the fidelity and
scrupulous care in the discharge of this responsible service
must in a great measure be attributed the complete success
of the enterprise.   The results of these expeditions form the
most important contribution which has yet been made to the
determination of the zero of longitude for the western continent." Messrs. Coolidge and Tuttle left Boston in the
steamer Asia at noon on Wednesday, Aug. 15, 1855, and
arrived at Liverpool, Saturday, August 26.   They returned
in the Africa, which left Liverpool at noon, Saturday, September 1, and reached her dock in Boston, Wednesday, the
12th of that month.

Mr. Tuttle kept a diary on his voyages to and from
England, and during his brief stay there.   His keen powers
of observation are shown by his graphic entries, which
have frequently a touch of humor.   The peculiarities of
his fellow-passengers, of whom, when he went on board, he
did not know a single person, with the exception of Mr.
Coolidge, are well described.   His chief attraction, however,
seems to have been the wonders of Nature.   A few of his
descriptions are here extracted : —

The wind is apparently blowing from the southeast.   It looks
finely now.   A cumuli stratus is dissolving into fine cumuli,

making that 'beautiful semblance of a flock at rest,' of Bloomfield. They do not appear so round as those seen on land, but only jagged and torn. The sun is approaching the horizon, and the ocean beneath it looks like liquid gold. . . .

A golden sunset. The sun went down amidst a gorgeous array of clouds. The sky was covered mostly with broken clouds, except near the horizon, where they were solid and unbroken. The sun seemed to break up the uniformity except where it went down and made a passage-way glorious to behold. The soft rose-color of the under side of the clouds fading away into gold and purple seemed to exceed anything I had ever seen. There is a landscape painting in the Athenæum representing the setting of the sun, and a flock of sheep lying down and standing up, on a little knoll, which I have frequently looked upon with much satisfaction, more especially perhaps on account of the peculiar softness of the colors of the clouds. The clouds at sunset to-night were scattered and tinted like those in that picture, which I well remember, having seen it this morning. . . .

Fog! Fog! Fog! Sometimes we see the sun glimmering through the mist, and then we hope for a speedy clearing up. But all of a sudden it disappears, and the fog gathers up close to the ship, so that we can see but little beyond the sides of it. I am tempted to think that we are in the land of Ossian, and I sometimes look for the ghosts through whose shadowy forms the stars are said to have "dim twinkled." . . .

It is impossible to describe the beautiful appearance of the several groups of gulls, with their snowy breasts rising and sinking in the blue waves. We passed a great many, and they made no effort to get far from us. Now and then a solitary one looked exceedingly beautiful. How contented they seem here in the solitude of the Atlantic. The storm and the winds give them no concern.

I cannot help leaning over the railing at the stern, gazing upon the path which the ship makes. We have heard of the trackless ocean; but for a mile the waters show the terrible track of the monster ship. When it is cloudy, or when the sun is east of the meridian, there may be seen splendid emerald tints over which liquid silver is gliding in a thousand different forms. . . .

I am not surprised at the murmurs of the sailors of Columbus's little expedition, when they had been many days at sea, at the improbability of return, and the dark uncertainty before them. I cannot look at the distant horizon, although I am well aware of what is beyond, without feelings bordering on the melancholy. There is something wonderfully sublime in looking at a horizon which has no bounds, and seems to terminate with the blue arch of heaven; the dark-blue waters foaming in the tempest, and the lonely gull gliding over the burnished summits of the billows, and skimming without effort the vales between them. . . .

This afternoon the clouds gathered as for a storm, and the ship rolled more than it has before on the voyage. At about four o'clock it commenced raining, and the ship began to roll more violently. The clouds were somewhat broken up in the west, and the sun went down giving them a crimson hue of indescribable beauty. Later it began to rain hard, and the clouds became thicker and blacker as the darkness of the night came on. At nine o'clock, ship's time, on deck, it was truly sublime. It rained very fast, and there was great darkness on every side. The sails were of inky blackness, and as the wind did not blow in a right direction to fill them, they flapped occasionally with a great noise, partly owing, I suspect, to their being wet. The officer of the deck, who had always heretofore had a numerous company of passengers about him, was now deserted. He was silent, walking or leaning over the railing of the ship, and I could see as he passed, by the light of the binnacle, his long oil-cloth coat glistening with rain-water. The wake of the ship for a great distance was a brilliant galaxy sparkling with meteoric stars. Indeed, it resembles one very much, and seemed a reflection of that "high and ample road" whose "dust is gold, and pavement stars." . . .

The waves are often compared to mountains; and though this is an exaggeration so far as size is considered, in every other respect the comparison is correct. The ship is now riding immense billows, the result of the storm yesterday, and they do indeed resemble mountains. . . .

A couple of extracts about his fellow-passengers must suffice.

I could not help observing what a jolly set of fellows the French passengers are. They are always lively in all sorts of weather. If they play cards, they talk and laugh continually, while a party of English close by, doing the same thing, sit in mopish silence. When these fellows walk the deck, they frisk all about, joking each other as they pass and repass. . . .

Just in the rear of the smoke-pipe, on the saloon deck, is the place for smokers, story-tellers, and loafers in general. The Yankees generally assemble there to talk of monetary affairs, which gives them a heart content for a while. The others consist of every nation under the sun, I believe, judging from their appearance and accent. . . .

They stopped at Halifax, Nova Scotia, on their voyage, and Mr. Tuttle gives a graphic description of his adventures there. On board, he witnessed some experiments in table-tipping. The vessel passed a number of steamers and sailing-vessels, the incidents in connection with which are duly recorded. He had expected to find much time for reading, but other things engrossed so much of his attention that he read but little. He spent a good part of one day in reading a recently-published book by a Northern man in defence of slavery. This he pronounced "a detestable book." "The Southerners," he adds, "cannot but be disgusted with it. It is the weakest apology for slavery I ever read."

Mr. Tuttle spent only a week in England. All the time not required on the chronometers, which were placed at the Liverpool Observatory, was devoted to visiting historic places with which his reading had made him familiar. His diary shows that he saw and understood, in the few days he was able to devote to sight-seeing, more than many a traveller has done in a month. This was owing to the fact that what he had gathered from books was so carefully treasured in his mind that he had it always at his command. London and Stratford-on-Avon were the only places at which he allowed himself to spend much time.

He made an early visit to Westminster Abbey, and looked with reverence on the graves and monuments of the illustrious dead of England. He was particularly attracted to Poets' Corner. He also heard in the chapel an impressive service. He visited the Tower of London, and saw the room in which Sir Walter Ralegh was confined; the Bloody Tower, where the young princes were murdered; the ancient armor and weapons of war, the crown jewels, and the other curiosities of the place. Somerset House, which then contained the rooms of the Royal Society and of the Royal Astronomical Society, was visited, and he saw there some of Newton's hair, and the reflecting telescope constructed by that illustrious man.   In St. Paul's he viewed the monuments, and went up to the Whispering Gallery, and also to the Golden Gallery, from which he looked out "over the length and breadth of London" on the people in the various streets who "appeared like mice," and it made his "brain turn to look at them."   He records also his visit to the British Museum, with its Gallery of Sculpture from Greece, Egypt, and Nineveh, — "the disinterred remains of three and four thousand years;" the Gallery of Animals; and the innumerable things besides these, all curious and instructive.   His visits to the National Gallery, to St. James Park, and the Suspension Bridge, are all noted in his diary.   The Parliament House and Westminster Hall were closed, and he could only see the exterior.

The localities which had been hallowed by the presence of those master minds, Shakspeare and Milton, seem to have had peculiar attractions for him.   Bread Street, where the latter was born, was visited, as was also St. Giles's Church, Cripplegate, where he and his father are buried.   I quote from Mr. Tuttle's diary this entry: —

When Paradise Lost and Comus enraptured me in America, I would gladly have gone any distance to pay my *devoirs* to so great a mind.   Here I was in the very church in which perhaps when he was in the flesh he may have bowed to Him whose

"Light discerns abstrusest thoughts."

John Fox the martyrologist is buried here, and some other persons of more or less note ; but all are obscure beside the "sun-brightness" of Milton ; Milton ever glorious, Milton whose Paradise Lost, "itself instinct with spirit," has been the source of so many happy hours to me, — hours whose values are inexpressible

"By numbers that have name."

All hail, Great Milton! The sweetness of thy voice never will cease to delight my ears. No!

"With thee conversing I forget all time,
All seasons and their change : all please alike."

While at London, Mr. Tuttle went to the Princess' Theatre, Oxford Street, where he saw Charles Kean and his wife, Mrs. Ellen Tree Kean, in Shakspeare's tragedy of Henry VIII. Mr. Kean took the part of Cardinal Wolsey, and Mrs. Kean that of Queen Katharine. He liked them both, but especially Mrs. Kean, who "acted nobly." The trial scene and the dream he pronounced "exquisite."

Mr. Tuttle also witnessed a parade of the Horse Guards, which he thought "grand," but not worth the delay it had caused him.

He left London Wednesday afternoon for Stratford-on-Avon, and arrived at midnight at the Shakspeare Hotel in that town. The next day was a perfect autumn day, and Mr. Tuttle was delighted with the beautiful scenery and pure atmosphere. He spent it in visiting the places connected with the memory of the bard of Avon. Early in the morning he went to the fields to hear the wonderful song of the skylarks, but was disappointed, being told that it was the season for them to moult, when it is rare to hear them sing. The scenery interested him much. He then visited the house where Shakspeare was born, and saw the various apartments in it. His feelings when the guide on entering a room said, " This is the room in which Shakspeare was born," are thus described in his diary : —

I stood for a moment in silence, reflecting upon the great event which had transpired in this room, — an event which gave to the world a poet unrivalled in every grace of language, and the master of every passion that moves the human breast.

After having thoroughly examined the house in which Shakspeare was born, he went to the church in which he was buried. After entering the Church of the Holy Trinity, he found himself among the sculptured memorials of celebrities of more or less note; but these did not detain him long. The guide advanced towards the railing before the altar, and said, " This is the great object which visitors come to see." At the same time he pointed with his hand to the north wall. " I raised my eyes," he writes, " and beheld the renowned monument of Shakspeare. The celebrated bust which preserves for us the lineaments of the great bard looked down upon me from its niche in awful majesty." The guide then rolled up a straw carpet which covered the floor directly in front of Shakspeare's monument, and Mr. Tuttle's eye rested on the famous inscription beginning, " Good friend, for Jesus' sake forbear," which covers his dust. "Awful lines," Mr. Tuttle calls them, "such as never before guarded the resting-place of mortal. It is useless," he adds, " to attempt to describe my feelings while I gazed upon the inscription. No one has dared to violate the dreadful injunction by opening his grave." The brass tablet bearing the epitaph of Shakspeare's wife, and the memorials

4

of other members of Shakspeare's family, and of other persons connected with his history, were reverently examined, as the diary shows.

Mr. Tuttle passed the site of New Place, where Shakspeare lived after his return from London, and where also he died. The building, which was ruthlessly demolished more than a hundred years ago, is called in early conveyances the " Great House," and Mr. Tuttle remarks : " It cannot but give the highest satisfaction to the admirers of ' the myriad-minded poet,' that his last days were passed in the best house that his native town afforded." The site is now a garden enclosed by high walls. He visited the Town Hall, " every part of which showed its antiquity," and saw, among other things, the pictures of Shakspeare, Garrick, and others. He then went to a house in Bridge Street, where various relics of Shakspeare were collected, — a family that formerly occupied the house in Henley Street, where Shakspeare was born, having removed them to this place. An " arm-chair without arms," in which it is claimed the bard used to sit ; a table much cut away, said to have been his ; a veritable piece of the mulberry-tree said to have been planted by Shakspeare himself ; and other relics of more or less authenticity, are noted in the diary. Here he found the registers of visitors to Shakspeare's birthplace in Henley Street, from 1812 to 1820, and noted many American names. Mr. Tuttle also made a pilgrimage to Shottery, to see the building claimed to be " Anne Hathaway's cottage."

He left the town that afternoon to return to Liverpool, taking the stage-coach for Leamington from Stratford at the Red Horse tavern. While waiting here for the coach he entered into conversation with an Englishman who had dined with him at the Shakspeare Hotel. Perceiving by the address on Mr. Tuttle's trunks that he was an American, he asked him if he had been to the Crystal Palace at Syden-ham. On his replying in the negative, he exclaimed, "Why! I should rather have gone there than come here to Strat-ford to see 'Shakspeare's house.'" Mr. Tuttle said nothing; but when the Englishman asked him why so many Ameri-cans came here to "see Shakspeare," he briefly told him of the high estimation in which Shakspeare's writings were held by every intelligent American.

After his return to America Mr. Tuttle published in the Dover Gazette a series of articles on the historic places he had visited. One article is entitled, A Few Hours in West-minster Abbey; the title of another is, A Visit to the Tower of London; while four articles are devoted to A Glimpse at Stratford-upon-Avon. They show a familiar knowledge of history, acute observations, and just reflections.

The sea-voyage and a long period of comparative rest improved his eyes, so that after his return from England he was able, in November, 1855, to enter the law office of the Hon. Harvey Jewell, of Boston, and complete his law studies. In 1856, at the March term of the Massachusetts Superior Court, held at Boston, he was admitted a member of the Suffolk bar, and authorized to practise in the courts of this State. He began practice that year at 20 Court Street, Boston, but removed to Newburyport in the spring of 1857, where he continued to practise his profession. Two years later he returned to Boston, where he practised till his death. His first office was at 46 Washington Street.

Here he remained till Jan. 1, 1860, when he formed a law partnership with the Hon. Richard S. Spofford, Jr., and removed to No. 81 in that street. They had also an office at 31 State Street, Newburyport. In November, 1860, they removed their Boston office from Washington Street, and took one at 27 Tremont Row, where they were joined by the Hon. Caleb Cushing. In July, 1864, Mr. Tuttle removed to 47 Court Street, where he remained nearly five years. In 1869 he took an office at 32 Pemberton Square, from which place he removed, about 1870, to 25 Bromfield Street. In the spring of 1872 he returned to 27 Tremont Row, which was his law office till his death.

On the 15th of October, 1858, he was admitted to practise in the United States Circuit Court, and on motion of Mr. Cushing, March 1, 1861, to practise in the Supreme Court of the United States. In October, 1860, he was appointed a United States Commissioner, in place of Mr. Sidney Webster, who had resigned the office. On the 18th of November, 1874, the United States Court of Alabama Claims appointed him a commissioner to take testimony to be used before that court.

In 1865 he was elected a member of the New England Historic Genealogical Society, and from that time took an active part in its proceedings. He was a member of the board of directors from January, 1867, till his death, and was for a time its secretary. He was also a member of the publishing committee, served on various special committees, and read papers at meetings of the Society. In 1873 he was chosen a member of the Massachusetts Historical Society. Here he was a member of the Council, acted on

special committees, read papers at its meetings, and otherwise contributed to the work of the Society. He was also
an honorary member of the New Hampshire Historical
Society, and a corresponding member of the State Historical Societies of Maine and Wisconsin, besides being a
member of various other associations.[1] On the 8th of September, 1859, he was elected a member of the Ancient and
Honorable Artillery Company. In 1872 he became a member of the Prince Society, in which he successively held the
offices of treasurer and corresponding secretary; was active
in procuring its act of incorporation in 1874, and his name
appears in the act. In 1854, while connected with the Observatory, he received from Harvard College the degree of
Master of Arts. He is said to have been "the youngest
person that had ever received an honorary degree from that
College." In 1880, Dartmouth College conferred upon him
the degree of Doctor of Philosophy.

He early became interested in the history of his ancestors.
In the Dover Enquirer, Nov. 25, 1854, appeared an article

[1] The following is a list of the historical societies of which he is known
to have been a member: 1. Essex Institute, Salem, Mass., elected Dec. 9,
1863, corresponding member; 2. New
England Historic Genealogical Society,
Boston, Mass., April 5, 1865, resident
member; 3. State Historical Society of
Wisconsin, Madison, March 20, 1868,
corresponding member; 4. Pemaquid
Historical Monument Association, Bris-
tol, Maine, April 3, 1872, honorary; 5.
Massachusetts Historical Society, Bos-
ton, Feb. 17, 1873, resident; 6. New
Hampshire Historical Society, Concord,
Jan. 17, 1874, corresponding; 7. Maine
Historical Society, Portland, July 22,
1874, corresponding; 8. Maine Genea-
logical and Biographical Society, Au-
gusta, Feb. 7, 1876, corresponding; 9.
Newport Historical Society, Newport,
R. I., Oct. 23, 1877, corresponding; 10.
Antiquarian and Historical Society of
Old Newbury, Newburyport, Mass.,
Feb. 20, 1878, corresponding; 11. New
Hampshire Historical Society, Concord,
July 16, 1880, honorary. He may have
belonged to other historical societies.

He was also elected a member of the
two following associations: 1. Boston
Society of Natural History, Boston, Jan.
20, 1859, member; 2. Appalachian
Mountain Club, Boston, June 15, 1876,
active member.

by the Rev. Dr. Quint, on John Tuttle, his emigrant ancestor, one of the founders of Dover, N. H.[1] Mr. Tuttle was
able, with the aid of public and private records, and the
memory of his relatives, to connect himself with this John
Tuttle, and began collecting everything he could find relating to the history of the family. On the 2d of October,
1865, he issued a circular, "To the Living Descendants of
John Tuttle," stating that he had collected details relative
to upwards of five hundred descendants, extending to the
ninth generation. He solicited further genealogical records
to complete the work, and also subscriptions to a book he
intended to prepare, the cost of which would be not far
from a dollar and a half. He adds:—

> Through the medium of wills and deeds I have ascertained the
> site and homestead of our emigrant ancestor on Dover Neck. It is
> a charming spot, forming a part of a wonderfully beautiful and pic-
> turesque landscape. I suggest that a granite monument, with ap-
> propriate inscriptions, be erected there to mark permanently a site
> forever memorable in the annals of our family, and to commemorate
> the name and memory of one in whom we all have an equally affec-
> tionate interest. A small contribution from every descendant would
> procure a column commensurate in size to the end proposed. The
> completion of such a monument might be made the occasion of a
> family reunion at that place, so much desired by many members
> of the family.

Mr. Tuttle published an article on The Tuttle Family
of New Hampshire, in the New England Historical and
Genealogical Register, for April, 1867; but the intended

---

[1] This was No. 146 of Historical
Memoranda, a series of articles com-
menced in that paper by the Rev. Alonzo
H. Quint, D.D., July 31, 1850.

volume was never completed. In his genealogical researches he found that he was a descendant of Ambrose Gibbins, the trusted agent, at the settlement on the Pascataqua, of Capt. John Mason, the founder of New Hampshire. This fact awakened in him a deep interest in Mason himself, of whom the accounts were very meagre, and he began to collect matter relating to him. In April, 1871, he announced, in the New England Historical and Genealogical Register, his intention of writing a memoir of Captain Mason, and on Wednesday evening, the 14th day of the following June, he read before the New Hampshire Historical Society at Concord a paper on Mason, embracing much new matter which he had collected from English and American sources. The paper was repeated before the New England Historic Genealogical Society, April 3, 1872, additional matter obtained by subsequent researches being introduced.

Mr. Tuttle also prepared a paper on Capt. Francis Champernowne, which was read for him by Gen. John Marshall Brown, before the Maine Historical Society at Bath, Feb. 19, 1873. The next year he began writing a series of articles on Champernowne, three of which appeared in the Historical and Genealogical Register for April, July, and October, 1874. Another paper on which he bestowed much laborious research is entitled The Conquest of Acadia by the Dutch. It was read before the Maine Historical Society at Portland, March 22, 1877, and repeated before the Newport Historical Society, Oct. 24, 1877, the New England Historic Genealogical Society, June 4, 1879, and before the New York Historical Society, Nov. 4, 1879.

Mr. Tuttle continued to collect materials for his Life of Capt. John Mason, with the intention of issuing a volume on the Founders of New Hampshire. In 1873, while he had the matter under consideration, he was invited by the Prince Society, of which he was an officer, to prepare for the Publications of that Society a volume on Mason, in which should be embodied a reprint of Mason's tract on Newfoundland, first published in 1620, his only known publication; the several American charters in which he was a grantee; and other papers illustrating the history of Mason and his colonization enterprises. This invitation Mr. Tuttle accepted, and continued his researches as he had opportunity. He delayed, however, to prepare the work for the press, in the hope of obtaining more materials. His principal hope was that the English Commission on Historical Manuscripts, which had brought to light many important documents found in private hands, would discover valuable manuscripts illustrating the life and services of Capt. John Mason, and that possibly the papers of Mason himself, as well as those of Sir Ferdinando Gorges, would be found. These would throw much light not only on the events of Mason's life, but upon the early history of New England.[1] After Mr. Tuttle's death his unfinished work on Mason was placed in my hands to be prepared for the press. This task I performed to the best of my ability, and in the autumn of 1887 the work was given to the public by the Prince Society, as one of its Publications. It is evi-

---

[1] The many difficulties encountered by Mr. Tuttle in these researches are narrated in his remarks before the New Hampshire Historical Society, at its annual meeting in 1880, printed in the Boston Evening Traveller, Oct. 9, 1880.

dent, from the materials which he left, that he intended to make it a more elaborate work than it was deemed advisable to attempt. No one regrets more than his editor that Mr. Tuttle did not live to complete the book and carry it through the press.

Some of the more important articles by him in the Historical and Genealogical Register are the following: The Tuttle Family in New Hampshire, 1867; The Isles of Shoals, 1869; Col. Nathaniel Meserve, a Memoir, 1869; Christopher Kilby, a Memoir, 1872; John Alfred Poor, a Memoir, 1872; Sketches of Capt. Francis Champernowne, 1874. Among the articles in the Proceedings of the Massachusetts Historical Society may be named Edward Randolph, 1874; Belknap's House at Dover, N. H., 1875; William Blaxton, 1875; Historic Mansions in Devonshire, 1876; The Spelling of Sir Walter Ralegh's Surname, 1877; Hon. Benjamin F. Thomas, 1878; The Indian Name, Pascataqua, 1878; Hon. Caleb Cushing, 1879; Hon. George S. Hillard, 1879; Report of the Committee on a Circular Letter from the Superintendent of the United States Coast Survey, on Restoring and Preserving the Ancient Names of Places, 1879; Indian Massacre at Fox Point, 1879; The Establishment of a Court of Vice Admiralty over America, 1879. One of the articles printed in the New England Historical and Genealogical Register, and three that appeared in the Proceedings of the Massachusetts Historical Society, were reprinted as separate works. Among Mr. Tuttle's manuscripts are lists of his contributions to the Historical and Genealogical Register; the Proceedings of the Massachusetts Historical Society; Notes and Queries, published in London; the Historical Magazine; the American Historical Record; the Magazine of American History; and the Maine Genealogist and Biographer. I intend to deposit with the New England Historic Genealogical Society, and the Massachusetts Historical Society, manuscript copies of these lists.

He frequently lectured before lyceums. These lectures were delivered at Boston, Newburyport, and other places. In the spring of 1861 he delivered in Boston a course of public lectures on the Astronomy of Comets. On the 19th of April, 1880, the anniversary of the battle of Lexington, he delivered an address at the Hawthorne Rooms, Boston, on Hugh Percy, Lieutenant General in the British Army. In the following December he delivered the Bi-Centennial Address before the New Hampshire Historical Society, commemorating the establishment, in 1680, of the first civil government over that province.

He contributed articles to Dr. Gould's Astronomical Journal, to Dr. Brünnow's Astronomical Notices, and to various antiquarian and historical magazines. He was a frequent contributor to the newspapers of elaborate articles on astronomical and historical subjects. He wrote for Johnson's Cyclopædia valuable historical articles. He contributed also many articles illustrating the history and genealogy of New Hampshire, and particularly of Dover, to the series which the Rev. Dr. Alonzo H. Quint had begun in the Dover Enquirer, under the head of Historical Memoranda.[1]

[1] The articles by Mr. Tuttle in the Historical Memoranda, seventeen in number, are Nos. 246, 248 to 258, 262, 265 to 267, 292. They appeared in the Dover Enquirer between July 19, 1866, and Jan. 18, 1877.

A year before Mr. Tuttle's death he prepared a list of the works upon which he was engaged, which was printed in the New England Historical and Genealogical Register for July, 1880. Since his death one of these works has been prepared for the press, and printed; namely, Capt. John Mason, published by the Prince Society, as before stated. His Life of Champernowne, his account of the Conquest of Acadie by the Dutch, and other papers, have been edited by Mr. Tuttle's friend, Albert H. Hoyt, A.M., and will be printed with historical documents in the present volume.

The following is a list of Mr. Tuttle's publications in separate form: —

   I. Christopher Kilby. A Memoir. Boston, 1872. 8vo, pp. 15. Reprinted from the New England Historical and Genealogical Register, January, 1872.

  II. Caleb Cushing. 8vo, pp. 6. Reprinted from the Proceedings of the Massachusetts Historical Society, January, 1879.

 III. Indian Massacre at Fox Point in Newington. 8vo, pp. 6. Reprinted from the Proceedings of the Historical Society, June, 1879.

 IV. New Hampshire without a Provincial Government. 1689–1690. An Historical Sketch. Cambridge, 1880. 8vo, pp. 13. Reprinted from the Proceedings of the Historical Society, October, 1879.

  V. Capt. John Mason, the Founder of New Hampshire: including his Tract on Newfoundland, 1620; the American Charters in which he was a grantee; with Letters and other Historical Documents, and a Memoir. By Charles Wesley Tuttle, Ph.D. Edited, with Historical Illustrations, by

John Ward Dean, A.M. Boston : Prince Society. 1887. Fcp. 4to, pp. xiv + 492.
VI. Historical Papers. Edited by Albert H. Hoyt, A.M. [The present volume.]

Mr. Tuttle's contributions to historical literature are of great value. Their trustworthiness is a marked characteristic. He was always ready to follow truth, though it led him to give up preconceived opinions. His researches were thorough and unremitting. His temperament prevented him from leaving a subject before he had exhausted it as far as there was a possibility of doing this; before he had gathered all the facts concerning it within his reach; in fact, before he had seen it on all its sides. Another characteristic was a breadth of thought which enabled him to comprehend all the bearings of the subject on which he was engaged. He was critical in the use of language, and bestowed much labor on the construction of his sentences, and in correcting and polishing them. The result was that he expressed his ideas with clearness and perspicuity, and yet with beauty and grace.

The Rev. Andrew P. Peabody, D.D., LL.D., of Cambridge, has furnished me with the following reminiscences of Mr. Tuttle : —

I first knew Mr. Tuttle as a young lawyer in Newburyport, where he was held in very high regard by the best people. After I became a resident of Cambridge I saw him often, and he soon became, and continued through the residue of his life, a not infrequent visitor at my house. I became greatly interested in him as a man of superior scientific attainments, literary taste, and general culture, and as thoroughly conscientious, upright, high-minded, and true-hearted. At an early stage of my intimacy with him he delivered a course of lectures on astronomy, in Boston, to a small but intelligent audience. I commenced attending the course for his sake; I continued attendance for my own. The lectures showed a strong grasp and clear comprehension of the science, and a rare capacity of statement and exposition. With the advantages of voice and manner, which he lacked, he might have commanded and delighted large audiences. I had from time to time conferences with him on historical subjects, especially on matters appertaining to the early history of New Hampshire, in which we had a common interest. His honesty would not suffer him to perform any work in that department otherwise than faithfully to the utmost of his ability; and he had a love for such work that enabled him to perform it with no reference to any possible revenue of reputation or of gain, but solely as a labor of love. I of course knew nothing in detail of his professional standing, but I have been told, by those who knew, that he was a well-read lawyer, and capable, prompt, and trustworthy in the discharge of business. In my estimate of his character, he seems to me to have possessed a large endowment in talents of pure gold, while his chief deficiency was in brass, which, if not the most precious of metals, is often needed to keep gold in currency.

The Hon. Charles Levi Woodbury, of Boston, well known as an able lawyer, who shared Mr. Tuttle's historical tastes, thus wrote concerning him:—

Mr. Justice Clifford, who had in his youth practised law at Newfield, Maine, where Charles had lived, feeling a sympathy for his already distinguished and peculiar career, very kindly gave him the appointment of a Commissioner of the Circuit Court of the United States. The duties of this position were those of a committing magistrate under the United States penal laws, and the taking of depositions, etc., in civil matters,—a kind of Master in Chancery work. Mr. Tuttle very readily acquired a familiarity with these duties, and obtained good success in attending to them. Particularly useful to him was the employment of taking down and presiding over the long examinations of the numerous witnesses and experts in some of the contested patent cases. I have myself sought his service in such cases, and indeed perhaps I was one of the first to do so. This was many years ago. I know that afterwards he had some patent cases himself, which he attended to with model assiduity.

Mr. Tuttle had considerable and varied business in the State Courts, and also in the Federal Courts, both here and at Washington. This he performed with scrupulous care, and with a skill that indicated a knowledge of the principles and practice of the profession. As his historical studies grew upon him, he formed a resolution to banish them entirely from the usual business hours of the day; and he kept this resolution with an admirable self-control. The consequence was not so well for him. Before and after office hours a second day's work would go on, earnestly and without self-restraint, until tired nature drove him to his bed exhausted, to rise the next day and renew the routine. The bow was ever strung, and the tough hickory failed at last.

Though Mr. Tuttle could not be called an orator, he argued a point very well. Occasionally, many years ago, he indulged in political oratory on the stump with decided success. This was due more to his straightforward honesty and blunt sincerity than to the conventional rules which Quintilian and David Paul Brown have laid down for the forensic art. Though always attractive and amiable, he would not sacrifice his opinions to please others. He enjoyed the respect of the Courts where he practised, and the esteem of his comrades at the bar. He was a good talker; and whenever he concentrated his attention on a subject, he showed natural powers of mind that made him the peer of any other laborer in the particular field.

He had a strong affection for New England. I recall that when the executors of General Cushing wished to employ him to go to Minnesota, and look after the titles, etc., of the large landed property of the estate there, he declined, remarking, with decided emphasis, that he did not wish to cross the Hudson River ever again in his life!

The Hon. Richard S. Spofford, of Newburyport, who for some years was a law-partner of Mr. Tuttle, furnishes the following reminiscences : —

My acquaintance with Charles Wesley Tuttle began in 1858, when, being several years my senior, he was practising law at Newburyport. Absent from the city during his earlier residence there, I had nevertheless heard much of Mr. Tuttle's character and acquirements before I had seen him, and also of the warm friendship between himself and my own family, growing out of his intimacy with my honored father, and arising from studies congenial to both, especially that of astronomy. I was thus prepared, on my first introduction to Mr. Tuttle, to greet him with cordiality, and begin the experience of that heart-warm regard which subsisted between us until his death. Having continued for some months subsequently to the period of which I have spoken, in the successful practice of the law at Newburyport, Mr. Tuttle afterward changed his residence to Boston, leaving behind him a host of admiring friends. Here soon after he formed a partnership with myself. We began business in what is now the Rogers Building, where we remained about a year, removing then to 27 Tremont Row. During our occupancy of the latter offices, in common with Hon. Caleb Cushing and Mr. Nicholas St. John Green, then in the pride of his success as a lecturer in the Law Schools of Boston and of Cambridge, our neighbors on the same floor were a group of remarkable men with whom there was daily a delightful intercourse ; among them, Theodore H. Sweetser, that Dantonesque legal advocate and leader of the bar; Governor Andrew, fresh from his wonderful civic career; and William S. Gardner, that upright judge and urbane gentleman, whose recent death numbers all except myself with the great majority. With but brief interruption we continued in these offices, although not in the relation of partners, to the hour of Mr. Tuttle's death.

In the earlier years we were not only in the constant association of office life, but we occupied common quarters for our place of residence; and I can therefore speak, as one having full knowledge, of his private character, his public relations, and his abilities and attainments; there was that about him, at the time, which made him an object of peculiar interest to all who knew him. Having already achieved high eminence as an astronomer, he had been obliged through the failure of his eyes to abandon his lofty pursuit, and to look to the profession of law as the means of obtaining a livelihood, and of gratifying his ambition. He was thus, as it were, an involuntary exile from the region of his pride and aspiration; and it was not to be expected that in his new surroundings he could wholly divest himself of his early predilection for scientific studies, in which he always continued to feel a profound and active interest, — a predilection, indeed, constantly kept alive, and in a measure gratified, by the success attending the career of his eminent brother, Horace Parnell Tuttle. One of my most pleasurable remembrances is that of the meetings of the two brothers, and their mutual enthusiasms, when some new astronomical discovery brought them together. Almost totally uninformed on the subject which at such times they discussed, and even of the terms employed, I had my share of the enthusiasm in my appreciation of theirs, to say nothing of the offhand names with which we would christen, to suit our fancies, some newly-discovered asteroid, or a comet that had been waiting for I know not how many thousands of years to be discovered by one of the Tuttles. But while thus cherishing his astronomical tastes, he was never neglectful of his professional obligations.

Much of our business was in connection with important cases, in which Mr. Cushing — then but recently having closed his term of office as Attorney-General of the United States — was engaged, and than whom no one more highly appreciated Mr. Tuttle, whether in his professional or other relations. During our partnership we were employed in many suits in which Mr. Cushing was principal counsel, of which the most notable were the Federal Street Church case ; certain amicable suits to obtain a judicial construction of the will of John Quincy Adams ; the Portland City case, involving the title to Portland City, Oregon ; the Myra Clarke Gaines case ; and others of no inconsiderable magnitude. Always a patient and conscientious worker, Mr. Tuttle's zeal in his profession was not less earnest than that exhibited while engaged in his astronomical labors. He neglected no interest intrusted to his oversight, and shrunk from no labor which any professional exigency demanded.

I need not speak further of Mr. Tuttle in his professional relations. But how can I sufficiently portray his qualities of a social and friendly character? The sweet simplicity of his nature, the integrity of his life and convictions, his earnestness and enthusiasm, his apprehensive mind and sound judgment, the originality of his intellectual perception, illustrated by an enlarged erudition, and interpreted with a splendid diction modelled on that of his favorite authors, Milton and Burke, — all of these high qualities combined to make him, to the recognition of those who came within the range of his companionship, and especially of his friendship, "the continent of what part a gentleman would see."

It was not until the later years of his life that his historical studies began to exert that emphatic influence which induced him to bestow so much time on them, and to dedicate himself with such self-forgetting earnestness to the special objects of this character which had enlisted his thought. But if ever such pursuits were to their devotee an exceeding great reward, these were such to Mr. Tuttle ; and it is a melancholy reflection that, aside from this reward, he had little other for labors as valuable, as original, and as instructive as any which have claimed the attention of the histo-

rian and genealogist. He was as a youth among the elders of the
leading historical societies of Massachusetts and of other States;
but there was no immaturity in his intuitions, endeavors, or accom-
plishment. His unexpected death in the midst of his labors was
the more deplorable as it left in an incomplete condition work to
which he had given years of effort, and which made his loss yet more
deeply felt than did his remarkable personal qualities.

For myself, I can only add that, thus endeared by so many ties
of personal intercourse and relationship, and so many years of un-
marred friendship, his loss was an irreparable one, and my sense
of it as keen as that of the Latin poet when he declared that the
departure of his friend took away "Animæ dimidium meæ,"— the
half of my soul!

Mrs. Harriet Prescott Spofford, the well-known author,
wife of the writer of the preceding recollections, thus wrote
to Mrs. Tuttle concerning her husband, — the subject of
this memoir : —

When I first saw Charles, the impression that he made upon
me had a strange romance about it. He had come to the place
where I lived, a comparative stranger, but we all knew that he
had been compelled to abandon the aim of his life and the dream
of his heart, owing to threatened blindness, and to open a new
path for himself; and that fact gave him a sort of heroic cast in
our thoughts. I never divested him of a certain poetry that hung
about him then; he seemed to belong to the region of great unknown equations, to be a part of the world of stars, out of which
he had come into our more common and prosaic life. He had
lived among those stars ever since he was a child, fashioning with
his own hand, when a boy, the tubes for a telescope, to buy the
lenses of which he had saved all his pennies; but when he took
it out, finished for its trial, his excitement was so great that he
could not look through it, and another, who had been nearly as

much interested in it as he himself was, had to take the first view
of the satellites of Jupiter and the phases of Venus.

He was just as eagerly intent on everything he undertook all
his life long. On the Observatory roofs he used the astronomical
instruments till his eyes were nearly destroyed by the star and
lunar rays; and later in life he made his historical studies and
research with the same rapt ardor, pursuing a theory or hunting
down a fact to the absolute forgetfulness, for the time being, of
almost everything else in life, with small idea of the passage of
time or the value of money. Perhaps his leading characteristic
was this eminent single-mindedness; and the power of concen-
trating thought belonging to it gave him a singular force. The
mathematical habit of his mind produced in him a rare discern-
ment and discrimination almost like another sense,—the sense of
truth; and when he stated a thing positively, you would be sure
that it was as fixed and demonstrable as one of the immutable
facts of the universe. With this, moreover, there was the trans-
parency and the guilelessness of a child, although far from him
were all childish things; for the nature of his own pursuits made
everything less noble appear frivolous to him, and it seemed indeed as if he never saw such things, but that his extended vision
looked over them and beyond them. His mind was a treasure-
house of great ideas and realities; and, earnest, passionate, and
natural to the last degree, he never could fit the words to them
fast enough, as they poured forth in any moment of enthusiasm.
His affections partook of this general earnestness of his nature;
where he had once bestowed them, the fibres of his being went
with them; and unlike most of the promoters of science, he was
singularly tender-hearted. He loved a child, a singing bird, a
flower, as he loved a star; but it was the star that led him away
into regions where he saw the beckoning hand of God; for he
had his times and seasons of that devoutness which the poet
Young thought must seize every student of the nightly heavens
who is not mad.

I never shall forget a night that I spent with him, in the company of my husband, — who was long in close professional and family relationship with him, a most tender attachment being cherished between them, — in the Cambridge Observatory, looking through the immense telescope there. It would have been ho different had we gone into the realm of unreal things, and among the arcana of magic, while that great engine tipped at the touch of the finger, while the swift sliding stars shot like meteors over the field before the clockwork was attached, while the iron dome turned and crackled as if the heavens rolled together like a scroll, while we had the freedom of the vast outer universe where double stars resolved their separate splendor, and nebulæ shed their shining vapors and hung revealed a moment. In his knowledge, his enthusiasm, his gentleness, his genius, I thought of him that night as a greater wonder himself than the wonders he showed us; he seemed like the lord of the domain, into which one night years afterward he was so swiftly and fortunately translated; and I think of him now only with those of whom the old Rosicrucian legend speaks, "Astra castra, Numen lumen."

Mr. Frank W. Hackett, of Portsmouth, N. H., writes me as follows: —

You have asked me to give you my impressions of the character of our late friend, Charles W. Tuttle. I take pleasure in so doing.

In my boyhood at Portsmouth I used to see Mr. Tuttle occasionally, and I looked up to him with a boy's admiration. My recollection is (though I may be wrong) that he was then connected with the Observatory at Cambridge. I distinctly remember that from the first he used to speak warmly, I may say enthusiastically, of Portsmouth and its neighborhood, so that somehow I got from him an idea that it was highly creditable in me to have been born there. Of course, I later saw plainly enough that it was the rich historic material, and the associations of the early period, that most attracted him.

When I had begun the practice of the law at Boston, a little more than twenty years ago, I had frequent opportunity of meeting Mr. Tuttle. I shall not forget how cordial and encouraging were his greetings, and how kind were his inquiries for my professional success. Leaving Boston in 1871, it was my fortune to be there three or four times every year, and I often availed myself of the occasion to call at his office for a friendly chat. He was, as you well know, genial and simple in manner, and very fond of his friends. The conversation was more likely to turn upon Champernowne and Capt. John Mason than what was going on in the courts. He loved to talk about Strawberry Bank, speaking with animation and respect of our antiquary, Mr. John Elwyn, of John Scribner Jenness, and others. You know that it was owing to the advice and encouragement of Mr. Elwyn that he undertook to investigate the history of Francis Champernowne. He once said of Elwyn: "I have walked with him again and again over all the venerable acres of old Strawberry Bank, and far beyond, and heard him discourse, as no one else could, of the olden time." I could not thus meet with Mr. Tuttle, and listen to what he said, without feeling that he was imparting to me somewhat of his ardor for a study of our early annals.

Our friend, I should say, had a warm, sympathetic nature that laid hold of an acquaintance and soon made of him a friend. He was quick to detect in another a taste for his favorite pursuit, and he inspired one with a confidence that he sought accuracy above all things, sparing no pains to be accurate, even in matters of apparently trifling moment. A lover of truth, no man surpassed him in the relish with which he set about its discovery.

I think I do not err when I characterize him as having been remarkably unselfish in his method of exhuming and using historical facts. By this I mean that he cared nothing for gaining the credit of finding a paper or a book, as a first discoverer, — thought little

of enlarging his repute as an antiquary; he was intent only that
the fact should be brought to light for what it might be worth, not
to him, but to the world. Indeed, he displayed a generosity in this
field that was most admirable. Mr. Tuttle was tolerant. He may
have been impatient of the blunders of others, but so far as I observed, nothing in word or tone escaped him that savored of harsh
criticism. His thoughts and energies seemed to be concentrated
on the men of the early time and their doings, rather than on what
was going on around him; and he welcomed every worker in the
field of historic research who sought his aid or advice.

Of his affectionate nature others can better speak than I; but
even one who but slightly knew him, felt its ever-present charm.
His untimely death is sincerely mourned, and the memory of him
is precious. As the years go by, and the early history of the
Pascataqua becomes more clearly outlined, the value of Mr. Tuttle's labors will be all the more appreciated. His personal traits,
however, lend an indescribable delight to what he has written;
and it is but simple justice to his memory, that his warm-hearted,
lovable nature should be known of by those who in future years
will recur to the treasures he freely gathered for lovers of history.
I feel that it is scarcely possible to say too much in his praise.

The Rev. Edmund F. Slafter wrote a Memoir of Mr.
Tuttle for the Massachusetts Historical Society, which
has before been quoted. I make the following extract:

In his social relations Mr. Tuttle was gentle, modest, and un-
assuming. He was warm-hearted, and always overflowing with the
spirit of kindliness. He was moderately reticent, and had little
ambition for seeming to impart to others information which he
did not possess; but on themes that lay within the sphere of his
personal observation, particularly those to which he had given a
scrutinizing investigation, he was warmly responsive, and ready
freely to unfold all the rich treasures of his accumulated knowledge.

He was simple and dignified in his bearing, faithful in his friend-
ships, a genial and instructive companion; and his death, in what
seemed to be the prime of his career of usefulness, will long be
deplored by a large circle of scholars who knew him well and
appreciated his excellent and rare qualities.[1]

Prof. Truman H. Safford, of Williams College, Williams-
town, Mass., writes of him: —

I first met Mr. Tuttle at Cambridge in 1849, when I was
thirteen years old. At that time I was much at the Observatory.
Mr. Tuttle was then at his carpenter's trade, near my parents'
home at Mt. Auburn, in the edge of Watertown, and visited me
there, showing me a telescope which he had himself constructed.
In a few days I went with him to the Observatory, and introduced
him to the Bonds. They were pleased with him, and shortly after
asked me if he would not be a good man to come to the Observatory on a small stipend, — I think five hundred dollars yearly, —
and be generally useful in the work of the Observatory; receiving
the stipend, at first on the order of the Director, and afterwards
as a permanent thing, in the regular way, on the College pay-
roll. He was in fact invited to accept the position — I suppose
provisionally — before he went "as a student" and received the
appointment from the Corporation, when it was found that he
was practically ready for a fixed position. His first position was
in fact that of an "Elève," as it is called in some places abroad, —
a highly promising learner under pay.

In his position at the Observatory he made great progress
outside of his specified duties. He discovered one comet in 1853,
independently of Father Secchi, at Rome, who preceded him by
two days; and his calculations of the orbits of these bodies are
still kept upon record in the catalogues of such works, published

---

[1] Proceedings of the Massachusetts Historical Society, xxi. 411, 412.

in Germany. He went once to Europe in charge of the chronometers which were sent backward and forward in the interest of the longitude-work of the Coast Survey. This was a mission that required a very good observer, as whoever went was obliged to take observations at Liverpool, in company with Mr. Hartnup, the astronomer there. Mr. Tuttle had also great mechanical skill, which was called into play in various ways on this mission, as well as at the Observatory. For myself, Mr. Tuttle's leaving the Observatory was a personal loss, as I was much there during his term of office, and his companionship was very pleasant.

Prof. Sylvester Waterhouse, LL.D., of Washington University, St. Louis, Mo., wrote of him : —

My acquaintance with Mr. Tuttle began in 1853. Towards the close of my last year in Harvard University our class was invited to visit the Observatory. It was on the occasion of this visit that I first met Mr. Tuttle. He was then an assistant of Professor Bond. An accidental conversation led to a friendship which lasted through life. His sterling virtues endeared him to me. The modesty of his nature, the loyalty of his friendship, the strength of his intellect, and the accuracy of his scholarship were traits that could not fail to win regard. Apart from my sense of personal loss, it is a profound regret that a man so capable of public usefulness was removed in the prime of his powers. The constant expansion of his mind was fitting him for broader work. Had his life been spared, doubtless his later labors would still more conspicuously have illustrated the clearness and breadth of his intelligence.

Mr. Tuttle was married, Jan. 31, 1872, to Mary Louisa Park, only daughter of the Hon. John C. Park. Her interest in his literary labors, and in his reputation as an author, is shown in the careful preservation of his manuscripts after his death, the collection of facts illustrating his life, and the provision in her will for editing and printing his unpublished manuscripts.

His health had been failing for a year or more before his death, and in the spring of 1881 he made a brief trip to the island of Bermuda, partly for his health, and partly to search the records for facts which his friend, the Hon. John Wentworth, L.L.D., was desirous of obtaining. He did not long survive his return, dying at Boston on Sunday morning, July 17, 1881, aged 51. Services were held in King's Chapel, the Rev. Edward H. Hall officiating. His funeral was attended by many relatives and friends, among whom were members of various societies with which he was connected. His remains were deposited in Forest Hills Cemetery.

The death of Mr. Tuttle was announced to the New England Historic Genealogical Society, at the first meeting after his decease, Sept. 7, 1881, by the President, Hon. Marshall P. Wilder, LL.D. Feeling tributes were paid to his memory by Hon. Charles Levi Woodbury and Mr. Frank W. Hackett, and a committee was appointed to prepare resolutions for future action. At the next meeting, on the 5th of October, Mr. Jeremiah Colburn reported resolutions, which, after remarks by President Wilder, the Rev. Dorus Clarke, D.D., and the Rev. Edmund F. Slafter, were unanimously adopted. The speakers expressed a high opinion of Mr. Tuttle as a man of ability and integrity, and as an historical writer, with a deep regret that he had been cut off in the midst of his usefulness. The resolutions are as follows : —

7

Resolved, That the death of our associate member, Charles Wesley Tuttle, A.M., Ph.D., is a great loss to the historical literature of New England. He took a deep interest in the early colonial history of this country, particularly in that of the colonies of New Hampshire and Maine, and devoted the energies of a mind singularly clear and free from prejudice to its investigation. He was never wearied in the pursuit of the truths of history, and was only satisfied when he had exhausted all possible sources of information upon the points he was investigating. His Life of Capt. John Mason, the Founder of New Hampshire; his Conquest of Acadia by the Dutch; his Life of Francis Champernowne, and other works which he had undertaken, and on some of which he had bestowed years of patient toil, would have added much to the reputation he had already gained as a truthful historian, had he lived to complete them.

Resolved, That this Society loses in him a valued member, who took a deep interest in its objects, and who was always ready to perform his share of its labors, and unselfishly to aid his brother members and others in their researches.

Resolved, That a copy of these resolutions be sent to the family of Mr. Tuttle.

At the first meeting of the Massachusetts Historical Society after the summer recess, Sept. 8, 1881, the President, the Hon. Robert C. Winthrop, LL.D., announced the death of several members since the last meeting of the Society, and accompanied the announcement with brief tributes to their memory. That to Mr. Tuttle was as follows: —

Mr. Charles Wesley Tuttle, who was born in Maine, Nov. 1, 1829, died, most unexpectedly to us all, on the 17th of July last, at his residence in this city. There are others of our number, who knew him more intimately than I did, who will bear testimony to his character and accomplishments. But I cannot forbear expressing briefly my own sense of his devotion to the work in which we are engaged. I knew him first while I was—as, I believe, I still am—one of the Visiting Committee of the Astronomical Observatory at Cambridge. He was there as one of the corps of observers, and distinguished himself by the discovery of a telescopic comet, in 1853. In the following year he was attached to the United States expedition for determining the difference of longitude between Cambridge, in New England, and Greenwich, in Old England. In this relation he made several contributions to the Astronomical Journal, and to the Annals of the Harvard Observatory. Finding, however, that he had taxed his eyes too severely, he was compelled to abandon his scientific pursuits, and after a year or more at the Dane Law School, he was admitted to the Suffolk Bar in 1856, and entered at once on the successful practice of his profession. He soon began to evince an eager interest in New England history, and contributed many historical articles to the Register of the New England Historic Genealogical Society, of which he was long an active member. Our own Proceedings bear abundant evidence of the earnestness with which he entered into our labors after he became a member of this Society in 1873. He was rarely absent from our monthly meetings, and was a frequent contributor of interesting and valuable matter to our volumes. At the time of his death he was engaged in preparing a Memoir of his friend the late Hon. Caleb Cushing, and other biographical works, which it may be hoped will not be lost. He was a man of great intelligence and energy, valued by us all as an associate and friend; and his death, at only fifty-one years of age, is a serious loss to the working corps of our Society.

Mr. Winthrop, with the authority of the Council, offered resolutions of respect to the memory of the resident members, which were unanimously adopted. That on Mr. Tuttle was as follows:—

Resolved, That we have heard with deep regret the announcement of the death of our valued associate and earnest fellow-worker,
Charles W. Tuttle, Esq., and that the President appoint one of our
number to prepare a Memoir of him, for our Proceedings.

On this occasion Mr. Winslow Warren paid the following
tribute to Mr. Tuttle: —

MR. PRESIDENT, — I labor under the same difficulty that many
of us experience, in attempting to add anything to your own admirable remarks; but my friendship for our deceased associate,
Charles W. Tuttle, leads me to a few simple words of recognition
and respect. It is a great regret to me that our friendship had
not begun at an earlier period, that I could have done more ample
justice to his early fame as an astronomer and scientific man; but
of that portion of his life, so full of promise, and of performance
also, I have little knowledge other than as gathered from the regrets
of his many friends and co-workers, that he should have been
compelled to forsake a career opening so brilliantly, to tread the
more prosaic paths of the law. Mr. Tuttle was admitted to the bar
of Suffolk County in 1856, and upon my own admission, a very few
years later, I became acquainted with him through a similar practice in the courts. The intimacy thus formed, continued without
interruption to the time of his most unexpected decease, and gave
me full opportunity to see and appreciate the strength and purity
of his character. Very early in my interviews with him at his office
or elsewhere, I became impressed with his earnest devotion to the
interests of his clients, and with the persistent energy in which
he delved at the very foundations of principles of law involved
in the cases with which he was connected. He gave to his clients the utmost of his abilities, and those of no mean order,
and he left untried no honest method for success. Wherever the
study of the law led, as it often does, along the paths of history,
his ardor was so enkindled anew, and all the enthusiasm of his

nature so fully aroused, that in his earliest practice one wondered whether the lawyer would absorb the astronomer, or the historian the lawyer.

He was a man of great simplicity of character, and with an un-obtrusive modesty that gave charm to social intercourse, though in some degree perhaps obscuring marked abilities, and proving a hindrance to professional success. His true field was that of the historian and scholar, rather than of the busy man of affairs. He possessed a remarkable fund of historical knowledge, more particu-larly of matters connected with the early settlement of Maine and New Hampshire, was critical and accurate, and indefatigable in investigation of nice and doubtful points.

For some years before his admission to this Society, in 1873, he had been a member of the New England Historic Genealogical Society, and of several State Historical Societies; and their records attest the value and constancy of his work. To this Society I feel that his loss is a very great one. Probably not many here present knew him well; but those that did know him, appreciated the ex-tent of his attainments, the power for work there was in him, and the promise of important historical contributions to our collections. Of the younger members there are but few whose attendance has been more constant, whose interest more active, and whose contri-butions more valuable; and if in the full maturity of his powers he had been enabled to devote himself more completely to those his-torical researches so congenial to his tastes, his rank would have been among the highest of our laborers in the field of history. At the time of his death he was engaged upon a life of Capt. John Mason, and had made a very extensive collection of material. It is to be hoped that this may not be lost to the world, and that his work was so far advanced as to make its completion by others possible.

Our friend has been taken almost in the prime of his strength, but he has left a worthy example of an earnest, painstaking, labo-rious life, and furnished a rare instance of a man combining the astronomer, the lawyer, and the historian, and achieving a good degree of success in each profession.

At a meeting of the Council of the Prince Society, held at Boston, March 13, 1882, the Hon. Charles H. Bell, LL.D., of Exeter, N. H., a vice-president of the Society, offered the following resolutions, which were unanimously adopted : —

Resolved, That the Council of the Prince Society desire to place upon record their deep sorrow at the death of one of their associates, the late Charles Wesley Tuttle, Ph.D., which occurred on Sunday, the 17th of July, 1881. Mr. Tuttle became a member of this Society in 1872. He was its treasurer from 1873 to 1874, and its corresponding secretary from 1874 to the time of his death. He had prepared a monograph on Capt. John Mason, the patentee of New Hampshire, to be printed by the Society. An enthusiastic student of history, a profound and painstaking explorer of ancient records, a conscientious and accurate writer, his loss will long be felt, not only by this Board, but by numerous historical associations, and by all who appreciate the value and importance of historical studies.

Mrs. Mary Park Tuttle survived her husband nearly six years. She died at Brookline, April 25, 1887, and her remains were laid by his side. Over the place where Mr. Tuttle's body reposes, on Clematis Path, Forest Hills, is an unhewn block of granite, placed there by his widow. It bears, on a bronze tablet, this inscription: —

CHARLES WESLEY TUTTLE

1829 ✠ 1881

ASTRA CASTRA, NUMEN LUMEN

BIOGRAPHICAL SKETCH

OF

MARY LOUISA PARK TUTTLE.

BY

HARRIET PRESCOTT SPOFFORD.

MARY LOUISA PARK TUTTLE.

MARY LOUISA PARK, of whose devotion to the memory of her husband, Charles W. Tuttle, this book is a witness, was the daughter of the Hon. John C. Park, a distinguished member of the legal profession, and was born in Boston, on the 5th of May, 1840. On her mother's side she was a lineal descendant of Christopher Kilby, of colonial fame; and the very romantic and picturesque story of her own immediate ancestry — as Mr. Tuttle's Memoir of Christopher Kilby exhibits it — led her to take a warm interest in genealogical studies, such as those which her husband pursued. She was married to Mr. Tuttle in the Arlington Street Church, by the Rev. Dr. Peabody, on the 31st of January, 1872, and her companionship and love and care were of inestimable value to him, surrounding him always with those tender observances without which it would have been impossible for him to continue his researches and work as he did. In her youth possessed of much beauty, Mrs. Tuttle was still, at the time of her death, of elegant and attractive personality, with peculiar grace and dignity. But her chief charm lay in an apprehensive intelligence, a perfectly equable disposition, a quick wit, and a lively sense of humor that made a dull hour in her society impossible. Unselfish to a marked degree, her great patience and strength of character were shown throughout the lingering illness — an affection of the heart — of which she died on the 25th of April, 1887, and whose acute sufferings she bore with an almost saintly sweetness. Through the generous love of her friend, Mrs. Carrie E. Evans, a very comfortable income was for many years assured to her; and, as the following paragraph of her will shows, a portion of the principal was set aside by her for the purpose of publishing the works of her husband, to be found in this volume.

Item Third. In memory of my beloved husband Charles W. Tuttle, that some of his historic works should be published, I hereby direct that my said executor shall cause to be published "Francis Champernowne" and other works, if he and my husband's friend, John Ward Dean, think advisable; and I hereby request that the said John Ward Dean select such other work or works as he in his judgment deems best to be published, and that he either edit the same, or cause some competent person under his supervision to do the same, and to see that such work or works be properly published. I further direct that as to the manner and form of their publication the said Dean shall consult with my husband's friend Thomas Weston, Jr. I hereby direct my said executor to pay out of my estate all proper expenses attending such editing and publishing the said "Francis Champernowne," and such other of said historical works of my beloved husband as the said Dean shall direct to be so published.

It was a large-souled and large-minded woman who in exemplifying her appreciation of her husband, and in her desire to gratify his friends by giving them works of his which otherwise might never see the light, dictated this provision. She was indeed one who, if devoted and fault-less as a wife, was not less so as a daughter, sister, friend. She made the world brighter while she lived in it, and sadder when she left it.

CAPTAIN FRANCIS CHAMPERNOWNE,

HIS ANCESTRY AND KINDRED,

WITH A SKETCH OF HIS LIFE.

BY CHARLES W. TUTTLE.

CAPTAIN FRANCIS CHAMPERNOWNE.

I.

HIS ANCESTRY AND KINDRED.

THE spectacle of families living with a broken hearth-stone, one fragment resting in the Old World and the other in the New, the affections and sympathies of kindred remaining unsevered, is one of the most impressive in the domestic lives of our ancestors. It is a scene that cannot be contemplated without emotion and concern. The history of those who left their fatherland in the period of early colonization to find homes and graves in the American wilderness, is invested with a melancholy and fascinating interest. Life under such circumstances is surrounded with new perils and strange incidents, and subjected to new vicissitudes. The career of the immigrant, fresh from the influence of venerable traditions, customs, and feudal limitations, is dramatic and interesting in proportion as it mingles with historical movements and events which come within the range of our sympathies and solicitude. An interest verging on the romantic gathers around him if he happens to be a scion of an ancient or noble family, or to bear a name made illustrious by his European ancestors.

More than two centuries ago, in the reign of Charles I., the people of the ancient, picturesque, and almost sea-girt counties of Devon and Cornwall in England were closely allied with the dwellers in New England, especially those living between the Merrimack and the Penobscot rivers. One was the offspring of the other; similar relations subsisted between them, although separated by a wide waste of waters, as now subsist between the people of the same stock in the Atlantic and the Pacific States. So frequent and continuous was the communication between these people, that the domestic circle was scarcely broken. Vessels sailed periodically between Dartmouth, Plymouth, Falmouth, and harbors bordering on the Bristol Channel, and from the Pascataqua, the Isles of Shoals, and harbors to the eastward, laden with merchandise and passengers, and bearing tokens of affection and remembrance. Nature seems to have designed these ancient counties to form some intimate relations with the New World, by thrusting them far westward into the Atlantic ocean. Their territory lies nearer to America than that of any other shire of England.

In the fore part of the reign of Charles I., when the tide of English emigration set strongly towards New England, more persons originating in Devon and Cornwall, and perhaps Somerset, were living on the sea-coast of Maine and New Hampshire, and on the adjacent islands, than

from all other counties in England. Looking over the family names in our early records, one would imagine he was between Land's End and Bristol in England, so numerous are the coincidences in this respect. These immigrants transferred to their new homes local names dear to them, and for ages to their ancestors, as memorials of their birthplaces. Before the time of King Philip's War, which happened more than two centuries ago, the names of Devonshire, of Somersetshire, and of Cornwall had been formally affixed to maritime districts lying in Maine, divided by great rivers, and having the functions and organization of English counties. The names of many towns and cities within those ancient shires had also been transferred to places in these new counties. Indeed the entire social, commercial, and political aspects of these new settlements were strikingly similar to those of the southwest of England. Perhaps the similitude in extent was not then to be found in the other English settlements in America.[1]

To Devon, more than to the other two counties, these immigrants to the shores of the gulf of Maine owed their origin, their knowledge of commerce and of the arts of life. This shire was then distinguished above all others of England for navigation and agriculture, mining and manufactures, — employments which admirably fitted the people for new settlements in America. Its inhabitants were accounted "bold, martial, haughty of heart, prodigal of life, constant in affections, courteous to strangers, yet greedy of glory and honor." Fuller, comparing them with the

---

[1] Compare Williamson's Maine, and Folsom's Saco and Biddeford.

inhabitants of other shires of England, declares that they were distinguished for having universal genius; and Queen Elizabeth used to say of the Devon gentry, " They were all born courtiers with a becoming confidence." [1]

The nobility and the gentry of Devon had no superior in England as regards ancient lineage and historic renown. The Hollands and the Seymours, the Carews and the Courtenays, and others, dukes and earls, fill a considerable space in the history of this shire. Its gentry shine with steady lustre through all periods of English history.[2] The memorable deeds of Ralegh[3] and of Gilbert, of Drake and of Hawkins, — and to these may be added the ever honored name of Gorges, — are sufficient to prove the quality of the people of this shire in the age of Elizabeth and of James.

In antiquity and splendor of descent the family of Champernowne[4] is surpassed by few, if any, in the west of England.[5] It is of Norman origin, and takes its name from the parish of Cambernun in Normandy, where it long flourished. Antiquarian and historical writers of the age of Elizabeth, and later, take notice of the several lustrous branches then flourishing in Devon, and of its

[1] Fuller's Worthies of England, Devonshire; Westcote's View of Devonshire, 42, 55.

[2] Among these were the Champernowne, Fulford, Bampfylde, Ralegh, Grenville, Gilbert, Drake, Hawkins, Cary, and Gorges families.

[3] Sir Walter Ralegh must be allowed to be the best authority for the mode of writing his own surname: I follow him.

[4] The last syllable of this name is variously spelled. I have adopted the spelling of Captain Champernowne himself in the only undoubted autograph signatures I have seen. In the old provincial records, contemporary with him, in New Hampshire and Maine, the recording officer has quite uniformly spelled the name as in the text. In Carew's History of Cornwall, printed in 1602, in the English State papers of this period, and in Burke's Landed Gentry, the name is usually in this form. The family now in possession of the ancestral manor of Dartington write it this wise.

[5] Burke's Landed Gentry, Champernowne.

alliances with distinguished families. The learned Camden styles it a "famous and ancient family," having the inheritance and possession of the town of Modbury in his time. Westcote, a Devon antiquary of great authority, writing in the first year of the reign of Charles I., speaks of the "clarous and knightly family of Champernowne," of Devonshire; and Prince, the author of the Worthies of Devon, in a later reign, speaks of the "eminent persons of this name and family, the history of whose actions and exploits, for the greatest part, is devoured by time."[1] While the mists of antiquity conceal the remote generations of this family, from the long and memorable reign of Henry II. the stream of descent in Devon is clear to this day, throughout a period of more than seven hundred years.[2] Dynasty after dynasty has come and gone, and yet this family has survived. During this long time the name of Champernowne winds like a silver cord through the naval annals of England.

Before the reign of Henry VIII. the family of Champernowne, having the lineage of many illustrious houses, even that of the royal house of the Plantagenets, had united by marriage with the ancient families of the Gilberts and the Raleghs, and thence sprang Sir Humphrey Gilbert and Sir Walter Ralegh, the two foremost names in Anglo-American history.[3] Near the end of the reign of Elizabeth,

[1] Westcote's View of Devonshire, 392, 406, 408 *et seq.;* Prince, Worthies of Devon, 192, 194; Lower's Family Names; Camden's Britannia.

[2] Tuckett's Devonshire Pedigrees, Champernowne; Burke, *ubi supra.*

[3] Tuckett, *ubi supra;* Edwards's Life of Sir Walter Ralegh, vol. i., chapters i. and ii., and the authorities there cited The descent of the Champernownes from King John, through Richard, King of the Romans, is undisputed. (See Westcote, 469, 589, and Tuckett, *ubi supra.*) Curiously enough, a corre-

an alliance with the old and knightly family of Fulford
issued in a son, Francis Champernowne, whose destiny it
was to share in the perils and fortunes of colonizing the
New World, and to leave his name in the early annals of
New England.[1]

The Champernowne family lived with dignity and splendor in Modbury, — a parish about midway between the
great commercial towns of Plymouth and Dartmouth, —
during many centuries. It was accounted ancient there
in the reign of Henry VII. Sir Arthur Champernowne,
great-grandfather of Francis, was a younger son of Sir Philip
Champernowne and Katherine, daughter of Sir Edmund
Carew, Baron of Carew,[2] a gallant soldier who fought in
the memorable battle of Bosworth Field, under the victorious banners of the Earl of Richmond. This Arthur was
one of the many distinguished sons of the Modbury house
of that period. In his younger days he was concerned
with his cousin, Sir Peter Carew, in the western con-
spiracy against Queen Mary of England and her match
with Philip II., — a very notable event in her short reign,
— and was sent to the Tower. In the reign of Elizabeth
he was vice-admiral of the west, and otherwise much
employed in public affairs. He was associated with his
celebrated nephew Sir Humphrey Gilbert — son of an
elder sister — in making plantations in Ireland, and was
connected with many other famous enterprises at home and

spondent living in Greenland, N. H.,
where Captain Champernowne lived
more than two centuries ago, informs
me that tradition reports his "descent
from royalty." On the other side of
the Pascataqua River, in Kittery, Maine,
where he also lived, tradition says he
was the "son of a nobleman."
[1] Westcote, 434, 614.
[2] Baron Carew was slain in France,
in 1513.

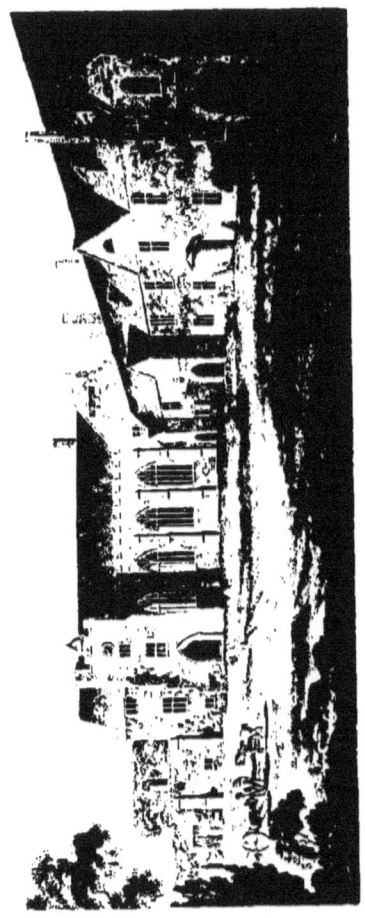

DARTINGTON HOUSE, DEVON.

abroad. For some public service, most probably, he was rewarded with the gift of the Abbey-site of Polsloe, near Exeter, one of the monastic spoils of Henry VIII. This he exchanged, early in the reign of Elizabeth, for the historic barony of Dartington, situated on the western bank of the beautiful river Dart, two miles above Totnes and ten from Dartmouth, where his name and posterity continue to this day. Traditions of his illustrious family connections, and of his baronial and cavalier style, linger in the neighborhood of his residence. A stately monument of alabaster in the parish church of Dartington commemorates his name and deeds.[1]

From the Conquest this barony had been the seat of illustrious families, — the Hollands, of royal lineage, Dukes of Exeter, being the last. Dartington House, the baronial and ducal mansion, a very ancient and stately structure, is seated on an eminence in the peaceful and romantic scenery of the Dart, overlooking the town and vale of ancient Totnes. It still bears the marks of feudal grandeur and power, and it ranks among the most famous of the antiquities of Devonshire. The original buildings were arranged in quadrangular form, enclosing a full acre of ground. The architecture, grand and massive, belongs to a period anterior to the reign of the Tudor princes. Viewed in connection with the parts now lying in ruins, the whole structure in its palmy days must have been imposing and magnificent, the fitting residence of the

---

[1] Prince, Worthies, 168, 192, 500; Burke's History of the Commoners, ii., 273; Calendar of State Papers (Domestic), 1547-1580; Westcote, 408; Froude's History of England, vi. 146, 148; ix. 365, 366. It is worthy of note that Mr. Froude, the historian, was born in Dartington. See note 1, p. 76, *postea*.

princely Dukes of Exeter.[1] These venerable buildings, thickly overgrown with ivy and patched with moss, now wear a picturesque and romantic aspect, differing but little from what they were in the days of James I., when the youthful Francis Champernowne played among their ruins, gambolled in their antique halls, and listened to the tales of their ancient glory. This is now the seat of Arthur Champernowne, Esq., having descended to him from his distinguished ancestor Sir Arthur, the proprietor in the reign of Queen Elizabeth.[2]

John Champernowne, of Modbury, heir of the house, the elder brother of Sir Arthur, of Dartington, married Katherine, a daughter of the Lord Mountjoy, while his sister, Katherine Champernowne,[3] by two marriages, became the mother of five knights, — among whom were the renowned Sir Humphrey Gilbert and Sir Walter Ralegh. How august a title to our reverence and to that of future generations has this English Cornelia! She alone would suffice to make the name of Champernowne illustrious; and she is as deserving of a statue to her memory as was the great Roman matron.[4]

---

[1] Prince, *ubi supra.* A view of the Dartington House is in Polwhele's Devon, and in Lyson's Devon : also in Moore's History of Devonshire, from which this heliotype view is taken.

[2] Since this was written, Arthur Champernowne, Esq., has died. See note 1, p. 76. *postea.* — H.

[3] Katherine Champernowne's first husband was Otho Gilbert, of Greenway, and their sons were Sir John, Sir Humphrey, and Sir Adrian Gilbert. Her second husband was Walter Ralegh, and their sons were Sir Carew

and Sir Walter Ralegh. She is buried in Exeter Cathedral. Tuckett's Pedigrees, *ubi supra;* Pole's Devon, 310.

[4] "There lived then a remarkable woman, — remarkable for having two sons of different fathers, whose heroic temperament and versatile talents must have been derived from their common mother. The half-brothers, Humphrey Gilbert and Walter Ralegh, were more alike in tastes and genius than is often seen in a nearer relationship. It was the blood of the Champernownes, — a name that has a place of its own in our

DARTINGTON HOUSE, DEVON.

Sir Arthur Champernowne,[1] the first proprietor of Dartington, married Mary, the daughter of Sir Henry Norreys, the widow of the heroic Sir George Carew,[2] and had several children, — among whom were Gawen and Elizabeth, both destined to advance the interests and the honor of the family. Elizabeth Champernowne became the wife of Sir Edward Seymour, Baronet, of Berry Castle, a grandson of the Duke of Somerset, Lord Protector of England. A stately monument in the church of the parish of Berry Pomeroy, hard by Dartington, perpetuates her memory and that of her husband and children. Her descendants, the present ducal house of Somerset being among them, have been high in rank, and have filled eminent stations in England down to the present time. Her grandson, cousin to Capt. Francis Champernowne, is the subject of eulogy by Lord Macaulay in his history of England. " An adversary," he says, " of no common prowess was watching his time. This was Sir Edward Seymour, of Berry Pomeroy Castle, member for the city of Exeter. Seymour's birth put him on a level with the noblest subjects in Europe. He was the right heir-male of the body of that Duke of Somerset who had been brother-in-law of King Henry VIII., and Protector of the realm of England.

Colonial history, — and not that of the Gilberts and Raleghs, which made them what they were." (Dr. Samuel F. Haven, Lowell Institute Lectures, 1869, p. 134.) — H.

[1] Sir Arthur Champernowne died in 1578.

[2] Sir George Carew, a noted and accomplished naval commander, perished in the celebrated Mary Rose, the pride of the English navy, sunk off Portsmouth in 1545. He was the commander of this ill-fated ship at the time, and went down with all on board. His widow, Mary, the daughter of Sir Henry Norreys, was sister to Henry, Baron Norreys, Queen Elizabeth's ambassador to France. Sir Arthur Champernowne, of Dartington, was cousin to her first husband.

From the elder son was descended the family which dwelt at Berry Pomeroy. Seymour's ,fortune was large, and his influence in the west of England extensive. Nor was the importance derived from descent and wealth the only importance which belonged to him. He was one of the most skilful debaters and men of business in the kingdom. He had sat many years in the House of Commons, had studied all its rules and usages, and thoroughly understood its temper. He had been elected Speaker in the late reign under circumstances which made that distinction peculiarly honorable. During several generations none but lawyers had been called to the chair; and he was the first country gentleman whose abilities and acquirements enabled him to break that long prescription. He had subsequently held high political office, and had sat in the Cabinet; but his haughty and unaccommodating temper had given so much disgust that he had been forced to retire." Gawen Champernowne inherited a passion for martial life.[1] In his youth he and his distinguished cousins, Sir Walter Ralegh and Henry Champernowne, served with the English contingent in France, commanded by the famous Huguenot general, the Count of Montgomery, whose misfortunes alone would suffice to make his name memorable.[2]

In a grand tournament held in Paris, on the occasion of a great festival in honor of the marriage of one of the royal family,[3] the King of France, Henry II., having vanquished several princely antagonists, challenged the young

---

[1] Two Champernownes were crusaders.

[2] Tuckett and Burke, *ubi supra;*

Westcote, 406 *et seq.;* Edwards's Life etc., *ubi supra.*

[3] Margaret, sister of the King and the Duke of Savoy.

Count of Montgomery, then Captain of the Guards, to
break a pair of lances with him. The Count reluctantly
accepted. The King and his gallant subject met in full
array, in the presence of the noblest assemblage in France;
and on the first tilt a fragment of the lance held by the
Count struck the King in his left eye, at the instant when
the sudden shock had moved the visor of his helmet, and
he fell mortally wounded. Upon this awful mishap the
Count retired, first to Normandy, and then into England,
filled with the deepest grief for what had only accidentally
happened. While in England he became a convert to
the reformed religion; and when the civil war broke out in
France a few years later, he joined the Prince of Condé
and the Admiral Coligny in the cause of the Huguenots.
The Champernowne family, like many others in the west
of England, espoused the cause of the reformers in France,
and aided it with their fortunes and their valor. The marriage of Gawen Champernowne, A.D. 1571, and the Lady
Gabrielle, the beautiful and accomplished daughter of the
Count of Montgomery, united the interests of the two
families. He followed the fortunes of his father-in-law
through many years of civil strife, until the latter was
taken prisoner at Domfront, in 1574, and publicly executed
in Paris, by the victorious Guises. Gawen Champernowne
now returned to England bereft of considerable of his
fortune hazarded in the strife, while his wife lost all, the
vast estates of her father having been confiscated. His military experience while in France enabled him afterward to
render good service to his country in the war with Spain,
which came on a few years later, and he was intrusted by

10

the Queen with many responsible military offices in Devonshire. He was associated with the renowned Sir Francis Drake in several public employments; and such was his friendship for this great navigator that he bequeathed to him in his last will a ring of gold.[1]

Gawen[2] Champernowne and the Lady Gabrielle, daughter of the Count of Montgomery, had nine children, who lived to adult age. Arthur, the father of Captain Francis, was the only son and heir. Seven of the eight daughters were married, all to gentlemen of ancient families, several of them being of the rank of knights of England.[3]

Arthur Champernowne succeeded to the ancestral manor of Dartington on the death of his father, which happened in a few years after the memorable Spanish Armada threatened England.[4] He was no less fond of adventure, and endowed with no less mental capability, than his ancestors; but these personal qualities were displayed in quite another way. The losses of his father and grandfather in the religious wars of France had diminished his patrimony to some extent; and this circumstance probably directed his energies into fields of enterprise calculated to restore the ancient opulence of his house, and to provide a home in the New World for some of his many sons.[5] To commerce and to plantations in America was an easy transition, for

---

[1] Edwards's Life, etc., *ubi supra;* Nouvelle Biographie Générale, Montgomery; Browning's History of the Huguenots; Calendar of State Papers (Domestic), years 1583–1584; Will in Prerogative Office, London.

[2] Gawen is an old surname in Wilts and Somerset, and came into this family from the Carews. Sir Gawen Carew, a distinguished person at the court of Queen Elizabeth, was a son of Sir Edmund, Baron Carew, the great grandfather of Gawen Champernowne.

[3] Tuckett's Pedigrees, *ubi supra.*

[4] Calendar of State Papers, A.D. 1592.

[5] Edwards's Life of Ralegh, *ubi supra.*

one of his shire, from arenas of martial and political strife. His illustrious kinsmen had distinguished themselves in both fields of enterprise, and had raised to eminence both these employments. He was the owner and joint owner of many vessels of Dartmouth. Alexander Shapleigh, of Totnes or Dartmouth, — the same, probably, who came to the Pascataqua about the year 1640, where descendants continue in high esteem to this day, — was joint owner with him of the ship Benediction, of Dartmouth.[1]

In November, 1622, Arthur Champernowne had a commission from the Council for New England permitting his vessel, the Chudleigh, an ancestral name, to trade and fish in the waters of New England.[2] This vessel did not sail, it is likely, before the following Spring; and she may have the forgotten distinction of bearing to the Pascataqua some of the fathers of that early settlement, begun at this time. It is probable that this vessel, and other vessels belonging to him, made voyages to New England before and after this date. He became very well acquainted, through his commercial undertakings, with New England and the various proprietary interests therein. Sir Ferdinando Gorges, captain of the castle, and also of the Island of St. Nicholas, at Plymouth, was most active and largely concerned in planting and settling the country, and ready to give information and to encourage adventurers. Besides, they were brothers-in-law, having married sisters of the ancient and knightly house of Fulford, a circumstance that accounts

---

[1] See Calendar of State Papers, Domestic, from A.D. 1625 to 1631. Champernowne's vessels were the Chudleigh, St. Nicholas, Mary, Bridget, Benediction, and others, all of Dartmouth.
[2] Proc. Am. Antiquarian Society, April, 1867, p. 70.

for the origin of Arthur Champernowne's interest in New England.

In the last year of the reign of Elizabeth, Arthur Champernowne married Bridget, daughter of Sir Thomas Fulford, of Great Fulford, in Devonshire, Kt. This family is not inferior in antiquity and in historic lineage to the Champernowne family; and both flourish to this day in the seats of their ancestors.[1] Westcote, the old historian, speaks of the "knightly and dignous family of Fulford of his time," and says that he had seen evidence of its great state and splendor in the age of Richard Cœur de Lion.[2] "This right antient and honorable family," says Prince, writing in the reign of William III., "have held this seat by the name of Fulford from the days of King Richard I. to this day, — upwards of five hundred years; in which long tract of time the heirs thereof have matched with the daughters of divers of the nobility, — as of Courtenay, descended from the Earl of Devonshire, Lord Bourchier, Earl of Bath, Lord Bonville, Lord Paulet, and others."[3]

[1] These ancient families are now represented in England as follows: Arthur Champernowne, Esq., of Dartington, educated at Trinity College, Oxford, magistrate of Devon, lord of the manors of Dartington, Umberleigh, and North Tawton, and patron of one living, to whom the writer is much indebted for information respecting the subject of this memoir, and his ancestors; and Baldwin Fulford, Esq., of Fulford, educated at Exeter College, Oxford, magistrate of Devon, lord of the manor of Dunsford, and patron of one living. The Rev. Richard Champernowne is the Rector of Dartington, and to him also the writer is indebted for valuable information. See Walford's County Families of England for 1873.

[The Rev. Richard Champernowne, of Christ Church, Oxford, 1839, was Curate of Dartington Parish from 1845 to 1859, when he became Rector, succeeding Archdeacon Froude, father of Mr. Froude the historian. Arthur Champernowne, Esq., mentioned above, died May 27, 1887, and is succeeded by his son Arthur. — H.]

[2] Westcote's View of Devonshire, 434 et seq.

[3] Prince, Worthies, 393. In the church of St. Mary, at Dunsford, there

The Fulford family is of Saxon origin, and is said to derive its name from the place of its ancient residence and possessions in Devonshire. The name is conspicuous in the history of the English Crusaders in the twelfth century. Sir Amias and Sir Baldwin Fulford shared in these romantic adventures, and achieved personal distinction in the Holy Land. Sir Baldwin, a Knight of the Sepulchre, gained renown by the courage and valor which he displayed in a memorable combat with a giant Saracen, as well as by the victory which he won over the infidel. The contest involved the honor and liberty of a royal lady in a besieged castle; and the whole affair forms a curious and interesting chapter of romance and chivalry in the history of that age. In commemoration of his heroic achievement, two Saracens were made the supporters of the arms of the Fulfords, — a distinction that belongs to but few families below the rank of nobles.[1] In all reigns members of this family have been distinguished in military and naval enterprises, as well as in offices of Church and State. It flourishes to this day in the seat of its remote ancestors, the male line continuing unbroken from the Knight of the Sepulchre. The late Right Reverend Francis Fulford, D.D., Lord Bishop of Montreal and Metropolitan of Canada, was of this family, and was born on the ancestral manor.[2]

is a magnificent monument to the memory of Sir Thomas Fulford, Kt., and his lady, Ursula, the daughter of Sir Richard Bampfylde, consisting of effigies of himself, wife, and children, with armorial symbols and banners. These are the maternal grandparents of Capt. Francis Champernoowne. — Polwhele's Devon, i. 80.

[1] Sir Baldwin (sheriff of Devon, 38 Henry VI., 1460), Knight of the Sepulchre, and Under Admiral to Holland, Duke of Exeter. High Admiral of England, married Elizabeth Bozome, and had issue, Sir Thomas Fulford, Knight, who married Philippa, daughter of Sir Philip Courtenay.

[2] Burke's Visitation of Seats and

Great Fulford, in Devon, the cradle of the race and the seat of the family from the Conquest, is nine miles south-west of Exeter, the ancient capital of the west of England. Fulford House, the family mansion for centuries, is still in excellent preservation, although built early in the reign of Queen Elizabeth. Some part of the venerable pile is of even greater antiquity. It is an imposing structure, standing on rising ground, near a beautiful sheet of water, in the midst of a fine landscape. Early in the great civil war Sir Francis Fulford, maternal uncle of Capt. Francis Champernowne, converted it into a military fortress, and garrisoned it in behalf of King Charles; but it was finally taken by the parliamentary forces under Sir Thomas Fairfax, after a siege of two weeks, without being destroyed.[1]

Such, in brief, is the lineage of Francis Champernowne, whose career belongs to the history of New England. Few persons in that age could claim an ancestry more ancient and more renowned. He could trace his descent from the period of the Conquest through more than fifteen generations of ancestors, finding among them, in every reign, historical personages whose blood ran in his own veins. His descent from the noble family of Montgomery of France infused the sprightly Gallic blood into his English veins, and connected him with historical families and great events in that kingdom. The venerable names of Champernowne and of Fulford had come down from remote antiquity side by side, always among the foremost in

Arms, i. 189, 190; Lyson's Magna Bri-   [1] Burke, *ut supra;* also, Devonshire
tannia, Devonshire. 171, 172; West-   in Beauties of England and Wales,
cote, 434, 613; Walford's County Fam-   where a view of Fulford House may be
ilies. See Fulford, in Prince, Worthies   seen.
of Devon.

ENTRANCE TO FULFORD HOUSE.

FULFORD HOUSE, DEVON.

Devonshire. Both families were descended from ancestors who derived lineage from the royal house of the Plantagenets; and both had been fountains of some of the noblest houses then in England. At the period of his birth, in the reign of James I., there was scarcely a noble or a distinguished family in the west of England not allied in blood with one or both of these ancient families. Their connection with the Gilberts, the Raleghs, and the Gorges, historic names that belong to both hemispheres, must ever excite fresh interest in their history on this side of the Atlantic.

Nor was Francis Champernowne less fortunate in the place of his birth. Nature and art had striven together to make the historic barony of Dartington one of the most romantic and picturesque sites in the west of England.[1] It lay in a favorite region, between the Tamar and the Teign, Dartmoor and the English Channel, and for centuries was known as the Garden of Devonshire.[2] The barony was a feudal gift of William the Conqueror to one of his Norman favorites. Before the Champernownes came hither from Modbury, a long line of great dukes and great barons dwelt there during many centuries; and they had built in successive reigns from the time of the Conquest, for shelter and defence, a stately structure, curious in de-

---

[1] "And now Dart with due respect salutes the barony of Dartington, which Martin possessed, together with Kemys in Pembrokeshire: then was it the seat of the illustrious family of Holland, Dukes of Exeter: very delightfully seated for prospect, as overlooking the town of Totnes; now it glories in the knightly tribe of Champernon, who married Fulford: his father, Gabrielle, the daughter of Count Montgomery, France: his grandfather, in the noble house of Norris." — Westcote's View of Devonshire, 408, anno 1630.

[2] Beauties of England and Wales, *ut supra.*

sign and workmanship. Several times between the Norman and the Tudor reigns it had returned to the Crown by forfeiture of its owners, and formed a part of the royal demesne and often served as a royal residence. Its splendor culminated while in the possession of the powerful family of Holland, Dukes of Exeter, a princely race issuing from the reigning house of Plantagenet. While held by this family it was the seat of imperial authority; for while Richard II. sat anointed on the throne, his half brothers, the able and ambitious Hollands, contrived to wield the sceptre of England.[1] Thomas Holland, the first Duke of Exeter, was a son of the Fair Maid of Kent, grand-daughter of Edward I., afterwards wife of the renowned Black Prince, and mother of Richard II. This Duke married a daughter of the famous John of Gaunt, son of King Edward III., and father of Henry IV. His son, the second Duke of Exeter, was Lord High Admiral of England. The third and last Duke of this family married a sister of King Edward IV., and came to a melancholy end in France. The chief part of the old baronial structure now standing, and known as the Dartington House, was built by the first Duke, half brother of Richard II.[2] The heraldic devices of its various possessors may still be seen carved on its antique walls. The badge of the Black Prince is yet conspicuous in the great tower.

[1] Hume's England, chap. xvii.

[2] Lyson's Magna Britannia. lxxxii. xcv. 152: Burke's Extinct Peerage. Joane Plantagenet, from her extraordinary beauty styled the Fair Maid of Kent, was the daughter of the Earl of Kent, a son of Edward I. She was married thrice: first, to the Earl of Salisbury; second. to Sir Thomas Holland, K. G., by whom she had a son, John, Earl of Huntingdon, and first Duke of Exeter; and third, to Edward the Black Prince, by whom she had Richard II.

When the first Stuart came to the throne of England, this venerable pile had lost much of its original splendor. The violence of the wars of the Roses, anterior to the reign of the Tudor monarchs, had destroyed the integrity of this princely habitation; and fame and age were striving for the mastery of it when Francis Champernowne first saw light within its ancient halls.

Hard by Dartington was the ancient barony of Berry, another baronial creation of the Conqueror, the gift by him to a favorite officer, Ralph de Pomeroy. Berry Castle, built by this Norman favorite, became one of the most splendid castles in Devonshire in the reign of Elizabeth. It stood on a rocky eminence beyond the Dart, its proud and lofty towers overlooking the landscape of Dartington. For a period of five hundred years this castle was the stately residence of the historic family of Pomeroy, descended from the Norman baron. But by an act of treason of Pomeroy the proprietor, in the reign of Edward VI., this ancient family fell from its high estate, and the castle with all its domains passed to the Duke of Somerset, uncle of King Edward and Lord Protector of England, in whose issue it continues to this day.[1] Sir Edward Seymour, grandson of the Duke, inherited the castle, and married Elizabeth Champernowne, of Dartington. This union of the Seymour and the Champernowne families in the reign of Elizabeth made the possessors of Berry Castle and of Dartington House one kindred in the reign of James I.[2]

[1] Lyson's Magna Britannia, lxxxii. cvi. 43. See Pomeroy, in Prince, Worthies. of Berry Pomeroy is now a magnificent ruin, having been destroyed during the great civil war.

[2] Prince, Worthies, 9, 10. The castle

This beautiful region of South Devonshire had been celebrated for generations as the cradle and nestling place of naval genius. Those renowned navigators, Sir Humphrey Gilbert, Sir Francis Drake, Sir John Hawkins, and Capt. John Davys, the glory of the English marine in the reign of Elizabeth, were born here. The ancestors of Sir Walter Ralegh were also of this region; but he was born beyond the river Exe in this shire. The memorable sea adventures of these heroic men had awakened all maritime England to a sense of the value of commercial intercourse with America. Nowhere was this new field of enterprise sooner and better appreciated than in Devonshire. Under the inspiring genius of these illustrious men Plymouth and Dartmouth had grown to be great commercial stations at the close of the sixteenth century. In no part of England was there a livelier interest felt in geographical discovery and in commercial undertakings. To the hazards and rewards of foreign commerce Gilbert and Ralegh had the merit of first joining schemes of English colonization; and in both these enterprises the people of this shire had largely shared. They had been with Gilbert on the bleak shores of Newfoundland, and with Ralegh in Carolina and Guiana; with the venerable George Popham at the Sagadahoc, and with David Thomson at the Pascataqua. A preference for the gains of the American fisheries and peltry trade limited their intercourse in the fore part of the seventeenth century to the maritime region of Norumbega, afterwards New England.[1] In the reign of King James their commerce had expanded into settlements and plantations between the Penobscot Bay and Cape Cod. In the memorable year of 1607, under fresh

[1] Collections of Maine Historical Society, Second Series, i. 231, 283.

authority from the English Crown, they had undertaken to make a settlement at the mouth of the river Sagadahoc, in Maine, and to hold a vast domain carved from the continent. This memorable undertaking awakened new adventurers in this bold and hardy enterprise ; and it was soon followed by further discoveries and settlements on these shores.[1]

The year of the birth of Francis Champernowne coincided with a year of memorable occurrences in New England. The adventurous and enterprising Capt. John Smith, whose memory is worthy of our reverence for what he did for New England, sailed early in the spring of the year 1614 for the northern shores of Virginia, — the name of the English possessions in America lying on the Atlantic coast between the thirty-fourth and the forty-fifth degree of north latitude, — on a voyage of traffic, fishing, and discovery. Never was a sea expedition formed of such slender materials, and undertaken solely for the purpose of private gain, fraught with greater results. The maritime parts of this remote and vast country were fully explored, the geographical features delineated on a map, and the whole described and named. Soon after reaching to the lofty and picturesque Isle of Monhegan, the western landfall of Penobscot Bay, Captain Smith designed a survey of the American coast, trending away to the southwest. Having set his crew to the work of fishing, he took a small boat and only eight men and explored every considerable harbor, river, and island between Monhegan and Cape Cod.[2] At the same

---

[1] See Popham Memorial Volume, 86 *et seq.*

[2] Captain Smith says: " I passed close aboard the shore in a little Boat." (Description of New England.)

time he carried on a fur trade with the natives along the coast, gathering from them much information of the interior of the country and its productions. Among the Indian countries which he visited was one bearing the barbaric name of Pascataqua, next west of Agamenticus. While in this wild region, so well known a few years later, he must have recognized, and perhaps explored, the large and nameless island lying close to the main land, and fronting several miles on the ocean, on the east side of the Pascataqua River, and forming the extreme southwest corner of the State of Maine. Braveboat Harbor and Champernowne's Creek, later names of the two picturesque water passages leading to the rear of this island, were inviting streams to his party, bent on trade and discovery of the country. On the bosom of these quiet waters, parting the island from the main,[1] Indian canoes laden with furs and native handiwork rocked gently and securely while their savage owners parleyed and trafficked with the English adventurers. What pleasure it would have been to this enthusiastic and veteran explorer, if then he could have had a vision of the future of this place ; could have foreseen that a child in Devonshire, then unborn, of the kindred of Gilbert and of Ralegh, was destined to come over the sea to this virgin island, take possession as proprietor, confer on it his own name, and dwell here for nearly half a century!

At the same time Captain Smith surveyed that group of isles lying in the sea, a few leagues distant, bestowing on them his own name, over which thirty-five years later

---

[1] Twice every day the sea lovingly embraces the island, throwing its watery arms entirely around it, as if never intending the main land to claim it.

Francis Champernowne was a civil magistrate. The circumstances that determined his choice of this solitary group of
rocky isles for his own name and propriety, when there were
so many nameless islands, harbors, rivers, and countries far
above these in importance and dignity, remain to be discovered.[1] Whatever they may have been, the selection implies
some pre-eminence in these isles at that period ; and the
name of their renowned proprietor, so deliberately given
to them by himself, ought never to have been disturbed.
Smith's Isles is a more euphonious name than the one they
now bear, besides the memorable and even romantic historical associations which must ever cluster around it.   Having
completed his survey of the entire coast, he sailed for England with his treasures of geographical and commercial information and a well-laden ship, arriving in the harbor of
Plymouth at the beginning of autumn.   Here he found Sir
Ferdinando Gorges, commander of the castle, whose interest
in the country just explored amounted to a passion, and communicated to him his discoveries on these shores.   Gorges
and his associates, representing the colony of North Virginia,
were so much pleased with him, his successful voyage, and
his report of the barbarous country, that they immediately
took him into their service and made him Admiral of Virginia for life.   Anxious to distinguish this country, and to
secure for it special favor among his countrymen in England, Captain Smith gave it the auspicious name, NEW
ENGLAND,—a name so apt that it immediately supplanted all

[1] By nameless, I mean, wanting
English names. It is to be observed
that Prince Charles and Captain Smith
gave to other isles on the coast the
names of eminent persons.   See the
admirable Historical Sketch of the Isles
of Shoals, by John S. Jenness, Esq.,
for full historical and descriptive information of this very interesting maritime
region.

others, barbaric and European, and survives to this day, the most venerable and attractive name on our shores.[1] New Spain and New France[2] were names that had long designated vast domains in North America claimed by Spain and by France; and now New England designated a considerable part of the domain claimed by England under the name of Virginia. The applause which greeted Smith's discoveries in northern Virginia, now New England, was softly echoed by domestic rejoicings over a new-born life in the venerable halls of Dartington.

Thirteen children, six sons and seven daughters, were born of the marriage of Arthur Champernowne and Bridget Fulford. Francis, the ninth child and youngest son, destined for the New World, was the first, and, so far as we know, was the last of his name and race in America. He was baptized in St. Mary's Church at Dartington in the month of October, 1614, a year memorable in the annals of New England. The church record is now so worn or defaced that the day[3] of the month of this event cannot be read. His Christian name, and the names of several of his brothers and sisters, came of his maternal kindred.

Of his youth and education nothing is definitely known.

[1] While Captain Smith has the merit of first applying the name of New England to this part of North America, it appears from his own statement that it was suggested to him by New Albion, a name given by Sir Francis Drake, thirty-five years before, to our western coast in the same latitude. See Smith's Description of New England, and New-England's Trials; and also his General History, ii. 176 *et seq.*

[2] The idea of transplanting the national name to American dominions was excellent. It kept up the interest of the emigrants.

[3] Tuckett's Pedigrees; and MS. letter of Arthur Champernowne, Esq., of Dartington, lord of the manor, to Mr. Tuttle. [Since the author's death it has been stated upon high authority that Francis Champernowne was baptized Oct. 18, 1614. (See the Visitations of the County of Devon, part v. 163, edited by Lieut.-Col. J. L. Vivian.) — H.]

It may be assumed that he received a mental discipline and physical training befitting his rank and station in life. His home and his surroundings were calculated to educate and to liberalize him without effort. A baronial style of living in that age implies the possession of an abundance of solid English luxuries, and a hospitality that entertains without stint the greatest and most worthy persons in the kingdom. In the peaceful reign of James I., Dartington House must have been the scene of many festive occasions, when the kindred and friends of the great house of Champernowne made merry together in the ancient halls of the princely Dukes of Exeter.

Being the youngest of six sons, there was only a bare possibility of his succeeding to the possession of the fair inheritance of Dartington; and therefore the devotion of his manhood to some profession was determined at his birth. That his youthful inclinations harmonized with the enterprising genius of his illustrious kinsmen, Sir Humphrey Gilbert, Sir Walter Ralegh, and Capt. John Davys,[1] and that he early selected the sea and its fortunes for his own, may be inferred from his career.

From his birth he must have heard much of the New World, its boundless domains, its vast treasures and deep mysteries. The famous sea-adventures of Gilbert and Ralegh, of Drake and Davys, which had occurred within the memory of generations then living, were still matters of cur-

---

[1] Captain John Davys of Sandridge, Devon, his great uncle, had made three voyages to discover a northwest passage to Asia, and had left his name forever connected with his great dis- coveries in the arctic seas of America. See Markham's Voyages and Works of Capt. Davys (Hakluyt Soc.), London, 1880; and Stephen's Dic. of National Biography. — H.

rent conversation and wonder throughout the realm.   The
El Dorado of tropical America, that mythical region of silver
walls and golden towers, was still a subject of interest and
speculation among all classes of persons.   His father was
the owner of many vessels, some of which were engaged in
New England commerce ; and it must have been a common
occurrence for his intelligent sea-captains to visit Dartington, only ten miles from the haven of Dartmouth.   Nothing
is more probable than that Captain John Smith was a guest
there when he went over the west of England distributing
his map and his description of New England, and encouraging persons to adventure in commercial and plantation
enterprises in this region newly explored by him.   He may
have pointed out and described the great river of Pascataqua and the fair islands therein.[1]

Besides, there was a near kinsman of our Champernowne,
Capt. Ralegh Gilbert, a worthy son of the renowned Sir
Humphrey Gilbert, who had been one of the leaders in the
great enterprise of procuring royal authority for settling
plantations in North America, and of sending in 1607 to the
wilderness of Norumbega the first English colony.   Captain
Gilbert had been president of this colony at the Kennebec
River, and had been commended by Sir Ferdinando Gorges
for ability and humanity.   He was named a grantee in the
charter of New England, and of the Council.   By the death
of his elder brother, Sir John Gilbert, the ancestral estates of
Greenway, on the banks of the Dart, came to him, and there
he lived during the youth of Francis Champernowne, never
losing his interest in American colonization.   The Sey-

[1] Captain Smith's General History, 1st edition, 228.

mours of Berry Castle were also interested in colonization, Sir Edward Seymour being named a grantee in the New England charter of 1620.[1]

Francis Champernowne was hardly six years of age when an event in the Fulford family may have determined his future career. The celebrated Sir Ferdinando Gorges, then in command of the royal defences of Plymouth, married, for his second wife, Mary Fulford, relict of Thomas Achim, of Cornwall, and a sister to the mother of Francis Champernowne.[2] This alliance brought nearer together the families of Gorges and Champernowne.

It seems probable that Francis Champernowne was a favorite with his maternal kindred; for he inherited a cherished Christian name, then borne by Sir Francis Fulford, the worthy head of that ancient house. His aunt Gorges could not fail to bring to the notice of her illustrious husband a favorite nephew, one of the kindred of Gilbert and of Ralegh, and to commend him to his new uncle. Although she died in a few years, Sir Ferdinando to the end of his life continued his regard and attachment for her nephew, styling him, even in formal instruments, his "trusty and well-beloved nephew Francis Champernowne." This connection, and the

[1] Tuckett's Pedigrees, Gilbert: Gorges's Brief Narration, chap. viii. See the Virginia and the New England Charters, in Popham Memorial Volume.

[2] My thanks are due to the Rev. Frederick Brown, M.A., of Fern Bank, Beckenham, Co. Kent, England, for this and other valuable information respecting Sir Ferdinando Gorges and his family, as well as for some interesting facts relative to the Champernownes and the Fulfords, derived from his own original researches. [The Rev. Frederick Brown was much interested in Mr. Tuttle's researches, and communicated generously to him, as he did to other American correspondents, the results of his own careful and extended investigations. His researches into the history of Somersetshire families especially yielded fruit of the most valuable character. Mr. Brown died after a very brief illness at Fern Bank, Beckenham, April 1, 1886. See New England Historical and Genealogical Register, July, 1888. — II.]

12

future relations between them on the great theatre of American colonization, demand some notice of Sir Ferdinando Gorges, whose life and memorable actions have been strangely neglected by historians.

Various circumstances have combined to obscure the fame of this great man, and to exclude his name and character from that exalted station among the English worthies of his age to which they are justly entitled.[1]

Gorges is the name of one of the old patrician families of England, grown in the course of many ages into her institutions and history. This name is conspicuous in the annals of the west of England, in the days of the greatest of the Plantagenet kings. In the reign of Elizabeth many branches of it were living in the western shires, all flourishing and distinguished. In the reign of James I. one branch was elevated to the baronetage and afterwards to the peerage of England. Knights of various ranks and orders there have been in every age.[2]

In his own person Sir Ferdinando Gorges represented the highest lineage of England. He was descended from that ancient and knightly family of Gorges which had been seated many centuries at Wraxall, near Bristol, in Somersetshire. Sir Ralph de Gorges, the founder of this house, was a distinguished warrior, and was intrusted with great and responsible charges by his sovereign. He attended in 1277 Prince Edward, afterwards Edward I., in his memorable

[1] The Prince Society announces two volumes for its series, containing a Memoir of Sir Ferdinando Gorges, his Tract entitled A Brief Narration, 1658, the American Charter granted to him, and other papers, to be edited by James Phinney Baxter, A.M. This will be welcomed by historical students everywhere. — H.

[2] Compare Collinson's History of Somersetshire ; Lyson's Devonshire and Cornwall in Magna Britannia ; Hutchins's History of Dorset ; and Hoare's History of Wiltshire.

campaign to the Holy Land. Sir Edmund Gorges, Knight of the Bath, a lineal descendant, and successor to the inheritance of Wraxall, married the Lady Anne Howard, daughter of the first Duke of Norfolk, and sister of the renowned Earl of Surrey, the hero of Flodden Field, and continued his race.[1] By this marriage Sir Ferdinando Gorges, a lineal descendant of Sir Edmund, issued from the illustrious ducal families of Mowbray of Howard, and through them from Edward I., King of England. The splendor of his lineage throws a halo of romance around his name, and gilds his long and illustrious career, reaching into the reigns of three great sovereigns of England, with imperishable glory.[2]

Sir Ferdinando Gorges was born probably at Clerkenwell,[3] in the year 1565, the year of the birth of his future sovereign, James I. He was a younger son of Edward Gorges, Esquire, whose father, Sir Edmund, a grandson of Sir Edmund Gorges and the Lady Anne Howard, inherited the manor of Wraxall. Having finished his education, he went to the wars in the Low Countries, a favorite resort, in that age, of young gentlemen of quality and chivalrous courage. While there, on some occasion in the summer of 1588, he was taken prisoner with other persons of note by the Span-

[1] Compare Collinson's History of Somersetshire, 156, 157; Hume's England, chap. xxvii.

[2] Compare Berry's Hampshire Pedigrees, part i. 125, 127; Collinson's History of Somersetshire, ii. 293, and iii 156 *et seq.*, and Collins's Peerage of England, i. 63 *et seq.* It is worthy of note that John Howard, first Duke of Norfolk, ancestor of Sir Ferdinando Gorges, was slain at Bosworth Field, fighting on the side of Richard III., while Sir Edmund, Baron Carew, ancestor of Francis Champernowne, fought in the same battle on the victorious side of the Earl of Richmond, afterwards Henry VII.

[3] His father was residing at Clerkenwell when he died, Aug. 29, 1568. See New Eng. Hist. and Gene. Register, xxix. 44. — H.

iards, and his release was procured by exchange of prisoners.[1]
Three years later he was captain in the English forces
sent to aid Henry IV. of France in his war against the
Leaguers. At the attack on Noyon, the birthplace of the
immortal Calvin, he behaved with great bravery; and while
making a heroic effort to enter that town, after taking the
Abbey, he was badly wounded and taken prisoner. In this
campaign he displayed both courage and military capacity,
and his valor was rewarded by the Earl of Essex, commander of the English forces, who knighted him in the presence
of the army, on the 8th day of October, 1591, before the
besieged city of Rouen.[2] He continued in the armies of
Elizabeth, serving at home and abroad, often charged with
special duties of importance, until the autumn of 1595, when
the Queen rewarded him with the captaincy of the Castle or
Fort, and also of the Isle of St. Nicholas, at Plymouth in
Devonshire. This castle, the key to the kingdom and the
most important in the realm, had recently been constructed,
probably under his direction.[3] The office of captain was
one of high rank, being directly connected with the supreme
government of the realm, and intrusted for the most part to
noblemen of responsibility having intimate and confidential
relations with the sovereign. This was the occasion of his taking up his residence at Plymouth, then the leading commer-

---

[1] Calendar of State Papers, Domestic Series, A.D., 1581–1590, 542.
[2] Camden Miscellany, i. 27, 68, in
Camden Society Publications.
[3] Calendar of State Papers, 1595–
1597, 90, 194, 196, 362. Jewitt's History of Plymouth, Eng., 131. As early
as 1591, before the castle was finished,
the mayor and inhabitants of Plymouth

petitioned the Queen to appoint Sir
Arthur Champernowne, of Modbury,
commander. Sir Arthur was a brave
and accomplished person, and second
cousin to Arthur Champernowne, of
Dartington, father of the subject of this
memoir. Prince has an account of him
in his Worthies of Devon. See also
Jewitt's History of Plymouth, 126.

cial and naval station in the southwest of England, and immediately connected with enterprises of discovery and trade in America. Unquestionably this event had much to do with directing his spirited genius to colonization beyond the Atlantic ; for it brought him in contact with navigators, merchants, and others, whose interests were drawing them to enterprises in the New World. That he soon formed acquaintance with the Champernownes of Modbury and of Dartington, as well as with the Gilberts and the Raleghs, is probable. Nor was he without kindred of his own name and lineage in his new home ; for his great-uncle, Sir William Gorges, a distinguished naval commander, had married Winifred, a co-heiress of the ancient house of Budokeside, of St. Budeaux, near Plymouth, and there had lived and died, leaving several sons — Sir Arthur, Sir Edward, Tristram, and Robert — to inherit his estate and name. Roger Budokeside, father of the wife of Sir William Gorges, had married Frances, daughter of Sir Philip Champernowne, of Modbury, a sister of Sir Arthur, of Dartington, and of Katherine, mother of Sir Humphrey Gilbert and of Sir Walter Ralegh; and so the worthy blood of the Champernowne race was coursing in the veins of this branch of the Gorges family. Upon the death of his second wife, Mary Fulford, in 1623, Sir Ferdinando married Elizabeth, daughter of Tristram Gorges, of St. Budeaux, and resided at Kinterbury, in that parish.[1]

Sir Ferdinando Gorges held command at Plymouth until the year 1629, a period of thirty-three years, with honor to himself and to his nation.[2] In the mean time he was

---

[1] Tuckett's Pedigrees, 130; Westcote, 466 ; Lyson's Devonshire, 88. [2] Calendar of State Papers, 1628–1629, 596.

concerned in many transactions of public importance, besides
his great enterprise of colonization in America. He was one
of the general officers of the great naval fleet designed to act
against the Spaniards in the summer of 1597, commanded
by the Earl of Essex, the vice-admiral being Lord Thomas
Howard, and Sir Walter Ralegh the rear-admiral.[1]   The
Queen appointed Gorges one of the six counsellors to the
Earl of Essex in this expedition.   He sailed with the fleet
from Plymouth, but was driven back by a dreadful storm,
and sickness prevented his sailing the second time, when the
fleet went to the Azores.

Gorges was concerned in the famous insurrection of the
Earl of Essex, which cost that nobleman his life, and the
lives of many others involved with him.[2]   His sympathies,
undoubtedly, were with the misguided Earl, with whom he
had been associated in many campaigns by sea and land,
and at whose hands he had received knighthood ; but his
allegiance was due to Elizabeth.   His position was a difficult one, and his escape from the anger of offended majesty, marvellous.   He was suspended from his captaincy in
Plymouth, but was soon pardoned and restored.[3]   His conduct in this affair was much censured.   He wrote an able

[1] Sir Arthur Gorges's Narrative,
Purchas, iv. 1940 *et seq.*   The name of
Sir Arthur Gorges occurs frequently in
history.   He was cousin german to the
father of Sir Ferdinando Gorges, being
a son of Sir William Gorges, of St.
Budeaux, and second cousin to Arthur
Champernowne.   His first wife was the
Lady Douglas Howard, daughter of
Viscount Binden, and his second, the
Lady Elizabeth, daughter of Henry,
second Earl of Lincoln.   For several
generations the family of Gorges and

the family of Clinton, Earls of Lincoln,
were connected by intermarriage.   Sir
Arthur married as above.   John Gorges,
son of Sir Ferdinando, married the
Lady Frances, daughter of Thomas,
third Earl of Lincoln : and Theophilus,
fourth Earl, married Elizabeth, daughter of Sir Arthur Gorges by his first
wife.

[2] Hume's History of England, chap.
xliv.

[3] Calendar of State Papers, 1601–
1603.

defence of it, wherein he displayed ability and excellent literary taste, and showed a high order of intellect.[1]

In the opening year of the reign of Charles I. he became conspicuous by his opposition to the wishes of the court party to supply the King of France with English vessels to aid in reducing the Protestants in Rochelle. On this occasion he went to France in his own ship, the Great Neptune, and there behaved with great courage and independence, utterly refusing to allow his ship to fight against the people of Rochelle.[2]

During the war with Spain and France, which immediately followed this event, his position in Plymouth was one of much responsibility, requiring great and constant exertion. Although now more than threescore years of age, he was active during the contest, displaying as much zeal for the public welfare, and as much ability, as he had done thirty years before in the wars of Elizabeth.[3] Early in 1629 he resigned or surrendered his captaincy at Plymouth, and retired to Ashton Phillips, in Long Ashton, in his native Somersetshire. He now devoted himself to furthering his enterprises of colonization in New England. Among other things he wrote an historical narrative of his own and of his associates' efforts in settling English plantations in America, which was not published until after his death. This, his chief literary performance that has come down to us, shows him to have been an accomplished man, a superior writer, and thoroughly candid in his statements. He died at Ash-

---

[1] Folsom's Early Documents relating to Maine, 118–137.

[2] Hume's History of England, chap. l. ; Rushworth's Historical Collections, i. 175; Calendar of State Papers, 1625–1626, 66, 75, 80 *et seq.*

[3] See Gorges's official correspondence during this war, in the State Paper Office in London.

ton Phillips, at the venerable age of eighty-two years, and was buried on the 14th day of May, 1647.[1]

At the age of twenty-five he married Ann, daughter of Edward Bell, of the county of Essex, and by her had four children, two sons and two daughters. John Gorges, the eldest son, married the Lady Frances, daughter of the third Earl of Lincoln, and had children, among whom was Ferdinando Gorges, Esquire, who succeeded his grandfather as lord proprietor of the province of Maine in New England. The second son, Captain Robert Gorges, was appointed by the Council for New England governor of its dominions in America, and came hither in 1623. The two daughters died young. Sir Ferdinando married thrice after the death of his first wife in 1620, but had no other issue.[2]

Gorges had lived to witness and be an actor in many great events in his time, but none more memorable than that of English colonization in America, mainly effected through his own agency. He had lived to see a vast region in the New World inhabited by wandering savages and claimed by Spain and France, annexed to the English em-

[1] Gorges's Brief Narration in second volume of Maine Historical Collections ; Hutchins's History and Antiquities of Dorset, iii. 33 *et seq.*

[2] Sir Ferdinando Gorges married, first, at St. Margaret's, Westminster, Feb. 24, 1589-90. Ann, daughter of Edward Bell, of Writtle, County of Essex; she died Aug. 6, 1620, and was buried in St. Sepulchre's, London. By her he had four children, viz.: 1. John, born April 23, 1593 ; 2. Robert ; 3. Ellen ; 4. Honora. The last two children probably died young He married, second, Mary Fulford, daughter of Sir Thomas Fulford by Ursula Bampfylde, and widow of Thomas Achim, of Hall, in Cornwall ; she died 1623. He married, third, Elizabeth Gorges, daughter of Tristram Gorges, of Budockshed, Devon ; she had married, first, Aug. 1, 1614, at St. Budeaux, Edward Courtenay, and on his death, married —— Blithe; she died 1629. He married, fourth, at Wraxall, Sept. 23, 1629, Elizabeth, daughter of Sir Thomas Gorges, and widow of Sir Hugh Smyth, of Ashton Court, County of Somerset ; she died 1659. (Letter of the Rev. Mr. Brown, of England, to Mr. Tuttle.)

pire, and settled with men of his own race and nation.
From the wilds of Norumbega he had carved a province
for himself, and sent there his kindred and his countrymen
to colonize it. On the banks of the beautiful river of Agamenticus, the city of Gorgeana, the capital of his province,
was rising to perpetuate his name and memory when he
passed from the scene of his earthly activity.

The latter years of his life were clouded by the domestic
dissensions in England, which brought him trouble and personal suffering. The venerable old knight, "sorrowing in
the highest degree to find such a separation threatening,"
beheld with grief his kindred and friends falling around him,
and venerable institutions, civil and ecclesiastical, menaced
with destruction.[1] The fate of his beloved province in
New England, the fruit of more than forty years' labor, was
involved in this mighty civil war raging around him. His
kinsmen and his colonists were coming from thence and joining in the awful conflict; and while the issue of this dire in-
ternecine struggle was still uncertain, the grave closed over
this great man. The events which followed obscured his
memory and wasted his fortune; and for more than two
centuries his merits and his misfortunes excited but little
public interest.[2]

But the fame of Sir Ferdinando Gorges belongs to both
worlds. England owes to his memory the applause due to
a noble spirit thoroughly devoted to her interests and her
glory; and New England, the reverence and homage due to

[1] Gorges to Lord Fairfax in Bell's
Memorials of the Civil War, i. 299;
Josselyn's Two Voyages, 197.
[2] Folsom's Early Documents relating to Maine, 22; Brief Narration,
book ii. chap. 3. George Folsom and
John A. Poor have in our time ably
vindicated the merits of Gorges.

the founder of English empire in America. Without the action of this enterprising man at an exigent moment, it is doubtful whether England would ever have come peaceably into the possession of a single acre of American territory. The great commercial nations, Spain, France, and Holland, were intent on seizing and holding America to their own use. The memorable attempts of Gilbert and of Ralegh to plant English colonies in America in the time of Elizabeth languished and came to an end with her reign. When James I. ascended the throne of England, there was not an English settlement or habitation between the Straits of Magellan and the arctic snows. Virginia was then the romantic name of a wild region, with shadowy boundaries, hanging on the skirts of foreign dominions. English possession, if not title, had departed from it many years before. Spain and France held the entire continent of North America, under the grand names of New Spain and New France, claiming title in virtue of prior discovery and occupancy. While these great kingdoms were diverse in their political interests, they were one in religion; and both interests favored immediate colonization in their respective American provinces. The empire of the Latin race and religion was extending everywhere outside the limits of Europe, while the English race and the reformed religion remained shut up in the British Isles. Had the Tudor Princes been worthy of their enterprising and chivalrous subjects, especially such as dwelt in the western maritime shires, England would not only have been the first to lead the way to America, but the actual possessor of it long before this epoch.

Such was the aspect of colonization in the New World, and such the condition of England when Sir Ferdinando Gorges, moved by a noble desire to enlarge the English empire and to extend his race and religion, formed his great design of planting colonies in North America. As the origins of mighty rivers are obscure, so are the beginnings of mighty enterprises : the current is passing before our eyes ere we suspect its existence.

Time has concealed the first steps of Gorges in this great enterprise of colonization ; but they clearly lie among the first years of his residence at Plymouth. His public employments there brought him much in contact with Sir Walter Ralegh, whose memorable efforts to plant colonies in America must have been well known to Gorges. Ralegh was still looking to the New World for the aggrandizement of England, although his own enterprises to this end had not been successful ; and it is not improbable that he may have imparted a portion of his spirit to Gorges. At all events, in a few years Ralegh became disabled by his imprisonment in the Tower from further prosecuting his designs, and Gorges appears his successor on the scene.

Of all maritime towns in the kingdom, Plymouth was the fittest to awaken and nourish a spirit of foreign adventure. This ancient haven had been the theatre of preparation of those memorable fleets of discovery and colonization which had made its name as widely known as the name of the metropolis of England. Only eighteen years before, Sir Francis Drake had sailed from this port with a fleet which circumnavigated the globe, — a feat regarded with wonder in that age. Soon after Drake's return Sir Humphrey Gilbert sailed with a commission from Elizabeth to take possession of such barbarous parts of the New World as were not in the possession of any Christian prince or people. The several fleets of Sir Walter Ralegh had fitted here with all the appliances of colonization, and sailed in the track of Gilbert, marking the "course of empire" to America. The interest in colonization which these great enterprises awakened in Plymouth had not subsided when Gorges assumed command of its royal defences.

II.

HIS LIFE IN NEW ENGLAND.

On the 12th of December, 1636, Arthur Champernowne, father of Francis, became interested in New England. Sir Ferdinando Gorges, the proprietor of New Somersetshire in New England, granted[1] to him two large tracts of land lying on the sea-coast, on the east side of the Pascataqua River.[2] One of these, comprising "five hundred acres more

[1] See York Deeds, bk. iii. fols. 97, 98; also for the same grant under date of June 14, 1638, see fols. 98, 99.

[2] For more than a century and a half the name of the river which divides the extreme southern portion of Maine from New Hampshire has been commonly written Piscataqua. The name is of Indian origin, and according to Capt. John Smith (Description of New England, 1616) was *Passataquack*. In the 17th century, and in the early part of the 18th, the name was variously spelled: Pascataqua, Pascataway, Pas-cataquack, Pischataquacke, Pischataway, Piscataway, Piscataqua, etc. The last form means nothing, while Pascataqua is sufficiently accurate to represent and preserve the meaning which the aborigines intended to convey by the word; namely, "a divided tidal-place." If it be borne in mind that both by the aborigines and the early settlers the word was applied to the territory on both sides of the stream as well as to the river itself, and that the latter near its mouth is split into two streams by the rocky island New Castle, the significance and

or less," extending northeasterly to Braveboat Harbor,[1] and entirely surrounded by salt water, was to be called Dartington,[2] doubtless in honor of his native parish in Devonshire. The other tract, containing about five hundred acres of marsh land, was situate on the northeast side of Braveboat Harbor. This was to be called Godmorock.[3]

appropriateness of the name will be apparent. It is desirable that the meaningless corruption — Piscataqua — be eliminated from our geographical nomenclature. (See Mr. Tuttle's Com. in Proc. Mass.Hist.Soc., Nov 1878.) — H.

[1] No satisfactory explanation of this name has been given. — H.

[2] This tract of land, lying in the town of Kittery, in Maine, was, so far as we can learn, never called Dartington, but during the lifetime of Captain Champernowne, and for some years subsequently, was styled Champernowne's Island. A portion of it was called Elliot's Island in 1721. For a long time the island has been popularly supposed to be two islands, and the two parts have respectively borne, as they now do, the names of the families which for many generations owned and occupied them; namely, Cutts and Gerrish; but it is in fact one island, the two parts being joined together by a solid isthmus over which the sea never flows. Cutts Island contains about 350 acres. In the year 1700, this tract, with 500 acres on Raynes's Neck, was conveyed to Richard Cutt by deed from Mrs. Mary Champernowne, widow of Francis, and her daughter Elizabeth Witherick, both then being residents of South Carolina. Since that date the larger portion of the tract continued in the possession and occupancy of descendants of Richard Cutt for six generations. The larger part of the tract is now owned by Mr. John Thaxter (a son of Mrs. Celia Thaxter, the well-known writer), who

has erected a dwelling-house on the traditional site of Captain Champernowne's "upper house." He has happily named his land Champernowne's Farm. Champernowne's "lower house" was situated on the main land and near the mouth of Chauncey Creek. It was standing down to a time within the memory of men still living, and was then known as the house of Col. Paul Lewis. That part of the island which bears the name of Gerrish comprises about 1000 acres. Robert Elliot bought this land of Mrs. Champernowne, and presented it to his daughter Sarah, on her marriage with Col. Timothy Gerrish, and it has continued in the possession and occupancy of their descendants until recently. It is gratifying to learn that Mr. William H. Goodwin, of Boston, who owns a portion of " Gerrish " island, has bestowed upon it the name Dartington, given to the whole island by Gorges. — H.

[3] Godmorock is presumably the original or an early form of Gomerock. " On the eastern side or shore of the entrance to Dartmouth Harbor [Eng.] is Gomerock, formerly Gomerock Castle, where one end of the chain stretched nightly across the harbour's mouth for protection (to maintain which chain, privileges were granted to Dartmouth by royal charter) was secured; the other end being connected with a windlass in the Round Tower of Dartmouth Castle, on the opposite shore." (MS. Letter of Mr. T. Lidstone, of Dartmouth, Eng.) — H.

Whether it was the design of Arthur Champernowne to come hither and improve this grant does not appear; but his sixth and youngest son, Francis, came in the year 1637, partly or wholly in the interest of Sir Ferdinando Gorges, and lived for many years, and died on the premises granted to his father. He seems to have had a fondness for maritime life and adventure, and to have held at one time some position in the royal navy. The title Captain was given to him in all official and private documents from his first coming here. It is probable that he came[1] to Boston in company with the young Lord Ley, afterwards third Earl of Marlborough, with whom he subsequently sailed as commander at sea. It was at this time that Gorges sent out a commission to Winthrop and others for the government of his Province of New Somersetshire. Two months later he writes of his nephew Champernowne as being in New England.[2]

As early as March, 1639, Captain Champernowne was regarded as one of the leading inhabitants in the Pascataqua plantations; for he was one of the persons there to whom the General Court of the Massachusetts Bay addressed letters relative to Capt. John Underhill[3] and others in that region, who were denying and resisting the authority in civil and religious affairs which the Bay Colony was then claiming the right to exercise over the settlers within the territory granted to Capt. John Mason.[4]

While his father, as we have seen, was the proprietor of a

---

[1] In June, 1637.
[2] MS. Letter of Arthur Champernowne, Esq., of Dartington, to Mr. Tuttle; Winthrop's Hist., i. *231; Maine Hist. Coll., i. 544. — H.

[3] Belknap's Hist. of New Hampshire, Farmer's ed., 17–28; Palfrey, i. 459, 487, 591; ii. 359, 378.
[4] Mass. Rec., i. 254.

large tract of land on the east side of the mouth of the
Pascataqua, which Francis probably was authorized to look
after, he selected for his principal residence at this time [1] a
tract of land lying in a picturesque region on the southerly
side of the Great Bay and east of Winnicut River, within
the present town of Greenland, then a part of Strawberry
Bank, now Portsmouth, in New Hampshire.[2] This farm, comprising about four hundred acres, he purchased of Robert
Saltonstall and others, owners of a portion of the "Squamscott Patent," so called.[3] This estate he immediately im-

[1] It is not improbable that Champernowne was also interested in behalf
of the heirs of Capt. John Mason, and
for this and other reasons settled upon
land which was included in Mason's
grant. When the owners of the so-called
"Squamscott Patent" asserted their
title he purchased of them this land in
Greenland. — H.

[2] Portsmouth was incorporated May
28. 1653, by the General Court of Massachusetts Bay, which at that time
exercised civil authority over the settled
portions of New Hampshire. The first
considerable settlement in New Hampshire was made on Great Island, lying
between the two mouths of the Pascataqua, and there for the next seventy-
five years was the seat of the government of the Province. A fort was
erected at an early day, and was popularly named the Castle. In 1693 Great
Island was set off from Portsmouth,
and incorporated as a town by the
name of New Castle. The fort or
castle had been enlarged and newly
equipped the year preceding the incorporation of the town, and this fact,
it is believed, suggested the name of
the new town. There certainly is no
ground for supposing, with some writers,
that the name was conferred in honor of
the Duke of Newcastle, or suggested by
the English city Newcastle. The name

is properly written in two words, as
above. See Albee's New Castle. — H.

[3] On the 12th of March, 1629 (O. S.),
the Council for the Affairs of New England in America granted to Edward
Hilton, a planter at Dover in New
Hampshire, and his associates, a considerable tract of land on the Pascataqua River. In 1632 the grantees sold
their patent, and the purchasers, through
their resident agent or agents, proceeded
to lay out and bound their patent. They
located the greater part of it on the
southerly side of the Pascataqua River
and the Great Bay. This portion of the
Hilton patent came to be known in
popular language as the "Squamscott
Patent." The present town of Greenland and other towns were claimed as a
part of this grant. This patent, or the
claims set up under it, became the
source of much controversy and liti-
gation, and the true construction of the
patent, its location and extent, have
long been a matter of discussion. The
original of the Hilton patent has undoubtedly perished, but a copy, or what
purports to be one, made by a careless
or illiterate copyist, was discovered a
few years ago by the Hon. Charles H.
Bell, among the court papers at Exeter,
N. H., and a transcript of the same
was printed in the New England Historical and Genealogical Register for

proved by building a dwelling-house and other structures thereon. The farm was then usually called Greenland,[1]

July, 1870. (See Belknap's History of New Hampshire, Farmer's Ed., 9 ; Provincial Papers of New Hamp., i. 211, 221, 223 ; Mass. Rec. iii. 409–412.) For an elaborate and interesting discussion of the Hilton Patent, see Notes on the First Planting of New Hampshire and on the Piscataqua Patents, by John S. Jenness, Portsmouth, 1878. Mr. Jenness's contention is, that the Hilton Patent was fraudulently construed by the purchasers to include territory south of the Pascataqua River and the Great Bay, and that the authorities of Massachusetts Bay connived at and profited by this construction. But this charge against Massachusetts, in the form made, does not appear to the editor to be warranted by any facts known to him.

The late Hon. Samuel D. Bell, Chief Justice of New Hampshire, one of the most learned and critical students of the history of that State, was of the opinion that the Hilton Patent was not intended to cover any territory south of the River Pascataqua. (Prov. Papers of New Hamp., i. 29.) It is not certain, however, that Judge Bell had seen the full text of the Hilton Patent.

The subject is too large for full discussion in a foot-note : but this in brief may be remarked : If it be objected that this grant to Hilton and his associates conflicted with existing grants from the same grantors, the reply would be that similarly conflicting grants were made of territory in Massachusetts and in Maine. What were the motives and considerations that induced Warwick, President of the Council, to issue these grants, perhaps in some cases without the consent or even knowledge of his associates, can only be conjectured. A clause in the grant reads as follows : " All that part of the River Pascataquack called or known by the name of Wecanacohunt or Hilton's Point, with *the south side of the said River up to*

the Fall of the River, and three miles into the main land with all the breadth thereof." Mr. Jenness contended that the boundary line ran up " the southerly side of that river to the lower or Quampegan Falls [not the Squamscott Falls in Exeter, — ED.], a distance of some seven or eight miles, and reached back into the interior country three miles along the entire river frontage ;" and that the " name *Piscataqua*" was never " applied by the English or the Indians to the Exeter River, on which the Squamscott Falls are situated." But the fact whether or not the Pascataqua River was understood at the time to extend to Quampegan Falls, and not to include Exeter River, — which empties into the Bay at its extreme southwestern limit, — is the point on which the controversy mainly turns. This question needs to be more thoroughly investigated. The strangest fact in this matter is, that some twenty months later than the date of the grant to Hilton and his associates, the same grantors (the Grand Council for the affairs of New England) conveyed to Sir Ferdinando Gorges, Capt. John Mason, and others, territory on both sides of the Pascataqua, and including the larger part of the land embraced in the " Squamscott Patent," and there are no words of reservation in the later grant. This fact, it has been urged, is quite conclusive as to the location intended in the Hilton Patent. For the Grant and Confirmation of Pescataway, see Tuttle's Captain John Mason, Prince Soc., 198–204 ; also Jenness's Notes on the First Planting of New Hampshire, 82–84. For a remarkable chapter of the history of conflicting territorial grants in Massachusetts, see the paper on the Patent of Mariana, by the Hon. Charles Levi Woodbury, in Tuttle's Mason, cited above, 45–52. — H.

[1] Greenland as the name of a hamlet

SITE OF CAPT. FRYE'S CAMPAIGN AT CHAMPERNOON'S POINT 1745-6.
GREENLAND, NEW HAMPSHIRE.

and this name was communicated to a portion of the town in which it lay.

On the 3d of April, 1639, Sir Ferdinando Gorges received from King Charles a patent of the territory lying between the Pascataqua and the Kennebec rivers, with full powers of government, being himself made lord palatine over the same.[1] For some reason not apparent, the old name, Province of Maine, bestowed on this territory in the grant of the same in 1622 to Gorges and Mason by the President and Council for New England, was restored, and the name New Somersetshire disappeared. By this change New Hampshire was thereafter the only English province in America named for an English county.

In September of the same year (1639) Gorges issued a commission for the government of his province, appointing Sir Thomas Josselyn[2] Deputy Governor, who declined the

or of a parish is not unknown in England. There was anciently a cove or dock in the harbor of Dartmouth called "Greenland Dock." The name must have been familiar to Champernowne from his boyhood days, and he it was undoubtedly who bestowed the name on his farm at the Great Bay. The name appears for the first time on the records of Portsmouth under the date of July 10, 1655, and it came at length to be applied to the western part of Portsmouth; and when that part was erected into a township it retained, as it still retains, the name bestowed by Champernowne. It has been repeatedly stated in print that Greenland was incorporated as a town in 1703. This is an error. It was set off as a separate parish in 1706, but the rights and privileges of a distinct township were not granted till 1732. See Town Papers of New Hampshire, ix. 320-328; xii. 64. — H.

[1] The charter of 1639 from the King was a confirmation of the grant by the Council for New England in 1635. It has been said that never before nor since were so ample powers of government granted to a British subject. A comparison of the terms of this charter with the other charters of that period confirms the statement. For the charter, see Hazard's Collections, i. 443-445; Sullivan's History of District of Maine. 397-408. See also Williamson's History of Maine, i. ch. vi., and Palfrey's History of New England, i. 524. — H.

[2] Until the publication of Folsom's Collection of Original Documents relating to the Early History of Maine, in 1858, it had been the understanding that Sir Thomas Josselyn never visited New England. Under date of Sept. 3, 1639, and attached to a copy of the commission and ordinances sent by

14

office, and afterwards his cousin Thomas Gorges,[1] and
several well-known residents in the Province, Councillors,

Gorges to his Province in Maine, is the following memorandum : "Whereas, Sir Thomas Josselyn, Kt. was named chief in the said Commission and Ordinances, and he being now returned to England, . . . Thomas Gorges is put in his room with the same powers," etc. This raised the presumption that Sir Thomas did visit New England. The publication of the Trelawny Papers by the Historical Society of Maine in 1884, clearly showed that he came in 1638, with his son John Josselyn, the author of An Account of Two Voyages to New England, and of other well-known works. See the valuable communication respecting Henry Jocelyn and the Josselyn Family, by Mr. William M. Sargent, in the New Eng. Hist. and Gene. Reg., xl. 290–294; Dr. Charles E. Banks' memoir of Edward Godfrey (1887), 16, 17, note ; and note 2 *postea*, p. 112. — H.

[1] Thomas Gorges was the eldest son of Henry Gorges, of Battcombe Manor, near Cheddar, Somersetshire, by Barbara Baynard, his wife, which Henry Gorges was grandson of Sir William Gorges, Kt., Admiral. He was born about 1618. He went to Maine in 1640, and was the first mayor of York. Governor Winthrop speaks of him as "a young Gentleman of the Inns of Court . . . sober and well disposed." He returned to England in 1643. He and his brother John Gorges were elected members of Parliament for the borough of Taunton, Somerset, in 1654, and he was again elected for Taunton in 1655, along with Robert Blake, the celebrated General and Admiral of the Parliament. They are mentioned in Thurlow's State Papers, v. 302. In Harl. Miscellany, iii. 430, is "a Narration of the late Parliaments," 1657, and a list of "those serving for England, sitting in the House,

that have civil employments and salaries from the State ;" among these is Col. Thomas Gorges, "one of the Commissioners for the New Building : " "His advantage thereby cannot well be known till he and his Brethren have racked the Consciences, flayed off the skins, and broken the bones of the poor people, making them swear ag[s] themselves." He is mentioned among those who spoke in the House of Commons, in the Diary of Thos. Burton. 1656–1659, published 1828. There are letters of his to his brother Dr. Robert Gorges, secretary to H. Cromwell, Lord Lieutenant of Ireland, in the Lansdowne MSS., British Museum, Feb. 15 and March 1, 1658. In 1659 he and his brother John Gorges were feoffees of the town lands of Taunton. In 1658 and 1660 he was M.P. for Taunton ; he had two wives.

Thomas Gorges married, first, Mary Sanford, daughter of Martin Sanford, Esq., of Nynehead Court, Somersetshire, near Wellington. This marriage took place before 1649. She was buried at Nynehead.

He married, secondly, Rose Alexander, daughter of Sir Jerome Alexander, Kt., and widow of Rawlin Mallach, Esq., of Cockington, Devon. Heavitree, near Exeter, register of marriages : "1656, March 23. Mr. Thomas Gorge and Mrs. Rosse Mallach were married." She died a few months after her husband, and is buried at Heavitree.

An old gravestone in Heavitree Church records that "Here lyeth the Bodyes of Thomas Gorges of Heavitree, Esq[re] and Rose his wife. He departed this life Oct. 17, 1670, and shee April 14, 1671.

'The loving Turtell having mist her mate
Beg'd shee might enter, ere they shut the
gate.

one of whom was his nephew Francis Champernowne. Thomas Gorges came over in the summer of 1640, and a

Their dust here lies, whose soules to Heaven are gonne, And wait till angels rowle away the Stone.' "

Sir Jerome Alexander, in his will March 23, 1670, mentions "his daughter Rose Gorges," and her children Rawlin and Ann Mallach, and Alexander and Elisab. Gorges.

The will of Thomas Gorges of Heavitree is dated Sept. 25, 1669, proved April 1, 1671, by Rose Gorges his widow. He speaks of his brother Capt. Ferdinando Gorges, of London. He bequeaths various estates to his eldest son Thomas Gorges, then under 24, and " one great silver Tankard with the Whirlpoole ingraven on it, being the ancient coate of my family." He bequeaths money to be raised from various estates "to bind my son Ferdinando an apprentice, and for the carrying on of the Trade to which he shall be bound." " To my son Henry, whose hitherto unguided temper hath carried him to Barbadoes, where he is at present," £200 and a tenement in Hemyoch, Devon. Also "to my son Thomas Gorges — whereas I have a good and indefeasible estate of Inheritance in 5000 acres of Land lying on the River Ogarhogg, otherwise Ogungigg, in the Province of Maine in New England, granted unto me for consideration in my Deed thereof, bearing date Aug. 4, 1641, under the seal of the Province, therein expressed by Sir Ferdinando Gorges, the Lord Provincial of the said Province of Maine according to the power and right he had then to the said Province and every part thereof, which said Deed of Feoffment being now in my custody, one also then enrolled amongst the Records of the said Province, and of which 5000 Acres I took peacable and quiet possession Aug. 18, 1642, all which lands and cattle thereon I give unto

my son Thomas Gorges." " To my son Ferdinando Gorges a two handled cup of Silver with the Covering, having on it the arms of Gorges and Sanford. To my daughter Susannah, now the wife of Rawlin Mallach of Cockington, Devon, £700 and plate and various books. To my two Children Alexander and Elisabeth Gorges my Manors of river Trewynt and Nether Trewynt in the Parish of Poundstock, Cornwall."

On June 2, 1676, another Commission to administer other goods of Thomas Gorges was issued to Ferdinando Gorges, son of the deceased Thomas Gorges, Rose Gorges, his widow, having died.

The eldest son of Thomas Gorges of Heavitree was Thomas Gorges, born about 1651, as his name appears amongst the Oxford graduates as son of Thomas Gorges, Esq., of Heavitree, Devon ; entered Wadham College, Oxford, in 1668, aged about 17. The second son was Ferdinando Gorges, whom his father wished to be bound apprentice in trade. He had property bequeathed to him " in St. Audrey's, Somerset, given him by his God Father John Tynte, his Father's kinsman." The third son was Henry Gorges, a scapegrace, living in Barbados in 1668. His eldest daughter was Susanna, born 1649. Marriage allegations, Vicar-General's Office, May 25, 1669: " Rawlin Mallach of Heavitree, Devon, Esq., Bachelor, aged 21, and Susan Gorges of the same place, Spinster, aged 20." Rawlin Mallach was probably the son of her stepmother, Rose Mallach, *alias* Alexander. She died April 17, 1673, and was buried at Heavitree, April 20, and is described as " daughter of Thomas Gorges of Battcombe, Somerset, Esq." Rose Mallach had also a daughter Ann, who married Martin Greenwood. The children of Thomas Gorges and Rose Mallach were : 1. Alexander Gorges, born July 29, 1660,

government was organized. The records do not show that Champernowne was present at any of the meetings of the Governor and Council while this government subsisted.

In the absence of a general government of New Hampshire at this period, the inhabitants of the several plantations were compelled to enter into combinations for the preservation of order and the protection of personal rights. A new combination of residents on the upper part of the Pascataqua was formed October 22, 1640. Captain Champernowne was one of the forty-two signers of this compact.[1]

Edward Saunders was his agent, and in 1644 rented the whole or a part of the Greenland farm for a term of years. In the mean time the Colony of Massachusetts Bay had extended its jurisdiction over the settled parts of New Hampshire. Champernowne was undoubtedly displeased with this proceeding; for, being a Churchman and a stanch royalist, he had no sympathy with the Bay colonists in either political or religious matters. In a manuscript record made before 1680, describing with considerable minuteness the leading residents on both sides of the Pascataqua River, I find Captain Champernowne set down as "a man always for the King, and was a commander at sea under the Lord of Marlborough many years ago."

I find no record of him as being in New England later than November, 1641, and before 1648. It is therefore probable that he returned into England on the breaking out of the civil war, and accepted a command in the King's fleet under the Earl of Marlborough. This fleet, in the

---

and baptized at Heavitree ; 2. Elisabeth Gorges. born April 14, 1662, and baptized at Heavitree ; 3. Edward Gorges, born May 15, 1666, and buried at Heavi-

tree, June 14, 1667. (Com. to Mr. Tuttle by the late Rev. Frederick Brown.)

[1] See Appendix, No. 1.

years 1644 and 1645, hovered about the Madeira Islands, and annoyed the shipping of the Massachusetts Bay, known to be engaged on the side of Parliament. When the King's cause had become desperate and Parliament everywhere supreme, Champernowne returned to his Pascataqua plantations, and began or resumed commercial undertakings.

In December, 1648, he appears again in the public records, making a conveyance in his own right of one half of all the land in Maine granted to his father by Gorges. This conveyance was to Capt. Paul White, a Pemaquid trader, in consideration of £200 sterling. It does not appear how the title to this land vested in Captain Champernowne, but probably it was by gift from his father. The island which was formally named Dartington in the grant by Gorges twelve years before was called Champernowne's Island in the conveyance to White, — a name which attached to it until the reign of Queen Anne. Houses and other buildings had already been erected on the island, as well as on the tract beyond Braveboat Harbor. In this deed Champernowne agreed to place fifteen swine on the island, and to divide the same and the increase with White. The result of this transaction was a lawsuit, and the return of the premises to the grantor.

As early as the year 1650 Captain Champernowne went to Barbados, and was absent until the spring of 1654, leaving his affairs in the charge of Thomas Withers of Kittery,[1] one of the principal men in Gorges' province. In

---

[1] Kittery lies partly on the sea-coast of Maine, and has the Pascataqua River for its southern boundary. It originally comprised, besides its present territory, that of the following towns; namely, Eliot, Berwick, South Berwick, and North Berwick, all of which was known at the time of the first settlement, in 1623, as a portion of the region lying partly in New Hampshire and partly in Maine, called the Plantation of Pascataqua. It is one of the most picturesque, and in summer one of the most attractive, portions of Maine, whose

November, 1650,[1] Withers leased Champernowne's farm on the Great Bay in New Hampshire to Samuel Haines,[2] for ninety pounds, for the term of two years. In a division of public lands of Portsmouth made in 1653, Champernowne's share was fifty acres, being the largest number of acres that fell to any one inhabitant.

In 1655 the town made to him a further grant of three hundred and seventy-five acres of "marsh, meadow, and upland." This grant was laid out in the same year, and was referred to in conveyances of land in Greenland for more than half a century as Champernowne's "new farm."[3] While

entire coast line is wonderfully indented with bays and coves, while the numerous islands lying near the mainland add greatly to the beauty of the scenery. A portion of Kittery is rocky and sterile, but other portions are under a fair degree of cultivation; and the town is now, as it has been from the first, inhabited by an intelligent, industrious, orderly, and remarkably homogeneous population. The name was probably given to it by Champernowne, or by Alexander Shapleigh. "Kittery Court is situated on the eastern shore of the river Dart, immediately southward of the ancient village of Kingsweare (which faces the town of Dartmouth), and, owing to a turn in the river there, it (Kittery) faces the narrow mouth of the Dart, the entrance to Dartmouth harbor from the English Channel. . . . The bend of the river at Kittery Court forms a point called Kittery Point" [a name applied also to a part of Kittery, in Maine. ED.]. (MS. Letter of Mr. T. Lidstone, of Dartmouth, Eng.) — H.

[1] For a notice of Thomas Withers, see Trelawny Papers, 238, note; also the authorities there cited. — H.

[2] Samuel Haines, born in England about the year 1611, came from Westbury, Wiltshire, to New England in 1635. He was a passenger in the ship Angel

Gabriel, which was wrecked at Pemaquid (now Bristol) Maine, Aug. 15, 1635. He was at Ipswich, Mass., in 1635-1636, at Dover, N. H., 1640-1649. and settled near the Great Bay, in what is now Greenland, in 1650, where he died about 1686-1687. He was a worthy and trusted inhabitant of Portsmouth, — holding various and responsible offices by the choice of his townsmen, and was one of the founders and a deacon of the first Congregational Church, at its organization in 1671. He was a neighbor and friend of Captain Champernowne. He owned much land in Greenland, which he divided among his children while living. He was the progenitor of the Haineses in New Hampshire, and of nearly all who bear the name in Maine and Vermont. Two of his descendants of the sixth generation — the late Hon. William P. Haines, of Biddeford, Me., and the Hon. Andrew M. Haines, of Galena, Illinois — have published valuable papers relating to the Haines family, and the early history of Greenland, in the New Eng. Hist. and Gene. Register (xxii. 451-455; xxiii. 151-169, 430-433; xxviii. 251, 415; xxix. 30-40). — H.

[3] Greenland is one of the most attractive of the towns in eastern New Hampshire. Especially is this true of

Champernowne was absent, several civil suits were brought against him, which were stayed by the court until his return.

He lived on his Greenland farm until the month of July, 1657, when he conveyed it to Valentine Hill, upon some agreement with Hill to satisfy a claim of Captain White, and for other considerations. Hill immediately conveyed the farm to Thomas Clarke and William Paddy, merchants of Boston. It is probable that some condition in the sale to Hill was broken, and the title again vested in Champernowne; for in March, 1669, he conveyed the same premises to Nathaniel Fryer, Henry Langstaff, and Philip Lewis.

From the Greenland farm he removed to Kittery, and settled on that portion of his estate which is now known as Cutts Island.

the farms lying on the shores of the Great Bay, — a large tidal lake fed from the sea through the Pascataqua River. One of these farms, comprising about four hundred acres, includes the "old farm" of Captain Champernowne. The natural features of the region, so similar to what he had been accustomed in Old England, could not fail to captivate his mind. "Here dwelt, for many years, in something of antique breadth and state that relative and almost companion of Ralegh and Gilbert; that noblest born and bred of all New Hampshire's first planters. Grand old English oaks, planted, as tradition has it, by the Captain's own hands, still lift their brave vigorous heads over the fertile meadows, — true Herne's oaks, as we exclaimed at the first glance, — unique in New Hampshire; a scene as beautiful as that from Windsor Castle over Datchet Mead." (Jenness's Notes, 69-70.) The "old farm" has been in the possession and occupancy of the Peirce family since the year 1809, and is now owned by the heirs of the late Col. Joshua Winslow Peirce. (See New Eng. Hist. and Gene. Register, xxviii. 367-372.)

The "new farm," also mentioned in the text, comprising nearly four hundred acres, included the southerly portion of the site of the village, and extended from a point on the easterly side of the road leading to Hampton in a north-westerly direction to, or nearly to, Winnicut River. A portion of the road here referred to is about seven rods wide. This extraordinary width was provided for in the vote of the town of Portsmouth making the grant, in 1655. "The Capt⁀ is to allowe the waye through the sayd lott to be seuen pols wide and to be commone to his naighbors." Portsm. Rec., i. 31 : Deed from Partridge and Packer to Matthias Haines, Sept. 20, 1717 (Reg. of Deeds, Exeter, ix. 648). — H.

His removal to Kittery nearly coincided with the restoration of Charles II. to the throne of England; an event which was immediately felt in New England by all parties, and especially by the Gorges and the Mason interests. Their respective territories, as we have seen, had been for many years under the rule of the Massachusetts Colony, asserted and forcibly maintained on a baseless claim that they were included in the patent of Massachusetts Bay. Champernowne was a devoted royalist, zealous and active in the interest of young Ferdinando Gorges, who had applied to the King to compel Massachusetts to restore to him the Province of Maine granted to his grandfather, Sir Ferdinando Gorges, with powers of government. Gorges issued a commission,[1] May 23, 1661, to Francis Champernowne, Henry Jocelyn,[2] Nicholas Shapleigh,[3] and Robert Jordan,[4]

[1] Maine Documents (Folsom's Coll.), 41.

[2] Henry Jocelyn, who was prominently and honorably connected with the interests of Gorges and the early affairs of Maine, was a son of Sir Thomas Josselyn (see note 2, *antea*, p. 105), and brother of John Josselyn, the author. His autograph signature, in every instance that has come to the knowledge of the editor, shows that he used the form of his surname given in the text. For a sketch of his life, see New Eng. Hist. and Gene. Reg., xl. 290-294; Williamson's Maine. i. 682; also, Trelawny Papers, 8, note. — H.

[3] Nicholas Shapleigh was a large landowner in Kittery, and other parts of Maine, a prominent ship-merchant, and exercised much influence. He held various offices under the government instituted by Gorges and his deputies, and likewise under the authority of Massachusetts. He was born about the year 1610, at or near Dartmouth, Co. Devon, and emigrated to Maine probably some time previous to 1640. His father, Alexander Shapleigh, a shipowner, and largely interested in the trade and plantation of the Province, was permanently settled in Kittery as early as 1640. Nicholas married Alice, daughter of Mrs. Ann Godfrey, wife of Edward Godfrey, sometime Governor of the Province. He died in Kittery on the 29th of April, 1682, leaving no children. The foregoing is chiefly extracted from a very valuable paper on "the Descendants of Alexander Shapleigh," communicated to the editor by J. Hamilton Shapley, Esq., of Exeter, N. H. His paper is deposited with the New England Historic Genealogical Society. See also Williamson's Maine, and The Trelawny Papers. — H.

[4] Notices of the Rev. Robert Jordan may be found in the Jordan Memorial, Willis's Portland, Williamson's Maine, Trelawny Papers, and the New Eng. Hist. and Gene. Register. — H.

authorizing them to take charge of his interests in the Province of Maine. They accepted, and met at Wells on the 27th day of December following.[1] They drew up a declaration setting forth their determination to proclaim King Charles in the Province; to collect the rents due the proprietor; to adopt the laws of England; and to maintain the rights of the proprietor, and of the freeholders of the Province.[2] Champernowne took the lead in this work of restoring and retaining the jurisdiction and authority of Gorges as lord proprietor of the Province of Maine. Neither his zeal nor his labors abated while there was any prospect of success in these efforts.

In March, 1662, Champernowne and his associates, acting under a commission from the lord proprietor, Ferdinando Gorges, issued a warrant to the marshal commanding him to seize all roll-books, records, and public writings, and deliver the same to Captain Champernowne. In a few weeks the marshal made return that he had executed the warrant.[3]

In May of the same year Champernowne and his associate commissioners issued a formal protest against any and all proceedings in the Province not derived from the King's authority.[4] The authority of Gorges was wellnigh again established by his commissioners when the Massachusetts Colony, in 1663, awoke from the stupor into which it had been thrown by the restoration of the King to the throne of his ancestors, and the contempt shown for its authority in its subjugated territory. That Colony despatched three of its magistrates into Maine, directing them to hold court and

---

[1] Maine Documents, 41.
[2] Maine Documents, 42.
[3] Maine Documents, 42.
[4] Maine Documents, 45.

to re-establish the authority of the Colony there.[1] This was successfully done in spite of all remonstrance on the part of Champernowne and others. The Massachusetts agents proceeded with a high hand. Champernowne and his associates — all leading citizens — were indicted by the court, and fined for these acts in behalf of the lord proprietor.[2] But this arbitrary and unjust procedure did not in the least abate his zeal for Gorges' and the King's interests. This year, and again in 1665, his name appears among the signers of the petitions of the inhabitants of New Hampshire, praying the King to free them from the usurped rule of Massachusetts. His name leads on the latter petition, and it is not improbable that it originated with him.[3]

In June, 1664, the King commanded Massachusetts to surrender the Province of Maine to Gorges or his commissioners.[4] This order brought joy to Champernowne and the other royalists in the Province, as well as to all those who were in the Gorges interest.[5] On the 5th day of November following, Champernowne and his old associates again united in issuing a proclamation setting forth the King's order relative to Gorges, and forbidding any acts inconsistent therewith, and especially

---

[1] Thomas Danforth, William Hathorne, and Eleazer Lusher.

[2] Folsom's Saco and Biddeford.

[3] Maine Documents, 57.

[4] It must be a cause of ceaseless wonder to every candid student of New England history that the leading men of Massachusetts — men eminent for their intelligence and personal integrity — could have made and enforced the claim that their charter covered the territorial grants to Mason in New Hampshire, and to Gorges in Maine. At the same time candor will compel the admission that both these Provinces were better governed, and were more orderly and prosperous, under the political administration of the Bay Colony, than they had ever been before that authority was extended over them ; and, further, that it would have been better for the people of these Provinces, if that authority had been left undisturbed. — H.

[5] Maine Documents, 64.

forbidding any interference with the affairs of the Province by Massachusetts.[1]

In June, 1664, the Royal Commissioners[2] appointed by the King arrived in New England. They were empowered to hear and determine all complaints, appeals, and other matters coming before them, whether civil, military, or criminal; to proceed therein "according to their good and sound discretion," and to "settle the peace and security of the country."[3] In the following year three of the Commissioners proceeded to New Hampshire and Maine.[4] They were cordially welcomed by Champernowne, and by all others who were upholders of the authority of the King and the interests of Gorges.[5]

On the 21st day of June Champernowne and Jocelyn issued a summons to the inhabitants of York, calling on

[1] This proclamation is here reproduced. It well illustrates the spirit and purpose of the men who signed it, and reflects no discredit upon its author. — H.

"Whereas his Gracious Majesty King Charles the Second hath been pleased to confirm by his immediate order unto Ferdinando Gorges, Esq., the Government & territories of the Province of Maine for ever, & to Command a resignation from all persons usurping the foresaid Government whereof we are Commanded to give signification: Wee do therefore give notice to all persons of the unlawfulness of any such act, more particularly to the Governor and Councell of the Massachusetts Colony; protesting against their intermedling with the government thereof as they will answer the Contrary at his Majesty's indignation: Which is done in the name of Ferdinando Gorges, Esq., Sole Proprietor thereof, & declared so to be by the forementioned Act of Grace; for proof & in the maintenance whereof we do appeale to his Majesty's honorable Commissioners: Colonel Richard Nichols, Sir Robert Carr, George Cartwright, Esq., Samuel Mavericke, Esq., from whom wee shall all expect equal justice.

"Dated Nov. 5, 1664.
    FRAN: CHAMPERNOWNE *Com'r.*
    HENRY JOCELYN *Comr.*
    JOHN ARCHDALE *Com.*
    ROBERT JORDON *Com.*
    EDW: RISHWORTH *Com'r.*
    FRAN: RAYNES *Com'r.*
    THOM: WITHERS *Comr.*"
       [Mass. Arch., iii. 264].

[2] Col. Richard Nichols, Sir Robert Carr, George Cartwright, and Samuel Mavericke.

[3] Hutch. History, i. 459, 460; Hazard's Coll., i. 638; Williamson's History, i. 409 (note); Palfrey.

[4] Carr, Cartwright, and Mavericke.

[5] For a thorough understanding of the grounds on which the Royal Commissioners were appointed, the history of their proceedings, the obstacles they encountered, and the results of their intervention, the historical student will

them to assemble the next day and hear the formal publication of the authority of the Royal Commissioners.[1] The Commissioners, having heard the various parties who came before them in regard to the several complaints, and other matters submitted to them by the inhabitants of the Province, resolved, pursuant to their instructions, to place the government under the King's immediate protection and control. Accordingly, on the 23d day of June they formally appointed and commissioned eleven of the principal inhabitants of the Province justices of the peace, giving them authority to hear and determine all causes, civil and criminal, and to order all the affairs of the Province. These were the first officers of this title in New England, and it is believed that never before nor since anywhere were such large powers given to officers bearing this title.

Captain Champernowne was the first justice named in the Commission. He and his associate justices continued to act according to their commission without serious interruption until the summer of 1668, when Massachusetts made another and a successful struggle for the government of the Province.[2] On the 6th day of July the Massachusetts Commissioners invaded the Province, supported by an armed force, and undertook the administration of government.

not be content with any partisan statement. Nothing in the history of the relations of the King and his advisers to the New England colonies at this period is more remarkable than that the Royal Commissioners should have been so ignorant of the spirit and purpose of the leaders in the several colonies as to come with the instructions they bore, but without any armed force to execute said instructions, or maintain their own authority. Indecision and imbecility marked the proceedings of the King and Council in regard to American affairs for nearly half a century. That this was largely due to the fact that some of the trusted advisers of Charles I. and Charles II. were in the pay of the colonies, or influenced by their paid agents, is hardly open to doubt. — H.

[1] Mass. Archives, iii. 67.
[2] Maine Documents. 78.

Champernowne and his associate justices put forth a formal protest against this usurpation;[1] but the protest availed nothing against superior force. The Massachusetts Commissioners fully established the authority of that Colony over the Province.

Champernowne never relinquished his hope of seeing the Province again under royal authority. He lived to see it return on the forfeiture of the Massachusetts Charter, and to hold a high position in the government.

In the year 1672 Champernowne and Jocelyn again endeavored to have a royal government established over both Maine and New Hampshire;[2] but the effort was fruitless. Five years later Ferdinando Gorges sold his interest in the Province to the Massachusetts Bay Colony.[3] This act, which was highly displeasing to the King,[4] and the frequent and distressing Indian wars,[5] put an end for

[1] Maine Documents, 80.

[2] Maine Documents, 14

[3] This sale was consummated March 13, 1677, and the purchase was ratified and confirmed by the General Court of Massachusetts in the following October. The sum paid was £1250 sterling. In this transaction John Usher, a Boston trader, acted as broker for Massachusetts. The negotiations had undoubtedly been in progress for some time. The fact that the bargain had been concluded between Gorges and Usher was communicated by Robert Mason to a member of the Privy Council a few days later (Jenness's Original Documents, 83). Fifteen years before this, Daniel Gookin. in behalf of Massachusetts, had urged Gorges to sell his proprietary rights (Maine Documents, 55). See Coll. Maine Hist. Soc., ii. 257–264; also the letter of John Collins, of London, to Governor Leverett in 1674

(Hutch. Coll., Prince Soc. ed., ii. 183), and Williamson's Maine, i. 451, note. — H.

[4] See the King's letter to Massachusetts, Hutch. Coll. (Prince Soc. ed.), ii. 260. Williamson (History of Maine, i. 554) says: "The purchase was open and fair." Palfrey (History of New England, iii. 312) says: "Massachusetts had outwitted the King." It could hardly have been an "open" transaction by which the King and his Council were taken by surprise. At the best it was a case of sharp practice, from which, it is safe to say, Massachusetts in the end derived no political benefit: nor can it scarcely be doubted that this transaction was one of the elements that embittered the controversy which resulted in the abrogation of the Charter. — H.

[5] For an interesting account of Philip's War, see Palfrey's New England, iii. chaps. v. and vi. Williamson (His-

a time to all efforts to secure the re-establishment of the royal authority in Maine.

In the Spring of 1678, Captain Champernowne, Nicholas Shapleigh, and Nathaniel Fryer[1] were appointed commissioners to settle a treaty of peace with Squando and other Indian chiefs in Maine. The parties met at Casco, now Portland, and agreed upon the terms of a treaty, and signed the same on the 12th of April.[2] This is the only instance where Champernowne exercised any authority derived from Massachusetts or from any local source. Nor do I find that he ever held any local office, or exercised any public authority not derived directly or indirectly from the Crown.[3]

In October, 1676, Edward Randolph reported to the Privy Council of England that "among the most popular and well-principled men who only wait for an opportunity

tory of Maine, i. chap. xx.) gives a summary and substantially accurate statement of the Indian hostilities in Maine at this period, and the terrible sufferings and losses resulting therefrom. The student of Philip's War will find a large body of valuable material, most of which had never before been printed, in the series of papers contributed by the Rev. Geo. M. Bodge, A.M., to the New Eng. Hist. and Gene. Register, xxxii. *et seq.* — H.

[1] For a sketch of the life of the Hon. Nathaniel Fryer, see Coll. New Hamp. Hist. Soc., viii. 353-356. — H.

[2] Belknap (History of New Hampshire, Farmer's ed., 83) says: "The terms of the treaty were disgraceful, but not unjust, considering the former irregular conduct of many of the eastern settlers," etc. Williamson follows Belknap substantially, and agrees with him

in thinking that, however humiliating the treaty may have seemed, it was preferable to a predatory warfare and "its consequent deprivations and calamities." Lieutenant-Governor Brockholls of New York, in a letter to Captain Knapton, under date of June 7, 1678, says: "The Agreement of peace made by the Gents. of Piscataway and the Indian Sachems . . . I think is a good piece of work." (Coll. Maine Hist. Soc., v. 24.) The original and all copies of the treaty seem to have perished. — H.

[3] The early records of Portsmouth show that at a general town meeting held on the 27th of March, 1654, Captain Champernowne was chosen one of the selectmen for that year. At that time he was a resident of Portsmouth, and living on his Greenland farm. Whether or not he accepted the office, does not appear. — H.

to express their duty to his Majesty," in New England, was "Captain Champernowne."[1]

In May, 1684, Cranfield, Lieutenant-Governor of the royal Province of New Hampshire, nominated Champernowne as a member of his Council, and recommended his confirmation to his superiors in England.[2] It does not appear what, if anything further, was done in the premises. Cranfield left the Province a few months subsequently. His character and standing is further illustrated by the fact that in the month of July of this year Champernowne was made one of five trustees, for the benefit of the inhabitants of Kittery, of all the lands or properties within the bounds and limits of said township, formerly granted by Sir Ferdinando Gorges, Knt., or by any of his agents, or by the General Assembly of Massachusetts. This was done by an indenture, in which Massachusetts was represented by Thomas Danforth, President of the Province of Maine. The same year the charter of Massachusetts Bay was

---

[1] As to Randolph, see pages 277–326, *postea;* and Tuttle's Life of Capt. John Mason, edited by John Ward Dean, A.M. (Prince Soc. 1887), 102, note 197, and the authorities there cited. — H.

[2] It has been supposed and assumed hitherto, that, after leaving his Greenland farm in New Hampshire, Captain Champernowne continued to be a resident of Maine until his death; and it has always seemed strange that Governor Cranfield nominated him to be of his Council. But there cannot be much doubt that Champernowne did return to Portsmouth and remained for some time, attracted thither most probably by the presence there of men in power under royal commission. The language of Governor Cranfield in his letter to the Privy Council would seem to establish the fact. "And [I] do recommend for your Lordships' confirmation [as Counsellors] Mr. Francis Champernowne and Mr. James Sherlock. Mr. [Nathaniel] Fryer having gone to live in the other Province [Maine], the number doth not exceed seven" (Jenness's Original Documents, 156). As a possible further confirmation, it may be stated that a portion of a rough draft of his Will (still preserved), directs that his body be buried in Portsmouth. This draft may have been made while he was temporarily resident at Portsmouth, *circa* 1684. — H.

annulled by legal proceedings, and the authority of the corporation came to an end.[1]

Champernowne was now seventy years of age, too old to be again active in restoring the royal authority over Maine, now certain to take place. His capacity, ability, and loyalty were recognized in England, as well as at home, and when President Dudley's commission issued in 1685,[2] to govern New England, Champernowne was named in the commission a member of his Council of State, — a high and responsible office. He was continued in this office under Sir Edmund Andros, the successor of Dudley, and held it until his death in 1687.

Some time subsequent to the year 1675, Captain Champernowne married Mary, the widow of Robert Cutt,[3] a prominent citizen and merchant of Kittery. It does not appear that he had married before. He had no children;

[1] The proceedings for the annulment of the charter were begun by a writ of *quo warranto*, issued June 27, 1683, returnable into the Court of King's Bench. But the writ was defective in form, and not seasonably served. This method of procedure was abandoned, and a writ of *scire facias* was issued from the Court of Chancery, April 16, 1684, and an *alias* on May 12. It was under this writ that the Charter was vacated, by the decree of the Lord Keeper, on June 21, which decree was confirmed October 23. See Palfrey, iii. 376–394. — H.

[2] President Dudley's Commission was dated Oct. 8, 1685. He presented a copy of it to the General Court on May 17, 1686. The General Court, on May 20, sent to Dudley and his Council a communication (Mass. Rec., v. 515–516), criticising the terms of the Commission, and his language to them, and thereupon

dissolved. On June 15, the new Government issued an " Order for the Holding of Courts and Execution of Justice." This Order, in point of style and phraseology, is one of the best official papers issued in Massachusetts in the seventeenth century. The copy of the Commission referred to above seems to have disappeared from the State archives, and the original has also perished or passed out of sight. A partial copy will be found in Coll. Mass. Hist. Soc., v. 244–246. Prov. Papers of New Hampshire, i. 590–592, and R. I. Rec., iii. 195. — H.

[3] The early generations of the family spelled their name Cutt; the later generations have added the letter *s*. For historical and genealogical notices of the family, see Brewster's Rambles about Portsmouth, The Wentworth Genealogy, and Savage's Gen. Dic. — H.

... I doe declare and publish this to be my last Will and Testament annulling
and makeing void all former and other Wills and Testaments ... In witnes
... whereof I have hereunto put my hand and seale the ... day of September in the
... yeare of ... God one thousand six hundred and eighty six ...

... Charles ... Doctor and published as to the
... last Will and Testament of Francis Brampton ... Mr Newstam Mitchell
... named ... In the presence of ... Mr Newstam Mitchell
... William Mitchell ... made oath the 28 December
... 1687 ... Exr die Jan: 5:
... Edm Gook ...

Franc Bramptonroure

... Exr die ...
1720 ...

... Brampton upon Sea ... In the other side ... Francis
... Will with a ... Brampton upon ... being in full and ...
... The Will of Brampton ... that they ... the above
... Notwithstanding ? ... the said Instrument as Will or ...
... hands to the said Instrument ... Frek: Slotherby

Frances Hooke jun: ...
... Thomas Scottow Exr

but he had a great affection for his wife's children by Robert Cutt, and often speaks of them as his own, which fact has misled some writers.[1]

His principal residence in Kittery was within a few miles of Gorgeana, now York, the metropolis of the Province. A narrow stream separated his homestead from that of Edward Godfrey,[2] sometime Governor of the Province. In 1666, the town of Kittery granted to him five hundred acres of land near his residence, and, in 1669, three hundred acres additional at Kittery Point.

The latter part of his life was devoted chiefly to the care of his plantation, while the ostensible interest which drew him to New England, and to which he devoted his younger years, was commercial.

Captain Champernowne lived in New England half a century. This period was about equally divided between Portsmouth and Kittery. Tradition still preserves his name and memory in both of these places. There is no contemporary account of him, nor any portrait extant. His form and features can be restored only by fancy, but his character may be inferred with considerable certainty from his acts, and the respect shown him by his contemporaries.

On November 16, 1686, he made his Will, devising his island home in equal parts to his wife and her daughter,

---

[1] Williamson (History of Maine, i. Appendix, 667), erroneously states that Champernowne had three daughters. Other writers have copied this error. — H.

[2] Edward Godfrey was for many years very prominent in the affairs of the Province. There was much that is pathetic in his career, and especially in his closing days in London. For a full account of his life, see Edward Godfrey: His Life, Letters, and Public Services, 1584-1664, by Charles Edward Banks, M.D., privately printed, 1887. — H.

Elizabeth, the wife of Humphrey Elliot.   This island, now known as Cutts, was soon after Champernowne's death conveyed to his wife's son, Richard Cutt, whose descendants have owned the larger part, and resided upon it until recently.   He made his wife's grandson, Champernowne Elliot, his heir-at-law and residuary legatee.[1]

Captain Champernowne died sometime in the Spring of 1687, the day and month not now known.   He desired to be buried on his island where he died.   No other monument marks his last resting-place but a heap of stones, which some friendly hand placed above his grave, where they may be seen to this day.   In a large open field sloping to the south, a rude stone wall encloses a small area, dotted over with mounds, indicating the graves of some of Champernowne's contemporaries, or of succeeding owners and occupants of the land.   In the northerly corner a large oblong pile of moss-covered stones denotes his own burial-place.

> "THOMAS DE CAMBERNON for Hastings field
> Left Normandy : his Tower sees him no more !
> And no Crusader's Warhorse plumed and steeled
> Paws the grass now at Modbury's blazoned door :
> No lettered marble nor ancestral shield —
> Where all the Atlantic shakes the lonesome shore
> Lies our forgotten, — only Cobblestones
> To tell us Where are Champernowne's poor Bones ! "[2]

---

[1] For Champernowne's Will, see Appendix No. 2. For notes on the Elliot, Cutt, and Elliott families, see Appendix No. 3.

[2] The author of these lines, the late John Elwyn, Esq., of Portsmouth, N. H., was born at Clifton, near Bristol, Eng., Feb. 1, 1801. and died in Portsmouth, Jan. 30, 1876. His father, Thomas Elwyn, Esq., a native of the city of Canterbury, Eng., and a graduate of Trinity College, Oxford, came to the United States in 1796, while a young man. After completing his travels, he

The waves on the sandy beach not far off continuously throb a monotonous requiem, while from the vast expanse of the ocean in full view come deeper and more solemn sounds. Here rests the first and the last of his name in New England, — the kinsman of the immortal Gilbert, Ralegh, and Gorges.

read law in Philadelphia. There he made the acquaintance of the family of the Hon. John Langdon, an eminent citizen of New Hampshire, and at this time a Senator in the Federal Congress. He married Governor Langdon's only child, Elizabeth, and she was the mother of Mr. John Elwyn. Thomas Elwyn settled in Portsmouth, and died there in 1816. John Elwyn was graduated at Harvard College in 1819. While in College, and for many years afterwards, he wrote his name, John Langdon-Elwyn. He lived nearly all his life in Portsmouth, and was buried on his estate at the head of Sagamore Creek. This estate he inherited from his maternal grandfather. It had been owned and occupied by the Langdons from the early years of the settlement of New Hampshire. Mr. Elwyn was a life-long and diligent student, and his acquirements in the languages, both ancient and modern, of Europe and of Asia, were extraordinary in extent. He was remarkably well-informed respecting the genealogies of the old families of England. He was no less well-informed in regard to the genealogies of the old

families and the antiquities of the Pascataqua region, and his information was always at the service of those seeking his aid.

In his second volume of "Poems of Places — New England," Mr. Longfellow inserted the verses above quoted, under the title : "The Grave of Champernowne," with a prefatory note from Mr. John Albee (Harv. Theo. School, 1858), of New Castle, New Hampshire, but inadvertently Mr. Longfellow located the grave in New Castle. In his charming monograph on New Castle, Mr. Albee pays an appreciative tribute to the character, learning, and poetic ability of Mr. Elwyn.

The fine sonnet on the page following this, from the pen of Mr. Albee, is here reproduced with his consent. It fitly concludes this paper on Champernowne by his friend, Mr. Tuttle. Among Mr. Albee's published works are the following: St. Aspenquid of Mount Agamenticus, an Indian Idyl (Portsmouth, N. H., 1879); Literary Art (New York, 1881) ; Poems (New York,1883) ; New Castle, Historic and Picturesque, illustrated (Boston, 1885). — H.

AT THE GRAVE OF CHAMPERNOWNE.

BY JOHN ALBEE.

HERE poise, like flowers on flowers, the butterflies ;
  The grasshopper on crooked crutch leaps up,
  The wild bees hum above the clover cup,
The fox-grape wreathes the walls in green disguise
  Of ruin: and antique plants set out in tears —
Pink, guelder-rose, and myrtle's purple bells —
  Struggle 'mid grass and their own wasting years
To show the grave that no inscription tells.

Here rest the bones of Francis Champernowne ;
  The blazonry of Norman kings he bore ;
His fathers builded many a tower and town,
  And after Senlac England's lords.   Now o'er
His island cairn the lonesome forests frown,
  And sailless seas beat the untrodden shore.

CAPT. FRANCIS CHAMPERNOWNE'S GRAVE.

Champernowne's Island.

Kittery, Maine.

CONQUEST OF ACADIE.

CONQUEST OF ACADIE.

WE need not look beyond the breach and end of the treaty of triple alliance, — that famous league of the three great Protestant nations of Europe, — for the causes of the events I am now to relate. England, the United Provinces, and Sweden enjoyed a few years of supremacy and tranquillity under the moral strength of that memorable international alliance. "All Europe," says Hume, "seemed to repose herself with security under the wings of that powerful confederacy."[1]

But the inconstant temper of the English king, Charles II., would not suffer him long to adhere to any policy or connection. Hatred of the Dutch and love of the French were the most steady passions in the breast of this monarch.[2] Less than two years after joining the triple league, — an act so much applauded by his subjects, — he was in secret council with Louis XIV., who was then plotting the destruction of the United Provinces. In this scheme of

[1] Hume's History of England, chap. lxiv.
[2] The reader will recall Hume's brief but masterly summing up of the character of Charles II., at the close of the sixty-ninth chapter of his History. — H.

perfidy, outrage, and ambition England was to have the province of Zealand, and France all the other provinces except Holland, which was to be reserved for the young Prince of Orange, if he would come into the arrangement.

With these views and purposes, not publicly declared, the English monarch and his ministers joined the ambitious King of France[1] in a war of conquest against the United Provinces, the old and faithful ally of England, — her ally in more than one crisis when without this great political and military support she had been without a friend in all Europe This most unjust and cruel war was publicly declared by France as well as by England, in March, 1672. Of the events which followed, I am concerned with those only which occurred in the New World and affected the American colonies of these belligerents.

When the war began in Europe, the Dutch possessions in America were not large. That famous Batavian Province, the New Netherlands, had already been wrested from the United Provinces by the English eight years before.[2] The Curaçoa island, or islands, in the West Indies, and Surinam[3] in South America, were all that now remained to the United Provinces in the New World.

The French possessions were immense. New France stretched from the Gulf of Mexico to the Gulf of St. Lawrence, its great eastern frontier pressing heavily on the

---

[1] "The King of England." said Louis to his ambassador D'Estrades (Jan. 25, 1662), "may know my forces, but he knows not the sentiments of my heart. Everything appears to me contemptible in comparison of glory" (Hume, chap. lxiv.). — H.

[2] The surrender was made Aug. 29, 1664.

[3] By the Treaty of Breda (July 10, 1667) the possession of Surinam was confirmed to the Dutch, and New Amsterdam to the English. — H.

English maritime provinces lying between the Penobscot Bay and Florida. Of this vast extent of French empire the most eastern division bore the provincial name ACADIE. Under this name were comprehended what is now the Province of Nova Scotia, New Brunswick, and the eastern half of the present State of Maine.[1]

Acadie had been explored and settled in some parts by the French before a permanent English settlement had been made in America. Castine, Champlain, and DeMonts had achieved fame in this region before the English, so far as we now know, had set foot on any part of Acadie. It was valued for the advantages it offered as a military position, for its great rivers and harbors, for its illimitable for-

---

[1] Prior to the year 1632 the boundaries of Acadie were not so defined as to make it perfectly clear what the French seriously claimed under that title. They had missions, stations, and trading-posts among the Indians as far west at least as the Kennebec; and whenever, subsequent to 1632, the western limits of Acadie came in question, the French insisted upon making that river the western boundary. But if persistent occupation of points on the coast to the eastward of the Kennebec gave title to anybody, that title rested in the English; and the Dutch, who had at different times made settlements and engaged in trade at various points on the coast, might, for the same reason, lay claim to portions of the territory between the Kennebec and the Penobscot. When, pursuant to the third article of the Treaty of St. Germain de Ley (in 1632), Acadie was restored to the French, the English surrendered no portion of the territory west of the Penobscot. And the same is true of the restoration made by the Eng-

lish pursuant to the Treaty of Breda in 1667. From and after 1632 the French never exercised any authority, political or military, in the territory lying between the Kennebec and the Penobscot. The extreme French claim was renewed whenever it served a purpose, and notably so in the years 1750–1753, when the question of the northern and western boundaries of Acadie formed the subject of an extended and exhaustive investigation by the commissaries of the courts of England and France. The argument of the English commissaries covers the entire history of the question, and seems to be complete and unanswerable. See The Memorials of the English and French Commissaries concerning the Limits of Nova Scotia, or Acadie (London, 1755); also Murdoch's History of Nova Scotia, or Acadie, i. 1, 2, and chapters x., xvi., and xvii. In regard to the bibliography of the Memorials, see Narrative and Critical History of America, iv. chap. iv., and the Catalogue of the Athenæum Library, Boston. — H.

17

ests, for its rich furs and inexhaustible fisheries, and for its proximity to the Old World. No wonder it was coveted by France, by England, and by the United Provinces, — the three greatest commercial nations of Europe. For a century and a half the English and the French contended for the possession of Acadie. It was repeatedly conquered by the English, who, however, kept possession only a short time; for Acadie always had a steady attraction for the French, its first explorers and possessors.[1]

In the Summer of 1654 the English again, and for the third time, became masters of Acadie. Upon some complaint made in 1653 against the Dutch of New Netherlands by the New Haven Colony, Cromwell sent hither a small naval force under command of Major Robert Sedgwick[2] and Capt. John Leverett, both of Massachusetts, with instructions[3] to obtain reinforcements in New Eng-

[1] "They knew the intrinsic value of its mines, fisheries, lands, forests, and fur trade. They saw, also, that the peninsula was important to them in checking the progress and disturbing the security of the New England colonies, and as a rampart and outwork to defend their own highly-prized colony of Canada" (Murdoch's Nova Scotia, i. 352). — H.

[2] Robert Sedgwick was the son of William and Elizabeth (Howe) Sedgwick of Woburn, Bedfordshire, England, and was baptized in St. Mary's Church in that town, May 6, 1613. He was one of the first settlers of Charlestown, Mass., in 1635. His business was that of a merchant. He served as a deputy in the General Court for several years. Before coming to New England he was, it is said, a member of the Artillery Company of London. He was one of the organizers of the Ancient and Honorable Artillery Company of Boston in 1638, and its captain in 1640; commanded the Castle in 1641, and the Middlesex regiment in 1643; and in 1652 was commissioned Major-General. In 1643–44, in connection with John Winthrop, Jr., he established furnace and iron works at Saugus (Lynn), which were the first, or among the first, in New England. Going to England, subsequent to 1652, he made the acquaintance of Cromwell, and was employed by him to expel the French from the Penobscot in 1654; was engaged in the expedition against the Spanish West Indies when Jamaica was taken; and just before his death, which occurred in Jamaica, May 24, 1656, he was promoted to the rank of Major-General in the British Army. See New Eng. Hist. and Gene. Register, xlii. 67, 184. — H.

[3] Coll. Mass. Hist. Soc., xxxii. 230–232.

land, then to proceed to "extirpate the Dutch," England then being at war with the United Provinces. The fleet proceeded to Boston, where it arrived in June, 1654; and while Massachusetts was beating up five hundred men for recruits, news came of peace with the Provinces,[1] and put an end to this design.

But this expedition, augmenting the land and naval force at the disposal of Massachusetts, must needs accomplish something against friend or foe. It forthwith proceeded against the French of Acadie, and, taking them by surprise, made an easy conquest of all the strongholds of that province,[2] although there was then no war existing between France and England. A thunderbolt from a clear sky could not have been more unexpected by the Acadians than this sudden onset by the English. Historians have said that the commanders of this expedition had secret orders from Cromwell to make conquest of Acadie; but they have not cited a particle of evidence to sustain the assertion. In the absence of any such testimony, it must be inferred that the design originated with the authorities of Massachusetts, and was executed under the great name and assumed authority of Cromwell. That Colony knew his temper well enough to venture in a struggle the issue of which was sure to be in favor of England, and to add still further to the military fame of the Protector.

One of these commanders, Capt. John Leverett, afterwards Governor of Massachusetts, remained in command of Acadie until Sir Thomas Temple was appointed governor of the

---

[1] The Articles of Peace were signed on April 5, 1654, and the news reached Boston, June 29. — H.

[2] Port Royal capitulated Aug. 16, 1654. — H.

conquered French Province, the name of which was now changed to Nova Scotia.

While Acadie, or Nova Scotia, remained an English Province, the people of New England, especially of Massachusetts, carried on there a large peltry trade, and were engaged in the fisheries, paying a reasonable charge for this privilege. Eighty thousand livres had been paid annually by the English for leave to fish in the waters of Acadie.[1]

Massachusetts came to regard the Province as a necessary part of her own domain. Soon after the conquest she instructed her agent, Leverett, to beg it of Cromwell if there was any prospect of its being surrendered to France. By dilatory pleas, seconded by Massachusetts, Governor Temple — a man who had the address to make himself equally acceptable to the Puritan and to the Royalist — delayed the surrender of Acadie to the French three full years after the Treaty of Breda. At last King Charles sent a peremptory order to him to deliver the Province to the French, and this was executed in the Summer of 1670.[2] The commission issued to the French governor made the Kennebec River the western limit of his government.

Massachusetts now saw with alarm this attempt to advance the frontiers of New France still nearer her own settlements. This construction of the western limit of Acadie included lands and trading-stations of some lead-

---

[1] Charlevoix, iii. 138; N. Y. Coll. Doc., iv. 476.

[2] The King's letters to Temple, directing him to surrender Acadie, were dated, respectively, Dec. 31, 1667; Aug. 1, 1668; March 8, 1668-9; Aug. 6, 1669. The surrender was formally made by Temple (who was in Boston), July 7, 1670. The fort at Pentagoet surrendered Aug. 5, 1670; Gemesic (on the river St. John), Aug. 27; and Port Royal, Sept. 2. See Memorials of English and French Commissaries; and Murdoch's Nova Scotia. — H.

ing men of Massachusetts between the two rivers. But, without waiting for the courts of France and England to settle the question of boundary between the two nations, Massachusetts boldly went to work to fix the western limit of Acadie. The northern limit of the Colony of Massachusetts Bay, as defined by its charter, was a line running east and west three miles north of the Merrimack River. She had already determined this line to be three miles north of the northernmost part of the Merrimack, and had thus unlawfully taken into her bounds, and exercised jurisdiction over, Mason's Patent of New Hampshire and nearly all of Gorges' Province of Maine. The east and west line of this unwarranted extension fell into the ocean, on the east, at Casco Bay, now Portland.

One of the magistrates, Capt. Thomas Clarke, of Boston, was a large proprietor of lands and trading-houses lying between the Kennebec and the Penobscot; and these were put to hazard by the French claim. The General Court of Massachusetts forthwith appointed this Captain Clarke to run "our north line from Casco Bay as far as he sees convenient eastward."[1] Hutchinson, the historian of Massachusetts, says: "The Court always thought it the part of good governors, as well as of good judges, to amplify their jurisdiction;"[2] and Edward Randolph said, about this time, "The present limits of Massachusetts are as large as that government please to make them."[3]

This survey was executed in 1672, twenty years after the previous survey, made by authority, had fixed the eastern

---

[1] Mass. Col. Records, v. 987.
[2] Hutchinson's Hist. of Mass., i. 239.
[3] Hutchinson Papers (Prince Soc. Edition), ii. 222 [487].

bounds of Massachusetts at Casco Bay. To the surprise of everybody concerned, except the people of the Bay Colony, the eastern limits were now found to be in Penobscot Bay. Thus the northern line — stretching from the Atlantic to the Pacific — was rolled backward several miles from points fixed by the first survey. The new surveyor, in his report to the General Court, said that if the Court " pleased to go twenty miles more northerly in Merrimack River, it would take in all the inhabitants and places east." By this survey and extension of jurisdiction the interests of the merchants and traders of Boston would be saved. And these interests, regarded as paramount to all other rights and claims, Massachusetts was resolved to defend.

The General Court forthwith erected the new territory into a county, and, yielding to the prejudices of the inhabitants, named it Devonshire. Governor Leverett immediately informed the Count de Frontenac, then Governor of New France, of this extension of Massachusetts limits northward and eastward, and warned the French not to venture therein.[1] There is hardly a bolder and more daring act recorded in the annals of Massachusetts. Who ever, before or since, heard of a remote and infant colony attempting thus to set the limits of empire between two proud and powerful nations?

On taking possession of Acadie in 1670, the French repaired the forts which the English had built, and also those built by themselves previous to the English conquest. A small military force was placed in each of them, to protect the country and its commercial interests. A provincial gov-

---

[1] Mass. Archives, lxi. 514.

ernor[1] was sent there, whose chief residence was Pentagoet, now Castine. Thus stood affairs between Massachusetts and Acadie, — between England and France, — in the year 1674, when the Dutch came and made conquest of Acadie.

The strife in Europe had already begun when England and France publicly proclaimed war with the United Provinces.[2] France was to bring armies into the field, and England was to cope with the Dutch on the sea. The Dutch navy was large and powerful, and commanded by able and experienced admirals. The fame of De Ruyter and Van Tromp was already spread through the maritime world; and with such opponents on the sea the enemies of the United Provinces might well have fears for the issue. From the Dutch navy the English justly expected much injury, especially in her numerous American colonies.

The King forthwith wrote[3] to the Governor of Massachusetts, announcing his declaration of war, and directing that proclamation be made there, and also issued like orders to the other English colonies. He also said that there was a report that a considerable number of men-of-war were fitting out in Zealand, designed to annoy the English planters in the West Indies.

The King's letter and declaration reached Boston the last week in May, while the General Court was in session. The Court immediately ordered " That the King's declaration sent to us against the States General of the United Provinces be published by the Marshal General in the three

---

[1] Hubert d'Andigny, Chevalier de Grandfontaine.

[2] War was declared by the King, March 7, 1672.

[3] See Appendix, No. 4.

usual places in Boston by sound of trumpet."[1] This is said to be the first instance of a public declaration of war in the Colony of Massachusetts;[2] and because that Colony had not been accustomed to pay very prompt respect to either the orders or the requests of the sovereign, it may be inferred that the quick compliance with the King's order in this case was due to a hostile feeling towards the Dutch.

In the Spring of 1673 the Zealand and Holland fleets, of which King Charles had advertised the Colonies, accidentally met at Martinico in the West Indies, — both sailing under the colors of their enemies, the one wearing a French ensign, the other an English. They prepared to fight, each believing the other to be, what its colors represented, an enemy. But an accident occurred, just as the conflict was to begin, which discovered their true character to each other, and saved them from mutual destruction.[3]

Without doing anything memorable in those waters, the two squadrons united and sailed for Virginia about midsummer. They seized many English vessels there, and one from New York, by which they gained the information of the weak state of the defences of that Province. Although they had not contemplated making a re-conquest of their ancient Province of New Netherlands, they now resolved on it; and the end of July, 1673, saw the colors of the Prince of Orange waving over Manhattan Island, to the great joy of the Dutch inhabitants. The conquest soon extended over every part of the Province of New York. A Dutch government was established, and the name New

[1] Mass. Records, v. 517.   [2] Hutchinson's History, i. 259, note.
[3] Hutchinson's History, i. 258, note.

Netherlands restored to the Province; while, in honor of the Prince of Orange, now at the head of affairs in the United Provinces, the name New Orange was given to Manhattan, or New York, formerly New Amsterdam.[1]

While this news sent a thrill of joy throughout the United Provinces, it sent a thrill of sorrow and mortification over England and her American colonies. Upon information of the operations of the Dutch fleet in the waters of Virginia, the authorities of Massachusetts at once took measures to defend the Colony from attack or injury.[2]

The people of England were already weary of this war when this event happened. Parliament now forced King Charles and his ministers to make peace with the United Provinces. The Treaty of Westminster was signed Feb. 9, 1674, nearly two years after the war began, and six months after the Dutch conquest of New York. It was agreed by the parties to this treaty that the Dutch might retain possession of New Netherlands until the English were ready to assume the government. It was not until the last day of October, 1674, that Sir Edmund Andros personally received the surrender.

About midsummer, 1674, Capt. Jurriaen Aernouts, commander of the Dutch frigate Flying Horse, being at Curaçoa in the West Indies, received a commission from the Dutch Governor of those islands, authorizing him, in the name of the great Prince of Orange, "to take, plunder, spoil, and possess any of the garrisons, towns, territories,

[1] This change of name was made Aug. 12, 1673 (N. S.). The Dutch now again introduced the New Style of reckoning time into New Netherlands. For a condensed and interesting history of the re-conquest of this Province, and of the proceedings of the Dutch authorities thereupon, see Brodhead's History of the State of New York, ii. 206-271. — H.
[2] See Appendix, No. 5.

privileges, ships, persons, or estates of any of the enemies
of the great States of Holland." His commission expressly named England and France as public enemies of
his great master.[1] The news of the Peace of Westminster,
made a few months before, had not reached Curaçoa when
this authority was granted.

With this provincial commission, Captain Aernouts sailed
for New Orange, little dreaming of so memorable an affair
in future as the conquest of a rich province of France in a
few months. The Flying Horse arrived at New Orange in
the fore part of July. There her commander was surprised
to hear that peace was proclaimed between England and the
United Provinces, made nearly six months before; and that
New Orange was to be surrendered to the English. He
found that his commission was now of no force against
the English, it having been granted before the treaty of
peace; but that it was good authority to proceed against
the French, peace not having been made with them.

While the Flying Horse was recruiting and preparing
for sea in New York, — or New Orange, as the Dutch
loved to call it, — Capt. John Rhoade, of Boston, an adventurous character, a pilot of some experience, made the
acquaintance of Captain Aernouts. He told the captain
that he was well acquainted with Acadie and all the French
defences therein; that it would be an easy conquest with his
force, if taken by surprise; that it was a great fur country,
and would make a fine Dutch province. Rhoade had recently been at Pentagoet, and had exact knowledge of the
strength of the French garrison there. After considering

---

[1] See Appendix, No. 17.

this scheme of conquest presented by Rhoade, and remembering what glory the conquest of New York not two years before shed on Dutch arms, Captain Aernouts submitted the plan to his officers and crew, and they were unanimously in favor of it.

Captain Aernouts now resolved to attempt the conquest. Rhoade took the oath of allegiance to the Prince of Orange, and was made chief pilot of the Flying Horse. With a company of one hundred and ten men he sailed from New York, and reached Pentagoet the 1st of August. He forthwith landed, and attacked the French fort, commanded by the veteran M. de Chambly with a small force of thirty men, and was soon master of it.[1] Chambly was wounded. The garrison surrendered to the Prince of Orange. The Dutch captain could not spare any of his force to garrison the fort, and he thereupon destroyed it, and also several houses, taking the cannon, ammunition, and other articles of value away with him. The French inhabitants of the humbler sort submitted to be subjects to the Prince of Orange, and were allowed to remain and trade, and keep possession till further orders, or some of the captors should return.

M. de Chambly, who was Governor of Acadie, and his principal officers were taken on board the Flying Horse. A thousand beavers were demanded as the price of his ransom; but he was unable to furnish them. He was allowed to despatch his ensign, with Indian guides, to Quebec, to acquaint Count Frontenac of his unhappy situation, and to request ransom from his captors. This ensign was

---

[1] This occurred August 10. See 254; Murdoch's Nova Scotia, i. 154; Charlevoix (Shea's ed.), iii. 187, 188; Williamson's Maine, i. 580. — H. Brodhead's History of New York, ii.

no less a person than the young Baron St. Castine, famous in later history.

Before leaving Pentagoet, the Dutch commander placed a copy of his commission, with a brief account of his conquest made in the name of the Prince of Orange, in two glass bottles and buried them in the earth, as a memorial of his seizure.

The Flying Horse then proceeded eastward, making conquest of every French fort and trading-place to the St. John River in the Bay of Fundy. The last considerable fort taken was at Gemesic,[1] in this river, commanded by M. de Marson, lieutenant to M. de Chambly. This fort was destroyed and its officers made prisoners. The poorer inhabitants having submitted were allowed to remain and trade, under conditions similar to those imposed at Pentagoet.

Bottles were here also buried in the earth, containing a copy of the captain's commission, and a brief account of the Dutch conquest made in the name of the Prince of Orange. Acadie was now proclaimed to bear the name of New Holland, another European name hitherto unknown in the annals of that region. No attempt was made on Port Royal, probably on account of its capacity to defend itself.

Thus was Acadie, lying between the Penobscot and St. John rivers, a favorite Province, again wrested from the French, after having been held by them only four years. The French had only got well established there and begun to enjoy a large revenue from the fur trade and fisheries, when this calamity befell them.

---

[1] This name is variously spelled in the histories. — H.

Count Frontenac received the news of the capture of M. de Chambly, and of the conquest of Acadie, near the end of September, with mingled feelings of surprise and mortification. Both had been but a short time in these high stations. The former was appointed in 1672 and the latter in 1673. Frontenac hastened to provide a ransom for the Governor of Acadie out of his own private fortune. The equivalent of a thousand beavers was subsequently negotiated at Boston, and Chambly was released.[1]

Only one month of navigation remained when this unhappy intelligence reached Quebec. Even had it been otherwise, Frontenac was not in condition to send help to Acadie. He however despatched some persons in canoes to discover what further calamities had befallen Acadie, to bring away some of the family of M. de Marson, and others of the garrison in the St. John River, and to carry letters to Boston.[2] In his letter to Governor Leverett of Massachusetts, Frontenac stated his belief that Boston, being jealous of the proximity of the French, and offended at the restraints which had been put on the English trade and fishing in Acadie, had employed this Dutch expedition against them, and furnished the pilot. He condemned in strong language the action of Boston in suffering the Dutch to return there with their French prisoners and plunder while peace existed between England and France.[3]

The Flying Horse, laden with the plunder of Acadie, and having its Governor and his chief officers on board,

---

[1] See Appendix, No. 6, for orders and letters of Frontenac in regard to this affair. — H.

[2] Frontenac's letter to Colbert, Nov. 14, 1674 (N. Y. Coll. Doc., ix. 119, 120). — H.

[3] See Appendix, No. 6.

sailed for Boston, reaching that place some time in September. Captain Aernouts applied for leave to come up to town to repair his ship and dispose of his plunder. He showed Governor Leverett his commission, which authorized him to make conquest of French territory and to make prize of French goods. Governor Leverett had already some weeks before been made acquainted with the conquest of Acadie.[1] He suffered Aernouts to bring the Flying Horse into the inner harbor. The Colony gladly purchased the cannon taken from the ruined forts of Acadie for the castle in the harbor, which had been destroyed by fire a few months before.[2] The inhabitants or traders of Boston purchased the rest of the plunder.

No sooner had Captain Aernouts reached Boston than the fur traders applied to him for leave to trade in Acadie, now New Holland. This was refused. The subordinate Dutch officers and men claimed that the conquest had been made by the sword, at the hazard of their lives, and that the trade, which was valuable, belonged to them. The Boston traders, however, hurried away their vessels to Acadie without leave or license, and without paying therefor. The French had always exacted large customs for this liberty.

When Captain Aernouts was ready to sail, about the last of October or the first of November, he went to take leave of Governor Leverett. The Governor boldly asked him if he had left any of his men to keep possession of Acadie, or New Holland. The captain replied that he had not. The

[1] Governor Leverett's letter to John Collins, Aug. 24, 1674 (Hutchinson's Coll., Prince Soc. Ed., ii. 465).
[2] March 21, 1673-4, "Our Castle fell on fire and was burned; only the powder saved, and most of the officers' and soldiers' goods" (Hull's Diary, in Archæol. Amer., iii. 235). — H.

Governor then asked him if he had given a copy of his commission to any one; and he said he had not, nor would he, for he would not be responsible for the actions of others. This is Leverett's version of this conversation.

The Flying Horse sailed from Boston, and I have no further account of her or of her commander. She left in Boston two of her men, afterwards styled Dutch officers, — Peter Roderigo and Cornelis Andreson, — both destined to have a notable career during the next twelve months. Capt. John Rhoade, the pilot, and John Williams, a Cornishman, were also left behind. Before sailing, Captain Aernouts gave these men and their associates authority to return to New Holland, and there trade and keep possession till further order from their great master in Holland, or from himself. The two Dutch officers and Rhoade resolved to proceed to New Holland and keep possession and carry on trade with the Indians till a Dutch force and government should be sent there. They purchased one vessel and hired another, and armed as well as they could. They persuaded four or five Englishmen to join them in this enterprise. Governor Leverett suspected the design of these men, and sent for Rhoade and demanded of him what he intended. Rhoade told him he was going eastward to trade. The Governor then asked him whether he or any of his company did not go there to take vessels that were coasting and trading. Rhoade replied that they did not; that they had no commission to do so. This is the Governor's report of the conversation.[1]

---

[1] Answer of the Governor and Council, Oct. 5, 1676, to the King's letter of Feb. 18, 1675-6. See Appendix, No. 16.

By the 1st of December following, the flag of the Prince of Orange waved from the topmast of these two vessels making their way into the Penobscot Bay. They visited Pentagoet, where they had the first struggle with the French four months previous. They found the French inhabitants still quietly submitting to the authority of the Prince of Orange. The English at Pemaquid had been there during the absence of the Dutch, and treated the inhabitants with some insolence, and carried away the iron and other articles found in the ruins of the fort. Proceeding farther eastward, they soon met some of the Boston vessels that had been trading in Acadie. They recognized some persons who had been refused in Boston leave to come there. They seized these vessels, and took from them the peltry and other articles that had come from Acadie. They then dismissed the officers and crews, and bade them begone out of the jurisdiction of the Prince of Orange, for the trade and possession there belonged to the Dutch.

Of the four vessels seized and released, two were of Boston, one was of Salem, and one of Pascataqua. Both Boston vessels had been warned by the Dutch officer while in Boston not to go to New Holland under penalty of seizure and forfeiture.

At Machias they set up an establishment for trade, but it had not been there long when a Boston vessel put in, and, being the strongest, overcame the Dutch, pulled down the flag of the Prince of Orange, plundered and destroyed their house, and made prisoners of their men. Proceeding onward towards the St. John River, they met with informa-

tion that the French at Gemesic had revolted and returned
to their former allegiance, and that a Boston vessel had
transported thither a French force from Port Royal. The
two Dutch vessels appear to have kept away all traders that
came there afterwards, and the Dutch continued their trade
for the next four months without further disturbance.

Meantime news was carried to Boston of the seizure of
Boston vessels at the eastward by persons under Dutch
colors, and was attracting public attention in the New
England metropolis. The bark Philip,—an ominous name,
—seized by them, belonged to John Freake and Samuel
Shrimpton, merchants of Boston. Freake complained to
Governor Leverett that his vessel had been piratically
seized by John Rhoade and his associates, and asked
that a force might be sent to seize them and to bring
them to Boston. He desired that Capt. Samuel Mosley,
a person destined to achieve great eminence in Indian
warfare in a few months, might be put in command of
the force to be sent out.[1] Mosley had recently been in
command of an armed vessel which had cruised about
Nantucket, by order of the Massachusetts authorities, to
protect Boston interests against suspected hostilities by the
Dutch of New Orange. He was an able and experienced
officer.

The Governor and Assistants, after considering this
application, and seeing the advantage it would be to have
Acadie open to Boston trade, and not favoring the Dutch
for neighbors, ordered Captain Mosley to proceed there
with sufficient force, and to "seize and surprise, and bring

---

[1] His vessel was seized Dec. 4, 1674. See Appendix, No. 7.

19

them forthwith to Boston." All ships in Boston harbor bound eastward were ordered to stay till Captain Mosley had sailed; and great care was taken to prevent intelligence of the expedition getting abroad. This was the middle of February, 1674–5.[1] The master of Freake's vessel, the Philip, was George Manning; he was wounded at the time he was captured by the Dutch. After being taken he attempted to get away, and offered some violence to his captors. They proposed to set him adrift in a boat, and to keep his vessel. At length he offered to join them, and to let them have his vessel and crew at eight pounds per month. They agreed, and hired his men; Dutch colors were immediately hung out on the Philip, the Puritan trader.[2]

The first Spring month of the memorable year 1675 found everything going smoothly in New Holland. A brisk trade had been carried on with the Indians, and great gains were assured. The southern and eastern horizon was watched daily to discover the tricolored flag of the United Provinces over a fleet coming to the assistance of the men who were holding the territory against the French. Happy dreams of the future of this new and rich Province annexed to the Fatherland cheered this little company in their wintry toils. At length there suddenly appeared an armed vessel wearing an English flag, bearing down on them.

Captain Mosley had taken a French vessel to his assistance, and provided her with men and ammunition.

[1] See Appendix, No. 8.
[2] See Manning's Deposition, Appendix, No. 9.

Manning, who had gone into the Dutch service, at once revolted, and while yet the Dutch flag waved from his topmast, poured a fire into the Dutch vessels. The French vessel wore her national colors. The Dutch were thoroughly confused by the attack on them by vessels under different colors, and after a short and sharp conflict they surrendered to Captain Mosley.

The Dutch force were made close prisoners, and their vessels were plundered of the peltry gained by a winter trade, and of all the goods that remained for future use. These trade goods were taken by Boston traders of Captain Mosley's company, and the Indian traffic was continued by them.

Captain Mosley immediately sailed for Boston, with his captives and their vessels, where he arrived April 2, 1675. The prisoners were at once put in close confinement. The Governor and Assistants assembled in Cambridge on the 7th of the same month, to consider what should now be done in this matter. They ordered that four of the pirates, as they termed the captives, be confined in the prison at Cambridge; and that the Dutch vessels with their furniture be appraised and left in the hands of Mr. John Freake, the Boston merchant, who had made complaint of the alleged piratical acts of the Dutch in Acadie, and had suffered loss thereby.[1] All the prisoners were next examined as to their connection with the affair complained of, and their answers reduced to writing. They frankly declared what they had done, and justified their acts.[2] A special Court of Admiralty, consisting of the

---

[1] Mass. Arch., lxi. 80.   [2] See Appendix, No. 10.

Governor, Deputy-Governor, and Board of Assistants, was thereupon summoned to meet in Boston on the 17th of May, to try these men.

While the prisoners were waiting for trial, a dreadful calamity happened in Boston and saddened the whole community. On the fourth day of May, two weeks before the Court of Admiralty assembled, an English vessel arrived in the harbor from Virginia. While John Freake, the merchant who had set on foot the expedition against the Dutch in Acadie, and Captain Scarlett, a distinguished shipmaster and merchant, one of the appraisers of the Dutch vessels, were in the great cabin of this English vessel, she was suddenly blown up. Freake was taken up dead, and the supercargo survived only a few hours. Captain Scarlett died next day. Nine others were wounded.[1] The great Increase Mather preached a sermon, which is printed, "Occasioned by this awful Providence."[2]

On the day appointed, May 17, the Court assembled in Boston to try the prisoners. The Governor, Deputy-Governor, and the Assistants, ten in number, were present on the Bench. Every member of this judicial assembly bore a name that is historic in the annals of Massachusetts. At the head of the Court sat the venerable Governor Leverett, many years Major-General of the Colony, experienced in war and in civil affairs, the ablest chief magistrate the Colony ever had. As before stated, he had been a

[1] Hull's Diary (Archæol. Amer., iii. 240) ; Bradstreet's Journal (New Eng. Hist. & Gene. Reg., viii. 329).

[2] This was one of the first two works printed in Boston. Hitherto, printing in the Colony had been done at Cambridge. Mather was at this time one of the licensers of the Press. For the full title of this sermon, see Sibley's Harvard Graduates, i. 440. — H.

joint commander of the English fleet that made conquest
of Acadie in 1654, and for many years was military governor of that Province. Next to him sat Samuel Symonds,
the Deputy-Governor. Of the Assistants, the highest in
public regard was Simon Bradstreet, destined not only to
succeed Leverett in the office of chief magistrate, but to
live to be the Nestor of the Colony. Although then more
than threescore and ten years of age, it may be said that
in a large degree his eye was undimmed and his natural
force unabated. The other Assistants also were able and
venerable men known all over New England.[1]

This Court quickly declared the two Dutch vessels
seized by Captain Mosley, and their cargoes, lawful prize,
and decreed that they be delivered to the heirs of Freake
in satisfaction for the injury done to the Philip, the heirs
first paying the charges of the Court, officers' fees, etc.
The Court then adjourned one week.

When the Court reassembled, the grand jury presented
indictments against all the prisoners, Dutch and English,
charging them with having committed acts of piracy on
the high seas, and specifying their dealings with the captured vessels.[2] The trial proceeded against Peter Roderigo
and Cornelis Andreson, the two Dutch officers, chiefs of the
party. The foreman of the trial jury first named was John
Checkley, brother of Anthony Checkley, the first Attorney-
General of Massachusetts under the Charter of 1692; but on
objection by the prisoners Benjamin Gillam was substituted.

[1] Daniel Gookin, Daniel Denison, Richard Russell, Thomas Danforth, William Hathorne, Simon Willard, Edward Tyng, William Stoughton, and Thomas Clarke.

[2] Peter Roderigo, Cornelis Andreson, John Rhoade, Peter Grant, Richard Fulford (*alias* Fowler), Randall Judson, John Williams, and John Thomas. For the indictment in the case of Roderigo, and other papers, see Appendix, No. 11.

The jury returned a verdict of guilty against Roderigo, and the Court sentenced him to death. He prayed for leave to ask the General Court, then in session, for his life, and his petition was allowed.[1] A full pardon was granted to him before the end of the May session.[2]

Cornelis Andreson was found not guilty of piracy, as charged in the indictment. The Court, however, was not satisfied with this verdict, and, sent the jury out again with these instructions, — "to find what they could against him"! The jury found him guilty of "theft and robbery," on the evidence that he had taken several moose, beaver, and marten skins from one of the Boston vessels. He too was subsequently pardoned.[3]

This Cornelis Andreson is without much doubt that mysterious Dutchman mentioned by all our old historians and writers of that period, who figured so conspicuously in King Philip's War under Captain Mosley. Some of his exploits were heroic. Who he was or whence he came has not been known till now. It is not improbable that these men are the "Buccaneers" referred to by historians as going with Captain Mosley against Philip near the end of June.

The defence of these men before the Court was set down in writing, and fortunately the manuscript is preserved. The whole subject is handled with skill and learning, and with an enlightened and comprehensive view of the public law of that day. The facts are stated with clearness, and the arguments are both forcible and luminous.

[1] Records of Court of Admiralty in the files of the County of Suffolk.

[2] May 12, 1675 (Mass. Rec., v. 40).

[3] Mass. Arch., lxi. 109.

The main defence was that Captain Aernouts had lawful authority to make conquest of Acadie, and to hold the same for the States-General of the United Provinces; that Massachusetts had recognized the validity of this authority by permitting Captain Aernouts to bring the French prisoners and plunder to Boston after the conquest, and that in keeping possession and driving away intruders from Boston and elsewhere they acted as lawful agents of the Prince of Orange, who was their superior, and to whom any person or government should look for reparation for injuries. Under the circumstances of the case they rightly contended that they were not guilty of piracy, and that this was a matter of diplomacy to be settled between the governments of England and the United Provinces. Who prepared this defence I cannot even find ground for conjecture. Whoever it was, I should judge his vernacular was not English. Roderigo and Andreson were both illiterate men, and their English associates, except Fulford, were not much better.[1]

The Court adjourned — for what reason does not appear — to the 17th of June, and then took up the charges against the remaining six prisoners. On being brought to the bar each put in a plea of not guilty, and presented the written defence made in behalf of Roderigo and Andreson as his own, expecting, of course, an acquittal, or a pardon in case of conviction, as had been granted to the Dutch officers.

Richard Fulford, John Rhoade the Dutch pilot, Peter Grant, and Randall Judson were each found guilty of

[1] For the full text of this defence see Appendix No. 12.

piracy; and the Court at once passed sentence, directing them to be executed on the first day of July, "presently after the lecture," and ordered warrants to issue accordingly. The other two prisoners, John Thomas and John Williams, were acquitted and discharged.

When the day of execution of the four Englishmen arrived, the Massachusetts Government was wholly unfitted for the task it had assumed. King Philip had been one week on the war-path, and every person in eastern Massachusetts stood fearful of the awful issue presented by the enraged red man. Their execution was respited from time to time, till near the end of the year, when they were set free on hard conditions. Fulford was, however, early released without conditions. He belonged in Muscongus, and had married a daughter of Richard Pearce. I suppose him to have been originally of Devonshire, England, and of an ancient and illustrious family.[1]

Rhoade, Grant, and Judson were required to pay prison charges, and find sureties that they would leave Massachusetts and not return. If they failed in this they were to be executed on the last day of December, 1675.[2] They complied, and went into banishment.

When the Directors of the Dutch West India Company, in Amsterdam, heard of this conquest of the Dutch arms in Acadie, they awoke to new enterprises. Their first action, Sept. 11, 1676, was to recognize the services of John Rhoade of Boston, the famous pilot of the Dutch cruiser,

---

[1] Fulford was indicted, tried, sentenced, and pardoned, under the name of Fowler, and under this name he petitioned the General Court; but Mr. Tuttle had fully satisfied himself that "Fowler" was an assumed name. — H.

[2] Mass. Rec., v. 66.

in making the conquest. They authorized him to hold possession of Acadie, and to carry on unlimited trade with the natives.[1] A month later the Directors commissioned Cornelis Steenwyck, distinguished for eminent services in the late Dutch government of New York, to be Governor of Acadie.[2] More than two years had elapsed since the conquest was made, and the French had now fully repossessed themselves of Acadie. The return of the French was not probably then known in Amsterdam. Besides, peace had not been concluded between France and the United Provinces. If the West India Company indulged any expectation that Acadie would remain to Holland by the express terms of any treaty of peace, they were mistaken. The Treaty of Nimeguen was signed a year after issuing these commissions, and no mention is therein made of the Dutch conquest of Acadie.

The action of Massachusetts in this affair was prompted by a selfish policy, and a constant dislike of the French and Dutch for neighbors. Both these nations understood this, and then and there declared it to be their belief. While Massachusetts was separated from the Dutch by other English Colonies, she was content to let them alone; but when they removed into a district adjoining her at the eastward, she was not content till they were dislodged.

It was a monstrous thing to charge persons acting under the commission and flag of a foreign prince with acts of piracy, and hold them amenable to municipal laws. It was as if some foreign State should make the acts of the officers and men of one of our public vessels, done in pursu-

---

[1] See Appendix, No. 13. [2] See Appendix, No. 13.

ance of a commission or instructions from their superiors, piracy, and undertake to punish them in a foreign jurisdiction. Acts done in the manner of these Dutch officers and their associates were clearly a matter between the United Provinces and England, and so the matter was regarded outside Massachusetts Bay.

The Government of Massachusetts was sure to act on the safe side. Although there was peace between the Dutch and English, the former were still in a death struggle in Europe with the French, and hence had neither fleet nor army to spare, to avenge the act of Massachusetts. Besides, it knew well the indifference of Charles II. to any wrongs that might be inflicted on the Dutch.

But this affair did not end in Boston, nor with the trial and condemnation of the Dutch officers and their associates in the early Summer of 1675. When news of the capture of these persons by Captain Mosley under the authority of Massachusetts, and of their imprisonment in Boston, reached the States-General, they immediately instructed their ambassador in England to lay their complaint before the King, to demand that he visit the offenders with exemplary punishment, give orders for the release of the prisoners, and for the restoration to the Dutch of the forts captured by Captain Aernouts in 1674. The ambassador of the States-General accordingly, on the 5th of August following, obeyed the instructions given him.[1] It does not appear that immediate attention was paid to the complaint of the States-General, and it would seem that their ambassador renewed his presentation of the complaint on the

[1] See Appendix, No. 14.

22d of January, 1676. Thereupon, and perhaps for the first time, the complaint was considered by the King in Council; and on the 18th of February the King, through Secretary Williamson, addressed a letter to the Governor and Council of Massachusetts, inclosing a copy of the complaint, and required them "to return a speedy answer."[1]

The King's letter came to the hands of the Governor and Council Sept. 3, 1676. At a session of the General Court held on the 5th of October it was ordered that a reply be sent to the King in answer to the complaint of the Dutch ambassador.

The answer of the Governor and Council, probably drawn up by Governor Leverett, was characterized by assurance and indifference. It recited the principal facts, and claimed that the authority given to the Dutch officers by Captain Aernouts was restricted "to trade and keep the country and sail upon the coast, for doing which they were not seized and imprisoned, but for piratically seizing the vessels and goods that belonged to his Majesty's subjects." They said also that Cornelis Andreson was the only Dutchman of the party, and he was not found guilty of piracy; that Roderigo was a Flanderkin, and the others English; that they all had "acknowledged the justness of the Court's proceedings," and had their lives granted to them, and had been banished the Colony on pain of death; that what had been done was not because the English would not suffer any Hollanders to be near them (as was alleged in the said complaint), but to suppress piratical practices of English, Dutch, and other nations. The an-

---

[1] See Appendix, No. 15.

swer concluded by protesting that there had not been any violation of the peace between the two nations.[1]

This answer was sent to the King by the hands of two agents of the Massachusetts Colony.[2] It is probable that there was no further correspondence on this subject for a year or more. The States-General could not hope for any nice justice from the English Court at that time; and had the authorities of Massachusetts executed the sentences of the Court upon the Dutch officers and their associates, the result would not probably have been different.

It has already been mentioned that soon after the Dutch West India Company learned of the capture of Acadie by Captain Aernouts in 1674, they commissioned Cornelis Steenwyck, of New York, to be Governor of Nova Scotia and Acadie. His commission bears date Oct. 27, 1676. It has also been stated that on the 11th of September of the same year the Company, recognizing the services of the aforesaid John Rhoade, in connection with the proceedings of Captain Aernouts in 1674, had given him a commission "to take possession of the coasts and countries of Nova Scotia and Acadie, to trade with the natives, and all others with whom the aforesaid Company is in peace and alliance." Steenwyck was furnished with a copy of the commission given to Rhoade, and was instructed to respect it.[3]

It does not appear that anything was done by Steenwyck under his commission. Rhoade, however, undertook to use the privilege and authority conferred upon him, and got

---

[1] See Appendix, No 16.
[2] William Stoughton and Peter Bulkeley.
[3] For the commissions to Aernouts, Steenwyck, and Rhoade, respectively, see Appendix, No. 13.

into trouble. In the course of his proceedings he entered with a vessel and goods into the river St. George, it was alleged, which was in the territory claimed by the Duke of York, and undertook to trade there. For this he was taken prisoner by Capt. Cæsar Knapton, a relative of Sir Edmund Andros, then in command of that region, and together with his vessel and goods was sent to New York.

When the news of this proceeding reached the Dutch West India Company, they laid the matter before the Lords of the States-General. The latter instructed their ambassador at the English Court to demand the release and indemnification of said Rhoade, and that the King's subjects in America be interdicted from interfering with the Dutch commerce and other rights of the States-General in Acadie. This was on the 21st of May, 1679. This complaint and demand were renewed in August. The King responded, August 8, that he had directed an inquiry to be made into the affair, and when he had received a report he would then take such further measures as justice and the good correspondence between the two nations required. The correspondence on this subject was continued for some time, but it does not appear that any results followed.

There can be no doubt that if competent Dutch forces had promptly occupied the forts and coasts of Acadie after their conquest in 1674, the French of New France could not have expelled them. France herself was then too much occupied in her struggle in Europe with the United Provinces, to send aid to New France. It is highly probable, however, that Massachusetts would have joined the French in

the recovery of Acadie rather than have permitted the
Dutch to secure a permanent foothold there.   The prover-
bial industry and thrift of the Dutch people would soon
have made their New Holland a great Province, and worthy of its renowned namesake in the Old World.   It would
have been a formidable rival of Massachusetts and greatly
lessened her supremacy in New England.   Danforth, a
leading man in the Colony, expressed Massachusetts views
accurately when, a few years later, he wrote as follows : —

> There being no wars between Holland and France, some are
> fearful lest the Hollanders should essay the possessing themselves
> of Canada ; and though it is hopeful they may prove better neigh-
> bors than the French, yet, considering the damage that will thereby
> be sustained by the Crown of England, in loss of fishery, masting,
> furs, etc., it were better to expend two or three thousand pounds for
> the gaining that place, than that the French, or Dutch either, should
> have it.[1]

These events, which stretched over the whole period of
King Philip's Indian War, and involved the interests of
three great nations, have received but little attention from
our historians.   The magnitude of the war in Europe threw
into the shade all other and more remote transactions of
that time.   Hutchinson mentions this affair in a note of
four lines, in his history, and blunders by making two con-
quests of Acadie, — one in 1674 and another in 1676.
Williamson adds nothing to Hutchinson.   Neither Bancroft nor Palfrey refers to it.   Munro, in his History of
Nova Scotia, sets it down as one of Captain Kidd's adventures.   Charlevoix mentions it, giving some particu-

---

[1] Letter, April 1, 1690, to Sir H. Ashurst (Hutchinson's Hist., 1. 353).

lars, but errs in some of his conclusions, not knowing all the facts.

About twenty years ago the commissions to Aernouts and Steenwyck, with a copy of the commission to Rhoade,[1] came into the possession of the New York Historical Society. General De Peyster, of New York, an able writer, then read a paper before the Society on " The Dutch at the North Pole and the Dutch in Maine." He brought together from the historians above named whatever facts they relate bearing on this Dutch conquest, but he was obliged to leave to conjecture the nature of the transaction. The archives of the State of Massachusetts contain a large mass of papers relating to this subject, and from these I have gathered the principal details in the foregoing narrative. I have been fortunate also in obtaining from the British state-paper office copies of important papers, and a still larger number from the archives of Holland, and the most important of these papers will be found in this volume.[2]

In conclusion, it may be said that if the occupancy of Acadie by the Dutch had been maintained, it is not improbable that that Province would have passed permanently into the possession of the United Provinces. The terms of the Treaty of Nimeguen are certainly broad enough to cover and protect all the rights which the Dutch had acquired by this conquest. If this result had followed, it is not difficult to imagine how different would have been the history of Acadie and possibly of all New France.

[1] See Appendix, No. 13.　　[2] See Appendix, No. 17.

THE REPORT

OF AN

INDIAN MASSACRE

AT

FOX POINT, NEWINGTON, NEW HAMPSHIRE,

MAY, 1690.

THE REPORT

OF AN

INDIAN MASSACRE

AT

FOX POINT, NEWINGTON, NEW HAMPSHIRE

MAY, 1690.

I FEAR that I have too long delayed to make public [1] that, while examining the early records of New Hampshire, both printed and manuscript, several years ago, I most unexpectedly discovered substantial grounds for doubting the destruction of Fox Point [2] by a party of Indians in May, 1690, as alleged by Cotton Mather in his Magnalia. Mather says: —

But the Arrival of *Orders* and *Soldiers* from the Government stopt them from retiring any further; and *Hope-Hood*, with a Party

---

[1] Printed, by permission, from the Proceedings of the Massachusetts Historical Society, June, 1879. — H.

[2] Fox Point is the northwest angle of Newington where Little Bay and the Pascataqua River join. It is about half a mile long, ending in the river and forming a prominent headland on that side of the river and bay. Tradition says the name originated from the use formerly made of this point to snare foxes. Reynard, being once driven there, could not escape his pursuers without swimming the river or bay, much too wide for his cunning.

that staid for further Mischief meeting with some resistence here, turn'd about and having first had a Skirmish with Captain *Sherborn*, they appear'd the next Lord's-Day at *Newichawannick* or *Berwick*, where they Burnt some Houses, and Slew a Man. Three Days after they came upon a small Hamlet on the South side of *Piscataqua River*, called *Fox Point*, and besides the Burning of several Houses, they took half a Dozen and killed more than a Dozen of the too Securely Ungarrisoned People ; which it was as easie to do as to have Spoiled an ordinary *Hen-Roost*.[1]

For nearly two centuries this account of the massacre has circulated in our histories, unchallenged in any respect, and always on the authority of Mather. My inquiries led me to look for the names of the slain in this reported massacre, not doubting but that I should find some, if not all. After much research, covering a period of many years, I have not discovered anything whatever relating to this tragedy, beyond what is contained in the following letter written in the night by William Vaughan at Portsmouth, and despatched to Governor Bradstreet and the Council in Boston.

PORTS° 28th May 1690, ten at night.[2]

MUCH HON.ᴿᴰ I have Soe long & often Informed of the approach of yᵉ Enemy & Danger to wᶜʰ wee are expos'd for want of releif that am not like to be in a Capacity much longer to doe it. Capᵗ Gerrish, Heard, & Capᵗ Woodman the Frontier Garrisons of Cochecha & Oyster river have Stood their ground wᵗʰ longing Expectation of helpe but none Appearing Capᵗ Woodman was forc'd to break up Yesterday & forthwᵗ the enemy came down that way & by Canooes pass't over the river to our Side & this afternoon have been killing burning & Destroying wiᵗʰin 3 or 4 miles of Straw-

[1] Magnalia, Book vii. Art. ix. 73.   London Ed., 1702.
[2] Mass. Archives, xxxvi. 87.

berry bank. Bloody Point & the houses above & below are all burnt & the people most destroyed: One that Escap'd out of a house after it was burning saw 8 or 9 dead belonging to that familie, & the Succour we Sent to Weles for that Exigents has render'd us uncapable of relieving o' Neighbours or defending o'selves. Want of Assistance will make all o' Neighbours round us run away & Portsm° will quickly follow their Example unlesse pres.' Supply of men, provision & Amunition be Sent to encourage their Standing.

As for that 120 men you were pleased to Advise mee were coming this way understand they are wholly order'd to y° Province of Main & not a man to our Province who are not lesse Expos'd to the enemy than they, but neither those 120 men nor Cap.' Wiswall (wh.ch you have Soe often Advis'd off) have appeared to this day as I can hear, Save onley about 20 or 30 men that pass'd the great Iland this morning into the Province of Main.

The Ind.ns left Nechowonuck after having Dangerously wounded one man burn'd Sundry houses &c, Suppose they are the Same now upon us whose attempt is bold & Daring & wee not able to oppose itt. I can doe noe more than give Acc.ts hereof & Soe leave it. Remaining Much Hon.rd,

Yo' Most humble Ser.t

W.m VAUGHAN.[1]

All the evidence of this reported massacre that I can find is contained in this letter and in Mather's narrative quoted above. The letter was preserved in the public archives when Mather wrote in the year 1698. It seems likely that he obtained the substance of his information from it, notwithstanding he is more circumstantial in some matters, and limits the extent of the destruction of life and property.

[1] William Vaughan was a rich and prominent merchant in Portsmouth, and had been a member of the provincial council of President Cutt and Lieutenant-Governor Cranfield.

Both agree that the date of the event was May 28, 1690.[1]
Vaughan undoubtedly wrote in some haste, under much excitement, and with no better information than what could
be gathered from the flying reports on the tongues of an
alarmed people around him.   The expectation of an attack
prepared him to receive such intelligence, and to communicate it forthwith to the chiefs of the government of Massachusetts, under whose jurisdiction the Province of New
Hampshire had again been placed a few months before.
According to this letter it was believed in Portsmouth that
the whole collection of houses and nearly all the inhabitants were destroyed, a calamity too dreadful ever to be
forgotten.

The settlement reported to have been ravaged was an
ancient one, stretching along the south side of the river
from Fox Point to Bloody Point and beyond.[2]   Many of
the inhabitants were leading citizens of Dover, and their
posterity are there to this day.   The public road to Bloody
Point ferry passed through it, making it known to travel-
lers, by whom it is not unfrequently mentioned in ancient
records.   The settlements of Oyster River, Dover Neck,
and Strawberry Bank, now Portsmouth, lie around it, only a

[1] Dr. Belknap says, "Sometime in May." Farmer places this event after Aug. 22, 1690. So little was known of it among the best-informed writers in former times. See Belknap's Hist. of New Hamp., Farmer's Ed., 133, 144.

[2] All that territory now forming the northern half of Newington, bounded northerly and easterly on the Pascataqua River, was within the limits of Dover till 1714, and was generally known by the sanguinary name, "Bloody Point."

The inhabitants, however, even to this day, restrict the application of this name to that part of it along the river opposite Hilton's Point, now called, very improperly, Dover Point, more than a mile southeasterly of Fox Point. The historian Hubbard says that this "formidable name of Bloody Point" came from an occurrence there as early as 1633. It is certain that it has been in use there ever since. Coll. Mass. Hist. Soc., xv. 217.

few miles distant. Mather speaks of the comparative security of its position.

Only a week before this reported massacre a force composed of French and Indians had utterly destroyed Casco, now Portland. A party of the Indians concerned in that affair was reported to be advancing toward the Pascataqua settlements, killing and destroying on their way. Hundreds of persons had fled from the east into Portsmouth.[1] The inhabitants of that whole region, remembering the dreadful fate of Cocheco, and the still more recent one of Salmon Falls, were terrified, and put themselves in the best state of defence they could, carefully watching the approach of the Indians. In such an excited state of the public mind, a rumor easily started and soon became reported as a fact.

No one acquainted with the Indian mode of attacking settlements will readily believe the statement in the letter that this massacre took place in the afternoon; for the inhabitants were at such a time not only prepared to defend themselves, but to spread an alarm to other places, so as to cut off the escape of the Indians, then in the heart of the English settlements. The smoke of burning buildings would instantly spread information of the presence of the Indians to the neighboring settlements. There is hardly an instance recorded in the history of Indian warfare in New England where such attacks were not made in the morning, at daybreak or just before, taking the inhabitants by surprise and when least able to resist and give an alarm.

[1] Mass. Archives, xxxvi. 77.

The leading, if not the sole, object of the Indians in these attacks was to secure captives for the ransom to be had for surrendering them to their friends, and to seize and carry away as much plunder as they could with convenience and safety. Any frontier settlement contained all they desired, besides affording them great advantages of attack, and also of escape. In executing their wicked design they killed only such English as actually opposed them. But according to this letter the Indians, in this instance, took an entirely different course from what they ever did before or since. They passed a frontier settlement whose garrison they knew had withdrawn, crossed a broad river or bay with houses along the shores, and in the daytime destroyed an old settlement, and massacred the inhabitants with whom it does not appear they ever had the least difference.

Mather's account is brief and in general terms, too much so to have a real transaction for a basis. He does not give the name of a captive, or the name of one of the slain, nor mention the age and sex. Neither does he give the number slain. That he made Fox Point the scene of the massacre may be owing to his ignorance of the extent of the application of the local names in that region. Vaughan, who was well acquainted there, says that "Bloody Point and the houses above and below" were destroyed. This would include Fox Point.

It seems impossible that a tragedy of this magnitude should have happened, then and there, without leaving in the records of the time more direct evidence than a mere rumor, — for such the statement in this letter must be regarded. It is hardly possible that a family of eight or nine persons should be slain, and the name not preserved. So memorable an event ought to be found among the oral traditions of the present inhabitants of that region, many of whom are descended from the slain or their kindred, if the report be true.

I made inquiries for records and oral traditions of this reported massacre, and others did for me, of persons now living at Fox Point and the region around, without finding either. There is a belief among them that it actually occurred, because, as many said, it is related by historians, and the region has been known ever since as " Bloody Point"! No one there could give, or ever remembered to have heard, the name of any person slain or made captive; nor had they ever heard that any of their ancestors or kindred were among the slain or captive.

It is fair to presume that Dr. Belknap, who lived many years near the site of the reported massacre, and only three quarters of a century after it is said to have occurred, never found any evidence of it during his extensive historical researches, since he relates the affair wholly on the authority of Mather. Other historians before and since Belknap have related the story always on the same authority. Some have indulged in a little variation as to the sex and number killed, Mather having said nothing as to the former, and left the whole number killed indefinite, showing how slender his information must have been on these points.

The negative evidence seems to me strong. On the 30th of May Governor Bradstreet, to whom the letter was despatched on the night of the 28th of May, giving notice of the attack on Bloody Point, wrote a letter from Boston to

22

Jacob Leisler, then at the head of the government of New York, explaining the recall of the military force of Massachusetts Bay while on its way to Albany to join the army designed for the conquest of Canada. He says this was done to protect the eastern inhabitants from the Indians, who had already destroyed Casco, and made assaults on Wells and Kittery. He makes no mention of the destruction of Bloody Point, of which he had been informed the day before.[1] This makes it quite certain that contradiction followed upon the heels of Vaughan's letter.

Judge Sewall of Boston kept a diary in which most considerable matters of public concern are set down, particularly Indian massacres. He makes no mention of this affair, although he had often been at Bloody Point. Captain Lawrence Hammond of Charlestown, experienced in military affairs, also kept a diary at that time, in which no mention is made of this massacre. Both these original diaries are in the archives of this Society.

I will cite but one more authority, and that is conclusive, that no such destruction of Fox Point as Mather relates, ever occurred.

At the time of the reported massacre, the Rev. John Pike was living in Portsmouth, only four miles distant from the scene of the massacre, and was keeping a diary of current local events. This diary is now printed in the Proceedings of this Society.[2] Mr. Pike had only the year before removed from Dover, where he had been minister for many years. He afterwards returned, and was living there when Mather

---

[1] Documentary History of New York, ii. 259, 260.

[2] Proceedings Mass. Hist. Soc., Sept. 1875, 121–152.

wrote.   Fox Point as well as Bloody Point was in his parish, little more than a mile from his residence, and in plain
view.   He must have known every inhabitant there.   Yet
Mr. Pike makes no mention whatever in his diary of this
Indian attack, while his habit of recording events warrants
the mention of the least injury done by Indians to any of
his former parish.   Mather says he was indebted to Mr.
Pike for many passages in his history of that war.[1]   Certainly he did not furnish the facts for the lame account in
Mather's narrative, and omit to make record of such an
event in his diary.

I may add that I find no mention of this massacre in any
of the French histories of that period.

---

[1] Magnalia, Book vii. 65.

ESTABLISHMENT

OF THE

ROYAL PROVINCIAL GOVERNMENT
OF NEW HAMPSHIRE.

1680.

ESTABLISHMENT

OF THE

ROYAL PROVINCIAL GOVERNMENT OF NEW HAMPSHIRE.[1]

1680.

 HE event which we commemorate on this occasion is the most memorable in the annals of New Hampshire. This event is no less than the organization of the first lawful government over the Province of New Hampshire, the establishment of a political existence which has now endured for two centuries. It is no less an event than the emancipation of the first generation of settlers on this soil from the bondage of an usurper, and the recovery of their birthright and independence. The year 1680 is commonly regarded as the end of the first period of New Hampshire history. It

[1] This address was delivered before the Historical Society of New Hampshire, at a special meeting convened at Portsmouth, Dec. 29, 1880, — the two hundredth anniversary of the establishment of a royal provincial government over New Hampshire. The address has been printed by that Society in vol. i. of their Proceedings, 1876-1888, and is here reproduced with their consent. The author had intended to enlarge the address before its publication by the Society, but was prevented by his failing health and sudden death. — H.

seems to me this period is properly divided into two : The first, beginning in 1623, and ending in 1641, during which the first settlements were made, and four towns had arrived at maturity; the second period beginning with the extension of the jurisdiction of Massachusetts over the towns and the entire Province, and ending with the establishment of a government over New Hampshire, raising it to the dignity of a British Province in the year 1680. I shall now briefly consider the events of these two periods, particularly those leading to the establishment of a royal government in 1680.

In the year 1620 James I. of England granted to forty persons, consisting of nobles, knights, and gentlemen, all the territory in North America lying between the 40th and the 48th degree of north latitude, and between the Atlantic and Pacific Oceans, with power to govern the same. This association was styled " The Council established at Plymouth, in the county of Devon, for the planting, ordering, ruling, and governing of New England in America." To this vast extent of territory was given the name New England. Except a few scattered English settlements on the coast of Maine, it was still an unbroken wilderness throughout. The Council proceeded to make small grants of their territory along the Atlantic coast to such Englishmen as desired to make plantations in America. In 1622 this Council granted to Capt. John Mason, who had just returned to England from Newfoundland, where he had been governor of a colony of English for seven years, all the land lying along the Atlantic from Naumkeag River to the Merrimack River, and extending back to the heads of those rivers.

This tract of land was then and there named Mariana, and, I submit, in compliment to the Spanish Infanta, to whom Prince Charles of England was then affianced, and not in compliment to the Princess Henrietta Maria, as historians will have it. In 1622 the Council granted to Captain Mason and Sir Ferdinando Gorges all the land lying between the Merrimack River and the Kennebec River, extending sixty miles inland, and this was called the Province of Maine. This grant included what was afterward New Hampshire. Seven years later, in 1629, Mason and Gorges divided their grant of the Province of Maine, Mason taking that part lying between the Merrimack River and the Pascataqua River, and naming it New Hampshire. The Council confirmed this to him by a grant. This is the first appearance of the name New Hampshire in New England, and it survives to-day, the only name of an English county applied to any of the States.[1]

In 1628 the Council granted to several persons or associates, known afterwards as the Colony of Massachusetts Bay, a tract of land lying between Charles River on the south and the Merrimack River on the north, and extending three miles beyond these two rivers, and east and west from the Atlantic to the Pacific Ocean. The Council had never hitherto made a grant of such an enormous extent of territory and of limits extending beyond the rivers that bounded it. A patent so ample was regarded with astonishment, especially as it covered Mason's patent, Mariana, and also Capt. Robert Gorges' patent of Massachusetts Bay. This

---

[1] The State of New York was so named in honor of the Duke of York, afterwards James II. — H.

mischievous grant not only broke up the Council at last, but gave trouble for one hundred years to all the Colonies that bounded on it.

In the Spring of 1623, David Thomson, with a small company, established himself at Little Harbor, at the mouth of the Pascataqua River, on the large grant that had been made to Mason and Gorges only the year before. So far as known, this was the first settlement in this State. About the same time a settlement was made at Dover.[1] For fourteen years these were the only settlements in New Hampshire. Hampton was settled in 1637 by people from Massachusetts; Exeter in 1638 by Wheelwright and others banished from Massachusetts. Captain Mason had great expectations of making his Province worthy of his efforts. His employment at home as paymaster and treasurer of the army in the wars with Spain and France had prevented his visiting his American Province. He had sent agents and servants with all necessary articles to make a plantation and look for mines. In 1635 he was made Vice-Admiral of New England, and was preparing to come hither when he fell ill and died, to the great comfort of

[1] It is not possible, with our present information, to fix the date of the first settlement of Dover, or more properly Hilton's Point, now called Dover Neck. It was probably at least four or five years after the settlement made in 1623 by David Thomson and others at Pannaway, or Little Harbor, at the mouth of the Pascataqua. See Declaration of Allen, Shapleigh, and Lake, in Belknap (Farmer's ed.), 435, and Prov. Papers of New Hamp., i. 159; Notes on an Indenture of David Thomson and others, by Charles Deane, LL.D., in Proceedings of Mass. Hist. Soc. for May, 1876; Jenness's Notes on the First Planting of New Hampshire, 14-24; and Tuttle's Memoir of Capt. John Mason, 18. All these authorities discredit the vague statement of Hubbard, from which it has been inferred that he assigned the year 1623 as the date of the settlement at Hilton's Point. But see note 18 in Tuttle's Memoir of Mason, by the editor of that work, showing that for some time before his death Mr. Tuttle was inclined to place more reliance on Hubbard's statements. — H.

Massachusetts Bay. He was an unflinching royalist and churchman, — a neighbor that the Bay much disliked.[1]

No sooner was Mason dead, than dreams of aggrandizement visited the leading minds of the Bay. They had discovered that the Merrimack River, after running southerly fifty or sixty miles, turned and ran easterly thirty or forty miles to the Atlantic Ocean. They construed their patent to mean that their northern bounds should be three miles north of the northernmost point of Merrimack River, and from that point run east to the Atlantic Ocean and west to the Pacific. It was plain enough to see that such a construction would not only take into their jurisdiction all Mason's patent, but most of Gorges' in Maine. Their east line ran into Casco Bay, and all south of it, to the Pacific Ocean, was Massachusetts. They notified the people of New Hampshire that they were living within the Massachusetts patent, and threatened them that they would look into their northern boundaries, and would see how far north the Merrimack River extended.

The first thing was to seize upon the fair lands in Mason's patent, called by the Indians Winnicowitt, and grant it to their people. In 1639 they incorporated it a town, by the name of Hampton, and its allegiance was always claimed by the Massachusetts government. Massachusetts had resolved to get the three other towns under her jurisdiction by her policy of intrigue, without actual force. Portsmouth was strongly Episcopalian, and Episcopalians were royalists. Dover was divided, part Episcopalian and part Puri-

[1] For a complete presentation of all known facts in regard to Mason's interests in New England, see Tuttle's Memoir of Capt. John Mason, edited by John Ward Dean, A.M., and published by the Prince Society, 1887. — II.

tan.   The settlers of Exeter and Hampton were Puritans.
Massachusetts began to intrigue with Dover, and the Puritan element fell into her embrace, taking along with them
the royalists.   Portsmouth was persuaded to follow Dover,
some of the leading loyalists having been first tampered
with by the Puritan agents of Massachusetts.   Portsmouth
and Dover yielded to the jurisdiction of Massachusetts in
1641; Hampton was already there, but Exeter held out
till 1643.

New Hampshire, or Mason's patent, as it was frequently
called, was now entirely wiped out from the political map of
New England.   The only power to remedy this great abuse
was in the King of England.   He was now in arms and
about to enter into a death struggle with the Puritan parliament.   The heirs of Capt. John Mason were young, the
eldest not above ten years of age.   Massachusetts, having
gotten these four towns into her jurisdiction, then made her
territory into counties.   She formed all the towns north of
the Merrimack River, including Portsmouth, Dover, Exeter,
and Hampton, into one county, and named it Norfolk.

Prior to 1641 no general government had ever been
placed over the towns.   Each settlement, except Hampton, had associated and agreed upon articles by which they
would be governed till the King should otherwise direct.
The *jura regalia* were in the King.   Captain Mason was
expecting the destruction of the charter of Massachusetts,
and that a general governor would be placed over New
England.   This would have secured to his Province all the
government that was needed.   A period of nearly forty
years now followed, during which the name of New Hamp-

shire was seldom if ever heard.[1] New generations had
come upon the soil, and the people had become hardened
into Puritan usages.

The restoration of Charles II. to the throne of England,
in May, 1660, was received in all the New Hampshire towns
with joy by the Royalists that remained, and by all those
who longed for emancipation from the yoke of Massachusetts. The Puritan element joined Massachusetts in de-
ploring the event. In the month of July that Colony
received authentic information that the King was on the
throne of his ancestors, and immediately received into its
bosom two of the flying regicides. More than a year
elapsed before His Majesty was proclaimed King in that
jurisdiction. The time had now arrived when those persons, and those colonies in New England which had been
aggrieved by the acts of Massachusetts, could apply for
redress in England. The King was ready to hear the complaints of his loyal subjects and do them justice. No one
having interests in New Hampshire had greater and longer
grievances than Robert Mason, grandson and heir of Capt.
John Mason, the founder and proprietor of the Province.
His estate extended from the waters of the Pascataqua to
the Naumkeag River, and every inch was then under the
jurisdiction of Massachusetts. The first step towards recovering his estate was to get rid of the jurisdiction of Massachusetts and restore to the King his *jura regalia*. The
sympathy and good wishes of all the inhabitants impatient
of Puritan rule went with him, but they were unable to

[1] See Notes on an Indenture of Da-   Deane, LL.D., in Proceedings of Mass.
vid Thomson and others, by Charles   Hist. Soc. for May, 1876. — H.

assist him beyond expressing their wishes. A great political question was involved in Mason's undertaking. His
action, if successful, might lead not only to the recovery of his estate, but to the independence of New Hampshire; but if unsuccessful, then farewell to the Province
forever. What had been designed for a British Province
in New England had been for many years converted into a
frontier county of Massachusetts. The name New Hampshire could not be found on any political map of New
England.

Robert Mason set about his designs with a spirit worthy
of his ancestors. He suffered nothing to turn him aside.
Before the end of the first year of His Majesty's reign he
presented his claim for the territory of New Hampshire, in
its fullest extent, to the King. His Majesty submitted its
legal aspect to his attorney-general, who soon reported that
" Robert Mason, grandson and heir of Capt. John Mason,
had a good and legal title to the Province of New Hampshire." All well so far; but how was Mason to get possession of it? Massachusetts, the most powerful Colony in
New England, had long been in possession of the Province,
claiming it to be within her patent and jurisdiction. Here
was a new and untried difficulty, and before any solution
had been reached, His Majesty had been advised to send
commissioners to New England, with authority to examine
the many complaints which had been made to him, determine them where they could, and where they could not,
report the facts to His Majesty for his determination. Four
commissioners were sent in 1664 and were well received in
all the Colonies except Massachusetts, where they met with

steady opposition.[1] The King gave them no directions concerning Mason's claim to the territory of New Hampshire, neither did he forbid their attempting to compose the difficulty. Massachusetts having refused to treat with them on any question where she was concerned, nothing was accomplished by way of negotiation.

In June, 1665, the royal commissioners passed into New Hampshire on their way to Maine. The inhabitants received them kindly, and those opposed to the rule of Massachusetts prayed the commissioners to deliver them from that Colony. They received a petition signed by about thirty inhabitants of Portsmouth, among whom were Champernowne, Pickering, Sherburne, Hunking, and many other well-known persons, setting forth their grievances under Massachusetts laws and fanaticism, which had become oppressive, and praying for relief. Another petition, addressed to the King, was placed in their hands. It was signed by inhabitants of the four towns, praying His Majesty to take New Hampshire under his royal protection, that they might be governed by the laws of England.[2] The commissioners, being satisfied that Massachusetts was but an usurper in that Province, appointed justices of the peace, in the King's name, with power to act under the laws of England, and to continue until the King's pleasure should be made known, and departed into Maine. Massachusetts hastened to undo all that the commissioners had done in New Hampshire.

That Colony, seeing that Mason was persistent in seeking to recover from its grasp the Province of New Hampshire,

---

[1] See pages 115, 116.
[2] These petitions are printed in Jenness's Transcripts of Original Documents relating to New Hampshire, 48, 49. — H.

now resorted to intrigue with Mason's relative and agent, Joseph Mason, living at Portsmouth. For this purpose they first despatched their secretary, Edward Rawson, and afterwards Robert Pike. Their final proposition was to surrender to Robert Mason his lands if he would consent that Massachusetts jurisdiction might continue over them. Robert Mason unhesitatingly rejected the proposition when it was communicated to him. He had no wish to live under that government; he desired to restore his Province to the jurisdiction of English laws. Had Mason then and there yielded, there had been an end to New Hampshire. After some years, no progress having been made with the adjustment of the claim, Mason presented a petition to the King, stating that he had received no satisfaction and was wearied with the delay. Gorges had been equally unsuccessful in recovering out of the grasp of Massachusetts his Province of Maine. The King despatched copies of these complaints by the hands of Edward Randolph to the magistrates of Boston, and required from them an answer to Gorges' and Mason's claims. The Colony sent agents to England to make answer. The matter was referred to the Lord Chief Justices of England to hear and determine. To the surprise of all, the Massachusetts agents disclaimed title to the soil, but contended for jurisdiction over the Province. The judges decided that the jurisdiction of Massachusetts went no farther than the boundaries expressed in the patent, and those boundaries, the judges said, cannot be construed to extend farther northward along the river Merrimack than three English miles. This decision was approved by the King, and there was an end to Massachusetts jurisdiction over so much of New Hampshire.

No sooner was this decision reached than the Massachusetts agents made application to the King to settle the four towns, Portsmouth, Dover, Exeter, and Hampton, under Massachusetts, at the same time stigmatizing the "inhabitants of those towns as few and of mean estate," and therefore of little consequence to any one. Massachusetts bestirred herself and procured petitions to be signed by some inhabitants in all the towns, requesting this to be done, and forwarded the same to their agents in London, who presented them to the Lords of the Committee for Trade and Plantations, but it was to no purpose; the King had resolved that Massachusetts should have no more territory or jurisdiction. The Colony agents had approached Mason to buy his interest in the Province while the matter was pending before the Lord Chief Justices, and he refused to sell to them. They were more successful with Gorges.[1]

Mason was bound to stand by his interests in the Province. He had now pursued them since the restoration of King Charles II., eighteen years before. It was his earnest desire that the King should establish his government over the Province, and at length his wishes were gratified. In July, 1679, the King wrote to the Colony of Massachusetts, rebuking them for having purchased, without his knowledge or consent, Gorges' Province of Maine, and bade them prepare to deliver it to him, when he should be ready to receive it. He told them they need not expect the Province of New Hampshire would be annexed to that Colony; that he had in view the establishing there such method as would benefit and satisfy the people of that place. He ordered the

[1] See page 117 and note 3.

Colony to recall all the commissions they had granted for governing New Hampshire, and thus prepared the way for his royal government. The four towns in the Province now awaiting the new government contained only about four thousand inhabitants, although Portsmouth and Dover had been settled nearly sixty years before, and Hampton and Exeter forty years. No new settlement had been made while under the jurisdiction of Massachusetts, — proof enough of the blighting effect of Puritan rule over this Province. Most of the present inhabitants never knew any other government than Massachusetts, having been born and reared under it. But among the aged, forty years' captivity had not entirely destroyed their love and reverence for the English Church and the English laws.

It is a notable fact that the chief trade of the Province at this time was in masts, planks, boards, and staves. Fishing seems to have been laid aside altogether. The new government immediately urged His Majesty to make the Pascataqua River a free port, and annex the south half of the Isles of Shoals.

Charles II. and his ministers had now resolved to establish a government over that part of the Province of New Hampshire, which had been determined to lie outside the northern bounds of Massachusetts jurisdiction, and which contained within its limits only four towns; namely, Portsmouth, Dover, Hampton, and Exeter. Among the considerations that led His Majesty to this undertaking were the petitions of the loyal inhabitants sent to him from time to time, asking to be taken into his immediate care and protection; the determination to see that his faithful subject,

Robert Mason, had that justice done him which he had so long prayed for; and the preservation of those forests in the Province which had yielded for the royal navy during many years the finest masts in the world.

At that time three species of colonial government were in vogue among the British Colonies in America. There were chartered governments, like Massachusetts and Connecticut; proprietary governments, like the Provinces of Maine and Maryland; and provincial governments, like New York and Virginia. A provincial or royal government consisted of three branches, — a governor or president and a council, both nominated and appointed by the King, and an assembly chosen by the people. It is manifest that in this form of government the just prerogatives of the Crown and the constitutional privileges of the people are equally attended to. Such a government had been established in Virginia as early as 1619, and was hailed with applause. It has the distinction of being the first legislative assembly in America. It was an auspicious day for New Hampshire when Charles II. adopted for it a provincial government, — a government that continued over it for almost a hundred years. There had never been in New England, and there never was afterwards, a government of this kind. New Hampshire has the distinction of being the only royal government this side of the Hudson River, — a government administered by the King's commission, in the hands of his lieutenant.

The royal commission for the government of the Province of New Hampshire is dated Westminster, Sept. 18, 1679. It is in the form of other commissions for government, and is briefly as follows: "It inhibits and restrains the jurisdiction exercised by the Colony of Massachusetts over the towns of Portsmouth, Dover, Exeter, and Hampton, and all other lands extending from three miles to the northward of the river Merrimack, and of any and every part thereof to the Province of Maine; constitutes a president and council to govern the Province; appoints John Cutt, Esq., president, to continue one year, and till another be appointed by the same authority; Richard Martyn, William Vaughan, and Thomas Daniel of Portsmouth, John Gilman of Exeter, Christopher Hussey of Hampton, and Richard Waldron of Dover, Esquires, to be of the council, who were authorized to choose three other qualified persons out of the several parts of the Province, to be added to them. The said president, and every succeeding one, to appoint a deputy to preside in his absence; the president or his deputy, with any five, to be a quorum. They were to meet at Portsmouth in twenty days after the arrival of the commission, and publish it. They were constituted a court of record for the administration of justice, according to the laws of England, so far as circumstances would permit, reserving a right of appeal to the King in Council for actions of fifty pounds value. They were empowered to appoint military officers and take all needful measures for defence against enemies. Liberty of conscience was allowed to all Protestants, those of the Church of England to be particularly encouraged. For the support of government, they were to continue the present taxes till an assembly could be called; to which end they were within three months to issue writs under the Province seal for calling an assembly, to whom the president should recommend the passing of such laws as should establish their allegiance, good order, and defence, and the raising taxes in such manner and proportion as they should see fit. All laws to be approved by the president and council, and then to remain in force till the King's pleasure should be known, for which purpose they should be sent to England by the first ships. In case of the president's death, his deputy to succeed, and on the death of a councillor, the remainder to elect another and send over his name, with the names of two other meet persons, that the King might appoint one of the three. The King engaged for himself and successors to continue the privilege of an assembly in the same manner and form, unless by inconvenience arising therefrom he or his heirs should see cause to alter the same. If any of the inhabitants should refuse to agree with Mason or his agents, on the terms stated in the commission, the president and council were directed to reconcile the difference, or send the case, stated in writing, with their own opinions, to the King, that he, with his Privy Council, might determine it according to equity."[1]

The King was extremely desirous to compose the differences likely to arise between the inhabitants of the Province and Mason, the proprietor. He points out, in the commission, with some detail, what he wishes the president and council to do in the matter.

Who suggested to the King the names for president and council does not appear,[2] but there were not in the whole

---

[1] Belknap's History of New Hampshire, Farmer's ed., 88, 89. For the commission to President Cutt. see Coll. Hist. Soc. of New Hampshire, viii. 1–9. — H.

[2] It is probable the suggestion originated with Robert Mason or Edward Randolph. — H.

Province straighter Puritans or firmer friends of the Massachusetts Colony. They were avowed enemies of the Anglican Church, and they loved the laws and jurisprudence of England none too well. Every one had been in office under Massachusetts during the usurpation, and every one had signed the recent petitions sent to the King, praying to remain under the jurisdiction of that Colony. They hated Mason for detaching the Province from Massachusetts, and they hated his claim to the soil more. All had gained considerable estates, mainly by commercial transactions. The planters of New Hampshire had no representative in the executive part of this new government. The Massachusetts Puritans must have smiled grimly when they saw the names of their partisans in the royal commission.

Charles II. and his ministers had been completely duped;[1] and they found it out before the first year of the administration had ended. All the members of the executive government were born in England, and were now advanced in years. They had lived in the Province between thirty and forty years, and were well known in every part of it. John Cutt, named president in the commission, was one of three enterprising brothers whose names were already conspicuous in the commercial annals of Portsmouth. His whole life had been passed in commercial adventures. The sails of

---

[1] It does not appear that any deception or duplicity was used in procuring the nomination of Cutt and his councilors. They were leading men in the Province, and most capable of organizing the new government: and undoubtedly it was chiefly for this reason that they were selected. They expressly declared their reluctance to accept office under the commission. President Cutt was an honest and fair-minded man, and while he lived exerted his influence to have the King's wishes and commands, as expressed in the commission, faithfully observed. But his death, which occurred soon after the government was organized, put the control of affairs into the hands of men less wise and less moderate. — H.

his vessels had whitened every sea known to the commerce of New England. He had long been known as an eminent and opulent merchant. He was now well advanced in years, and lived in Portsmouth, the commercial metropolis of the Province. His spacious homestead on Strawberry Bank was part of the lands which had been reduced to cultivation by the agents of Captain Mason half a century ago. President Cutt had not seen much of public life. He appears to have avoided it. Once only had he been a member of the General Court of Massachusetts, and after a few days' service he got excused from further attendance. Occasionally he was a commissioner of the county court, and often a selectman of Portsmouth. In 1663 the town elected him constable, but he refused to accept, and paid his fine, five pounds. He was an active and a conspicuous member of the Rev. Joshua Moody's church. His name stands with the original members.[1]

Richard Waldron, one of the council, had no equal for ability and force of character in the whole Province. He had been longer a resident than any other member of the board, and was a steady adherent to Massachusetts. He had been many years a member of the General Court and seven years Speaker of the House of Deputies. He was strongly opposed to Mason's interest, and his influence in New Hampshire had always been great. The other five members of the council named in the commission, Richard Martyn, William Vaughan, Thomas Daniel, John Gilman, and Christopher Hussey, had had considerable experience in the local government under Massachusetts.

[1] See note 2, p. 120.

The royal commission having passed the seals, the King wrote a letter to the president and council, and placed both, with the provincial seal, in the hands of Edward Randolph, to carry to the Province of New Hampshire. The King also gave Randolph a portrait of His Majesty, and the royal arms to be set up at the seat of government. Randolph placed these somewhat bulky articles on a New England vessel which never reached its destination, and thus New Hampshire was deprived of these memorials of royalty.

Randolph's route lay by the way of New York. He sailed from England the last of October, and arrived in Portsmouth on the 27th of December, 1679, little more than three months after the royal commission had passed the seals. Randolph at once presented himself to Mr. John Cutt, "a very just and honest man," says Randolph, and acquainted him with his royal errand. Cutt lost no time in sending summons to the members of the council named in the commission to meet at his house and receive from Randolph His Majesty's communications. On the first day of January, 1680, the council assembled, and Randolph placed in their hands His Majesty's letter, and the royal commission for the government of the Province. The letter and commission being read, most of the council desired time to consider whether they would accept. Waldron and Martyn were decidedly opposed to the commission. President Cutt, and John Gilman of Exeter, were ready to accept the commission. Nearly three weeks were spent in deliberating the matter by the hesitating members of the council. At last, seeing that the president was determined to organize the government within the time required by the commission, and that their places were likely to be filled by others, they accepted, and took the oaths of office on the 21st of January. Meantime President Cutt notified the inhabitants of the Province to assemble at Portsmouth on the 22d day of January, and hear His Majesty's commission read and proclamation made of His Majesty's having received the Province of New Hampshire under his gracious favor and protection. This must have been a memorable day in Portsmouth, for it is recorded that great acclamation and firing of cannon followed the announcement that they were under His Majesty's government.[1]

On that day the organization of the executive government was completed. The president made choice of Richard Waldron as deputy president, and the number of the council was made complete by the election of three new members. Proclamation was then made that all persons holding office in the Province should continue in their places until further orders be taken by His Majesty's government. The next step was to summon an assembly. A warrant was despatched to the selectmen of all the towns, then only four in number, requesting them to send to the president and council a list of the names and estates of the inhabitants. This being done, the council selected from the selectmen's list the names of such persons as they judged qualified to vote for assemblymen, and returned these names to the

[1] Belknap's History of New Hampshire, Farmer's ed., 90-96; Paper by Charles Deane, LL.D., on the Records of the President and Council of New Hampshire, in Proceedings Mass. Hist. Soc., xvi. 256-260; Notes Historical and Bibliographical on the Laws of New Hampshire, by Albert H. Hoyt, in Proceedings of American Antiquarian Soc., 1876; and Jenness's Transcripts of Original Documents relating to New Hampshire. — H.

selectmen. Great complaint was made that many fit persons were deprived of the elective franchise. It is easy to see that the council had an opportunity to make the assembly, and probably did so The election was ordered to take place March 9, and not above three persons for the assembly were to be chosen in any one town.

The members of the assembly were summoned to appear at Portsmouth, on March 16, to attend to His Majesty's service. On that day the first legislature in New Hampshire assembled and was organized. It consisted of eleven persons, two from Exeter, and three from each of the other towns. Thus, in two and one half months after the arrival of the royal messenger with the commission, the government was completely organized over the Province, — a government that was destined to continue, with but few interruptions, for a hundred years. New Hampshire was restored to her place on the political map of New England, never again to disappear. She was raised to the dignity of a British Province in America.

Portsmouth had the honor to be the seat[1] of government during the entire period of the royal government. Here were the scenes of all that was splendid in a provincial court. Portsmouth gave of her citizens the chief of the new government, John Cutt, and she also gave the last royal governor, Sir John Wentworth. The provincial government was succeeded by a republican government, whose centenary is at hand. *Esto Perpetua.*

---

[1] The principal officers of the government resided, and the assembly convened, on Great Island (now New Castle), which until 1693 was included in the town of Portsmouth. See note 2, p. 103. — H.

NEW HAMPSHIRE WITHOUT PROVIN-
CIAL GOVERNMENT.

1689–1690.

NEW HAMPSHIRE WITHOUT PROVIN-
CIAL GOVERNMENT.

1689–1690.

THE political condition of the royal Province of New
Hampshire during the short period it was without
government, beginning with the deposition of Sir Edmund
Andros on the 18th day of April, 1689, and ending with
the re-annexation of that Province to Massachusetts on the
19th of March, 1690, — eleven months, — has received but
little attention from historians.[1] Dr. Belknap gives but little
space, — less than twenty lines, — in his admirable history
of New Hampshire, to the consideration of the civil affairs
of this period, and is not entirely accurate in this.   His relation of other events is more extended and correct.[2]

The fall of the government of Sir Edmund Andros over
New England, an event in which neither the Province nor
the people of New Hampshire had any part, left that Prov-

---

[1] This paper is reprinted, by permission, from the Proceedings of the
Massachusetts Historical Society, Oct.
1879. — H.

[2] Mass. Records, vi. 1, 3, 127, 128 ;
Belknap's Hist. of New Hamp., Farmer's
ed., 121, 122.

ince without any government. The provincial officers of
his appointment, civil and military, had no authority to act
after his overthrow by the action of the people of Massachusetts. The four ancient towns, Portsmouth, Dover,
Hampton, and Exeter, which then constituted that entire
Province, were again in a state of independence, as they
were when annexed to Massachusetts in the year 1641.
They were now stronger in population and in political
organization. Fifty years' experience had given them an
almost perfect system of domestic self-government. But for
the exigencies of the times, which required a bond of political union, and unity of action, they might have remained
in their independent state without inconvenience, so well
regulated were their domestic concerns, and orderly their
inhabitants.

The people of the other Colonies and Provinces in New
England, under the government of Sir Edmund Andros,
were likewise left without government; but they had systems of government under which they had long been accustomed to live, and which they could readily resume. In
less than one month after the overthrow of Andros, the
Colonies of Massachusetts, Connecticut, Rhode Island, and
Plymouth returned quietly to their former governments, and
recalled their former magistrates.[1]

New Hampshire had been a royal Province little more
than nine years when the revolution in New England occurred. During this period it had been governed by royal
commissions in the hands of officers appointed by the King
of England. Two entirely different systems of government

---

[1] Palfrey's Hist. New England, iii. 596, 597.

had been set over the Province, neither of which suited the genius and wants of the whole people. They were therefore without any system of government, suited to their desires, to fall back upon. The four towns remained eleven months without union, or any provincial government.

The war with the eastern Indians, begun in the Province of Maine in the summer of 1688, was only slumbering when the government of Sir Edmund Andros was overthrown in April, 1689. It was destined to break forth with great and terrible energy, supported by the moral strength, at least, of a new foe, before the summer ended, and to rage with little interruption till the Peace of Ryswick, more than seven years later.[1]

To add greater calamities to New England, on the 7th of May England declared war against France, — an act that finally led to a fierce and bloody conflict between their American Colonies, notwithstanding the treaty of colonial neutrality made between these two crowns less than three years before. This unhappy event in Europe encouraged the Indians in their war on the English, and darkened the prospect of all New England.[2]

A mighty scheme for the conquest of New York and of Hudson's Bay was already devised in France, although the treaty of colonial neutrality provided that, if the two crowns should break friendship in Europe, their colonies in America should remain in peace and neutrality. Actual collision with the French did not take place before November, — a delay more on account of Boston trade than on account of

---

[1] Belknap's Hist. of New Hamp., Farmer's ed., 131–143.

[2] Brodhead's Hist. New York, ii. 475, 545; Mass. Hist. Soc Coll., xxxi. 99.

the treaty stipulations. The blow then came from a squadron on the coast of Acadie, recently from France, and said to be designed to surprise Boston.[1]

The four towns in New Hampshire, nestling between Massachusetts and the Province of Maine, again under the jurisdiction of the Bay Colony, seemed far enough removed from either of the enemies of the English.

Suddenly, in the darkness of the morning of the 28th day of June, the third month after their government had been withdrawn, a body of Indians swooped down like a bird of prey on the frontier village of Cocheco, in Dover, and destroyed it; killing a large number of the inhabitants, and carrying away into captivity as many more. Among the slain was the venerable Richard Waldron, for more than forty years the admitted chief in civil and military affairs in the Province. Within one week after the overthrow of Andros, he had been appointed by the Council of Safety, in Massachusetts, Commander-in-Chief of the New Hampshire Regiment.[2]

A few hours after this memorable tragedy had ended, six of the principal gentlemen of Portsmouth received from Richard Waldron, Jr., a brief account in writing of what had befallen his venerable father and others at Cocheco, by the hands of the barbarous Indians. They immediately wrote a joint letter to Major Pike at Salisbury, the nearest

[1] Documentary Hist. of New York, ii. 47 ; Murdoch's Nova Scotia, i. 178, 179 ; Brodhead's Hist. New York, ii. 547 ; Mass. Archives, xxxv. 106.

[2] What political relation the Council of Safety regarded the Province to have to Massachusetts when this act was done does not appear. Nor does it appear that Major Waldron exercised over the militia any functions of this commission. Belknap's Hist. of New Hamp., Farmer's ed., 126, 129 : Pike's Journal in Proceedings Mass. Hist. Soc. (Sept. 1875), 124 ; Mass. Records, vi. 6.

military commander in Massachusetts, enclosing this account of the disaster, for the Governor and Council, and requesting assistance in this exigency of affairs, "wherein the whole country is concerned."

Major Pike wrote a short letter to the Governor, requesting speedy orders and advice, and forwarded it with the others to Boston.

Governor Bradstreet received the letters at midnight the same day of the massacre, and next day laid them before the General Court. Their contents were quickly considered, and a letter to the gentlemen of Portsmouth was prepared and forwarded. The Court expressed concern for their friends and neighbors, looking upon the affair as concerning all, but declined " to exert any authority in your Province." The letter concluded with advice to them to "fall into some form or constitution for the exercise of government for your safety and convenience." [1]

A few days later, the 2d day of July, seeing the defenceless condition of the Province, the General Court ordered that " drums be beaten up in Boston and the adjacent towns for volunteers to go forthwith for the succor and relief of our neighbor friends at Pascataqua, distressed by the Indian enemies." To encourage volunteers, the court offered to provide their sustenance, and gave them liberty to nominate their own officers. They were also authorized to receive from " the public treasury eight pounds for every fighting man's head or scalp that they shall bring in," and also to share all plunder taken from the Indians. [2]

This dreadful massacre — the greatest, in all points of

---

[1] Coll. Mass. Hist. Soc., xxi. 88–90.   [2] Mass. Records, vi. 53.

view, in the annals of the Province — spread terror among the inhabitants, and weakened their strength. It opened their eyes to the fact that their geographical position offered them no security from the blows of the barbarous enemy. It brought freshly before them their helpless condition by reason of the want of provincial government. Executive authority to raise military forces and provide for them, by impressment if necessary; to construct public defences and garrison them; to levy and collect taxes; and, above all, to make a treaty with other Colonies for joining in a common defence against common enemies, was now needed more than ever.

The magistrates and military officers in the Province, appointed by Andros, had undoubtedly exercised a feeble sway. The question had long been debated by the inhabitants whether their functions were wholly suspended. At length they generally concluded, " that we had no Governor nor authority in this Province so as to answer the ends of government, and to command and do in defence of their Majesties' subjects against the common enemy."[1]

The refusal of the General Court to exercise in the Province any of the functions of government, now so much needed there, the advice to form a government among themselves, and the great and pressing need of one at this juncture of affairs led to the first attempt to that end since the fall of Andros. Several gentlemen of Portsmouth and Great Island sent letters to the several towns in the Province, requesting them to make choice of fit persons to meet

[1] Nathaniel Weare's Letter to Robert Pike, in Coll. N. H. Hist. Soc., i. 135-140.

on the 11th day of July, and to "consider of what shall be adjudged meet and convenient to be done by the several towns in the Province for their peace and safety, until we shall have orders from the crown of England." Whatever should be agreed on by this convention was to be submitted to the towns for their approval. Nothing appears to have come of this.[1]

While the matter of provincial government was under consideration and debate in the towns, Massachusetts was actively preparing for the common defence of all the New England Colonies, against the French as well as the Indians.

On the 17th of July she summoned her ancient allies, the Colonies of Connecticut and Plymouth, to send commissioners to Boston, "according to the rules of our ancient union and confederation," to consider measures for "a joint and vigorous prosecution of the common enemy." The commissioners assembled on the 16th day of September, and carefully examined the causes of the Indian war. They formally declared "the same to be just and necessary on the part of the English, and ought to be jointly prosecuted by all the Colonies." They directed notice to be sent to the towns in New Hampshire of their meeting and action, with a request for their "concurrence and assistance in a joint management of the war," and adjourned to meet again on the 18th day of October.[2]

With the first month of autumn came another attack of the barbarians on the Province. On the 13th of September,

---

[1] Coll. N. H. Hist. Soc., viii. 399; cvii. 244; Coll. Mass. Hist. Soc., xxxv. Weare's Letter. 203, 212; Bradstreet's Letter to Governor Treat, Connecticut Archives.
[2] Mass. Archives, xxxv. 50; *Ibid.*, ernor Treat, Connecticut Archives.

the settlement on Oyster River — a place fated to feel the stroke of savage vengeance oftener and more severely than any other in the Province — was attacked by Indians, and eighteen persons were slain.[1]

On the 10th day of October, Governor Bradstreet carried out the request of the commissioners by direction of the General Court. He wrote a letter to Richard Martyn, William Vaughan, and Richard Waldron, principal persons in New Hampshire, acquainting them of what had been done by the commissioners of the United Colonies, and requesting a commissioner to be sent from that Province to meet the commissioners at their next meeting. On the 16th these gentlemen sent a joint answer, wherein they expressed their thanks for what had already been done for the defence of the country, and regretted that there was insufficient time for the towns to assemble and make choice of a commissioner before the next meeting of the commissioners. They declared their determination to communicate the request to the several towns forthwith, so that a commissioner might be chosen for any later meeting of the commissioners.[2]

Near the end of October the several towns held meetings

---

[1] Manuscript Letter of Maj. Robert Pike, in Mass. Archives, cvii. 314 ; Coll. Mass. Hist. Soc., xxxv. 212 ; Mather's Magnalia, lib. vii. 67 ; Belknap. Farmer's ed., 131. Major Pike says the garrison attacked was Langstaff's ; and that the number slain and carried captive was nineteen. Mather says it was Lieutenant Huckin's garrison that was attacked ; and that "Captain Garner" pursued the Indians. His statement has been accepted by all historians.

Capt. Andrew Gardner, of Boston, of the forces of Major Swayne lately sent into those parts, had a company of soldiers scouting there, whose headquarters were at Salmon Falls. Pike in his journal says it was James Huggin's garrison, and carries the event back into August, which is clearly wrong. The date of this attack has never before been fixed.

[2] Mass. Archives, xxxv. 50, 57.

and voted for a commissioner of the United Colonies of New England, — an act that gives the Province new importance in history. The votes of the towns were sent to Portsmouth, and it appeared that William Vaughan was elected commissioner.[1] Dover appointed John Tuttle agent to take the vote of the town to Portsmouth to be counted with the votes of the other towns, and to assist in giving instructions to the commissioner chosen as to the management of the war.[2]

The commissioners of the United Colonies now assumed the direction of the war, which was carried on at the joint expense of all. Connecticut had strongly hinted that Rhode Island should be invited to join the confederation. Governor Bradstreet was prevailed on to write to Governor Clark on the 2d day of August, setting out the necessity of making a joint defence against the common enemies of the English, and requesting advice and assistance. It does not appear that any ever came. Rhode Island had not been admitted to the confederation in former years.[3]

On the 6th of December the commissioners of the Colonies, Vaughan with them, assembled in Boston to consider the war with the French. Although this war had been declared seven months before in Europe, no considerable injury had been inflicted on New England till recently. Intelligence had now arrived that war had been publicly declared against the English at Port Royal, and that English

---

[1] N. H. Prov. Papers, ii. 30, 32; Mass. Archives, xxxv. 106.
[2] Coll. N. H. Hist. Soc., viii. 398.
[3] Mass. Archives, xxxv. 63, 106; *Ibid.*, cvii. 247; Colony Records of Conn., 1689-1706, p. 3; Church's Philip's War, pt. ii. 55, 58; Arnold's Hist. Rhode Island, i. 156, 157.

fishing vessels in that quarter had been seized, some kept and others sent to France; that the French were aiding and assisting the Indian enemy with arms and ammunition, thereby showing their intention, by all ways and means, to hurt and destroy their Majesties' subjects, — a thing they will continue to do so long as they have any considerable fortified fort or harbor near us. The commissioners therefore recommend that in the United Colonies and Provinces in these parts his Majesty's declaration of war against France be forthwith published, and that care be taken that the militia be well settled, and the fortifications in seaport towns be made serviceable. They also recommend that a committee of fit persons be appointed to inquire into the present condition of our French neighbors, and to find what measures need be taken in regard to them, so as to prevent their doing further injury, and giving further assistance to the Indians, and make report.[1]

On the 18th of December, Hampton was so sensible of the want of government that three of its principal inhabitants, namely, Nathaniel Weare, Samuel Sherburne, and Henry Dow, were selected to meet persons chosen by other towns, and consider and debate this matter of government, and make report at the next town meeting. Nothing, however, seems to have come of this, except that Hampton now began to be very jealous of the other towns.[2]

When the memorable year 1689 ended, the four towns in

[1] Mass. Archives, xxxv. 106; Doc. Hist. N. Y., ii. 47.

Our historians have omitted to mention the commissioners of the United Colonies and their action, as related here.

[2] N. H. Prov. Papers, ii. 31, 43, 44; Weare's Letter.

New Hampshire were still without union and without government. The prospect of having a provincial government set over them by William and Mary was no better than when the government of Andros was withdrawn from them, more than eight months before. A conflict of arms with the French was impending. The veteran Frontenac, the greatest soldier in the New World, now again the military chief of New France, had been three months in Canada, and was preparing to crush the English settlements in New England.[1]

At this juncture of affairs, Portsmouth, Dover, and Exeter came to an understanding that each should choose commissioners with full power to meet in joint convention and devise "some method of government in order to their defence against the common enemy."

Hampton seems to have been unreasonably jealous of the other towns, and to have delayed action in the matter of providing a provincial government. This applies to part, not all the inhabitants. Portsmouth, Dover, and Exeter elected their commissioners to the Convention ; and the commissioners of the two former towns were forced to request Hampton to elect her commissioners. She delayed action nearly three weeks in a matter of so much consequence, and finally brought all to nought.

Exeter sent four delegates, and the other towns six each, to the Convention, making twenty-two in all. They were the chief persons in the four towns of the Province, and heads of families. The commissioners met in Convention in Portsmouth, the metropolis of the Province, on the 24th

---

[1] Brodhead's New York, ii. 603, 606; Belknap, Farmer's ed., 132.

of January, 1690. How they organized, or who their officers
were, is unknown. The Convention unanimously adopted a
simple form of self-government, substantially like that set
over the Province by the royal Commissions of Charles II.
to President Cutt and also Lieutenant-Governor Cranfield.
To give their act the greatest force and authority, each and
every member of the Convention set his hand to the instrument in which was drawn the form of the new provincial
government. This celebrated document, the only remaining record of the Convention now known, is in the hand-
writing of John Pickering, a lawyer of Portsmouth, and a
member of the Convention.[1] Having finished its labors,
the Convention adjourned to meet again, after the election of officers for the new government, and count the
votes.[2]

This venerable State document, now printed here for
the first time, came to my hands many years ago, with some
manuscripts of John Tuttle of Dover, a member of the
Convention, and my paternal ancestor.[3] The Convention
being a novel proceeding, its records would not likely go
with the public archives of the Province. It is amazing
that so fragile and homeless a document should find its
way down to this time in such good state of preservation.
It could not have been seen by Dr. Belknap, otherwise he
would have related more fully and accurately the action of
the Convention.

[1] N. H. Prov. Papers, ii. 31–34;
Weare's Letter above referred to.
Also the original record printed on
pages 213, 214.

[2] Dover Town Records, January,
1690.

[3] A biographical sketch of John Tuttle is in the New England Historical and
Genealogical Register, xxi. 135–137.

The new government was to consist of a President, Secretary, and Treasurer to be chosen by the whole Province; also a Council of ten members to be chosen by the four towns, — Portsmouth and Hampton having three each, and Dover and Exeter two each, — and a Legislative Assembly.[1]

On the 30th day of January, 1690, six days after the adoption of the form of government, a town meeting was held in Dover to choose two members of the Council, and to vote for President, Secretary, and Treasurer. Capt. John Gerrish and Capt. John Woodman, two leading citizens, were elected members of the Council. The votes for the other provincial officers were given and sealed up, to be opened by the commissioners and counted with the votes of the other towns.[2]

About the same time a town meeting was held in Hampton to elect three members of the Council, and to vote for President, Secretary, and Treasurer of the Province. A majority agreed not to vote for any provincial officers, to the great surprise of the whole Province. The six commissioners of Hampton had agreed in Convention to the form of government, and subscribed the record. This action speedily put an end to the attempt to form a provincial government.[3]

The events of the war were thickening. Schenectady

---

[1] See the original record printed on pages 213, 214.

[2] Dover Town Records, January, 1690.

[3] Weare's Letter. It is worthy of note that the town records of Hampton, with the letter, so often cited, of Nathaniel Weare, furnish an outline of the political history of the Province during this period. Portsmouth and Exeter town records show but little of their action; while Dover records supply valuable information nowhere else to be found.

had been destroyed at one blow, and a French and Indian force was already on its way from Canada to the Pascataqua, though then unknown in the Province. A crisis had arrived. These towns must have a government over them.

Some of the leading gentlemen in Portsmouth drew up a petition, addressed to the Governor and Council of Massachusetts, praying for government and protection as formerly, till their Majesties' pleasure should be known, and declaring readiness to bear a proportion of the charge for defence of the country against the common enemy. This was now the 20th of February, 1690. The petition was quickly carried through all the towns, and received three hundred and seventy-two signatures. Fifteen members of the Convention, two thirds of the whole, signed it, — all from Exeter, and all from Portsmouth, except Robert Elliot; all from Dover, except John Tuttle, John Roberts, and Nicholas Follett; and all from Hampton, except Nathaniel Weare, Henry Dow, and Henry Green.[1] The original petition is preserved with the Massachusetts Archives.

Nathaniel Weare, a principal inhabitant of Hampton, and a member of the Convention, was much grieved at the action of Hampton in refusing to elect officers and complete the organization of the provincial government. He was in favor of the plan of self-government, and opposed to annexation to Massachusetts to the same extent as before. He says that this petition was brought to Hampton on the

[1] Coll. N. H. Hist. Soc., viii. 293–298 ; Mass. Archives, xxxv. 229. The names are very incorrectly spelled in the seventh volume of the Collections of the New Hampshire Historical Society.

26th day of February, while the militia were assembled there, and that many signed it without knowing what it was; and also that many children and servants there did the same. Hampton now clearly preferred to remain in her independent state.[1]

This petition was quickly taken to Boston by John Pickering and William Vaughan, and was presented to the Governor and Council on the 28th day of February. It was received, and the prayer of the petitioners granted. The Governor and Council forthwith appointed William Vaughan, Richard Martyn, and Nathaniel Fryer, known adherents to the Colony, magistrates over the Province; and Vaughan then and there took the oath of office.[2] Order was given for the towns to make choice of civil and military officers, to complete the new organization, and present their names to the General Court for confirmation, which was quickly done.

In a few weeks John Pickering was despatched to Boston in behalf of the Province, with a full list of officers, civil and military, and a joint letter of recommendation from William Vaughan and Richard Waldron, to lay the same before the Governor and Council and the Deputies. On the 19th day of March, 1690, both branches approved the action of the Governor and Council on the 28th of February, and confirmed the list of officers.[3] Only the day before, Frontenac's party of French and Indians had fallen on

---

[1] Weare's Letter. A biographical sketch of Nathaniel Weare, by the late Chief-Justice Bell, is in Coll. N. H. Hist. Soc., viii. 381-394.

[2] Sewall Papers, i. 312; Weare's Letter.

[3] Mass. Archives, xxx. 308; N. H. Prov. Papers, ii. 40, 41; Mass. Rec., vi. 127, 128; Belknap, Farmer's ed., 132.

the eastern frontier of Dover, and destroyed the village of Salmon Falls.

The Province was now again fully restored to its former relations with Massachusetts, and remained till the Commission of Samuel Allen as Governor of the Province was published there Aug. 13, 1692.[1]

During this period of suspended government over the Province, only one act of violence appears against any of the officers appointed by Andros. Richard Chamberlain was Secretary from 1680 to 1686, when the government of Joseph Dudley was extended over the Province, and that office abolished. He was then made clerk of the judicial courts, and held that office till the government of Andros was withdrawn. The records and files of the Province as well as of the courts were in his possession, having come there by virtue of his official station. The people resolved to get them from him, although no one had a better right to hold them. Capt. John Pickering, a resolute man, — the same mentioned in these pages, — with an armed force proceeded to Chamberlain's house, and demanded the records and files. Chamberlain very properly refused to give them to him without some legal warrant for his security and protection; thereupon Pickering seized them with force, and carried them out of the Province.[2]

---

[1] N. H. Prov. Papers, ii. 71.

[2] N. H. Prov. Papers, i. 590, 600; *Ibid.,* iii. 298; Belknap's Hist., Farmer's ed., 149, 150. A Memoir of Capt. John Pickering is in Coll. N. H. Hist. Soc., iii. 292–297.

[Form of Government.]

NEW HAMPSHIRE IN NEW ENGLAND.	At a meeting of the Committee chosen by the Inhabitants of the respective towns within this Province for settlement of a method of order and government over the same, until their Maj^{ties} take Care thereof, held in Portsmouth the 24th of January, 1689.

Whereas, Since the late revolution in the Massachusetts Colony, no order from their Maj^{ties} has yet arrived for the settlement of government in this Province, and no Authority being left in the Province save that of the late Justices of Peace ; which, considering our present circumstances, cannot answer the end of government, viz., the raising men, money, and so forth, for our defence against the Common Enemy,

Resolved, That a President and Council, consisting of ten persons, as also a Treasurer and Secretary, be chosen in the Province, in manner and form following : viz., for the Council, three persons of the Inhabitants of Portsmouth, three persons of the Inhabitants of Hampton, two persons of the Inhabitants of Dover, and two persons of the Inhabitants of Exeter ; which persons shall be chosen by the major vote of the Inhabitants of the town where they live, and the President, Treasurer, and Secretary to be chosen by the major vote of the whole Province, which President shall also have the power over the militia of the Province as major, and the President and Council so chosen, or the major part thereof, shall with all convenient speed call an assembly of the representatives of the people not exceeding three persons from one town, which said President and Council, or the major part of them, whereof the President or his Deputy to be one, together with the representatives aforesaid, or the major part of them, from time to time shall make such acts and orders, and exert such powers and authority as may in all respects have a tendency to the preservation of the peace, punishment of offenders, and defence of their Maj^{ties} subjects against the common enemy, provided they exceed not the bounds his late Maj^{ty} King Charles the Second was graciously pleased to limit in his Royal commission to the late President and Council of this Province.

ROB^T WADLEIGH,
WILL^M HILTON,
SAMUELL LEAUETT,
JONATHAN THING,

JOHN WOODMAN,
JOHN GERRISH,
JOHN TUTTLE,
THOMAS EDGELEY,
JOHN ROBEARTS,
NICH. FOLLETT,

HENRY GREEN,
NATH^{LL} WEARE,

SAMUELL SHUEBERN,

his
MORRIS ✕ HOBS,
mark
HENRY DOW,
EDWARD GOUE,

NATHAN^{LL} FRYER,
W^M VAUGHAN,
ROBT. ELLIOT,
RICH^D WALDRON,
JOHN PICKERIN,
THO. COBBETT.[1]

---

[1] The spelling and punctuation of this manuscript have been made to conform with modern usage in this printed copy. The names of persons are allowed to remain as they were written. A heliotype of the original manuscript is given in the Proceedings of the Mass. Hist. Society, Oct. 1879.

HOPE - HOOD.

HOPE-HOOD.[1]

SEVERAL years ago I was turning over the leaves of a venerable folio volume in the Registry of Deeds at Exeter, New Hampshire, when my eye accidentally fell upon the name Hope-Hood, or Hope Whood, as it was then written.[2] On examination, I found the name was in a deed conveying land now in the County of Strafford, New Hampshire, executed by Hope-Hood and three other Indians, calling themselves native proprietors of those parts of New England.

Hubbard says that Hope-Hood, the first-named grantor in the deed, was son of Robin Hood, a noted Indian of an eastern Abnaki tribe. This Hope-Hood first appears in history a few months after the breaking out of King Philip's war, leading an attack on a house in Berwick, Maine.[3] Mather

[1] Reprinted, by permission, from the Proceedings of the Mass. Hist. Society, February, 1880. — H.

[2] The name of this Indian is variously spelled. I follow Hubbard the historian. Hope-Hood was also known under the name Wayhamoo (Proceedings Mass. Hist. Soc., March, 1878). Mather's *alias* for him is Wohawa.

[To the letters of John Hogkins, a Penacook sachem, May 15, 1685 (Belknap's Hist., Farmer's ed., 508), his name is affixed as Hope-Hoth. But the spelling of Indian names depended very much on the ear of the scribe. — H.]

[3] Hubbard's Narrative of the Troubles with the Indians in New England, from Piscataqua to Pemmaquid, 14, 20.

28

styles him a "memorable tygre,"[1] and says he was accidentally killed in the summer of 1690.[2] Williamson says he
was "one of the most bloody warriors of the age." He
and his followers were with the French at the destruction
of Salmon Falls, and also of Casco, two months later, in the
spring of 1690.[3]

Hope-Hood was one of the Indian chieftains who signed
the treaty of peace made Sept. 8, 1685, between His Majesty's subjects inhabiting the Provinces of New Hampshire
and Maine, and the Indians dwelling in the same Provinces.
His name is also on each of the letters written May 15, 1685,
by Kankamagus, *alias* John Hogkins, to Lieutenant-Governor Cranfield, imploring protection from the Mohawk Indians. His mark standing for his signature to the treaty,
and also to the letters, is the same as on the deed to Coffin.[4]

The names of his three Indian associates, grantors in the
deed, are scarcely known. They appear, however, with his,
on the letters to Cranfield.[5] The name Ould Robin suggests
a family connection. Maybe he is the veritable Robin
Hood mentioned by Hubbard.

---

[1] Mather bestows also other seemingly well-deserved epithets upon Hope-
Hood: "that hellish fellow," "the
wretch," "that hideous *loup-garou*,"
"the villain," etc. He also states that
this savage was "once a servant of a
Christian master in Boston." (Magnalia, Bk. vii. Appendix, art. x.) — H.

[2] Magnalia, Bk. vii. Appendix, art. x.
p. 74. The only authority which supports
Mather in regard to the accidental killing of Hope-Hood may be found in
Public Occurrences, the first newspaper
printed in Boston, dated Sept. 25, 1690.
The circumstances of his death so much
resemble those of the accidental killing
of Kryn, the "Great Mohawk," about

that time, as to make it somewhat
doubtful whether Mather has not con-
founded these two Indians (N. Y. Col.
Doc., ix. 473-479). There is no mention of the death of Hope-Hood in the
French narratives of that time. Besides, a Hope-Hood from Norridge-
wock was present at the [making of the]
treaty with the English at Falmouth
[Maine]. in June, 1703.

[3] Williamson's History of Maine, i.
618-623.

[4] N. H. Provincial Papers, i. 583,
584, 588. [See note 3 on page 217.
— H.]

[5] N. H. Provincial Papers, i. 583,
584.

Peter Coffin, the grantee named in the deed, was one of the most considerable inhabitants of Dover, New Hampshire, and afterward chief justice of the Province. However contemptible an Indian deed may have appeared at that time in the eyes of Sir Edmund Andros, to the mind of Peter Coffin, a frontiersman, it was sufficient to give him the right and title to so much of the wilderness as was bounded and described therein. He was not a man to part with seven pounds for a worthless title.[1]

It is worthy of note that this Indian grant lay within the limits of Captain Mason's patent of 1629; and that his grandson, Robert Mason, was then contending in the judicial courts of New Hampshire for possession of all the lands lying within the patent, not granted by himself or his ancestors. Coffin's motive for buying the Indian title at this time may have been to anticipate the issue of Mason's suits.

While Hope-Hood hovered much on the eastern frontier of New Hampshire, he has not been supposed by historians to have had any connection with that Province, except as a raider and an enemy, during the Indian wars.[2] There is, however, one place in Dover, on the western bank of the Bellamy River, near where it falls into the Pascataqua, which has borne the name "Hope-Hood's Point" for nearly two centuries, — almost back to the date of this deed of conveyance.[3] This fact, and his act in conveying hereditary lands

---

[1] The author must here be understood as presenting the view which Coffin entertained. But it was an erroneous view. The title to the soil was in the King of England or his grantees. This was the law of England, and it was in harmony with the accepted public law of Europe at this period. Hope-Hood and his associates had received no grant, and therefore could convey no legal title. — H.

[2] I have shown that the (reported) attack on Fox Point, in 1690, which Mather charges that Hope-Hood led, never occurred. See pages 163–171.

[3] New Eng. Hist. and Gene. Register, xx. 373; xxviii. 203; xxxiv. 205.

in this quarter to Coffin, indicate that his savage ancestors or his tribe had been possessors of that region.

The spelling in the following deed is modernized, except the names of persons and places.

To all Christian people to whom this present writing shall come and appear: —

Know ye that the natives of New England or Indians whose names are known in the English tongue, are called by the name of Hoope Whood, and Samll Lines, and Ould Robbin, and Kinge Harry, now we, the before-named Indians and natives, as by our native right, are the proprietors of these parts of New England which do join and border upon the rivers called by the names of Newitchawanoke River, and Cochechow River, and Oyster River and Lamperill River, within the Province of New Hampshire. Now know all men that we, the said Hope Whood, Samll Lines, Ould Robbin, and King Harry, for and in consideration of the sum of seven pounds to us in hand paid by Mr. Peter Coffin of the town of Dover, in the Province of New Hampshire, the receipt whereof we acknowledge, and of every part and penny thereof, do free, acquit, and discharge the said Peter Coffin, his heirs, executors, and administrators. By these presents do give, grant, bargain, and sell and confirm unto the said Mr. Coffin and to his heirs, executors, administrators, and assigns for ever, all our right and title which we, the said natives ever had, have, or ought to have, unto all the marshes, and pine timber standing or lying, that is or shall be within the two branches of Cochecho and half way between northernmost branch of Cochechow River and Newchewanoke River, beginning at the run of water on the north side of Squammagonake old planting ground (and between the two branches) to begin at the spring where the old cellar was, and so to run ten miles up into the country between the branches by the rivers, all which said marshes, lands, and timber as is before mentioned, and expressed in the bounds aforesaid, shall be to the sole and proper use, benefit, and behoof of Mr. Peter Coffin, his heirs, executors, administrators, and assigns for ever, to have and to hold the premises aforesaid and all privileges and appurtenances thereunto belonging, and to every part and parcel thereof, and also we do warrant to make good, and maintain the before bargained and sold premises against all and all manner of natives or Indians which shall lay any claim or right or title to the same. In witness whereof we, the said Hoope Whood, Samll Lines, Ould Robbin, and Kinge Harry, do bind ourselves and every of us jointly and severally, and our heirs and successors firmly by these presents. Dated the third day of January, in the second year of the reign of our sovereign Lord King James the Second, over England, Scotland, France, and Ireland, King, Defender of the Faith, &c. Annoq. domini, 1686.

Signed, sealed, and	The mark X of	Hoope Whood,	[and seal.]
delivered in presence	℧℧	Samll Lines,	[and seal.]
of Benjamin Herd,	ꝗ	Ould Robbin,	[and seal.]
Test. John Evens.	O	Kinge Harry,	[and seal.]

Benjamin Herd personally appeared this seventh day of January, 1709-10, and made oath that he was present and saw these several sachems or Indians sign and seal the above written instrument and set to his hand as witness, and that Jno Evins also set to his hand as witness at the same time. Before me, Nathll Weare, Justice Peace.

Entered and recorded according to original, 18 January, 1709.

Wm. Vaughan, *Recorder.*[1]

---

[1] Provincial Deeds at Exeter, vol. vii. fols. 366, 367. The tract of land described in the deed lay just outside the northern limits of Dover. It is now within the limits of Rochester, Barrington, Strafford, and Farmington.

CHRISTOPHER KILBY.

CHRISTOPHER KILBY.[1]

THE capacity, public services, wealth, and liberality of Christopher Kilby place him among the worthies of Boston of the last century. While he lived abroad most of his days, and died there, and while most of his living posterity are now in England and Scotland, he was nevertheless a son of Boston, began his public life here,[2] remembered his native town in its affliction, bequeathed his name to one of its most public streets, and a few of his posterity still live here. Although his name appears frequently in the records of his time, is mentioned by Hutchinson and other historians, and is memorably associated with his native city, but little is publicly known of his career and his connections. His personal history derives fresh interest from the fact that his great-granddaughter was the first wife of the seventh Duke of Argyll, — the grandfather of the Marquis of Lorne, who recently[2] married Her Royal Highness the Princess Louise, of England.

<hr />

[1] Reprinted from the New England Historical and Genealogical Register for January, 1872.

[2] The reader will bear in mind that this Memoir was written in Boston, and published in 1872. Several persons mentioned by the author as living when he wrote, have since then died. (See page 235.) — H.

Christopher Kilby was the son of John and Rebecca (Simpkins) Kilby, of Boston. He was born May 25, 1705, and bred to commercial pursuits. In 1726 he became a partner in business with the Hon. William Clark,[1] a distinguished merchant of Boston, whose eldest daughter he married the same year. Mr. Clark carried on an extensive commercial trade with England and the West Indies; and Kilby was several times in those countries, on business of the firm, during the continuance of the partnership, which terminated on his return from England in 1735. In this period of nine years he passed three abroad, employed in commercial undertakings. He now formed a partnership with his brother-in-law, Mr. Clark's youngest son, Benjamin, and continued in the same business until he went to England in 1739 as agent for Massachusetts.

[1] The Hon. William Clark was brother of the Hon. John Clark, of Boston, for many years Speaker of the House of Representatives, and grandson of Dr. John Clark, an eminent physician, whose portrait is in the cabinet of the Massachusetts Historical Society. Mr. William Clark was a member of the House and of the Provincial Council. He was a merchant, and acquired a large estate. He lived in the largest, most elaborately finished and furnished house in Boston. It was a brick structure, standing on Garden Court Street, leading from Clark's Square, so called; next to the mansion-house afterwards occupied by Governor Hutchinson, at the North End. It was subsequently owned and occupied by Sir Henry Frankland, and is mentioned in one of Cooper's novels. Mr. Rowland Ellis, now of Newton Centre, Mass., who lived in it many years, has a fine exterior view of this famous house, and also several elaborate paintings taken from its walls; he also has the centre part of a wooden mosaic floor of the house, having the arms of Clark wrought therein. The late Mr. Peter Wainwright, of Boston, had among his collection of family portraits one of the Hon. William Clark, full size, painted in 1732. These portraits were destroyed, or much damaged, by the Boston fire in 1872. Mr. Clark died July 24, 1742. His first wife, the mother of his children, was Sarah, daughter of Robert Bronsden, of Boston, to whom he was married May 14, 1702. His second wife was Sarah, daughter of William Tyler, of Boston. She died about 1762. It is said that William and Sarah (Bronsden) Clark had fifteen children. Of these we have the following names: (1) Sarah, who married Christopher Kilby; (2) Robert; (3) Benjamin; (4) Rebecca, who married Samuel Winslow, June 8, 1729; and (5) Martha, who married Dea. Thomas Greenough, May 9, 1734.

In May, 1739, he was chosen representative to the General Court from Boston, his colleagues being Thomas Cushing, Jr., Edward Bromfield, and James Allen. The session of the Court began near the end of May, and continued, with several intermediate adjournments, to the end of the year, the domestic affairs of the Province being in a troubled state. Mr. Kilby served on all the important committees, and took an active part in the business of the session. Important questions relative to the issue of paper money and to the boundaries of the Province were discussed and acted upon. Governor Belcher had received instructions from the King to limit the issue of bills of credit to a period not exceeding in duration those current at the time of a new issue, and the consequence was that all became payable in 1741. The Governor declined to recede from his instructions, although the public distress was great. The last of September the House of Representatives resolved to send a special "agent to appear at the Court of Great Britain, to represent to His Majesty the great difficulties and distress the people of this Province labor under by reason of thus being prevented from raising the necessary supply to support the government and the protection and defence of His Majesty's subjects here." Thomas Cushing, a distinguished member of the House, and formerly its Speaker, was chosen agent; and a committee of eight, Mr. Kilby being one, was appointed to draw up his instructions. On account of continued ill health, Mr. Cushing declined the office, and Mr. Kilby was, on the 2d of October, chosen in his place.[1]

---

[1] Hutchinson's History of Massachusetts; Journal of House of Representatives, 1739.

The Province had always selected its ablest men to act as agents, the functions of the office being of a diplomatic character, requiring ability, sagacity, prudence, and a knowledge of public affairs. Mr. Kilby, then only thirty-four years of age, accepted the appointment, and Capt. Nathaniel Cunningham, an eminent merchant of Boston, was chosen to succeed him in the House.[1] Early in December Kilby received his instructions, and immediately sailed for England. He presented to the King in Council the petition of the House, praying for a modification of the royal instructions to Belcher concerning the issue of bills of credit; but the King could not be persuaded to make the change asked for.[2]

In October, 1741, Francis Wilks, long an agent of the Province in England, was dismissed, and soon after died, and Kilby was chosen in his place. About this time

---

[1] Capt. Nathaniel Cunningham was one of the richest merchants in Boston in his day. He died in London, Sept. 7, 1748, leaving wife Susanna, and children; namely, Nathaniel, who married Sarah Kilby; Ruth, who married the celebrated James Otis; and Sarah, who married Andrew McKenzie, of Boston, merchant, in 1749. His estate was valued at nearly £50,000. To each daughter he gave £10,000, and annuities for their support while minors; to Dr. Sewall's church sixty ounces of silver, to be made into a proper vessel for the service of the Holy Sacrament of the Lord's Supper, the expenses of making to be paid out of his estate; to the poor of the church, £500; the rest of his large estate to his only son Nathaniel. He mentions Charles Paxton, Esq., as his brother-in-law. Mr. Cunningham was one of the proprietors of the lands in the west parish of Leicester, where he built several fine houses. He gave the town, now Spencer, land for a meeting-house and training-field. (See Hist. of Spencer, and Suffolk Probate Records.) Susanna Cunningham, relict of Nathaniel Cunningham, Esq., and only sister of the Hon. Charles Paxton, Esq., died Feb. 13, 1770, in the 69th year of her age. She was his second wife. ¡Capt. Timothy Cunningham, a brother of Nathaniel, died Sept. 12, 1728, and by his will gave £200 to the "South Church in Boston." At the request of Nathaniel this money was expended for the purchase of the bell long used in the Old South. It was recast in London about 1816, and now hangs in the tower of the New Old South. — H.]

[2] Journal House of Representatives; Hutchinson's Hist. of Mass.; Mass. Archives.

Massachusetts took an appeal from a decision of the commissioners respecting the boundary line between it and Rhode Island. In January, 1742, Robert Auchmuty — an able lawyer of Boston — and Christopher Kilby were chosen joint agents to prosecute the appeal before the King in Council. Auchmuty continued in this service till April, 1743; and Kilby did not cease his exertions in the matter of the appeal till 1746.[1]

The removal of Governor Belcher was one of the questions which agitated the people here and in New Hampshire when Kilby went to England. He was one of the strong party opposed to Belcher, and he used his influence to displace him, and to secure the office for Shirley, who was appointed governor in 1741.[2]

Mr. Kilby continued to act as standing agent of the Province till the middle of November, 1748, performing many important services, among which may be mentioned the procuring from the British government reimbursement to the Province for expenses in the famous expedition for the conquest of Louisburg in 1745, commanded by Lieut.-Gen. William Pepperrell.[3] William Bollan, a lawyer of Boston, son-in-law of Governor Shirley, was chosen joint agent with Kilby to prosecute this claim for expenses in "taking and securing the island of Cape Breton and its dependencies." In the prosecution of this claim Kilby labored with untiring industry and energy. His official and

[1] Journal House of Representatives; Arnold's History of Rhode Island; Mass. Archives.

[2] Hutchinson's History; Kilby's Letters.

[3] Pepperrell resided with Kilby in London, in 1749. See Parsons's Life of Pepperrell, 222; and Papers relating to Lieut.-Gen. Pepperrell, Lieut.-Gen. St. Clair, and Admiral Knowles, in New Eng. Hist. and Gene. Register, xxviii. 451-466. — H.

private letters show this; and nothing but ignorance or jealousy has kept this fact from being more publicly known. In a letter to Secretary Willard, dated March 10, 1747, he says: " No other affair I am concerned in but what is made subservient to this important and most necessary point of reimbursing the Province and relieving it from distress which is not possible to be endured long, for I have an unshaken and immovable zeal for the welfare of my country." He writes to the Speaker of the House, from Portsmouth, England, where he then was in conference with Admiral Sir Peter Warren, under date of April 6, 1748, that the House of Commons passed a bill on the 4th inst., "granting to Massachusetts £183,649 02 7½, the time and manner of payment being left entirely with the treasury."[1]

The Duke of Newcastle promised the governorship of New Jersey to Kilby, on the death of Morris; but the friends of Belcher persuaded the Duke to change his purpose at the last moment, and Belcher got the appointment. While agent of Massachusetts he was member of the firm of Sedgwick, Kilby, & Barnard, of London. On the death of Sedgwick, the firm name was Kilby, Barnard, & Parker. The business of the firm was extensive, especially with the American Colonies.[2]

In 1755, Boston, having some grievances of its own, appointed Kilby its agent at the Court of Great Britain. He accepted the appointment, and performed the duties required of him to the entire satisfaction of his native town.[3]

[1] Mass. Archives ; Kilby's Letters.
[2] Kilby's Letters.
[3] A volume containing the original letter of instructions to Mr. Kilby from the town of Boston, with other papers relating to his agency, is among the MSS. in the possession of the New England Historic Genealogical Society. — H.

In May, 1756, England formally declared war with France. John Campbell, fourth Earl of Loudoun, was appointed commander-in-chief of the King's forces in North America, and governor of Virginia. Kilby was appointed "agent-victualler of the army" under the Earl, and sailed from Portsmouth, England, May 20, for New York, arriving there about the middle of July. The Nightingale man-of-war, having the Earl and his staff, and also Thomas Pownall, soon after appointed governor of Massachusetts, on board, sailed from the same port, and arrived at New York a few days later than Kilby. The organization of the army went forward, and great preparations were made for subduing the French in Canada and elsewhere on this continent. Kilby addressed himself to the furnishing of supplies for the army.[1]

In January, 1757, the Earl of Loudoun and many of his officers came to Boston to meet the commissioners of the several Provinces, to consult about raising an army, and other matters, for the campaign of that year. The Boston Gazette of Jan. 24, 1757, after speaking of the arrival of the Earl in Boston, adds: —

At the same time, and in company with the Earl of Loudo[u]n, arrived Christopher Kilby, Esq., who went from hence about 17 years past as Agent for this Province at the Court of Great Britain: the warm affection he has discovered for his countrymen, and the signal services he has rendered this Province during that space, has greatly endeared him to us. The Selectmen of the Town waited upon him as Standing Agent of the Town with their congratulations and Thanks for the Favors he has from Time to Time shown us. A

---

[1] Boston Gazette, July and August, 1756; Doc. Hist. of New York.

Committee of the General Court has invited him to Dine at Concert Hall this Day ; and his townsmen rejoice at the opportunity they now have of testifying the deserved esteem they have for him. With Pleasure we can acquaint the Publick that he is in a good measure recovered from the illness which attended him this Fall while at Albany.

Kilby probably remained in this country till the peace of 1763. He was in New York when the terrible fire occurred in Boston, in March, 1760, destroying many dwelling-houses and causing much distress. Upon hearing of this calamity Kilby sent two hundred pounds sterling to the sufferers, a sum that was regarded as enormous at the time. The district burnt over embraced both sides of " Mackerill Lane," so called. When this part of the town was rebuilt, and the lane widened and extended, it was called Kilby Street, by common consent, in compliment to Mr. Kilby for his generous donation, and for his zeal for the interests of his native town.[1]

On his return to England he purchased a large estate in the parish of Dorking, co. Surrey, where he " built a curious edifice called the priory, and several ornamental seats." There he lived many years prior to his death,[2] which took place in October, 1771. He left an immense estate, which he distributed among his seven grandchildren, after providing for his wife.[3]

Mr. Kilby was twice married. His first wife was Sarah, eldest daughter of the Hon. William Clark, whom he mar-

---

[1] Boston Post Boy, April 7, 1760.
[2] " Late of Tranquil Dale, so called, in the parishes of Betchworth and Buckland, in the county of Surrey."
[3] Allen's History of Surrey and Sussex, vol. ii. ; Whitmore's Heraldic Journal.

ried Aug. 18, 1726. Mrs. Kilby died April 12, 1739, about six months before her husband was sent as agent to England, leaving two young daughters, Sarah and Catherine.[1] A son William died young. In 1742 his father-in-law, Clark, died intestate. Kilby being in England, his warm personal friend, Thomas Hancock, an eminent merchant, and uncle to Gov. John Hancock, was appointed guardian of Sarah and Catherine Kilby, and secured for them their share of their grandfather Clark's estate. Five years later they were sent to England, their father receiving them at Portsmouth. Catherine appears to have died soon after her arrival.

Mr. Kilby was now married again, but had no other children. His second wife's name was Martha, and she survived him. Her family name is not known here. On Sarah Kilby, his surviving daughter, he bestowed every advantage that wealth could command. She received the best education England could afford; and in 1753 was betrothed to Nathaniel, only son of Capt. Nathaniel Cunningham, a merchant of the greatest wealth of any in Boston. His daughter Ruth married the celebrated James Otis, patriot and orator. Sarah Kilby returned to this country just before her marriage, which took place June 20, 1754. Mr. Cunningham settled in the fine mansion-house of his father, — now deceased, — situated on an eminence in Cambridge, now Brighton. In Price's view of Boston, taken in 1743, dedicated to Peter Faneuil, this house is a conspicuous object, and designated by name, being the finest mansion-

---

[1] " Last week dy'd suddenly Mrs. Kilby, Wife of Mr. Christopher Kilby of this Town, Merchant, and Daughter to the Hon. William Clark, Esq." — Boston Weekly News Letter, April 17, 1739.

30

house in the vicinity of Boston. Nathaniel Cunningham died near the end of the year 1756, leaving two infant children, Susanna and Sarah.[1] His widow died in Ayrshire, Scotland, July 15, 1779.

When the Earl of Loudoun visited Boston, a few months after this event, there came with him his aide-de-camp, Capt. Gilbert McAdam, as well as Kilby, who introduced his widowed daughter to Captain McAdam. He was of an ancient Ayrshire family, and uncle to John Loudoun McAdam, the inventor of macadamized roads. In September, 1757, Capt. McAdam married the widow Sarah Cunningham, and took her and her two children to New York, the principal headquarters of the army. At the close of the war, possibly before, Captain McAdam returned to Ayrshire with his family.[2]

Susanna and Sarah Cunningham were the special objects of Kilby's bounty and solicitude. They were sent to France, and there educated with care. Their domestic lives, and the lives of some of their descendants, are invested with an air of romance. Susanna was thrice married. Her first husband was James Dalrymple,[3] of Orangefield, Ayrshire, the friend and patron of Robert Burns. By this marriage she had one son, Charles Dalrymple, an officer of the British army. Through subsequent marriages, first with John Henry Mills,[4] and afterwards with William Cunningham,

---

[1] Susanna Cunningham, bap. May 1, 1755; Sarah Cunningham, bap. Aug. 20, 1756. — Trinity Church Records, Boston.

[2] Kilby's Letters; Family Papers.

[3] In one of Burns's letters he writes thus of Dalrymple: "I have met in Mr. Dalrymple, of Orangefield, what Solomon emphatically calls 'a friend that sticketh closer than a brother.'"

[4] John Henry Mills and Susanna his wife had son John and daughter Mary, who came to Boston, where Mary married Col. Abraham Moore (H. C., 1806), and had Susanna Varnum, and Mary Frances, who married the Hon.

both of Scotland, she is now represented in this country by her grandchildren, Mrs. Frances Maria Spofford, wife of the venerable Dr. Richard S. Spofford, of Newburyport, Mrs. Susanna Varnum Mears, of Boston, and Capt. Thomas Cunningham, of Somerville. Her sister, Sarah Cunningham,[1] married William Campbell, of Ayrshire, and had two daughters, the eldest of whom, Elizabeth, married the seventh Duke of Argyll, grandfather, by a second marriage, of the present Marquis of Lorne;[2] and the other daughter, Martha Kilby Campbell, married Charles McVicar.

The following is a copy of an original letter from Christopher Kilby to Thomas Hancock, before referred to.[3]

SPRING GARDEN, 18 July, 1746.

DEAR HANCOCK, — I am greatly oblig'd for the dispatch in Lumber and Bricks to Newfoundland, and for your advice of the vessels arrival there. The Louisburg affair is not in the deplorable case you have imagined. Capt. Bastide[4] is Engineer, and the thing lays with him and his officers; and I think you cannot fail of a season-

John Cochran Park (H. C., 1824). Their daughter, Mary Louisa Park, married Charles W. Tuttle, author of this Memoir. — H.

[1] "On the 19th current was married at Mount Charles, William Campbell, Esq., Jun., of Fairfield, to Miss Sally Cunningham, second daughter of the late Nathaniel Cunningham, Esq., of Boston." (London Chronicle, Nov. 3, 1772, p. 430.) She died in London, Dec. 31, 1781; her husband, William Campbell, had died before.

[2] Burke's Peerage and Landed Gentry.

[3] To the grandchildren of Susanna Cunningham, above named, I am indebted for permission to examine letters and family papers in their possession relating to the subject of this memoir. I am also indebted to Charles L. Hancock, Esq., for information contained in letters of Kilby and others, in his possession.

[4] John Henry Bastide, royal engineer for Nova Scotia. In April, 1745, Massachusetts granted him £140 for his services in the repairs of the forts in this Province. He was made director of engineers in 1748, and afterward raised to the rank of major-general.

able part if any advantage is to be had ; but these officers arriving and a great sum of Sterling money to be spent amongst you I should think Exchange must be constantly lowering till this service is over, and however that may be you 'll certainly not want as much of their money as I should think you would be willing to take. I have mentioned you to most of the Staff Officers on this Expedition.[1] Mr. Abercrombie,[2] who is Muster Master General, having directions to you in his Pocket-book, and if it should be necessary will introduce you to the General,[3] to whom indeed you 'll not need it, but apply to him as early as possible with the use of my name, and I hope he will receive you as my best Friend. We have been often together since his return to Town, and I believe he has a good opinion of my services in recovering the Expedition after it was laid aside.

Pray do him all the service you can, and if you find it not inconvenient offer him a lodging in your house for a night or two, till he can be otherwise accommodated. His Power is great and may be useful to you; he is honest, open, and undissembling; you 'll like him very well on increasing your acquaintance.

Belcher[4] has got the Government of the Jerseys ; it was done by Duke of Newcastle yesterday, which neither Dr. Avery[5] nor I expected two days before. I have not seen the Dr. since the appointment, nor shall till his return to Town on Tuesday next. The vessel

---

[1] This expedition was designed to proceed against Canada. A squadron under Admiral Warren was to go to Quebec by way of the St. Lawrence, and a land force to Montreal by way of Albany under the command of General St. Clair. The English troops collected at Portsmouth, England, and sailed several times, but returned. They finally sailed for France, and the Canada expedition was abandoned. Kilby's letter indicates that they were to come to Boston, — at least the principal officers.

[2] Gen. James Abercrombie ; he was next in command to the Earl of Loudoun in 1756; he commanded the English forces sent against Ticonderoga in 1758.

[3] Lieut.-Gen. James St. Clair. [For a further notice of Lieut.-Gen. St. Clair, see New Eng. Hist. and Gene. Register, xxviii. 451–466. — H.]

[4] Jonathan Belcher, provincial governor of Massachusetts from 1730 to 1741.

[5] Dr. Benjamin Avery, a man of the greatest influence at Court about this time.

that brought the News from Boston was several days below before
her bag of Letters came up, and its said the Advice was sent in the
mean time to Belcher's Friends. It's a shocking affair, and must
destroy any favorable opinion entertained of the Duke of Newcastle
by the People of the Colonies ; and I am of opinion it will lessen
Gov'r Shirley's Influence in his own and in the Neighboring Governments. There is a very worthy set of people in the Jerseys that
it will most fatally prejudice. I fear they have been almost ruined
by Law without a possibility of getting so far thro' it as to have an
appeal home, and I am mistaken if some of them have not defended
their possessions by fire and sword ; they will be in fine hands under
Belcher, who is to be the Tool of the Quakers, as they are one
would imagine of Satan. Some time past this seemed to be allotted
for me [1] by the desire of the Gentlemen who came from thence who
had engaged Dr. Avery's Interest to perfect it, and it was mentioned
to, and approved of [by], the Duke of Newcastle. The vacancy has
at last happened when it was impossible for me to accept it, and
after consulting the Doctor we had laid a Plan for keeping the appointment off till we could hear from our Friends, which neither he
nor I have done by the ships that bring the News of Morris's [2] death,
nor had many months before. But the Duke [3] differing in this Instance from every other circumstance of this sort during his Administration, has fix't the thing in the greatest hurry (on some other
motive certainly than the Interest of the Quakers). As the thing
concerns myself I am in no pain, not having been defeated ; but as
it may be hurtful to the honest people who are to fall under his Government and will stagger and discountenance the very best people

---

[1] Provincial governor of New Jersey. Kilby's aspirations were not behind those of other Massachusetts
agents, who always aspired for royal
appointments as soon as they got fairly
Anglicized.

[2] Lewis Morris, ancestor of a very
distinguished family, was chief-justice
of New York, and afterwards governor
of New Jersey. He died May 21,
1746.

[3] Duke of Newcastle, minister of
British America from 1724 to 1748.
" Newcastle was of so fickle a head and
so treacherous a heart that Walpole
called his name ' Perfidy.' " — Bancroft's History.

in our own and the neighboring Colonies, it gives me much concern. This Letter must be broke off here to go to Portsmouth, where the Ships tarry, and [if] anything occurs I shall back it by another, being, dear Sir,

Your most sincere Friend and obliged humble Servant,

CHRIS. KILBY.

To Mr. THOMAS HANCOCK,
    Merchant in Boston.

HUGH PERCY.

HUGH PERCY,

DUKE OF NORTHUMBERLAND, LIEUTENANT-GENERAL IN THE BRITISH ARMY.[1]

O NE hundred and twenty years ago the din of war and clash of arms still resounded along the frontiers of New England and New France. The fleets and armies of England were in deadly conflict with the fleets and armies of France, contending for empire in America. In 1760 this great and memorable strife had been going on with varying success, marked from time to time by dreadful barbarities of savage allies, five long and weary years. Throughout all the land, —

> " Each new morn,
> New widows howl; new orphans cry; new
> Sorrows strike heaven in the face."

At length England put forth anew her military and naval strength, and supported by her American Colonies moved

---

[1] By the invitation of a number of prominent citizens of Boston, Mr. Tuttle read the following paper before an audience in Hawthorne Hall, on Monday, April 19, 1880, — the one hundred and fifth anniversary of the British attack on Concord and Lexington. — H.

against the fleets and armies of France, which soon melted away. Wolfe and Amherst and Boscawen won immortal renown. The frontiers of the British Empire rolled westward to the Pacific Ocean, and northward to the frozen seas. The name of New France disappeared forever from among the Provinces of North America. The conquest was complete, and England rose to the highest pitch of renown and greatness. The end of this great and memorable conflict, known in our annals as the last French and Indian War, but in Europe as the Seven Years' War, was sealed with the Peace of Paris, in the year 1763.

At this great epoch in our history the English Colonies were as much attached to the English monarchy and government as were any of the shires and counties between the Humber and Land's End. The people of the Colonies, grateful for the sacrifices made by England in crushing forever their ancient hereditary foe in America, felt a new attachment to the mother country. But in this victory, so glorious and so memorable, there lay concealed from mortal vision the germ of an internal political strife that ten years later led to a fratricidal war, dismembering the English Empire, and turned the fruits of victory to bitterness and to ashes.

The expense of this great conquest in America had drained the English Exchequer; and the British ministry, in an evil hour, resolved to replenish it by taxation extending throughout the empire. They said that inasmuch as the war in America had been carried on at vast outlay of money for the protection of the American Colonies, and had resulted in crushing forever the ancient disturber of their peace, it was but reasonable that the Colonies should contribute towards paying the expense of the war. To this end a rigid enforcement of the old Acts of Trade and Navigation, limiting the trade of the Colonies to England, was immediately undertaken. A royal naval force was despatched to cruise between Newfoundland and Florida, to seize unlawful traders, and to assist the officers of His Majesty's customs in the execution of their duties. Parliament soon passed the famous Stamp Act, establishing a system of internal revenue in the Colonies, by which it was expected that £100,000 would annually thereafter flow into the English Exchequer.

Oppressive and galling to the colonial trade as the enforcement of the ancient Navigation Act was, there seemed no way of successfully resisting it; but as to the Stamp Act, a new method of taxation, nearly all the Colonies protested against it. They contended that taxation and representation went together; and that inasmuch as they had no representation in the British Parliament when the Stamp Act was passed, they were not bound to abide by it; and they resisted it, and it was reluctantly repealed in 1766. But the English ministry stoutly contended that they had a constitutional right to tax the Colonies, and immediately resorted to other methods of taxation through the royal custom-houses in the Colonies. Resistance to this new method of taxation was likewise made, and in Boston cargoes of tea sent from London were daringly cast into the harbor in December, 1773. This last act of violence and defiance of English laws made for the Colonies roused the English government to adopt measures of coercion. Parliament immediately

passed acts shutting up the harbor of Boston, curtailing
the charter rights of the Province, and ordering rebellious
subjects to be sent into England, or other Provinces, for
trial. These acts were ordered to be carried into immediate
execution, and a portion of the royal army and navy was
despatched to Boston in the spring of 1774.

Among the veteran regiments that responded to this call
was the Fifth Regiment of Foot, now and long since known
as the Northumberland Fusileers, but then stationed in Ireland and commanded by Col. Earl Percy, eldest son and
heir of the Duke of Northumberland. This regiment was
one of the oldest of the royal army. Its military annals
extended back to the reign of Charles II., a period of one
hundred years. Its origin was coeval with the formation
of the English standing army, and its history crowded with
thrilling events in the affairs of Europe. It was formed
out of the English forces engaged in that memorable struggle between the United Provinces and the allies France
and England. When England retired from that war of
conquest — for it was the design of the allies at the outset
to crush forever the nationality and independence of the
United Provinces — in the spring of 1674, this regiment
was one of several that were organized out of the English force then to be disbanded. At that time, on account
of the preponderance of Irish officers and soldiers in the
regiment, it was known as the Irish Regiment, its colonel
then being O'Brien, Viscount of Clare. Although it soon
lost its Irish character, yet it is probable that in memory of
its origin the green was continued in its regimental colors,
and likewise in its uniform.

This war still continued with France, and the States-General made arrangements with Charles II. to take this and other English regiments into their service as an auxiliary force. So, wheeling about, this English force turned its arms against the French, its old ally, and fought them till the Peace of Nimeguen in 1678. Under the banners of the Prince of Orange this regiment fought with desperate valor, sometimes in divisions commanded by the Earl of Ossory, and sometimes by the renowned Duke of Monmouth. When this war ended, the States-General continued to keep this regiment and some others in its service and pay.

In November, 1688, this regiment was called on to form part of that military force designed to accompany the Prince of Orange into England. It had revolted from the service of King James II. No one who has read Baron Macaulay's history of that bloodless campaign into England, need be told again of the conspicuous place of this regiment in that picturesque and gorgeous military cavalcade which escorted the Prince from Torbay to London, to ascend the throne of England under the title of William III. In that masterly narrative the Fifth Regiment is designated " Tolmash," the name of its then colonel. Afterwards it fought in the battle of the Boyne under the eye of King William, and was later at the siege of Athlone and Limerick. I need not recount the battles, sieges, and fortunes of this Fifth Regiment of Foot during the three quarters of a century which followed, ending with its embarkation for Boston in the fore part of May, 1774.

Earl Percy, colonel of this regiment at this last epoch, was descended not only from the noblest and most ancient houses

of England and France, but also from royal houses of both
kingdoms.   In France his lineage is traced back to Charle-
magne, a period of a thousand years.   He had in his veins
as much, and perhaps more, of the blood of the Norman, the
Plantagenet, and the Tudor sovereigns of England as had
King George III.   The histories of England and France
recount the deeds of his illustrious ancestors from the downfall of the Western Empire.   Among his lines of descent in
England is the ancient warrior-house of Percy, the founder
of which, William de Percy, a Norman baron, came into
England with William the Conqueror, founded the Abbey
of St. Hilda, and died in the Holy Land during the first
Crusade.   His descent in this illustrious family is through
all the famous historical Earls of Northumberland, who flourished between the reigns of Edward III. and James II.

At last, on the death of the eleventh Earl of Northumberland the honors and the wealth of this great house descended
to an heiress, the Lady Elizabeth Percy.   She married
Charles Seymour, the Duke of Somerset, descended from
the Protector Somerset.   Before this marriage, this proud
noble of a historical house was obliged to bend and give
his consent that he would surrender his great inherited
name and take that of Percy.   This, however, was waived
by his wife after marriage.   Their granddaughter, the Lady
Elizabeth Seymour, daughter of Algernon Seymour, also
Duke of Somerset and Earl of Northumberland, became
the heiress of both these illustrious houses, Percy and Seymour.   There was nothing that could add to her worldly
honors and estate.   Titles to six ancient baronies had descended to her, and all the castles and estates of the ancient
Earls of Northumberland.   " The blood of all the Percys

and Seymours swelled in her veins and in her fancy," says
Horace Walpole.

In 1740 this great lady was married at Percy Lodge to
Sir Hugh Smithson, a Yorkshire baronet of ancient family
and great possessions. The fortunes and vicissitudes in
the life of Sir Hugh Smithson have but few parallels in
history. This marriage conferred on him great distinction
in the estimation of his contemporaries; but it was only a
step to greater things.

On the decease of Algernon Seymour, his wife's father,
in 1750, the titles of Earl of Northumberland and Baron
Warkworth descended to Sir Hugh Smithson, pursuant
to a limitation in· the grant of these titles to Seymour,
making him a peer of England. At the same time Parliament enacted that his family name, Smithson, should be
changed to Percy, — the name contemplated in the marriage
settlement of the Baroness Percy and the proud Duke of
Somerset seventy-five years before, — and that he should
take and bear the arms of the ancient Earls of Northumberland, from whom his wife was descended. This now Sir
Hugh Percy, Earl of Northumberland, was soon made lord
of the bedchamber of George II., vice-admiral of Northumberland, knight of the garter, lord-lieutenant of Middlesex
and Westminster, and viceroy of Ireland. At this epoch he
appears, or rather should appear, in our American history;
for in 1764 he was appointed by the King vice-admiral over
all America.

When this appointment was announced here, Benning
Wentworth, royal governor of New Hampshire, in honor
of the Earl, soon bestowed the name Northumberland on a

new township in that Province. Two years later (1766) he
was created Earl Percy and Duke of Northumberland.
In 1784, as if no number of titles of honor could suffice,
he was created Lord Lovaine and Baron Alnwick of
Alnwick. Two years later he died; and his hereditary
titles and estates descended to his eldest son, Hugh Percy,
of whom I am discoursing. I may add that this great person was born, not only to leave his own name, but the names
of two sons, immortalized in the pages of American history, — one in the annals of the Revolutionary War, and
the other (James Smithson, founder of the Smithsonian
Institution at Washington) in the brightest pages of the
catalogue of public benefactors.

The number of castles, baronies, and manors of this
newly-married pair, in 1740, admitted of their having a
home in many parts of England. But in 1742 they were
living in the parish of St. George, Hanover Square, London,
where, on the 25th day of August (new style), their eldest
son, Hugh (then Smithson), was born. Before he was eight
years old he found his surname transmuted into Percy,
and his title, Lord Warkworth, — the second title of his
father, then Earl of Northumberland. By this title — a
title of courtesy — he was known to the public until 1766,
when his father was raised to a dukedom, and Lord
Warkworth became Earl Percy, by which title he is known
in our annals. Young Lord Warkworth was educated at
Eton, and was there with Earl Cornwallis, who was a British general in our Revolutionary War. A passion for war
seems early to have possessed him; and no wonder, when
he had read the deeds of his illustrious ancestors in the his-

toric pages of England, especially of the ancient Earls of Northumberland. Before he was eighteen years of age he had served one whole campaign in Germany, as a volunteer officer under Prince Ferdinand, in the Seven Years' War; and before he was twenty he was appointed lieutenant-colonel of the First Foot Guards.

In July, 1764, at the age of twenty-two years, Lord Warkworth married the Lady Anne Stuart, daughter of the Earl of Bute, late prime minister of England, and granddaughter of the renowned Lady Mary Wortley Montagu. In the month of December following he was appointed aide-de-camp to King George III. In the early part of 1768, Earl Percy, formerly Lord Warkworth, was elected a member of Parliament for Westminster; and again in 1774, while he was in Boston.

In November, 1768, he realized what all ambitious English soldiers much desire, — the colonelcy of the Fifth Regiment of Foot in the royal army. This was obtained through Lord Granby, the commander-in-chief. This appointment was not well received, especially among those who thought their military services entitled them to that place. Three months hardly passed before Earl Percy was astonished, and perhaps mortified, to see his name made conspicuous before the whole kingdom in a publication that ranks among English classics. A masked political writer, from his den of concealment, turned his baleful eye and scorching pen upon this act of Lord Granby. "Did he not," shouted Junius, "betray the just interests of the army in permitting Lord Percy to have a regiment?" Sir William Draper, a general in the army, came forward to defend his

chief, and to answer Junius. " In placing Earl Percy at the
head of a regiment," said Sir William, " I do not think either
the rights or best interests of the army are sacrificed and
betrayed, or the nation undone. . . . I feel myself happy
in seeing young noblemen of illustrious name and great
property come amongst us. They are an additional security
to the kingdom from foreign or domestic slavery. Junius
needs not be told, that, should the time ever come when this
nation is to be defended only by those who have nothing
more to lose than their arms and their pay, its danger will
be great indeed."

From the time of his marriage in 1764, to his appointment as colonel in the army, he had lived with his wife
at Stenwick. But now some domestic infelicity imbittered
his home, and he and Lady Percy entered into articles of
separation, and thereafter lived apart, having no communication whatever with each other. Lord Percy joined his
regiment in Ireland, and was in England only twice during
the four years which preceded his embarkation for America.

A few illustrative anecdotes are related of him at this
period, which place his character in an amiable light.
Hearing that there was in his regiment a private soldier of
good reputation, the son of a half-pay officer, Lord Percy,
at his own charge, procured for him the commission of
ensign, and presented it to the poor soldier. As his regiment was on the point of embarking for Boston, he stepped
forward and discharged all the debts of those officers who
had not the means at hand. Hearing that the wife of a
poor soldier was sick with the small-pox and must be left
behind, he generously gave eight guineas for her comfort

and support, and ordered her to be sent to her husband in
Boston, on her recovery, at his charge. Another anecdote
is related of him, supposed to illustrate his habit of econ-
omy. Horace Walpole spoke of him as "a penurious, un-
dignified young man in America." But Horace Walpole
did not love the Percys, and his sayings of them are to be
taken with much allowance for his antipathy. While in
Ireland, Lord Percy gave a dinner to the officers of the
garrison at Limerick, stipulating with the landlord that it
should not cost above eighteen pence per head for fifty persons. The officers, hearing of this arrangement, privately
made a contract with the landlord to provide an entertain-
ment that should cost a guinea a head, and if Lord Percy
failed to pay the difference, they would. When this ban-
quet was served, there was but one astonished person at
the board, and that was his lordship, who beheld a feast for
the gods, which he had ordered at eighteen pence per head.
On all sides he heard compliments of his generosity, the
excellence of the viands and wines. His health was drunk
with an enthusiasm that fairly bewildered him. When he
rose to return thanks it dawned upon him what had occurred to derange his expectations, and he enjoyed the
joke.

It was said at the time that Lord Percy came to America
at the special request of the King. This may be true; but
he was a soldier and a firm believer in using force to reduce
the rebellious Colonies to obedience. The King undoubtedly wished to avail himself of the moral effect of some
of those qualities mentioned by Sir William Draper on his
soldiers as well as on the people of the Colonies. Rank

and power, to awe the people of Massachusetts to obedience! King George did not know his subjects on this side
of the Atlantic!

On the 7th of May, 1774, Lord Percy embarked with
his regiment at Kinsale, in government transports, for
Boston in New England. Part of the regiment reached
Boston on the 1st of July; the remainder, in the same trans-
port with Lord Percy, on the 4th of July, — a day then in
no wise memorable in our political calendar, but destined
only two years later to take a rank never to be surpassed in
our annals! From the day he left Ireland for America to
the day of his return to England, — a period of three years,
— the eyes of the British people never turned from him,
whether he was in battle or in camp; nor was he less observed by the people of the Colonies. The Colonial press
everywhere heralded his coming. It was announced that
" a descendant of the never-to-be-forgotten hero who fought
the battle of Chevy Chase " (as he truly was, for he carried
the blood of Hotspur in his veins) was soon expected in
America with his regiment.

Tuesday, the 5th day of July, the weather, as is recorded,
was "fair and pleasant" in Boston. That day Lord Percy's
regiment landed at Long Wharf, marched through the
streets directly to the Common, and there encamped. This
martial pageant attracted the gaze of thousands of citizens,
and the spectacle was long remembered. While in Ireland
the regiment had earned for itself the significant name, "the
Shiners," from its extreme cleanliness and attention to dress.
The coats of the rank and file were faced with gosling
green, and medals of merit shone on the breasts of many

a veteran soldier. The officers were richly dressed in scarlet and gold. A green silken flag having thereon the figures of Saint George and the Dragon, with the ancient and expressive motto, *Quo Fata Vocant*, waved gently above the heads of these heroes of many battlefields. The grenadier company was led by a young officer who afterwards rose to be a lieutenant-general in the British army and a peer of the realm. This lieutenant, Lord Francis Rawdon, of ancient and noble lineage, a few years later commanded the royal troops in South Carolina, became governor-general of India, and the Marquis of Hastings.

There were already encamped on the fresh grass of Boston Common two veteran regiments of the British line, when Percy's went into camp. One of them was the Fourth, or King's Own, and it must have suggested no pleasant memories to Massachusetts men who knew its history. A century before it had been commanded during many years by the infamous Col. Percy Kirke, the same person who had been selected by Charles II. in the last months of his reign to be governor of Massachusetts, New Hampshire, and Plymouth, after the overthrow of the Charter in the year 1684. His name had been for generations a synonym in New England for all that was cruel and barbarous.

Earl Percy soon found one of the best houses in Boston for his residence. This fine mansion stood at the corner of Winter and Tremont streets, almost within the sound of my voice; and although standing back from both streets, leaving a fine lawn around it, its windows overlooked the Common. It was then owned by John Williams, a commissioner of His Majesty's customs in Boston. It had been the residence

of some very noted persons, Colonel Vetch, Winthrop, Ox-
nard, and others well known in the history of Boston.

There are many persons now living who remember that
venerable structure. Here Earl Percy lived in a style befitting his rank as an officer and a nobleman, besides spend-
ing a large sum in acts of charity and generosity, until he
quitted Boston with the army in March, 1776, a period of
nearly two years.

Soon after Earl Percy's arrival in Boston, Sir John Wentworth, the royal governor of New Hampshire, complimented
him by giving the name Percy to a new township in the northern part of that Province, adjoining Northumberland. For
more than half a century the town flourished under this
historic and romantic name. General Stark, hero of Ben-
nington and patriot of wide renown, had lain several years
in his grave without his name being attached to any mountain peak or any township. But in 1832 the patriotic citizens of New Hampshire could no longer endure this neglect
of the memory of their favorite warrior, and applied to the
Legislature of the State to substitute the name Stark for
that of Percy, and it was accordingly done. The name Percy,
however, still clings to that region. The Percy Peaks, two
conical mountains rising above all the adjacent region, bear
his name and proclaim themselves far and wide.

Boston must have been a dreary abode for his lordship,
in spite of all his ample means to make himself comfortable.
There was no place in the whole British Empire, whither
he could have gone, more gloomy and more rebellious than
Boston. The port had been shut more than a month when
he arrived, and all commercial transactions in this metropo-

lis of New England were at an end. Days of fasting and
prayer on account of "the present alarming situation of our
affairs" were proclaimed in the newspapers.   Droves of
cattle and flocks of sheep, the gifts of sympathizing persons
in the Colony to the needy inhabitants of Boston, poured
through the streets.   Breathings of defiance and hatred of
the English government could be heard on all sides and
snuffed in every breeze.   The inhabitants gazed sullenly on
the martial spectacle augmenting on the Common.   Every
day the breach between England and her Colonies widened.
Edmund Burke justly observed that as the number of acts of
Parliament increased, the number of His Majesty's subjects
in the Colonies decreased.   Had his lordship been in Boston
six years before, he might have witnessed a spectacle that
showed how these people detested the ministers of the
King whose acts had led to this state of affairs.   He
might have seen drawn through these very streets where
his regiment had so proudly marched the effigies of his
own father-in-law, the Earl of Bute, and of George Grenville, both in full court dress, saluted with every insult and
indignity that an angry people could suggest, landed at
the gallows on the Neck, and there burned amid the jeers
and shouts of the multitude.

When Lord Percy landed at Boston, General Gage, governor of Massachusetts, and commander-in-chief of the
British army in America, was staying at his summer residence near Salem.   He immediately put Lord Percy in
command of the royal troops in Boston.   This gave him
sufficient employment; for there were constant collisions
between the troops and the inhabitants, and many com-

plaints reached the attentive ear of Percy.[1] At the end
of the first week in August, about a month after his arrival,
the royal troops had poured so fast into Boston that there
were six regiments, besides several companies of artillery.
General Gage formed these regiments into two brigades,
and appointed Colonel Lord Percy a brigadier of the first,
and Colonel Pigot brigadier of the second.

The storm of war was approaching. Both parties were
collecting ammunition, especially the Provincials. General
Gage thought it good policy to get into his hands the ammunition of the insurgents. On the 1st of September he
sent a military force to the powder-house in Charlestown,
and took away all the powder which had been collected
there. Another force went to Cambridge and took away
two pieces of cannon. These acts produced an immense
uproar, and thousands of persons in the country seized their
arms and hastened towards Boston. The people refused
to be comforted. Gage at once fortified the Neck "to
protect His Majesty's troops and His Majesty's subjects."
This sudden and threatening movement was magnified in
London into an attack on Boston, and it was reported that
Lord Percy was slain. Bets were freely made and taken
on the event. Lord Percy was a candidate for re-election
to Parliament, and the election was at hand. Those opposed to him industriously propagated the rumor of his
death; but it availed not, for he was elected.[2]

[1] For several interesting references
to Earl Percy's intercourse with the
people of Boston, see the Letters of
John Andrews in Proceedings of Mass.
Hist. Society, viii. 316–412. — H.

[2] Dr. Franklin, writing from London,
under date of Oct. 12, 1774, to Joseph
Galloway, says: "It being objected to
one of the candidates for Westminster,
Lord Percy, that he was absent on the
wicked business of cutting the throats
of our American brethren, his friends

During the four months' civil administration of General Gage he had been industriously issuing proclamations with the view to stay the progress of the rebellion; but he failed in his purpose. Every act of his seemed to promote a collision. The reins of executive government were now falling from his hands. On the same day that he seized the powder and cannon he summoned the General Court to meet at Salem on the 5th of October. A week before that day came round he issued a proclamation forbidding it. The members of the Court met, nevertheless, resolved themselves into a Provincial Congress, and adopted measures by which they effectually called into being a government of the people. The authority of Parliament was no longer recognized.

The Provincial Congress, now wielding the executive and legislative powers of government, immediately took measures to organize a military force sufficient to oppose and repel the English troops now encamped in Boston. From this moment a steady preparation for hostilities went forward to the hour of the first conflict at Lexington, five months later.

But a single public occurrence worthy of mention took place in the career of Lord Percy between October and the memorable day at Lexington, in April, 1775. On the last day of March, 1775, at the head of his brigade, he made an excursion into the country, going as far as Jamaica Plain. The people became alarmed, and messengers were quickly sent hither and thither to give notice of this movement of

have thought necessary this morning to publish a letter of his expressing that he is on good terms with the people of Boston, and much respected by them. These circumstances [he had mentioned several] show that the American cause begins to be more popular here." (Franklin's Works, viii. 138, 139.) — H.

the royal troops.   Great numbers of the Provincials assembled, fully armed.   It was first supposed that the troops
designed to go to Concord to seize and destroy stores; for
rumor had some time before made known such an intent.
The most considerable complaint of this military movement
came from the farmers residing on the road through which
Percy and his troops passed.   While on the march the
soldiers found it convenient to do a good deal of flanking
service, at the expense of stone walls, rail fences, tender
shrubbery, and fields recently sown with grain.   The yeomanry of that region howled vengeance on the red-coats,
and may have gotten it near the end of the next three weeks.
Curses both loud and deep followed hard upon the heels of
their rear-guard.

The memorable conflict of the British troops and
Provincials at Concord and Lexington has been related
here so many times within a few years that you must know
it all.   Earl Percy shared in this first baptism of fire and
blood, of which this day is the one hundred and fifth anniversary.   He led reinforcements to Lexington, and he also
led the retreat to Boston.   That he conducted that retreat
according to approved military rules, that he showed courage
and coolness in the most trying moments, has always been
allowed.   That he escaped death, under a fire of several
hours, was regarded a miracle.   Indeed, a report went forth,
even to England, that he was killed.   "News came that
Lord Percy was dead and buried," wrote the minister of
Portland, Maine, Dr. Deane, in his diary of that date.

In the dreadful battle of Bunker Hill, two months later,
he was not a participant, his brigade not being summoned

to take part in that engagement, but left to protect Boston. His regiment, being in the brigade of General Pigot, was in that action, where, says General Burgoyne, who was a spectator of the battle, "it fought best and lost most." Percy was active in giving relief to the sufferers of that day. In the midst of all this suffering an Irish officer put the camp in a roar by exclaiming, "Indade, we have gained — but a loss!"

On the 10th of July, before news of the battle reached England, Percy was appointed a major-general in the British army in America. He had served in the capacity of brigadier-general almost from the time of his arrival. Eight months passed without any considerable event in his military life. The British troops were now shut up in Boston, with only a passage out by water, and guarded by no less a person than General Washington, who had arrived at Cambridge and taken command of the Provincial army.

I beg leave to read a single letter written by Percy at this time to General Haldimand in London, showing how cheerful he was, how attentive to the business of the army, and what pains he had taken to oblige a friend: —

BOSTON, Dec. 14, 1775.

DEAR SIR, — Since I did myself the pleasure of writing to you last, our situation is exactly the same. The Rebels, however, have been too fortunate in other places. Canada, as you will have been already informed, is in their hands. Besides this, they have been very successful at sea, having taken a brig loaded with military stores, and — what was to them still a greater prize — a ship from Glasgow with great quantities of blanketing, woollens, and shoes, all which they were before in great want of. As they have yesterday begun to fling up a work upon Phip's Farm, just opposite to Barton's Point, I fancy they mean to bring the mortar which they took in the ordnance brig. If they do, they may trouble us a good deal, as they are within about 1000 yards of the Town. It is very odd that Great Britain still persists in sending out vessells to this part of the world unarmed. The Transports with the troops from Ireland are not yet arrived. One, indeed, with 4 Companies of the 17th Reg., came in here about 6 weeks ago ; we imagine the rest are gone to the West Indies. Our Discipline is exactly the same as when you left us, which we shall begin to perceive now the Troops have got into winter quarters. I am extremely happy to find that your reception in London was agreeable to you ; you merited it. I had no doubt that His Majesty would do what was proper. I assure you, you are by no means forgot by your friends on this side the Atlantic. Gen. Howe, in the handsomest manner, in the Augmentation, appointed your nephew a 2nd Lieu! in his own Reg., imagining, as you had desired he might do duty with it, that such a step would be agreeable to you ; and yesterday he very obligingly appointed him a full Lieutenant in the 45th Reg., chusing particularly that Corps, as there were two situations vacant ; by which means your nephew would have a Lieutenant under him, and therefore would not be broke, tho' the youngest Company should be again reduced.

I have had the pleasure of being acquainted with Lt. Col. Monkton, and shall take care to particularly recommend Mr. Haldimand to his care. Adieu, my dear Gen. Keep yourself warm this cold weather, and be assured I am, with greatest truth,

Your sincere friend

And humble servant,

PERCY.

I beg you will be kind enough to make my very best compliments to Capt. Dorkins, and tell him the Engineers have not found it necessary to alter his works in the least, which have been found remarkably useful.

The next important military event in Boston in which Percy was concerned took place early in March, 1776, when the Provincial army took possession of Dorchester Heights. The British army was even more surprised to see our troops there than they had been to see them at Bunker Hill. And well they might be; for unless they were removed, the whole British force would immediately be prisoners to General Washington. General Howe resolved to attack them by night, and appointed Percy to command the troops. Percy proceeded to Castle Island to carry out the design; but the wind and wave prevented the attack, and it was given up. General Howe now resolved to evacuate Boston, and did so on the ever memorable 17th of March, 1776. Percy proceeded with the troops to Halifax. Ten days after he left Boston he was made lieutenant-general in the British army in America.

Although the British army had left Boston without accomplishing the purpose for which they had been sent, the British Ministry no more faltered in its purpose of coercion than the Colonies in their purpose to resist.[1] Back came

[1] The patriotic zeal of the people was greatly stimulated and sustained by the clergy generally. A few hours after the enemy retreated from Boston, the Rev. Abiel Leonard, D.D., chaplain to the Connecticut troops, preached at Cambridge a sermon before General Washington and others of distinction, from Exodus xiv. 25: "And took off their chariot wheels, that they drave them heavily: so that the Egyptians said, Let us flee from the face of Israel; for the Lord fighteth for them against the Egyptians." The Rev. Ebenezer Bridge, of Chelmsford, preached a discourse in Boston, March 24, 1776, having for his text 2 Kings vii. 7: "Wherefore they arose and fled in the twilight, and left their tents, and their horses, and their asses, even the camp as it was, and fled for their life." The Rev. Andrew Eliot, D.D., preached a discourse. on March 28, being the Thursday lecture (General Washington and the Council being present by invitation), from Isaiah xxxiii. 20: "Look upon Zion, the city of our solemnities: thine eyes shall see Jerusalem a quiet habitation, a tabernacle that shall not be taken down; not one of the stakes thereof shall ever be removed, neither shall any of the cords thereof be broken." — H.

this army, early in July, much refreshed, and prepared for a new campaign against the rebellious Colonies. It gave Boston a wide berth, landing at Staten Island. While Earl Percy was there celebrating the second anniversary of his arrival in America, the members of the Continental Congress at Philadelphia were signing an immortal Declaration, putting the war on a new issue, — Freedom, and Independence of England.

The British army, on receiving large reinforcements, was organized into three great divisions, Earl Percy, now a lieutenant-general, having command of one. General Howe attacked the Provincial army on Long Island with complete success, Earl Percy's division having a share in this battle. The British army, flushed with victory, followed the Provincial army to New York, and there again was successful. At the attack on Fort Washington, Earl Percy led his division into the thickest of the fight. His horse was shot under him. His valor was applauded.

On the 1st of December General Howe sent the fleet under Sir Peter Parker, and also six thousand men under the joint command of Earl Percy and Sir Henry Clinton, to take Newport, R. I. The large frigates passed outside Long Island, and the smaller ones, with the transports having the troops, inside. While this fleet stood off New London, so vast did it appear that it seemed as if the very waters groaned under its pressure. This was on the 5th of December, a day memorable in the life of Earl Percy. For on this day his mother, the Duchess of Northumberland, died in London, and the ancient baronies of Percy, Lucy, Poynings, Fitz-Payne, Bryan, and Latimer, which had come down with the blood of the ancient Earls of Northumberland, to his mother, descended to her son, Earl Percy. He was now a peer of the realm in his own right, and his title Baron Percy. A new election was ordered at Westminster to fill his place in the House of Commons.

The fleet and army were entirely successful. Newport fell into their hands with scarce a struggle. Sir Henry Clinton soon after left, and Percy succeeded to the command. Here occurred an event which led to his leaving America some months later. While Howe and Cornwallis were struggling with the Provincial forces in New Jersey, they suddenly needed reinforcements. Howe sent to Earl Percy for fifteen hundred men, and got only eleven hundred, Percy assigning as a reason for withholding men that he was daily expecting an attack by the Provincials, and that his garrison was already too weak to resist a resolute attack. General Howe was enraged, and wrote Percy a sharp reproof for not obeying his order to the letter. This reproof Percy thought undeserved, and he procured leave to return to England. He sailed from Newport on the 5th of May, 1777, and never returned to America.[1]

[1] On his departure from Rhode Island, a considerable number of the most respectable inhabitants of Newport presented the Earl with a formal address expressive of their high appreciation of his liberal and humane conduct, and of his personal character. After mentioning in terms of gratitude the good order and discipline he had maintained among his troops, they add: "The fear of offending (not insensibility) prevents us, at present, from attempting to express how much we are affected with your Excellency's great and amiable private virtues, with that spotless Integrity of Manners and uniform regard to Religion and Decency which would add Dignity to the meanest station, with that condescending Affability which stoops without any view to private Advantage; and above all, with that unbounded and well-directed Generosity which has so often procured for your Excellency the blessings of those who were ready to perish." (Newport Gazette, May 8, 1777.)

The Independent Chronicle (Boston), of Oct. 23, 1777, has the following: "It is impossible to express the regret of the army on the departure of Lord Percy. Provincials as well as our own people, if in distress, shared alike in his

In November he moved the address to the King in the House of Lords. Among other things he defended the officers of the British army in America from aspersions cast on them in England, and spoke encouragingly and hopefully of the war if prosecuted with vigor.[1] In 1779

benefactions. He kept open table for inferior officers. In short, he spent while in America ten thousand pounds of his own fortune, all his pay, and upwards of twenty-five thousand pounds remitted to him by the Duke and Duchess."

Soon after his return to England Lord Percy was fixed upon as a fit person to be placed at the head of the commission to negotiate with the Colonies, but this service he declined. (Gentleman's Magazine, lxxxvii. 182.) — H.

[1] The following, taken from Almon's Parliamentary Register, ix. 2–5, is the report of the Duke's address on the occasion referred to in the text. — H.

Lord Percy acquainted the House that it had fallen to his lot to have the honor of moving an address in answer to the most gracious speech now read. He acknowledged his own insufficiency for an undertaking which called for the most zealous and energetic language that House was capable of expressing itself in.

His Lordship observed an event had happened since they last sat there, which ought to give every noble Lord present the most heartfelt pleasure; that was the birth of a princess, as it was an additional security to the Protestant religion, and the enjoyment of those constitutional rights which were known to be so peculiarly the care of the amiable and virtuous sovereign on the throne, and were likely to be transmitted to the latest posterity through his illustrious house. . . . He acknowledged his obligations, in common with the officers serving in America, for the very gracious testimony which has been given of their services by their royal master, and the high confidence he expressed in the spirit and intrepidity

of his forces both by sea and land. He lamented, as a professional man, what a disagreeable situation persons serving in high commands stood in, when accidents which it was frequently not in the power of the greatest military skill or foresight to descry or prevent were attributed to neglect or incapacity. He lamented the fate of those brave and able men who were thus liable to suffer under unjust censures; and whose absence in a distant country necessarily prevented them from having an opportunity to defend themselves. From his own knowledge he could affirm that they were as cruel as ill founded. It was impossible, at this distance, to pass a judgment on the operations of war; it was injudicious and unfair to estimate their propriety by the events. It was with particular satisfaction, therefore, that he perceived His Majesty and his ministers, and he believed a very great majority of the nation, entertained sentiments of a very different kind. . . .

His Lordship expressed great sorrow for the occasion of the war, and the effusion of human blood, which was inseparable from such a state; but he was convinced, how much soever His Majesty, the Parliament, and the nation might feel on the occasion, the temper of America made it necessary; the people there had been deluded and misled by their leaders; and nothing, he feared, would compel them to return to their allegiance, but a continuance of the same decisive exertions on our part till we were fully enabled to convince them that as our rights were indisputably superior, so our strength was fully adequate to their full maintenance and support.

He concluded his remarks on the speech with passing great commendation on the humane, gracious, fatherly spirit which, he said, it breathed, and the invitation it held forth to our deluded Colonies to return

he procured a divorce from his wife, with whom he had not lived for ten years, and by whom he had no issue, and in the same year married Frances Julia Burrell, one of the daughters of a house not then distinguished for opulence, antiquity, or renown, but for making great matrimonial alliances.[1] He soon retired to Stenwick with his new wife, and there watched with much interest the American war and public affairs, without taking any part in them. He was much disgusted with the leaders of affairs in England, and was stung with neglect of the Ministry. In 1782 he wrote from Stenwick to his friend, the Right Hon. George Ross, as follows : —

What encouragement is there for any man of Rank to exert himself in the service of the King and country, when the only reward he is likely to meet with is a total neglect, and constantly to have the mortification of seeing every person without either weight, consequence, or merit, preferred before him in every instance, both civil and military. I may without vanity assert that there is not an officer in the army who has done his duty in the line of his profession, with more zeal and attention than myself ; and in consequence of that it is now fourteen years since I have received the smallest mark of approbation of His Majesty or his Ministers.

In 1784 he resigned the colonelcy of the Fifth Regiment, on being promoted to the command of a troop of the Grenadier Guards. In 1786 his father, the Duke of North-

to their loyalty and their former constitutional connection, and attachment to this country. His Lordship then moved an humble address.

[1] Frances Julia Burrell was the third daughter of Peter Burrell, Esq., of Beckenham, Kent, sister to the Marchioness of Exeter, the Countess of Beverly, and Lord Gwydyr. The issue of this marriage was five daughters, one of whom married Lord James Murray, second son of the Duke of Athol ; and two sons, whose names are given in the text. — H.

umberland, died, and Lord Percy succeeded to the title of
Duke and Earl of Northumberland, and other titles, and to
vast estates in Great Britain. In 1793 he was made a
general in the royal army. Above all, he was made knight
of the garter, — the most ancient and splendid order of
knighthood in England, if not in all Europe.

He was member of the House of Commons eight years,
and of the House of Peers forty years; yet if the indexes
to the journals of these Houses are correct, he spoke not
once in the Commons, and but twice in the House of Peers,
during all that time.

For the last twenty years of his life he was afflicted with
gout, and quite withdrawn from public view. He interested
himself with the organization of fifteen hundred of his tenantry in Yorkshire into a military body, whom he clothed,
fed, and paid, — showing a bias for military employments
to the last. The annual revenue from his estates was estimated at eighty thousand pounds sterling.[1]

[1] The following, extracted from the Gentleman's Magazine for July, 1817, gives additional facts in the life of the Duke. — H.

His time and attention have been chiefly employed in continuing and completing the improvements begun by his father in the princely mansions of Northumberland House, Zion House, and Alnwick Castle, in Northumberland, where, in his extensive domains, upwards of a million of timber and other trees were annually planted for many years. The large income of his Grace, estimated at not less than £80,000 per annum, was expended in these useful pursuits and in keeping up the ancient feudal splendor in the Castle of the Percys. During the late war with France he raised from among his tenantry in the country from which he derived his title a corps of 1,500 men, under the denomination of the Percy Yeomanry, the whole being clothed, appointed, paid, and maintained by himself; Government finding arms and accoutrements alone. To his tenants he was a most excellent landlord; and the monument just erected by them in honor of him will transmit to posterity the memory of his kindness and indulgence, and of their gratitude. One custom which he introduced among them cannot be too highly praised or too extensively imitated; it was that of providing for the industrious hinds of every large farm by giving them a cottage and ten acres of land, which proves an encouragement to industrious youth and a security against want in old age. In ready money his Grace was for years considered the most wealthy man in England; which he often employed in rescuing industrious families from ruin. . . . The personal property is sworn to as under £700,000.

Lord Percy died at Northumberland House in London, July 10, 1817, and a week later his body was borne to Westminster Abbey, with extraordinary pomp and solemnity, and deposited in the Percy vault in St. Nicholas Chapel.[1]

He left two sons, both of whom succeeded to his titles and estates. The eldest, Hugh Percy, who had already distinguished himself in Parliament, now became Duke of Northumberland, and died in 1847, without issue. The titles and estates then went to his brother, Algernon Percy, a naval officer, and a man of science and learning. He died in 1865, without issue. Thus ended the male line of Lord Percy. The titles and estates thence passed into the line of his youngest brother, Algernon Percy, Earl of Beverly.[2]

---

[1] An extended account of the funeral is given in the Gentleman's Magazine, lxxxvii. 83-85. — H.

[2] Since this Memoir was printed, the Annals of the House of Percy, from the Conquest to the Opening of the Nineteenth Century, by Edward Barrington de Fonblanque, issued in two volumes, for private circulation, have been noticed in the Quarterly Review for April, 1889. — H.

COURT OF VICE–ADMIRALTY OVER
` AMERICA.

COURT OF VICE-ADMIRALTY OVER AMERICA.[1]

WHILE looking into the details of the civil and military career of Lord Percy, who commanded the British reinforcements sent from Boston to Lexington April 19, 1775, some years ago, I found that his father, the Earl, afterward Duke, of Northumberland, had in 1765, and several years after, the official title, "Vice-Admiral over all America." No American and no English history that I had then or have since read, mentions any such officer.[2] I could not help turning for a while from my principal design and looking up the origin of this official station. Proceeding from one thing to another, I came at length upon the official announcement in the London gazettes of 22d December, 1764, that His Majesty had been pleased to appoint the Right Honorable Hugh, Earl of Northumberland, "Vice-Admiral over all America;" to which was added, " This appointment being made pursuant to a late act of Parliament."

---

[1] Reprinted, by permission, from the Proceedings of the Massachusetts Historical Society, December, 1879. — H.

[2] The author refers to general histories. The establishment of the Court is mentioned by Washburn in his Judicial History of Massachusetts (175).—H.

This was " An act for the granting certain duties in the British Colonies and Plantations in America," etc., and providing, among other things, for the punishment of breaches of the revenue laws.   By this act the Admiralty Courts in the several Colonies were authorized to take cognizance of breaches of the revenue laws.   It provided also for the establishment of a new Vice-Admiralty Court over all America, having jurisdiction of breaches of the revenue laws wherever the offence might occur in the British Colonies.

The Colonies at once objected to this extended jurisdiction of the Admiralty Court, and also to the proposed establishment of a Court of Vice-Admiralty.   But I find no mention, in the discussions of this subject at that time, or later, or in contemporary histories, of the organization of this new Admiralty Court.   It was therefore a surprise to me to find, in the London gazettes of 1764, the appointment, at various times, of a full board of officers of this great Court of Vice-Admiralty over all America, and a still greater surprise when I came upon a proclamation announcing the opening of this Court in Halifax, Nova Scotia, in October, 1764.

The following persons were appointed, at various dates between the passage of the act and the end of the year 1764, to constitute this Court: Vice-Admiral, the Earl of Northumberland; Judge, the Right Worshipful William Spry, LL. D.; Registrar, the Hon. Spencer Percival; Marshal, Charles Howard, Gent.   It is manifest that none of these officers expected to execute these offices in person: that was to be done by deputy.

Judge Spry, whose wife was niece of the Earl of

Chatham, arrived in Halifax, with his family, on the 25th of September, and on the 9th day of October following, opened the Court cf Vice-Admiralty, and on the 16th of October the Court issued the proclamation printed below. Whether this Court was opened for business in any other Province, as designed, I am not yet informed.[1] The passage of the Stamp Act the next year, and the riots it occasioned in America, together with the violence offered to the local Admiralty Courts, very likely prevented further extension of this new Court.

In 1767 Judge Spry was appointed Governor of Barbados. He removed there, and died in office in 1772. It is singular that the elaborate histories of Nova Scotia contain no account of this Vice-Admiralty Court over all America.

The proclamation mentioned above is as follows: —

WHEREAS, by an Act of Parliament, made and passed in the fourth year of His Majesty's Reign, entitled, "An Act for the granting certain Duties in the British Colonies and Plantations in America," etc., it is thereby, among other Things, Enacted and Declared, That from and after the twenty-ninth Day of September, A. D. 1764, all the Forfeitures and Penalties inflicted by that or any other Act of Parliament, relating to the Trade and Revenues of the said British Colonies, or Plantations in America, which shall be incurred there, shall and may be prosecuted, sued for, and recovered in any Court of Record, or in any Court of Admiralty, in the said Colonies or Plantations where such Offence shall be committed, or

---

[1] Mr. Washburn also states that the year following the proclamation given below, Judge Spry "made arrangements for removing from Halifax to Boston, to enter upon his duties there as Supreme Judge of Vice-Admiralty." Undoubtedly the cause of his not removing was the one suggested by Mr. Tuttle; namely, the political disturbances in Boston. — H.

in any Court of Vice-Admiralty which may, or shall be, appointed over all America (which Court of Admiralty or Vice-Admiralty are hereby respectively authorized and required to proceed, hear, and determine the same), at the Election of the Informer or Prosecutor ;

And whereas His Majesty, by Letters Patent, under the Great Seal of His High Court of Admiralty of Great Britain and Ireland, etc., dated at London, the fifteenth Day of June, A. D. 1764, has been pleased to appoint the Right Worshipful WILLIAM SPRY, Doctor of Laws, to be Judge of His Majesty's Court of Vice-Admiralty over all America, with Power to proceed, hear, and determine all Causes, civil and maritime, arising in any of the Provinces of America, or the maritime Parts thereof, and thereto adjacent, at the Election of the Informer or Prosecutor ;

PUBLIC NOTICE IS HEREBY GIVEN, That the Right Worshipful WILLIAM SPRY, Doctor of Laws, the Judge of His Majesty's said Court of Vice-Admiralty over all America, hath opened his said Court on the ninth Day of October, Instant, at Halifax, in the Province of Nova Scotia ; hath thought fit to fix the first and third Wednesdays of every Month as Term Days for the sitting of said Court at Halifax, aforesaid, when and where all Causes, civil and maritime, arising in any Province of America, or the maritime Parts thereof or thereto adjacent, may be prosecuted.

Of which all Parties concerned therein are hereby desired to take Notice.

By Order of the Court.

JAMES BRENTON, Dep. Registrar.

HALIFAX, 16th October, 1764.

EDWARD RANDOLPH.

EDWARD RANDOLPH.[1]

EDWARD RANDOLPH holds so conspicuous and so important a place in our colonial history, that anything concerning him is worthy of consideration, especially if new. It is surprising, in view of the extent of our historical inquiries, that the arch-enemy of Puritanism in all its aspects, the prime mover and the actual abettor of the overthrow of the first political and ecclesiastical establishments of New England, should have excited so little interest and be so little known. Measured simply by the results of his own undertakings, Edward Randolph is justly entitled to rank among the most remarkable men of his time. In that dramatic period of our history which embraces the closing scenes of the life of the first charter, he is the central figure and the chief actor, — not inaptly called the "destroying angel." His public acts are memorable, and they form the chief interest in the history of that time.

[1] Reprinted, by permission, from the Proceedings of the Massachusetts Historical Society for February, 1874. — H.

His career in New England may be characterized as meteoric in many respects; it certainly is without parallel in our history. He came suddenly into public view from beyond the Atlantic, the unwelcome bearer of a royal message having a menacing aspect, at a time when the Colonies were in a death-struggle with the Indian enemy. For a period of thirteen years he was regarded by our fathers as the most baleful and malignant luminary that ever appeared in the political skies of New England. His name was a synonym for something dreadful, and his fame — an ill one it was — extended to all the Colonies. On the records of that age no name is branded by writers with so many, so varied, and so strongly denunciative epithets as that of Edward Randolph. It is but just to his memory to say that his excessive zeal for the interests of the Crown and for the Church of England, his undaunted courage and uncompromising spirit, were the chief causes of his great unpopularity.

Whence he came or whither he went has hardly been thought worthy of inquiry by our antiquaries in a period of two centuries. His history, so far as known, begins and ends with his career in New England. Dr. Palfrey, who looked after many neglected worthies of our colonial times, as his History attests, made special search in the archives of England for some light on the early career of Randolph, but without success.

While collecting materials for my projected "Life of Captain John Mason," patentee of New Hampshire, I noticed in letters of Robert Mason, grandson of Captain Mason, and also in letters of Edward Randolph, expressions indicating some degree of relationship between them. Following up this hint, I came to the origin and parentage of Randolph himself,— singularly enough in the first Christian city and spiritual metropolis of England. He was the son of Edmund Randolph, Doctor of Physic, of the city of Canterbury. His mother was a daughter of Gyles Master, of the same city. Both parents were of gentle lineage, and of high character and standing. Edward Randolph married Jane Gibbon, of West Cliff, in the county of Kent. Her brother, Richard Gibbon, Doctor of Physic, married Anne Tufton, sister of Robert Mason. It is proper to observe that Robert Tufton assumed the surname Mason to inherit his grandfather Mason's estate in New England.

On the death of his wife, in 1679, Randolph again came to New England, bringing his family, designing, it would seem, to remain here permanently. He had been appointed by the Commissioners of Customs, collector of customs in New England. Having other public employments, he appointed his brother Gyles deputy in his place. Another brother, Bernard Randolph, also his deputy, was an author of considerable note in his day.

In 1691, Edward Randolph was appointed surveyor-general of customs in all the English Provinces in North America. This fact shows that he was recognized as an able and faithful officer by the English government.[1]

---

[1] Mr. Tuttle intended to write the life of Edward Randolph, but had made no progress in the work up to the time of his death.— H.

EDWARD RANDOLPH'S WILL.

IN the name of God, amen. This fifteenth day of June, in the yeare of our Lord one Thousand seaven hundred and two, I, Edward Randolph, Esq'., Surveyour-Gen^{ll} of Her Ma^{tie's} Customes in all her Plantations and Colonies in America, sound of body and memory, thanks be given to Allmighty God for all his mercies, yet nevertheless taking into my serious consideration the frailty of human life, and being about to make my seaventeenth sea-voyage to America, doe make this my last Will and Testament in manner and forme following. After having comended my soul, body, and estate to the mercies and protection of Allmighty God, hoping for salvation at my dissolution through the merits of my blessed Lord and Saviour Jesus Christ, I dispose of my temporall estate wherewith it hath pleased God to bless me, as followeth; viz. I doe hereby give and bequeath unto my youngest daughter, Sarah Randolph (whoe is otherwise unprovided for), all such summe and summes of money as are or shall be due to me of my sallary as Surveyor-General, payable from the Commissioners of Her Ma^{tie's} Customes for the time being, and which I have not allready given to my daughter Williams or to my daughter Deborah Randolph, which said salary is usually received and paid for me by my Worthy friend Richard Savage, Esq'. And in case it should please God that my said daughters Williams and Deborah, or either of them, shall happen to dye in the life-time of my said daughter Sarah, then I doe will and bequeath such parte and parts of my said sallary as I have ordred to be paid to them, or either of them, to be thenceforth paid to my said daughter Sarah; and I doe also give and bequeath unto my said daughter Sarah all my plate which I leave in the hands of my loving friend Mr. Edward Jones of the Savoy, and all such summe and summes of money as is or shall be recovered for my use of Gilbert Nelson, late Chiefe Justice of the Island of Burmuda, whether the same be in the hands of Mr. Samuell Spofforth or any other person whomsoever, and all such summes of money as shall be recovered for my use of George Plater, Esq'., living in Potuxent, in the province of Maryland, and which the said Plater hath or may receive for my use of Samuell Willson or any other person, and all and singular debts due and payable, or which shall be hereafter due or payable to me. But in case my said daughter Sarah shall happen to depart this life before she attaine the age of eighteen years, and be married (which I enjoine and require her not to doe without the consent and approbation of Mrs. Mary Fog, and Nathaniell Bladen of Lincoln's Inn, Esq'., thereunto in writing first had and obtained), then I will that my daughter Elisabeth Pim, and (if she be dead) her son Mr. Charles Pim, or her and his children, shall have all that is herein bequeathed to my said daughter Sarah. But if neither my said daughter Pim, nor her said son Charles, nor any child or children of hers or his shall be living, then I will that whatsoever I have herein bequeathed to my said daughter Sarah shall go to my daughters Williams and Deborah and their children equally, and I doe hereby constitute and appoint my said daughter Sarah sole executrix of this my last will and Testament, by these presents revoking and annulling all former wills by me made heretofore and declared by word or writing, and this only to be taken for my last will and Testament.

In witness whereof I have hereby declared and published this to be my last will and Testament, the day and yeare above written, in the presence of Humphrey Walcot, Gent., Mrs. Catherine Bladen, and Nathaniel Bladen.

ED. RANDOLPH, S.-G.

Witness, Humphrey Walcott,
Catharine Bladen,
Nathaniel Bladen.

7 Dec. 1703. Administration to Sarah, wife of John Howard, Guardian assigned to Sarah Randolph, a minor, dau' and Executrix named in the Will of Edward Randolph, late of Acquamat in Virginia, deceased.

(234 Degg.)

NOTES BY THE EDITOR.

THE Randolph family claims to be of Norman origin. Persons bearing this name figure conspicuously in English and in Scottish history. Sir Thomas Randolph is mentioned in Domesday Book as ordered to do duty against the King of France. In 1298 Sir John Randolph, Knt., was a commissioner to summon knights, and attended the coronation of Edward II. in 1307. In 1329 Sir Thomas Randolph, Earl of Murray, was with common consent made governor of Scotland, and died in 1331, universally lamented.[1] John Randolph, of Hampshire, connected with the Exchequer in 1385, was an eminent judge. Sir Thomas Randolph, son of Avery of Badlesmere, co. Kent, and cousin of Thomas Randolph the poet, was born in that parish in 1523. He rendered important public services in the reign of Elizabeth, having been employed by that sovereign in no less than eighteen different embassies. He died in 1590. One of his wives was a cousin of Sir Francis Walsingham. An Avery Randolph was principal of Pembroke College, Oxford, in 1590. On the roll of bishops of the Church in England appears the name of Dr. John Randolph, born in 1749, son of **Dr.** Thomas

---

[1] Douglas's Peerage of Scotland, 498.

(1701–1783), archdeacon of Oxford. He became the bishop of Oxford in 1799, of Bangor in 1806, of London in 1809, and died in 1813.

Edward Randolph — the subject of these notes — was a grandson of Bernard Randolph, who married Jane, daughter of William Boddenham, of Biddenden, Hundred of Barkly, co. Kent, and through this marriage became possessed of the estate of Lessenden in that place. Bernard died in 1628. This estate continued in the family until 1808, when it was sold by the then holder, the Rev. Herbert Randolph.

Bernard and Jane Randolph had several children, among whom were John, Herbert, and Edmund. It is a family tradition that John emigrated to Virginia. Herbert married Elizabeth, daughter of Gyles Master, of the city of Canterbury, and died in 1644. He had a son Herbert, who married Elizabeth Best, of Canterbury, and died in 1685.

The last-named Herbert had a son Herbert, who was a barrister, and held the office of recorder of Canterbury, and died possessed of Lessenden in 1726. He was twice married: (1) to Mary, daughter of Dr. John Castillion, dean of Rochester, of the Italian family of Castiglione; and (2) to Grace, daughter of John Blome, of Sevenoaks, Kent. He left two children by his first wife: Herbert, and Mary, who married Christopher Packe, M.D. By his second wife he had eight children: Thomas, D.D., archdeacon of Oxford, and president of Corpus Christi College; George, M.D., of Bristol; Francis, D.D., principal of Alban Hall, Oxford; Charles, bred to the law; and four daughters.

Out of this branch of the family sprang Bishop Randolph, above mentioned.

Herbert, son of Herbert and Mary (Castillion) Randolph, was of All Souls' College, Oxford, and rector of Deal, Kent, and died in 1755. He married (1) Catharine Wake, daughter of Dr. Edward Wake; and (2) Mary, daughter of Nathaniel Denew. By his first wife he had a son Herbert, rector of Croxton, Lincolnshire, and prebendary of Salisbury, who married Elizabeth Adcock, of Ashford, Kent, and died in 1803. The last-named Herbert, by his wife Elizabeth, had a son Herbert, fellow of Corpus Christi College, Oxford, rector of Letcombe Basset, Berks, and vicar of Chute, Wilts. He died in 1828, having married Jane, daughter of Benjamin Wilson, of Leeds, and sister of Gen. Sir Robert Wilson, K. M. T.[1] He had ten children, of whom two survive; namely, Francis and Edmund. The latter married Georgiana H. Sherlock, daughter of Col. Francis Sherlock, K. H.,[2] and has had issue five sons and one daughter, of whom one son, Herbert, is dead.

Edmund Randolph (baptized in the parish of Biddenden, Kent, in 1600), fifth son of Bernard, was a doctor of physic both of Oxford and Padua. He married at Canterbury, about the year 1628, Deborah, daughter of Gyles Master, of that city, and there followed his profession. He died in 1649, and was buried in St. George's church. The inscription on his monument, formerly existing in that church, was as follows: —

[1] Knight of the order of Maria Theresa.

[2] Knight of the Guelphic order of Hanover, instituted by George IV.

EDMUNDUS RANDOLPH EX ANTIQUA FAMILIA ORTUS
MEDICINÆ DOCTOR EXERCITATISSIMUS
ALIORUM I ROTELANDO VITAM DECURTAVIT SUAM.
NUMEROSA AUCTUS PROLE
FILIIS DECEM, MOLLIORISQUE SEXUS QUINQUE
MUNDUM SIMUL AC DOMUM LOCUPLETAVIT SUAM
HISCE LIBENS SOCIAM DEDIT OPERAM DEBORAH
FÆMINA, SI QUÆ ALIA, SPECTATISSIMA
D^{ni} ÆGIDII MASTER
NUPER DE CIVITATE CANTUARIÆ ARMIGERI
FILIA QUARTA
UXOR SEMPER FIDA, SEMPER IMPENSE DILECTA.

ULTIMA [1] LETHI
VIS RAPUIT RAPIETQUE GENTES.

FRUAMUR PRÆSENTI
ANNO D^{ni} MDCLXXXI.[2]

Edmund and Deborah (Master) Randolph had fifteen children. The three oldest were baptized at Biddenden, Kent, the five youngest at St. George's, Canterbury; namely, Mary, in 1639; Gyles, in 1640; Jane, in 1641; another daughter, in 1642; and Bernard, in 1645. Their fourth son, Edward, so intimately connected with the affairs of New England from 1676 to 1689, was baptized in the parish of St. Margaret, Canterbury, on the 9th of July, 1632.

Edward Randolph was married three times. His first wife was Jane, born in 1640, daughter of Thomas Gibbon,

---

[1] Hor. Odes, ii. 13. *Ultima* is substituted for *improvisa*.

[2] Although Dr. Edmund Randolph died in 1649, his monument was not erected until 1681. The delay may have been due to the political troubles of the intervening years.

of West Cliffe, Kent, by his wife Dorothy Best. Of the
issue of this marriage we have the names certainly of
three daughters, — Jane, Deborah, baptized July 6, 1661,
and Elizabeth, born in 1664. There was a fourth daughter by the first or by the second marriage; namely, Mary,
who is mentioned by Randolph in his letter of July 18,
1684, to Samuel Shrimpton.[1]

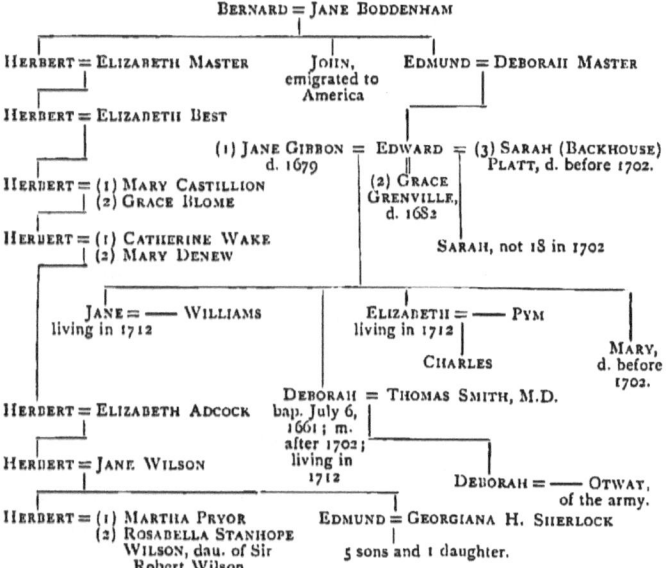

RANDOLPH

BERNARD = JANE BODDENHAM

HERBERT = ELIZABETH MASTER   JOHN,   EDMUND = DEBORAH MASTER
                            emigrated to
                            America

HERBERT = ELIZABETH BEST

                            (1) JANE GIBBON = EDWARD = (3) SARAH (BACKHOUSE)
                                   d. 1679   PLATT, d. before 1702.
HERBERT = (1) MARY CASTILLION   (2) GRACE
          (2) GRACE BLOME   GRENVILLE,
                                          d. 1682
HERBERT = (1) CATHERINE WAKE
          (2) MARY DENEW   SARAH, not 18 in 1702

        JANE = —— WILLIAMS   ELIZABETH = —— PYM
      living in 1712   living in 1712
                                          CHARLES   MARY,
                                                          d. before
                                                          1702.
                            DEBORAH = THOMAS SMITH, M.D.
HERBERT = ELIZABETH ADCOCK bap. July 6,
                            1661; m.
                            after 1702;
HERBERT = JANE WILSON   living in   DEBORAH = —— OTWAY,
                            1712   of the army.

HERBERT = (1) MARTHA PRYOR EDMUND = GEORGIANA H. SHERLOCK
          (2) ROSABELLA STANHOPE
          WILSON, dau. of Sir   5 sons and 1 daughter.
          Robert Wilson

[1] Coll. Mass. Hist. Soc., Fourth Se-   on my daughter[s] Betty and Mary.
ries, viii. 543. " Pray haue a strict eye   Their sister Jane hath shewn them a

Jane (Best) Gibbon was of the same family as the historian Edward Gibbon. Her brother Matthew had a son Edward,[1] and the latter also a son Edward, father of the historian. Another brother of Jane Gibbon, namely, Richard, married Anne Tufton, sister of Robert, who, pursuant to the will of his grandfather, Capt: John Mason, assumed the name of Robert Mason. Jane (Gibbon) Randolph died in 1679. The place of her death is not known.

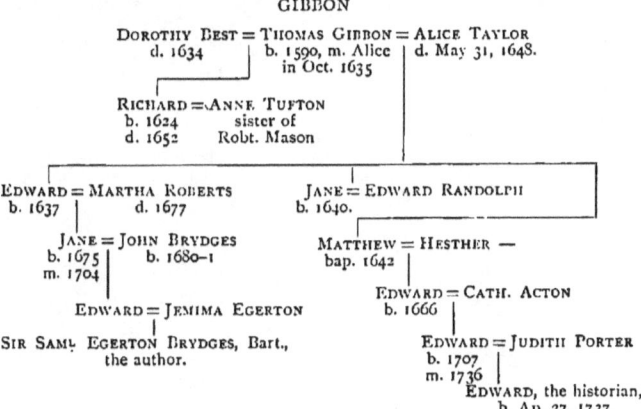

GIBBON

DOROTHY BEST = THOMAS GIBBON = ALICE TAYLOR
d. 1634   b. 1590, m. Alice   d. May 31, 1648.
in Oct. 1635

RICHARD = ANNE TUFTON
b. 1624   sister of
d. 1652   Robt. Mason

EDWARD = MARTHA ROBERTS   JANE = EDWARD RANDOLPH
b. 1637   d. 1677   b. 1640.

JANE = JOHN BRYDGES   MATTHEW = HESTHER —
b. 1675   b. 1680–1   bap. 1642
m. 1704

EDWARD = JEMIMA EGERTON   EDWARD = CATH. ACTON
    b. 1666

SIR SAML EGERTON BRYDGES, Bart.,   EDWARD = JUDITH PORTER
the author.   b. 1707
    m. 1736
      EDWARD, the historian,
      b. Ap. 27, 1737.

The Bests were also a Kentish family, with which the Randolphs have been several times allied. Edward's first

very bad example. and is a lost child to me. God give her grace to repent."

It is to be inferred that Jane and Deborah were at this time in England. Elizabeth and Mary were in Boston, and probably living in the family, or under the care, of Mr. Shrimpton.

[1] For a very full genealogical history of the Gibbon family, see Sir Egerton Brydges's essay on that subject in the Gentleman's Magazine, 1797, lxvii. 915–919, 1104–1107. The writer corrects several errors into which the historian Gibbon fell in his autobiographical account of his family.

ERRATA.

Page 286, first line, *for* Dorothy Best *read* Alice Taylor.
 287, first line, *for* Jane (Best) Gibbon *read* Jane (Taylor) Gibbon.
 288, line seven, *dele* Jane Gibbon = Edward Randolph.
 311, third line, *for* Elliott's *read* Eliot's.

cousin, Herbert, married one of them, namely, Elizabeth. The following table will show the relationship between Elizabeth and Dorothy Best: —

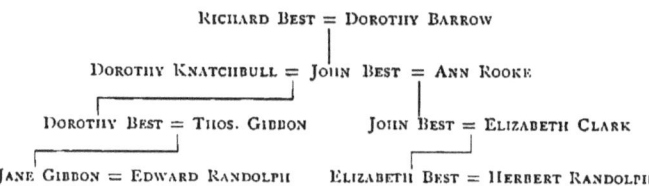

RICHARD BEST = DOROTHY BARROW

DOROTHY KNATCHBULL = JOHN BEST = ANN ROOKE

DOROTHY BEST = THOS. GIBBON   JOHN BEST = ELIZABETH CLARK

JANE GIBBON = EDWARD RANDOLPH   ELIZABETH BEST = HERBERT RANDOLPH

Ursula Best, sister of John Best, sr., was grandmother of Sir George Rooke, vice-admiral of England, the hero of Gibraltar. She married Thomas Finch, and their daughter Jane married Sir W. Rooke, Knt., father of Sir George.

The second wife of Edward Randolph was Grace Grenville, of the parish of St. Martin-in-the-Fields, London. The marriage occurred in that parish, Aug. 18, 1681. She died in Boston, New England, late in November, or early in December, 1682.[1] It is to her undoubtedly that Randolph refers in his letter of May 13, 1684, to Sir Robert Southwell: "I lost a wife in New England." And in his letter to the same, of Aug. 1, 1684, he says, "The troubles of 1681 [in New England] broke my wife's heart."[2]

Edward Randolph's third wife — to whom he was married in London, in 1684 — was Sarah Platt, the widow of

[1] New England Hist. and Gene. Register, xxxvii. 155-159, and note. She is mentioned by Judge Sewall in his Diary (Coll. Mass. Hist. Soc., vi., Fifth Series, 17 *): "Dec. 17: Foye arrives, in whom Mr. Randolph, and his new wife and family. 25: they sit in Mr. Joyliffe's pew, and Mrs. Randolph is observed to make a curtsey at Mr. Willard's naming Jesus, even in prayer-time."

[2] Proceedings Mass. Hist. Soc., xviii. 256, 257.

Peter Platt. Her maiden name is supposed to have been Backhouse, for the following license from the vicar-general of the Archbishop of Canterbury is preserved: " 1671-2, Jany. 31. Peter Platt of Swallowfield, Berks, Gent., Bachelor, aged about 30, and Sarah Backhouse of Aston, near Stafford, co. Stafford, Spinster, aged about 22, at her own disposal, to marry at St. Sepulchre's, London." The register of St. Sepulchre's shows that the said parties were married in that church Feb. 1, 1671-2. The burial of Peter Platt is recorded in the register of St. Martin-in-the-Fields, as of Nov. 3, 1681. The license for the marriage of Edward Randolph and Mrs. Sarah Platt is as follows: " 1684, Dec. 22. Edward Randolph of St. Margaret's, Westminster, Esq', widower, and Sarah Platt of St. Martin-in-the-Fields, widow, to marry at St. Martin-in-the-Fields;" and in the register of the last-named parish occurs this entry: " 1684, Dec. 24. Edward Randolph of St. Margaret's, Westminster, and Sarah Platt of this parish, by license from the Archbishop." The Backhouses were also of Swallowfield, Berks; and Sarah may have been a daughter of Sir John Backhouse, knight of the bath, who died in 1649. She was related to the wife of Edward Hyde, the Earl of Clarendon. The grandfather of Mary Castillion, who, as stated above, married Herbert Randolph, was Douglas Castillion; and two of his sisters married Hydes,—one being Sir Lawrence, —thus becoming aunts to Edward Hyde, for a brother of their husbands was his father.[1]

---

[1] The chief portion of the genealogical statements respecting the Randolphs in these notes has been gathered by the editor from letters addressed to the late Charles W. Tuttle, Ph.D., by Edmund Randolph, Esq., of the Isle of Wight.

Randolph's third wife was the mother of Sarah, "my youngest daughter," mentioned in his Will. In his letter to Sir Robert Southwell, under date of Aug. 19, 1683,[1] he writes: "I have now 4 daughters living." These were Jane, Deborah, Elizabeth, and Mary. As will be seen, he mentions four children in his Will; namely, Deborah, Mrs. Williams, Elizabeth Pim, and Sarah, and his grandson Charles Pim. His daughter Jane married a Williams, and was the "daughter Williams" named in the Will. Deborah married, subsequently to 1702, Thomas Smith of Maidstone, M.D.[2] Elizabeth married a Pim (or Pym). Mary, not mentioned in the Will, had probably deceased before 1702. Sarah was born after 1684, as she had not reached the age of eighteen at the date of the Will. It is to be inferred that he had other children who did not survive him. He left no son.

Two brothers of Edward Randolph came to New England and held office as his deputies; namely, Gyles and Bernard, both born in the city of Canterbury, the first named in 1640, the second in 1645. Bernard was a deputy collector of customs in 1683, and again in 1684, as appears by contemporary letters. He was suspected by Dr. Increase Mather of being concerned, with his brother Edward, in the authorship or transmission of the famous "forged letter" of Dec. 3, 1683, signed "I. M.," the authorship of which Dr. Mather denied.[3] In a letter from Edward Cranfield, royal governor of the Province of New Hampshire, to Mr. Secretary Jenkins, under date of June 19, 1683, it is stated that "Mr. [Edward] Randolph's Bro', who was left

[1] Proceedings, Mass. Hist. Soc., xviii. 254, 255.
[2] Gentleman's Magazine, lxvii. 1107.
[3] Coll. Mass. Hist. Soc., Fourth Series, viii. 100-110, 702-704; Palfrey, iii. 556.

here his Deputy, not being able to serue his Maj[tie] (as things
are now managed here, being dayly affronted and abused,
as I haue been an Eye Witness of), goes to England to
make his complaints to your Hon[r] and the Lords of the
Treasury."[1] And in a letter of the same date to the Lords
of the Committee of Trade and Foreign Plantations, Cranfield also says: "The bearer hereof, M[r] Bernard Randolph,
Deputy Collect[r], comes home with fresh complaints against
the Boston Governm[t] of things I have been an eye Witness
of. . . . I have sent another exemplification of Goue's tryall
by M[r] Randolph's Bro[r]: who has been so ill treated in the
Execution of his place that he is compelled to quit the
King's seruice."[2] His place was supplied by his brother
Gyles,[3] who was commissioned deputy-collector for New
England, Nov. 26, 1683.

Edward Randolph, writing from London under date of
July 18, 1684, to Samuel Shrimpton, of Boston, says: " I
send my brother ouer to succeed my brother Gyls."[4] From
this it would appear that Bernard Randolph came again to
New England and served as deputy collector. He was
the author of at least two works; namely, The Present
State of the Morea, Oxford, 1686, London, 1689, 4to;
and The Present State of the Islands in the Archipelago,
Oxford, 1687, 4to.

---

[1] Jenness's Transcripts, 151.

[2] Under date of June 13, 1683, Bernard wrote to his brother Edward as
follows: "I have received many affronts since my being in the office you
left me, and cannot have any justice.
I ordered Gatchell to go aboard a sloop
at Marblehead to search her. . . . The
constable had his staff taken out of his
hands; his head broke therewith. Gatchell was shrewdly [severely?] beaten.
. . . I have been very uneasy, but with
my life and fortune will ever serve His
Majesty." (Colonial Papers, quoted in
Palfrey, iii. 375.)

[3] Jenness's Transcripts, 157.

[4] Coll. Mass. Hist. Soc., Fourth
Series, viii. 525.

Of Gyles Randolph we learn nothing further, except that he married in America and had a son; but the son's history is not known.[1] It is supposed that Gyles died in Boston, or elsewhere in New England, late in the Spring of 1684. His death is reported by Governor Cranfield in a letter to the Lords of the Committee of Trade, dated May 14, 1684;[2] but in his letters written prior to May of that year he makes no mention of this event.

It has already been stated that it is a tradition in the English branch of the Randolph family that John, a son of Bernard and uncle of Edward, emigrated to Virginia. There were Randolphs in that Colony at an early period besides those descended from William Randolph, who until recently has been supposed to be the earliest immigrant of that name.[3] One of the descendants of this William, in the present generation, has united himself in marriage

---

[1] Letter from Edmund Randolph, Esq., of the Isle of Wight, to the editor.

[2] Jenness's Transcripts, 155–157.

[3] Sir Egerton Brydges, Bart., in his poetical work entitled The Lake of Geneva, etc., published in Geneva, Switzerland, in 1832, devotes much space to the history of the Gibbon family, with which he was allied. He had carefully studied the English parish registers and other sources of information for that purpose. In a note he says: "A sister of Edward and Matthew married a Randolph, and thence sprang the Randolphs and Jeffersons of Virginia." Of course this is an error. Edward Randolph was not the ancestor of any Virginians, so far as is known. In another note he says: "I suppose the manor of Westcliffe descended by *gavelkind* among all the sons; for *Matthew* had a share in it. I have a letter of his regarding the distress for rent, when Randolph, who married one of his sisters, fled to America." In the Gentleman's Magazine for the year 1797, Sir Egerton Brydges also states that "tradition relates that Mr. Randolph, having for some years rented the mansion and estate at Westcliffe, till by imprudence he was involved in considerable arrears of rent, fled to America, where he founded a family who have made figure in the Congress there." Edward Randolph, who is the "Mr. Randolph" here referred to, did not "flee to America," nor, it is hardly necessary to say, was he the founder of a family here. There is a strong probability, however, that the persistent tradition in the Randolph family of England that one or more of the Randolphs of Kent settled in Virginia, rests upon a solid foundation. See New England Hist. and Gene. Register, xxix. 233–237.

with the English Randolphs. The Rev. William Cater
Randolph, eldest son of the late Rev. Henry J. Randolph
and his wife Frances, eldest daughter of Beckford Cater,
Esq., married, in 1847, Grace, daughter of the Rev. Herbert
Randolph, mentioned above.[1]

Another person, who I am inclined to believe was a relative of Edward Randolph, resided for a short time in Boston.
This was Giles[2] Master, a lawyer by profession. As has
already appeared, Edward Randolph's mother was a daughter
of Gyles Master, of Canterbury. The latter had a son Giles,
or Gyles, and he would be likely to follow his father's profession, — the law. Of the attorneys practising in the courts
of Massachusetts at this period, besides Master, we have the
names of Benjamin Bullivant, Christopher Webb, George
Farewell, Anthony Checkley, James Graham, Hayman, and
King. Thomas Newton, who was employed as an attorney
in the early stages of the witchcraft trials, and who subsequently held various important offices in New Hampshire
and in Massachusetts, came a little later than the others
above named. He was an able and much respected man,
and a well-educated lawyer. As to the others, we know very
little concerning their professional qualifications.

[1] The descent of the Rev. William
Cater Randolph is as follows: Robert[1] Randolph of Hammes, Suffolk, m.
Rose Roberts of Hawkhurst, Kent;
their son William[2] (b. 1572, d. 1660),
by his first wife, Elizabeth Smyth, was
father of Thomas, the poet (b. 1605,
d. 1634), and by his second wife, Dorothy Lane, had Richard[3] (b. 1621, d.
1671), who m. Elizabeth Ryland. Richard and Elizabeth had William[4] (b.
1650, d. 1711), who m. Mary Isham.

This William was born in Warwickshire,
emigrated to Virginia, and died there.
William[4] and Mary had Isham[5] (b. 1687,
d. 1742), m. Jane Rogers, and their son
William[6] (d. 1791) m. Elizabeth Little,
whose son Henry Jones[7] (b. 1777) m.
Frances Cater, and had William Cater,
named in the text.

[2] He wrote his Christian name as it
is given in the text; but in the records
of the Superior Court of the county of
Suffolk, the name is invariably *Gyles*.

Amsterdam, accidentally came into my hands a letter from Boston, which I had time to copy.[1]

Randolph sent a copy of the letter to Judge Dudley of Massachusetts, who showed the same to Mather and subsequently furnished him with a copy. The following is the copy of the letter[2] furnished to Dr. Mather: —

LETTER TO REV. THOMAS GOUGE.

To my worthy ffreind Mr. G: in Amsterdam By way of Barbados.

BOSTON in New England,
the 3th of Xth 1683.

S[R], — I am obliged to you for your favour in writing me by o[r] Agents return, which letter I have received, and observe what you write concerning affairs in England, and how o[r] friends are there wrongfully abused. I am glad God hath preserved o[r] good friend Mr. Fergusson, and sent him over to y[r] side the water, where their malice cannot reach him. Wee have (before y[m] came to hand) heard the great sufferings of several of the servants of the Lord. What you say as to their intentment to root out God's word from amongst us, I will say with the Lord's Prophet, The Righteous also shall see this and fear, and shall laugh them to scorn. I am well assured of y[e] happiness of that great freind of God's cause, the Lord of Shaftsbury, who you say, dyed in our friend Mr. Kick's house. If they could, wee [he?] should certainly have bin cut off by those Evil doers, for they can now mould the lawe as [they] please,

---

[1] Palfrey's Hist. of New England, iii. 558.

[2] Mather Papers, Prince Coll., Boston Public Library. A copy of this letter was communicated to the New Eng. Hist. and Gen. Register for January, 1885, by G. D. Scull, Esq., of Oxford, England. That copy bears date "9th of y[e] 10th, 1683." It is to be noticed, however, that Randolph in two instances speaks of the letter as dated Dec. 3, 1683. The copy of the letter in the Register differs but slightly from the copy used at the trial; some words being left out in the latter, and others substituted; but the meaning is the same.

and make it their study more to please men then God. Corrupt are they, and are become abominable in their wickedness. There is none that doeth good. Jehovah looked down from Heaven upon the children of men, to see if there were any that would understand, and seek after him. No, all are seeking after vanity, and have not God before their eyes. Truly, I must say with you, never was any age gone so farr in whoring after their own lusts and pleasures. Yea, from the King y' sitteth on the throne to the beggar. An unwise man doth not well consider this, and a fool doth not regard it. It was a great greife to mee to hear the death of that good Lord Russel, and how barbarously the Earle of Essex was murthred in the Tower. Wee may see with halfe an Eye which way they intend to drive poor England. Well, we can onely say with holy David, O' God shall come, and shall not keep silence, there shall go before him a Consuming fire ; A mighty Tempest shall be stirred up round about him, to whom wee will Committ all our Concerns.

I thank you for the Care you have taken in getting those prints in readiness to send me by ye next shipping. Pray lett mee have the following books sent me with them. The new Covenant of Scotland, Caril upon Job, and Mr. Owen's last works, with some of yo' new Geneva prints, that I may collect of all to sweeten the milk to the Pallats of those good Christians, who, praysed bee God, receive with cheerfulness our administration. I am glad the Lord hath raised up a defender for his People in Hungary, and I am certain[ly] of opinion, the Lord's work will bee done by those heathen, and the whore of babylon shall fall. His late signs in the heavens did foretell such Works. My prayer shall bee continually for their victory, for certain it is his will it shall bee so. As to affairs in these parts, which you desire to have an account of; I shall tell you. The same week as our Agents arrived, Randolph did also arrive with a Summons from the King for our Charter. The next day after hee arrived, hapned a sad fire, which burnt down the richest part of the Town, which some believe was done by his means ; for hee went out of Town, or certainly hee would have

ended his dayes through some of y⁰ tumultuous sufferers. Hee
has made it his business to spread the King's declaration all about
the Countrey, and perswaded two Colonies to fall off from uniting
with us. A General Court hath bin called here, which has been
held fourteen dayes. The Governor and several of the Magistrates,
not regarding their oath to God and the Countrey, esteeming rather
to please his Majesty, have voted to surrender up their Charter, butt
y⁰ Deputy Governour with other Magistrates, and most of the
house of Deputyes, who fear God more then man, are for keeping
o' priviledges, which is my opinion also, for I cannot understand
why wee should give away what the Lord God hath afforded [us];
and whatever the Event may bee, wee ought to stand by y^m with o'
lives and fortunes,[1] for so Ahab required Naboth's vineyard. Wee
have had great encouragement from England, for several Good and
Worthy men among the Law Doctors have Councelled us to stand
it out at Law, which most give us hopes wee shall bee able to maintain, though the Charge bee very great. Butt in England Money
will do much.

This Randolph hath been a mortal Enemy to our Countrey, and
most say, if hee had not moved his Matie it would never have been
his Concern, for hee was satisfyed with our sending away the Com-
mission^n which came over some years past. It hath cost these
people a great deal of Money, and if two or three thousand Pound
will buy it off, wee have those who will give it. Wee have good
friends in England who will largely contribute, butt dare not bee
seen, for fear of troubles. Wee expect great quantity's of o' friends
to come over from England; God will certainly avenge the blood
of his Saints, and those who live shall see it, and fear our Great
Jehovah. Oh, that wee may not bow the knee to Baal, nor worship
any graven Image. Our God is y⁰ Great God, and Jehovah is his
name. Hee hath strengthned his people in the Wilderness, and

---

[1] This phrase, "our lives and fortunes," very frequently met with during
the last hundred years, was not common
in the seventeenth century. Bernard
Randolph in his letter (note 2, page
291) uses the words "my life and fortune." I do not find this expression elsewhere in the "Mather Papers."—H.

made his Power known amongst the heathen. Yett wee have some
who run a whoring after their own Inventions, and fall off from o^r
Church. Oh that God would send a Daniel to interpret the visions
which o^r King may dayly see in the Heavens, least it be said no
more, beware, beware, butt vengance fall upon the nation : I will
say with John the Divine, Here is Wisedom ; lett him that hath
understanding count the number of the Beast, for it is the number
of a man, and his number is six hundred, threescore and six, and
God will certainly fulfill his sayings. Pray when you see M^r
fferguson, give him my kind salutes. If hee continue his resolution
of coming over here, hee may bee sure of an hearty welcome ; butt
I fear hee must bee forced to change his name, for though wee have
power in our Charter to receive and protect who fly for persecution
sake, as wee did Gouff and Whaley, yett wee fear that Priviledge will
bee forced from us. God grant wee may have the Enjoyment of our
heavenly Charter, which Jesus Christ hath Purchased for us, and
would also bee demanded, if some dare venture, butt there wee shall
meet, and the Sheep shall bee known from the Goates ; butt now a
Jesuit is a Courtier, a servant, and what you will, so as hee bee no
Enemy of ye Court, hee may bee any thing. Some report here
that Mr Oates is out of favour for discovering the Popish Plott.
Had hee but sworn for them, hee would certainly [have] been a
Bishop, if Sr L. J.¹ had pleased. This comes to you by way of
Barbados, a Jew going thither, and so for your place, has promised
to deliver it into yor own hands. Pray give my hearty respects to
Good Mr. Kick, to whom I will write by a ship that may sayl about
three weeks hence. Mr. Kick's son 's a hopefull young man, and
one, I dare say, that fears the Lord. Randolph returns upon a ship
which will sayl about three weeks hence. God will certainly follow
him wherever hee goes, for hee has much prejudiced us. If hee
should miscarry, it is God's Just Judgment. Pray let mee hear
from you by all occasions, and lett your prayers bee for us as wee
continually pray for you, and all the true servants of ye Lord. I

---

¹ Leoline Jenkins.

will conclude in saying, the Lord liveth, and blessed bee my strong helper, and praysed bee the God of o' Salvation, Jehovah is his name. To him I commit you, and in all sincerity am

Yours in Christ Jesus, I. M.

Coppied out October 24, 1684.

Thereupon Dr. Mather addressed the following letter to Judge Dudley: —

WORTHY SIR, — I returne you my humble thanks for your civility, in letting me have a coppy of a letter pretended to be dated at Boston, the 3: 10: 1683, & subscribed I: M. which it seemeth to some that know me not, to have supposed me to be the Author of it, but I assure you it is none of myne. The forger of it begins with a lye, in the first line, for he speakes as if Mr. Gouge had written to me by our Agents, which he never did, and as if he had informed me as if the Earle of Shaftsbury died in Mr. Kick's house, when as no man ever writ any such thing to me. He represents me as a person well assured of Shaftsbury's happiness, and as esteeming him the great freind of God's cause. They that are acquainted with me knowe that I never had an high opinion of that Gentleman. This manifests the letter to be a peece of forgery. As for that reflection on his maj^{ty}, and what is added concerning the Lord Russell & Essex, they are the Expressions of the forger, and none of mine. He pretends as if I sent to Amsterdam for the New Covenant of Scotland, Carill upon Job, and Mr. Owen's last works. Now herein he has so grossly played the fool, soe as to discover the letter to be a meer peece of forgery. As for the new Covenant of Scotland, I never heard of such a thing, untill I saw it in this wicked letter, nor do I to this day vnderstand what is the meaning of it. Carill have been in my study this fiveteen years, & if I had him not, it is [not?] likely that I should send to Amsterdam, for Mr. Carill & Doct. Owen's works, which are here sould in Boston. I might obtaine them sooner and cheaper from London, then from

Holland, and whether such books are to be bought in Amsterdam or no, I knowe not. By this then onely he spitts some of his vennome against some of those excellent men, of whom the world was not worthy : but he addeth with some of the Geneva prints, that I may collect of all to sweeten the milke to the pallats of those good Christians, who receave with cheerfullness our administrations. This is extreemly foolish. I hope that no man that is acquainted with me, can suppose such ridiculous stufe had dropt from my pen. He farther represents me as that I knew by the signes in the Heavens, that the heathens should destroye the whore of Babilon. In this also he hath acted like a fool, for now all men may know that this letter was never written by me, since my judgment is declared in print express contradictory ; soe what is here pretended in my books of Commits, page 129 & 130, I endeavor to prove by the scripture that Rome shall not be distroyed by Mohemet, but by other hands ; and how often have I declared that the appearance of a blazing star is not to be slighted, that mortalls cannot tell what the particuler events are, that shall followe, yet such Phinominas are seen, when the forger of lies goes on & tells how Randolph was suspected to have had a hand in the last fier in Boston, & that if he had not gon out of towne, the tumultuous sufferers would have ended his dayes. Now these are things I never heard of before, therefore I could not write them. The letter forger saith that Randolph has perswaded two Collonies to fall of from vniting with us. This is a great vntruth, & some upon reasonable termes conjecture that no man except Randolph could tell such a impudent lye, when the whole Contry knowes the contrary. What he farther adds of the Governor & Dep[ty] Governor, as concerning the Hon[ble] Govern[r] is a scandelous falsehood, & so discovers the malice of the forger, not onely against me, but against this Collony, nor is it likely that I should speake of mens venturing their lives & fortunes,[1] that being an expression no wayes sutable to my genius. He also sheweth himselfe to be a child of the Divill, by what he writeth concern-

---

[1] See note 2, page 291.

ing Doct^r Oates, & S^r L: J:, of neither of whom did I write any thing. He pretends, in the close of his forgery, as if I had sent the letter by a Jew by way of Barbados. This doth moore fully demonstrate the forgery ; for I knew not that there was any Jew in Boston the last winter, nor did I learne that any Jew did go from thence to Barbados ; to be sure, I saw none, nor did I ever send a letter by any Jew in my life. Belike the Jew's name that carried the letter was either Edward, or Bernard Randolph. I shall take notice but of one passage more in this letter, which in sume respect is moor wicked then all the rest. He brings me in sending keind salutes to Mr. Ferguson, & assuring him of hearty welcome to New England, if he held his resolution of coming hither. Ferguson is a person with whom I have no manner of acquaintance I never sent salutations to him by any one, or at any time, nor did I ever heare that he had thoughts of coming to New England, vntill this letter-forger, who is not to be believed, said it. Whereas he addeth, we had power by our Charter to protect those, who flye for Protection sake, as we did Goff & Whaly, this dos suffitiently intimate who was the authur of this forgery, viz. that it was Randolph himselfe, for it is well knowne, he did once exhibit a complaint against this Collony, because in their Law-book it is declared, if men fly thether, being persecuted, they shall finde favour, and [the] lying comment that Randolph made vpon it, was by virtue of this law of the people in New England, in showing kindness to Goff & Whaley. Let all rationall men judge whether any one but Randolph was the Authur of this Forgery. Besides there is so much said of Randolph in this spurious letter, that giveth just cause to suspect him to be the Father of it. It is reported that he has a notable art in imitating hands, that he can doe it soe exactly, that a man cannot easily discerne the knavery, & that one of the Randolphs being detected of such villany, is lately fled, to save his ears. Whether, as some say, he has imitated my hand, in his forgery, I know not, or whether he has forged any moor letters with this, and fathered his Bratts upon me, only I hope that good will come out of it. However, tis good that all mankind will be convinced that Randolph is a great knave, for he that will forge such a bloody letter, that so he may do mischiefe, not only to an Innocent man, but to an honnest People, what wickedness & inhumanity will he not be guilty of, if he doth but think that his villany shall not be discovered. But I am not the first that have been thus abused. I finde in the History of Sham Plotts, in page 16 & 17, that treasonable letters w[ere] forged and laid to the charge of severall Nonconformist ministers, Mr. Baxter, Doct^o Conant, and other men of great worth; but the impious Authurs thereof were detected, to theire shame. And soe I dought not but it will be in this case, and rather because the forger has highly abused the Glorious name of the blessed God, not onely by a profane Cotation of many scriptures, which were not mentioned by me, but by mentioning the sacred title of the most high God, to serve a wicked designe. In the superscrition of his forgery he mentions the name of Jesus Christ, and four times he mentions the dreadfull name Jehovah, which is a name that for some reasons not needfull here to be exprest, I doe verry rarely mention, and that is a farther manifestation, that this letter was not of my Composure. Such has been the desperate prophaness of the Atheisticall Authur of this forged letter, that rather then not attempt the doeing of mischiefe to New England, and to me, who am one of the least of the ministers of God therein; he will attempt God himselfe, to vindicate his owne name upon him, but I beleeve as to your selfe, S^r, to whom I am knowne, I am certaine that before ever you spake with me about it, you were perswaded the letter was none of myne, since it was not written in my stile, and there are things in it obhorrid to my knowne Principles. You may communicate this to whome you please.

I am, s^r, y^r humble serv INCREASE MATHER.[1]

BOSTON, the 10th November, 1684.

When Randolph learned that Mather had written the foregoing letter to Dudley, he solicited and obtained a copy,

[1] The spelling of this letter is not Mather's. — H.

and subsequently brought an action of trespass on the case against Mather for defamation, laying his damages at £500. The writ was dated Dec. 24, 1687.[1] Mather was arrested by virtue of the following precept:—

SUFFOLK ss.

By Vertue of his Maj^{ts} Writt of Capias to me Directed, Returnable before his Maj^{ts} Justices at the Next Superior Court of Pleas, to be held in Boston on the Last Tuesday in January nexte, you shall Arest Increase Mather to Answer To Edward Randolph, Esqir: of a Plea of Trespas uppon the Case, to the Plaintiff's Damage five hundred pounds. Da^t the 24th of Decē. & in the Thirde year of his Maj^{ts} Reigne.

L. S.

> JAMES SHIRLOCK, Sher^{ff}.

Vera Copia. THOMAS LARKIN.[2]

During the pendency of the suit against Dr. Mather, he received from one of the lawyers whom he consulted the following "opinion" of the law applicable to his defence:[3]—

---

[1] The long interval between the date of Mather's letter to Dudley and the bringing of the suit may have been owing in part to Randolph's long and frequent absences from New England. In this connection the following letter from Dudley to Randolph is noteworthy, as coming from a justice of the court.

To Edward Randolph, Esq.

S^r,—I made my Excuse yesterday to Mr West [secretary of the Council] for my absence. I am this morning ill and uncapable to ride. You have already a copy of the letter you desire, and that which is in my hand is not Mr Mather's own writing, but only his subscription. What may be done with the one will alike be done by the other. Give my humble Seirvice to his Excellency. I wish his health while I want my own.

> Your serv^t,

15 Dec. 1687. J. DUDLEY.

[2] Prince Coll.

[3] The manuscript copy of this "opinion" is in the Prince Collection, and with other papers, letters, etc., relating to this suit, has been printed by the Mass. Hist. Society in the "Mather Papers." The manuscript copy is unsigned, and there is nothing to show who was the author. In the "Mather Papers," as printed, this paper is signed "C. C.;" but the copyist evidently misread the abbreviation "&c." for the initials of the writer. The handwriting in the manuscript somewhat resembles Bradstreet's, but it would seem probable that Checkley was the author. In order to make the sense clearer, quotation marks are now placed before and after the words taken from Mather's letter to Dudley of Nov. 10, 1684.

As to the Action of Defamation

Please To Know that as to things incertaine or dubious noe ꝑticular Action can be coͫenced vpon. Now 't is noe where asserted in that Lr̃e that Edward Randolph was the Forger of that Lr̃e. As to that (that "belike the Jewes Name was either Edward or Bernard Randolph;") 't is not ꝑticularly appropriated to Edward Randolph, soe that for the incertainctye thereof Noe Action can lye at the Suite of Edward Randolph, and "one of the Randolphs being detected of such villanye is lately fled to save his Eares," which cannot touch Edward, and that "Randolph is a great Knave," is too geñall to Coͫence an Action vpon, and that "'t is suspected that he may be the author thereof," is too geñall still to maintcyne an Action ; and as to an Action for words, it cannot bee, for that the ꝑper words for such action are (Retulit, p'palavit, & publicavit in auditu quam plurimorum subditorum Dñi Regis in his anglicanis verbis videlͭ &c.) ; then writeing of a Lr̃e barely to one I cannot vnderstand to be a publication, altho the ꝑson to whome the Lr̃e was Writt doe shew it to seuerall ; but he may be said to publish, &c.

But let them first prove the Lr̃e to be yours, which you need not owne, and you may safely plead, That you are not guilty (modo & forma ut querens versus eum queritur). Et de hoc poñ se sup. patriam &c.   In hast, I am Yrs, &c.

Just before or during the trial of the suit, Dr. Mather addressed the presiding justice the following letter. Such a proceeding in the present day would be regarded as extraordinary and highly improper. It contains one very significant and important statement (printed in italics), to be noticed hereafter.

These for the Honorable Joseph Dudley, Esq. in Roxbury.[1]

Sʀ, — I have for many years showed all the respect to yourselfe & yours which I could do, & have wished for an opportunity of doing more. Providence has so ordered that it is now in your power to do

---

[1] Prince Coll.

me a kindness. I desire nothing but what is just & righteous, & therefore am confident you will hearken to me. I then pray you to consider whether it can stand with justice in M.ʳ R[andolph]s case to find for him at all. For 1. I never did positively charge him with the forged letter ; only declared my suspicion. Now, except the charge be positive and particular the case is not actionable as a slander. *The truth is I never thought that hee (& therefore could not charge him,) but a brother of his was the forger,* only I wish he can *bonâ fide,* clear himselfe from being privy to that wickedness. 2. No man can say that my name was subscribed with my owne hand, or that the Scribe might not mistake several words, & send a wrong copy to yourselfe. 3. M.ʳ R. is legally guilty. Hee that has falsely to the Secretary of State and others, charged me with a letter which is a forged thing, is legally guilty of that Forgery. But M.ʳ R. has done so. In his letter to M.ʳ Bradstreet, (who has bin so kind as to give it to me) dated 7ᵇᵉʳ 4, 1684, he confesseth that hee informed Sir L[eoline] J[enkins] & several of the Lords, that I was the Author of that letter to M.ʳ Gouge. And in his letter to M.ʳ Shrimpton dated July 18ᵗʰ 84, (which I have by me likewise) hee accuseth me with that treasonable letter. I have little knowledge in the Statutes of the Land, but some acquaintance with the Laws of God I ought to have. If that statute, Deut. 19, 18, 19, 20, may take place, M.ʳ R. ought to dye the death for having falsly & maliciously accused me with a capital crime.

These things I thought it my concern humbly to suggest to you. I comend you to God, and rest, Sir,

Yours to serve you,   I. MATHER.

January 24, 1687[-8].

S.ʳ, — I must entreat you to be as kind to me as M.ʳ Bradstreet has bin, in giving me M.ʳ R.'ˢ letter to yourselfe with which hee sent the Forged Letter of mine.

The official record of the pleas, trial, and judgment in this suit has disappeared from the files of the court. Not a paper or line remains; but from fragmentary copies of papers preserved in the Prince Collection and in the State archives I am able to compile the following statement. The cause came on for trial at a term of the Superior Court for the county of Suffolk, on the last Tuesday of January, 1687–8. The Court consisted of Joseph Dudley, presiding justice, William Stoughton, associate justice, and several of the justices of the peace for the county aforesaid. Farewell and Hayman appeared for the plaintiff; Master and Checkley for the defendant. The jury chosen to try the case was composed of the following persons, all of Boston; namely, George Turfrey, Adam Winthrop, William Hobby, Gervaise Ballard, Robert Howard, William Gibson, Simeon Stoddard, Bozoan Allen, Humphrey Parsons, Thomas Stanbury, and Duncan Campbell.

The following note of the trial, hitherto unprinted, is, for various reasons, interesting:—

RANDOLPH Dec⁴ in Defamačon. Dam. £500. Checkley & Master
vs. for Def¹. plead not Guilty. Hayman for Pl¹ opened y⁵
MATHER. Declar. Farewell pursued & read y⁵ Letter. The Letter was wrott by y⁵ Def¹ to y⁵ Pres'd¹, but he Says he never published y⁵ Same to any.

To proue y⁵ publičon of y⁵ Letter M⁵ Farewell produces
Jn⁰ Hale of Beverley
Gyles Master.

Hale Objects ag¹ Swearing on y⁵ bible & was Admitted to Sweare by holding up his hand.

It was demanded of Hale if Euer he heard or Saw a Letter wrott by M⁵ Mather to y⁵ purports of that menčoned in y⁵ dec¹

Sayes that ab[t] 3 years agoe heareing of a Letter that was published in England in abuse of y[e] Def[t] & ab[t] which remarkes was made by y[e] observator, he asked M[r] Mather ab[t] it, who told him it was a false thing putt on him, & showed him a paper where in he had vindicated himselfe, w[ch] he delivered him to Shew to others & Satisfie them therein, & that he did both Shew it & declare it to Seurall persons, & y[e] writeing was Sometime out of his hands, but was after Returned to M[r] Mather againe. That y[e] writeing he receiued from M[r] Mather was a Letter directed to y[e] Presid[t], that it was Something like what he heard now read, but cannot remember eury Perticuler: that y[e] paper M[r] Mather gaue him Seem[d] to be a coppy of a Letter wrott to y[e] Presd[t], but whether it was a true Coppy or not does not know, nor whether y[e] Letter in y[e] dec[l] be diverse or y[e] Same.

The Letter being read in part, Some he remembers & Some does not. Says he Lent y[e] paper to Deacon Hill, & ab[t] 3 yeares Since, on M[r] Mathers desire, he Returned it to him againe; he after Says he lett M[r] Higginson & M[r] Cobbitt haue y[e] paper & to many others of meaner Rank.

Master Ownes y[e] Seeing y[e] letter long before y[e] accōn Commencs. Farewell Sworne. Sayes he Saw y[e] Letter ab[t] 9 months Since in Boston.[1]

As might have been expected under the circumstances, the plaintiff failed in his suit, and was compelled to pay the costs.

It has never been ascertained beyond a doubt who was the author of the forged letter. Independent of the contents of the letter itself, Dr. Mather's denial of the authorship should have been sufficient at the time, and must be

[1] Mass. Archives.

so regarded now. Was Edward Randolph the author? As we have seen, Dr. Mather says in his letter to Dudley (Jan. 24, 1687–8): "The truth is I never thought that hee [Edward Randolph] (& therefore could not charge him) but a brother of his was the forger." However inconsistent this statement seems to be when compared with the general tone of Mather's previous letter to Dudley, dated Nov. 10, 1684, it must be accepted as true. But Mather's denial as to himself, and his exculpation of Edward Randolph from the charge of forging the letter, must go together. It is testimony of the highest value in favor of Edward Randolph from one who had greatly suffered and was still suffering, as he believed, at Randolph's hands.[1]

It is remarked above (page 278), that "in the records of that age no name is branded by writers with so many, so varied, and so strongly denunciatory epithets as that of Edward Randolph." In the forged letter, falsely attributed to Dr. Increase Mather, the writer, using a phrase which had undoubtedly become familiar to his ears, speaks of Edward Randolph as "a mortal enemy" of New England. In his letter of Nov. 10, 1684, to Dudley, as given above, Dr. Mather calls Randolph "a child of the Divill," whatever

[1] In the elaborate note appended to the forged letter, in the eighth volume (4th series) of the Collections of the Mass. Hist. Society, the editor, Dr. Chandler Robbins, demonstrates beyond a reasonable doubt that Mather was not the author of the letter, and in that note and elsewhere expresses his belief that Edward Randolph was the author. He seems to have overlooked the letter of Mather to Dudley of Jan. 24, 1687, printed in the same volume, or to have regarded it as inconclusive. Dr. Palfrey (History, iii. 557) discusses the same subject, and comes to the conclusion that neither Increase Mather nor Edward Randolph was the author. His suggestion as to the possibility that Dr. Cotton Mather was the author is not likely to have much weight. Cotton Mather, although afflicted from boyhood with the disease known as *cacoethes scribendi*, and through his whole life the victim of pedantic tastes and the conceit of all knowledge "in half a dozen languages," was neither a fool nor a knave. We do not see any motive inducing him to write the letter.

that may mean, and "a great Knave." These are certainly vigorous epithets, and the more remarkable as coming from the amiable and courteous Increase Mather, who, unlike his famous son Cotton, was rarely "surprised in his cups"— of rhetoric highly spiced with capital letters and italics. Randolph himself was not incapable, when it served his purpose, of graphic or pungent phrases, an example of which occurs in his letter of July 18, 1684, to Shrimpton,[1] where he characterizes Mather as "the bellows of sedition." Cotton Mather, who is not open to the charge of undue affection for Randolph, nor of feebleness of invective concerning those whom he hated or disliked, had his last shot in 1724, when he wrote as follows: "I will here take my *Eternal Farewell* of him, with Relating That he proved a *Blasted Wretch*, followed with a sensible *Curse* of GOD wherever he came; Despised, Abhorred, Unprosperous." [2]

A collection of some of the epithetical phrases referred to above may not be altogether uninteresting; and the reader may perhaps discover who is entitled to the credit, if credit there be, of their primary use. The following list has been gathered in a somewhat hasty glance at the books:—

"Randolph, who, the people of New England said, 'went up and down to devour them.'" (Hutchinson's Hist., 1764, p. 319.)

"Messenger of death." (Hutchinson's Hist., 1764, p. 337.)

"Messenger of death." (By the unknown author of the British Dominions in North America, etc., London, 1773, p. 147.)

"The angel of death." (Belknap's Hist., 1784, i. 117.)

"The public accuser of those days." (Morse and Parish's Hist., 1804, p. 294.)

[1] Coll. Mass. Hist. Soc., viii., Fourth Series, 96.
[2] Parentator, or Remarkables of Dr. Increase Mather, 107.

"An enemy." (Holmes's Annals, 1805, i. 394.)

"The evil genius of Massachusetts." (Holmes's Annals, 1805, i. 410.)

"An active and implacable adversary to New England." (Elliott's Biog. Dic., art. *Randolph.*)

"The general enemy and accuser of the free." (Graham's Hist., 1827, i. 438.)

"The general enemy of American liberty." (Graham's Hist., 1836, i. 370.)

"The hated messenger." (Bancroft's Hist., ii. 124.)

"'The Evil Genius of New England,' or, as he is called, her 'Angel of death.'" (Washburn's Jud. Hist. of Mass., 129.)

"That indefatigable enemy." (Hildreth's Hist., 1849, i. 504.)

"The enemy." (Palfrey's Hist., 1864, iii. 289.)

In a letter of Randolph to Governor Winslow of the Plymouth Colony, dated January 29, 1679–80, he states that he had just returned to Boston from New Hampshire, where he remained from December 27 to January 22; and adds that he was "received at Boston more like a spy than one of His Majesty's servants. They kept a day of thanks for the return of their agents [Stoughton and Bulkley], but have prepared a welcome for me by a paper of scandalous verses, all persons taking liberty to abuse me in their discourses, of which I take the more notice, because it so much reflects upon my master, who will not forget it."[1] The following are the verses[2] to which he refers:—

RANDOLPH'S WELCOME BACK AGAINE.

WELCOME, S', welcome from y' eastern shore,
With a commission stronger than before
To play the horse-leach; rob us of our Fleeces,
To rend our land, and teare it all to pieces:

[1] Coll. Mass. Hist. Soc., vi. 92.
[2] Hist. Coll., by Farmer and Moore, iii. 30.

Welcome now back againe ; as is the whip
To a Foole's back ; as water in a ship.
Boston make roome, Randolph's returned, that hector,
Confirm'd at home to be ye sharp Collector ;
Whoe shortly will present unto y^r viewes
The Greate Broad Seale that will you all amuse, —
Unwelcome tidings, and unhappy newes.

New England is a very loyall shrubb
That loues her Soueraigne, hates a Beelzebub :
That's willing (let it to her praise be spoake)
To doe Obedience to the Royall Oake,
To pay the Tribute that to it belongs,
For shielding her from Injuries and Wrongs :
But you the Agent, S^r, shee cannot brook ;
Shee likes the Meate, but can't abide the Cook.
Alas, shee would haue Cæsar haue his Due,
But not by such a wicked Hand as you :
For an acknowledgement of Right, wee scorne
(To pay to our greate Lord a pepper-corn)
To baulke the Tearmes of our most Gratious Deed,
But would ten thousand times the same exceed.

Some call you Randall — *Rend-all* I you name,
Soe you 'll appear before you 've played y^r Game.
Hee that keeps a Plantaçon, Custom-house,
One year, may bee a Man, the next a Mouse.
Y^r brother *Dyer* [1] hath the Divell played,
Made the New-Yorkers at the first affraide,
Hee vapoured, swagger'd, hector'd (whoe but hee ?)
But soon destroyed himself by Villanie.
Well might his cursed name w^th *D* begin,
Who was a Divell in his hart for Sin,

---

[1] William Dyer (Hutchinson, i. 330, writes the name *Dyre*) was appointed surveyor-general of customs, Jan. 4, 1683. He came to New York with Gov. Andros in 1674. See N. Y. Col. Docs., iii. 221 ; Mass. Rec., v. 383, 386, 530 ; Mass. Hist. Coll., Fourth Series, viii. 533. — H.

And currantly did pass, by common vogue,
For the Deceitfull'st Wretch and Greatest Rogue.
By him you 're furnish't wth a sad Example —
Take heed that those you Crush don't on you trample.

Wee veryly belieue wee are not bound
To pay one Mite to you, much less a Pound.
If there were need *New England* you must know
Fiftey p. cent we 'ld on our King bestow,
And not begrutch the Off'ring, shee 's so Franck,
But hates to pay where shee will haue no thanke.
We doe presume Secundus Carrolus Rex
Sent you not here a Countrye's heart to vex.
Hee giues an Inch of power : you take an Ell.
Should it be Knowne, hee would not like it well.
If you doe Understand y^r occupation,
'T is to keepe acts of Trade from Violation.
If Merchants in their traffique will be Faire,
You must, Camelion-like, liue on the aire.
Should they not trade to Holland, Spain, and France,
Directly you must seeke for maintenance.

The Customs and the Fees will scarce supply
Belly and Back. What 's left for 's Majesty?
What you collect won't make you to look bigg
With modish Nick-Nacks, Dagger, Perriwigg ;
A courtier's garbe too costly you will see
To be maintained where is noe Gift nor Fee.
Pull downe the mill, rente the ground, you 'll finde
That very Few will come to you to grinde.
Merchants their Corne will always carry there,
Where the Tole 's easy, and the Usuage Faire.
Wee 'll Kneele to the mill-owner, as our Cheife ; ⎫
But doe not like the Miller ; he 's a Theife, ⎬
And entertaine him not wth joy, but Greife. ⎭

When Heauen would Job's signall Patience try,
He gaue Hell leaue to Plott his Misery,
And Act it, too, according to it's will,
With this exception, — don't his body kill.
Soe Royall Charles is now about to proue
Our Loyalty, Allegiance, and Loue,
In giuing Licence to a Publican,
To Pinch the Purse, but not to Hurt the Man.
Patience raised Job vnto the height of Fame,
Lett our Obedience doe for us the Same.

It is not intended in this place to enter upon an extended discussion of any one of the several questions involved in Randolph's connection with the affairs of New England from 1676 to 1689; nor to engage in a formal defence of his character or his acts against the accusations made by his enemies, and repeated by many historical writers since his day. Nor is it intended to discuss at length the conduct and motives of the leading public men of Massachusetts, during the period in question, in respect to those acts of omission or commission of which the King repeatedly complained, and on account of which he at last intervened. Whoever desires to learn the facts will resort to the original sources of information. The facts are detailed or referred to by Dr. Palfrey in his History of New England with sufficient fulness to enable the student to see very clearly whether or not the merits of that controversy were confined to one side. That able and justly esteemed author aimed to be candid and impartial; but the temptation to become the advocate of a party — a temptation that assails and triumphs over most writers of history — was not wholly resisted by him. His readers will fail to find any admission that in his judg-

ment there was a reasonable ground or proper justification
for the King's intervention.

The only other American writer of acknowledged weight
and historical learning who has treated the subject specially
and at length, is the author of a recent work on the Puritan Age and Rule in Massachusetts.[1] While naturally
disposed, it may be assumed, to make the best possible
showing for Massachusetts in that long and disagreeable
controversy which resulted in the forfeiture of the first
charter, he has stated the chief grounds of contention and
defence with fairness and frankness. The work referred
to is a contribution in the direction and in the interest
of a critical and impartial history of the period named,
and as such is a step towards a restatement of that
history.

When that restatement shall appear in a formal narrative,
as it must, we may reasonably believe it will be seen that
there were two sides to the controversy, as there were two
parties, and that by reason of their obstinacy and lack of
foresight, if not lack of statesmanship, the leaders of public
thought and action in Massachusetts were themselves chiefly
responsible for whatever of misfortune befell them in the
loss of their power and their government. But was the fall
of the theocratic government of the old Puritan leaders a
misfortune for Massachusetts or for New England? It
was based on an impracticable theory ; it had served its end,
and so was destined in the nature of things, or rather, as
we may more properly say, under the hand of Providence,

[1] The Puritan Age and Rule in 1629-1685, by George E. Ellis. Boston,
the Colony of the Massachusetts Bay,   1888.

to be removed out of the way sooner or later. It was fortunate for the people of New England that the end came when it did, and that the event was not marked by bloodshed or extreme violence.

We may also expect that some men who then rested and still rest under a load of distrust, and even hatred, will receive, when the evidence is more discriminatingly considered, a less rigorous treatment than has hitherto been visited upon them. Among these men Randolph, so long the target for invective, will probably receive a fairer estimate. His side of the case will also be presented. Justice demands that he should be fairly and fully heard.

It will appear that he was a man of no ordinary ability, and there is no evidence that he was open to reproach on the score of personal morality. It will be seen that he was not a volunteer in the mission that brought him to New England; that he came as the agent of the King, with instructions to do a prescribed work. As such he was entitled to a respectful reception and to respectful treatment. It was charged against him that he behaved rudely and arrogantly towards the authorities. The inquiry will have to be made whether or not the treatment he received would not be likely to goad a man of spirit, acting under the authority of his sovereign, into a display of intemperate zeal and the expression of irritated feelings. It was charged that he sent home exaggerated reports and malicious statements as to the motives and acts of the ruling men in New England. It must be conceded that many of his statements proved to be exaggerated; but this fault was not peculiar to Randolph. Malice is always more easily charged than proved. He wrote and probably uttered many harsh things concerning the men who resolutely and steadily labored to baffle his efforts and hinder him in the discharge of his office; but did he in any case give more than a "Roland for an Oliver"? Many other charges, more or less grave, were made against him. The question will be, whether the charges rest on credible evidence, or only on the assertions of his enemies.[1]

It will be borne in mind that he gained and retained the personal friendship of some men of good standing and influence in New England, and that he secured the confidence of three sovereigns in succession. If it be objected that to have been the trusted agent of Charles II. and of James II. reflects no credit upon him, it must be remembered that he had likewise the confidence of a better man than either, a more sagacious statesman, a far more respected sovereign,— William III., and that he died while holding an important commission from that monarch.

Of Randolph's early history little is known. It is evident that he had been educated in the classics. His occasional use of Greek and of Latin phrases, always accurate and pertinent, would indicate so much, at least. It would also appear that, previous to his coming to New England, he had been employed in the affairs of the Admiralty, and per-

---

[1] It appears that Randolph had one defect which has not been charged against him : he lacked the sense of humor. But in this he was not very different from the people among whom he lived a troubled life for ten years and more. The greatest boon for the Puritans would have been a daily newspaper, wherein the absurdities and insanities of the times might have been lashed out of sight, or out of hearing, by the whip of ridicule. One year's issue of *Punch* would have done more good than two synods, or half a dozen sessions of the General Court.

haps also in the department of Customs. His letters and reports compare favorably in style with similar papers of that day.

When Dudley was commissioned president of New England, Randolph was named as one of his counsellors, and he was also a member of the council in Andros's government. How far he was individually responsible for whatever was harsh, arbitrary, and oppressive in Andros's administration, does not appear.

The career of Andros was in most respects an ignominious failure. He and most of the men who came in his train, or were drawn about him as advisers, were singularly unsuited to the business intrusted to them. They were ill-fitted to deal with a people who aimed, even in that early period, at independence of the Crown and the Parliament, and acknowledged their allegiance only under stress or compulsion. A more conciliatory policy, a more moderate course of procedure, would in the end probably have accomplished all that the King desired.

Randolph was involved in the downfall of Andros's administration by the uprising of the people, and after a close and not very humane imprisonment in the common jail in Boston for nearly ten months, was, by the King's order, with Andros and several other prisoners, sent to England for trial. The order was dated the 30th of July, 1689, but was not complied with until the 9th of February of the following year.[1] No one appeared at the trial to support the

---

[1] Mass. Arch. xxxv. 231. The King's order required that " Sir Edmond Andros, Edward Randolph, John Trefry. and others our Subjects, that have been in like manner seized by the said People of Boston, and shall be at the Re-

charges made against the prisoners, and they were released without even a reprimand. Andros and Randolph were soon afterward appointed by the King to important offices in America.

As has already been stated, Randolph, though temporarily removed from America in consequence of the revolt against Andros's government, gained the confidence of his new sovereign, and returned to America with a new commission, and with larger powers than those previously conferred upon him. In 1691 he was made surveyor-general of His Majesty's customs in all the English Provinces and Plantations in America. How soon he entered upon the duties of his office does not appear, but it is

ceipt of these Our Commands detained there under Confinement, be forthwith sent on Board the first ship bound hither, to answer before us what may be Objected against them, and that you take care that they be Civilly used in their Passage from New England, and safely Conveyed to our Royall Presence." Some of the prisoners had been released. The order to Captain Bant to receive the prisoners, and his receipt, are as follows : —

To Gilbert Bant, Comander
  of the Ship Mehetabel.

Pursuant to his Maties Comands in his Gracious Letter of ye 30th of July last past, Copy whereof is above written, you are Required in their Maties names to receive into your charge & custody on board the Ship Mehetabel, whereof you are Comand^r, now bound for England, Sr Edmund Andros, K^{nt}, Joseph Dudley, Esqr, m^r Edward Randolph, m^r John Palmer, m^r John West, m^r James Grayham, m^r James Shelock, and m^r George Farewell, & every of them herewith delivered unto you by Cap^{te} John Fayerweather, and them safely to convay according to his Maties Comands in said Letters, which you are exactly to observe in

all Respects, hereof faile not, as you will answer the contrary at yor peril. Dated at Boston within the Colony of the Massachusetts Bay in New England the Fifth day of Feburary, 1689. In the First year of the Reign of our Sovereign Lord and Lady, William and Mary, by the grace of God King & Queen of England.

SIM: BRADSTREET, *Gov^nr*
  in the name of the Gen'all Cour.

By virtue of the withinwritten Precept Signed by the Honble Simon Bradstreet, Esqr, Governo^r, pursuant to his Majesties Comands I have received (together with the said Precept and Copy of his Maties said Comands thereabovewritten) into my charge and custody, on board the Ship Mehetabel, the severall persons named in the said precept, vizt. Sr Edmund Andros, K^{nt}, Joseph Dudley, Esqr, m^r Edward Randolph, m. John Palmer, m^r John West, m^r James Grayham, m. James Sherlock, and m^r George Farewell. As also a Letter from the Government directed to the Right Honble the Earle of Nottingham, One of his Maties most Honble Privy Councill and Princip^{ll} Secretary of State For his Ma^{es} Service. P GILBERT BANT.

BOSTON IN NEW ENGLAND,
ye 9th February, 1689 [1689-90].

probable that he came soon after receiving his commission.   From the glimpses we get of him after this time, he
would seem to have been almost constantly travelling from
one colony to another.   He was at Annapolis, Maryland,
Dec. 16, 1697, and in Philadelphia, March 17, 1698; in
New York, April 26 and May 21; in Rhode Island, May
24; in Boston, May 30; and again in New York, July 6
and August 25.   He appears to have been in London in
1699, and in 1702.   It will be observed that in his Will he
speaks of himself as about to make his seventeenth voyage
to America.   This would indicate that he crossed the ocean
many times after the date of his last commission.

Where Randolph fixed his principal residence subsequent
to 1691 has not been definitely ascertained.   Cotton Mather
says: "Anon he died in *Virginia*, and in such Miserable
Circumstances that (as it is said) he had only Two or Three
Negro's to carry him unto his Grave."[1]   If this statement
as to the circumstances of his death be true, it would seem
to indicate that he fell ill while on a journey, and died
among strangers, or at some point remote from English
habitations.   As his duties would lead him to the West
Indies, as well as to the southern Colonies, it may be he
had a residence in Virginia or in Maryland, at some place
convenient for taking ship.   It has been conjectured that he
had relatives of the same name living in Virginia, and for
that reason also fixed his residence in that Colony.   That
he did so, is rendered probable by a clause in the certificate
appended to his Will; namely, "Edward Randolph, late of
Acquamat in Virginia, deceased."   There is no place or

_____

[1] Parentator, or Remarkables of Dr. Increase Mather, 107.

district bearing this name. Doubtless Accomac is the name intended.

No complete collection of the letters and official papers of Edward Randolph has as yet been printed. His Narrative, covering his proceedings and voyages in connection with his agency in the King's affairs in New England between the years 1675 and 1687 is printed in the Andros Tracts, and in the Proceedings of the Massachusetts Historical Society for November, 1880. In the last-named publication there are also abstracts of Randolph's letters in the library of the late Sir Thomas Phillipps, of England. The Hutchinson Papers also contain letters to and from Randolph; and in the New England Historical and Genealogical Register for 1883 are other papers and letters from his pen. Several of his letters are preserved in the Bodleian Library, Oxford, and others are in the State Paper Office of England. The Historical Magazine for September, 1868, has a list of the manuscripts in the Bodleian relating to America, prepared by the late Joseph L. Chester, D.C.L. This list comprises nine papers and letters from Randolph; namely : —

1. Letter, from Boston, to Archbishop Sancroft, on the aversion of the inhabitants to the discipline of the Church, Dec. 11, 1682.

2. Letter to the same, relating to Patent of the Company for evangelizing the Indians in New England, March 26, 1684.

3. A General Account of the Patent granted to the Company mentioned above in No. 2.

4. Letter to Archbishop Sancroft, asking his assistance in raising money as bail in an action brought against him, dated Aug. 23, 1684.

5. Letter to Dr. Lloyd, Bishop of St. Asaph, on the state of affairs in Boston, March, 1685.

6. Letter to Archbishop Sancroft on the same subject, Aug. 2, 1686.

7. Letter to the same on the sad and distracted condition of New England, May 28, 1689.

8. Abstract of letters sent to Randolph from the inhabitants of Boston after the notice of the vacating of the Charter .

9. A short account of the state of New England.[1]

In the Andros Tracts[2] is a list of Randolph's letters and papers already printed, prepared by the editor of that work. This useful list, considerably enlarged, is here reproduced.

1676.

June	17.	Randolph's Letter to Sec. Coventry	Jenness's Transcripts, 60.
June	23.	Randolph's Letter to Gov. Leverett	Andros Tracts, iii. 218.
July	6.	Randolph's Letter to Gov. Leverett	Andros Tracts, iii. 219.
Sept. 20. } Oct. 12. }		Randolph's Report on the Colonies*[3]	Hutch. Coll. ii. 210.

1678.

July	9.	Randolph's Instructions from the Commissioners	Mass. H. S. Coll. xxvii. 129.

1679-80.

Jan.	4.	Randolph's Letters,—abstracts . .	Jenness's Transcripts, 84.

[1] Of the above papers, those numbered respectively 2, 3, 4, and 9 are printed in the New England Historical and Genealogical Register for April, 1883; those numbered 1, 5, 6, 7, and 8, in the Register for July, 1883. — H.

[2] Published by the Prince Society; William H. Whitmore, A.M., editor.

[3] The papers marked by an asterisk are printed in Bishop Perry's Papers relating to the Church in Massachusetts. — H.

1679–80.

Jan. 29. Randolph's Letter to Gov. Josiah Winslow relating to his proceedings at Pascataqua . . . . . Mass. H. S. Coll. vi. 92.

1680. Randolph's Instructions against the Bostoners . . . . Hutch. Coll. ii. 264.

1681–2.

Feb. 15. Randolph against Gen. Ct. of Mass. Hutch. Coll. ii. 265.

1682.

May 29. Randolph's Letter to Bp. of London Hutch. Coll. ii. 271.

June 14. Randolph's Letter to E. of Clarendon Hutch. Coll. ii. 275.

July 14. Randolph's Letter to Bp. of London Hutch. Coll. ii. 279.

Dec. 11. Randolph's Letter to Archbishop of Canterbury * . . . . His. & Gene. Reg. xxxvii. 267.

1683.

July 11. Randolph's Memorial to Archbishop of Canterbury . . . . His. & Gene. Reg. xxxvii. 268.

Sept. 2. Randolph's Letter from Gov. Leverett Palfrey's Hist. iii. 375.

Oct. 3. Randolph's Letter to Lords of Trade giving account of the Rebellion in New Hampshire . . . . . . Belknap, Farmer's ed. 463.

Dec. 13. Randolph's Letter to I. Mather . . Mass. H. S. Coll. xxxviii. 524.

1684.

Mar. 26. Randolph's Letter to Archbishop of Canterbury, with an account of the Company for Evangelizing Indians in New England * . . . . . . His. & Gene. Reg. xxxvii. 156.

Mar. —. Randolph's Short Account of Present State of New England * . . His. & Gene. Reg. xxxvii. 157.

June 19. Randolph's Letter to Gyles Randolph Tuttle's His. Papers. 325.

July 18. Randolph's Letter to S. Shrimpton . Mass. H. S. Coll. xxxviii. 524.

21. Randolph's Letter to S. Shrimpton . Mass. H. S. Coll. xxxviii. 525.

Aug. 23. Randolph's Letter to Archbishop of Canterbury * . . . . His. & Gene. Reg. xxxvii. 158.

Sept. 4. Randolph's Letter to S. Bradstreet . Mass. H. S. Coll. xxxviii. 527.

Dec. 3. Randolph's Letter to Lords of Treasury . . . . Mass. H. S. Coll. xxxviii. 530.

8. Randolph's Letter from Bradstreet . Mass. H. S. Coll. xxxviii. 527.

1684–5.

Feb. 9. Randolph's Letter to Dudley . Hutch. Coll. ii. 283.

1685.

Mar.	28.	Randolph's Letter to Bp. of St. Asaph, with abstract of Letters of S. Bradstreet and Richard Wharton *	His. & Gene. Reg. xxxvii. 268.
July	7.	Randolph's Report and Privy Council's Report	N. Y. Doc. iii. 362.
Aug.	3.	Randolph's Proposals about Quo Warranto	R. I. Rec. iii. 177.
	18.	Randolph's Proposals about Quo Warranto	R. I. Rec. iii. 178.
		Randolph's Articles against R. I. .	R. I. Rec. iii. 175.
Sept.	21.	Randolph's Commission	Mass. H. S. Coll. xxvii. 161.

1686.

May	27.	Randolph's Letter to Gov. Treat .	Conn. Rec. iii. 352.
July	7.	Randolph's Letter to Archbishop of Canterbury	Hutch. Coll. ii. 291.
July	28.	Randolph's Letter to Lords of Trade	Hutch. Coll. ii. 285.
		Randolph's Letter to W. Blathwayt	Hutch. Coll. ii. 288.
Aug.	2.	Randolph's Letter to Archbishop of Canterbury *	His. & Gene. Reg. xxxvii. 270.
	23.	Randolph's Letter to Lord Treasurer	Mass. H. S. Coll. xxvii. 154.
		Randolph's Letter to Board of Trade	R. I. Rec. iii. 205.
Oct.	27.	Randolph's Letter to Archbishop of Canterbury	Hutch. Coll. ii. 294.
Dec.	23.	Randolph's Letter to Gov. Treat .	Conn. Rec. iii. 375.
	28.	Randolph's Letter to Major Pynchon	Mass. H. S. Coll. xviii. 237.

1687.

May	21.	Randolph's Letter to Povey . . .	Hutch. Coll. ii. 297.
		Randolph's Letter to Blathwayt .	Mass. H. S. Coll. xxxviii. 531.

1687-8.

Jan.	24.	Randolph's Letter to Povey . . .	Hutch. Coll. ii. 299.
Mar.	10.	Randolph's Letter from Blathwayt .	Hutch. Coll. ii. 301.
	18.	Randolph's Letter from Povey . .	Hutch. Coll. ii. 303.

1688.

June	21.	Randolph's Letter to Povey . . .	Hutch. Coll. ii. 304.
Oct.	8.	Randolph's Letter to Lords of Trade	N. Y. Doc. iii. 567.
Nov.	9.	Randolph's Letter to Pen	Mass. H. S. Coll. xxxviii. 531.

1689.

May	16.	Randolph's Letter to Gov. of Barbados	Hutch. Coll. ii. 314.
	28.	Randolph's Letter to Archbishop of Canterbury *	His. & Gene. Reg. xxxvii. 273.

1689.

May 29.	Randolph's Letter to Lords of Trade	N. Y. Doc. iii. 578.
Nov. 25.	Randolph's Letter to Elisha Cooke .	Hutch. Coll. ii. 318.
Dec. 28.	Randolph's Letter to Brockholls . .	N. Y. Doc. iii. 664.

1692.

Sept. 28.	Randolph to John Usher . . .	Tuttle's His. Papers, 326.

1698.

April 26.	Randolph's Letter to Lords of Trade	N. Y. Doc. iv. 300.
May 16.	Randolph's Letter to Lords of Trade	N. Y. Doc. iv. 311.
30.	Randolph's Letter to Lords of Trade	R. I. Rec. iii. 339.

The following letters [1] from Randolph are now for the first time printed : —

EDWARD RANDOLPH TO GYLES RANDOLPH.

JUNE 19, 1684.

BRO. GYLES, — I have not further to trouble you by this ship only to acquaint my friends what was done in their Charter yesterday at y' Court of Chancery: A Rule for judgment to be as of this Term : but in case they shall appear by the first day of next Term & plead so as to go to tryall that Term, then the judgment not to be recorded. By the inclosed you see what is done with D' Oates. To-morrow Sir Thomas Armstrong is to be executed at Tyburn. Here was a flying report that Ferguson was taken, but that is contradicted. Be sure you [are] very exact in your ce[r]tificates for ships loaden for Barbados, Jamaica, etc : Sir Richard Dutton goes now aboard for Barbados. My blessing to my Dear children. Be careful in delivery of all my letters as directed, & believe that I am
Your very Lo: Brother,
ED. RANDOLPH.

My service to Mr. Shrimpton, Mr. Wharton, & Mr. Usher: & to all my friends.

[Endorsed, in the hand of John Usher :
" Edward Randolph's letter, 19 Ju: to Giles Randolph."]

[1] The originals of these letters are in the possession of Mr. Walter Lloyd Jeffries, who has kindly permitted copies to be taken for this volume. — H.

EDWARD RA?OLPH TO JOHN USHER.

BOSTON, Sept. 28, 1692.

SIR, — I have scarce wᵉd my mouth since eat a messe of good broath at your house foᵣny Breakfast: where your lady, son Jeffryes, your daughter Jefyes, Jenny, John, David, and little pretty Betty are all well: I ꜀ not question your manage[ment] every where, nor the respect ꜱown you by yᵉ Inhabitants where you have to do: yett we are no without some foolish sham discourse which no wise body believes, ho' many fooles employ themselves about it. I expected Mr. Hirst ꜰf Salem here to make out the truth of what he said to me about yᵉ Dutch bottom at Great Island & salt. But upon a second enq iry she was loaded with European goods and came directly from Cales [Cadiz] & was consigned to Mʳ Gedney & Mʳ Hirst, havirg Goods & bills for building a very large ship So that she is seizᴂle. Mʳ Brenton (Jᵗˢ· Court) [?] has appealed, but against a verdict ᴋ judgment in Court: & he can make nothing of it. Now, if Mʳ Elliott can prove her unlivery [unlading?] of Goods before Entry, pray upon your Establishing of Courts both ship & cargo of salt be prosecuted upon my Information, you will save the King's & your third part, & pay the charges of my journey & save Mʳ Brenton 100 £: which he will be forced to pay if Tho: Wilkinson obtain a confirmation of his verdict. You will hear from me befor I leave this place. I am, dear frind,

Your obliged humble s'v't,

ED. RANDOLPH.

Let Mʳ Newton be retained for me.

APPENDIX.

APPENDIX.

No. 1. Page 108.

COMBINATIONS FOR LOCAL GOVERNMENT IN NEW HAMPSHIRE.

THE grant of territory in New England to Capt. John Mason did not confer upon him any power of political government; but the grant of so much power as should be necessary to protect his own rights and the rights of his servants, as well as to preserve order, must be understood as implied in the concession made to him. In the absence of any general government, even of the simplest sort, the several communities or clusters of inhabitants in New Hampshire found themselves compelled at an early period to combine for self-protection. These separate communities were settled at and in the neighborhood of Strawberry Bank (Portsmouth), Great Island (New Castle), Exeter and Dover.

The Lower Pascataqua.

It is not possible, at the present time, to determine the year when the inhabitants on the lower Pascataqua, including Strawberry Bank, Great Island, and Little Harbor, first entered into a "combination" or local government. Hubbard[1] says, that "after Captain

---

[1] History of New England, 219, 220.

42

Neal's going away " to England (1633) the inhabitants entered into a combination for the better enabling them to live orderly one by another." They chose for their first governor " Mr. Francis Williams, an agent sent by Captain Mason, this Williams being a prudent man, and of better quality than the rest." He held this office for several years. In 1638 he exercised his authority, seemingly, however, beyond the limits of his jurisdiction, in quelling the violent disturbance at Dover, which grew out of the factious disputes between Larkham and Knollys and their respective partisans.[1]

It would appear that the inhabitants on the lower Pascataqua entered into a combination for a second time previous to 1643. The editor of the Provincial Papers of New Hampshire mentions an existing court record, bearing date the year last named, in which " John Pickering is injoyned to deliver the old combination of Strawberry Bank the next court." And in the grant of glebe lands by the " inhabitants of the lower end of Pascataquack," May 25, 1640, signed by " Francis Williams, Governor, Ambrose Gibbins, Assistant," and others, reference is made to an existing " combination."[2] The record of both the earlier and later combinations has undoubtedly perished, nor is there any record of their substance. When Massachusetts extended her jurisdiction over New Hampshire, all these combinations were dissolved, and some of the persons, like Williams, who had been prominent in the local governments, were appointed to civil or military offices under the government of Massachusetts.

Exeter.

In the year 1638 the Rev. John Wheelwright and others, who had been banished in the preceding year from the Colony of Massachusetts Bay, on account of their active participation in

---

[1] Belknap, Farmer's ed., chap. ii.
[2] Prov. Papers of New Hampshire, i. 111, 112.

the theological controversy incited by Mrs. Ann Hutchinson, or on account of their known sympathy for her doctrines, made a settlement at Exeter. They first instituted a church, concerning which Winthrop, under date of Dec. 13, 1638, says : —

> Those who went to the falls at Pascataquack gathered a church, and wrote to our church [in Boston] to desire us to dismiss Mr. Wheelwright to them for an officer ; but because he desired it not himself, the elders did not propound it. Soon after came his own letters, with theirs, for his dismission, which thereupon was granted. Others also (upon their request) were dismissed thither.[1]

The people whom the Rev. John Wheelwright led or early attracted to the "falls at Pascataquack," entered into a written combination for the purpose of government in 1639. Shortly afterward this instrument was altered to suit the views of those who were not inclined to profess in strong terms their allegiance to the King. But in the year 1640 there was a reaction in public sentiment, and the original combination " in substance " was readopted, with the following preliminary statement : —

> Whereas a certen combination was made by us, the brethren of the church of Exeter, wth the rest of the Inhabitants, bearing date Mon. 5th d. 4, 1639, w^h afterwards, upon the instant request of some of the brethren, was altered & put into such a forme of wordes, wherein howsoever we doe acknowledge the King's Majesty our dread Soueraigne & our selves his subjects : yet some expressions are contained therein w^h may seeme to admit of such a sence as somewhat derogates from that due Allegiance w^h we owe to his Hignesse, quite contrary to our true intents & meaninge : We therefore doe revoke, disannull, make voyd, and frustrate the said latter combination, as if it never had beene done, and do ratify, confirme, & establish the former, w^h wee onely stand unto as being in force & virtue, the w^h for substance is here set downe in manner & forme following. Mon. 2^d d. 2, 1640.

> Whereas it hath pleased the lord to moue the heart of our Dread

---

[1] Winthrop's Hist. of New England, i. 338.

Soueraigne Charles by the grace of god king of England, Scotland, France, & Ireland to grant license & liberty to sundry of his subjects to plant them selves in the Westerne partes of America : Wee his loyall subjects, brethren of the church of Exeter, situate & lying upon the riuer of Piscataquacke,[1] wth other inhabitants there, considering wth our selves the holy will of god & our owne necessity, that we should not liue wth out wholsome lawes & civil gouernment amongst us, of w^h we are altogether destitute, doe in the name of Christ, and in the sight of god, combine our selves together, to erect & set up amongst us such Government as shall be (to our best discerning) agreeable to the will of god : professing our selves subjects to our Soueraigne Lord King Charles according to the libertys of our English Colony of the Massachusetts, and binding our selves solemely by the grace & helpe of christ & in his name & feare to submit our selves to such godly & christian laws as are established in the Realme of England to our best knowledge : & to all other such lawes w^h shall upon good grounds be made & inacted amongst us according to god, y^t we may live quietly & peaceably together in all godlyness & honesty. Mon. 5th d. 4th, 1639.[2]

The following names were subscribed to the above : —

[1] It will be observed that Gov. Winthrop uses the phrase, "the falls at Pascataquack," and that the Exeter compact of civil government contains the expression, "Exeter, situate & lying upon the riuer of Piscataquacke." Both expressions refer to the stream now called the Exeter River, the Indian name for which was Squamscott. The falls in the river are still popularly called Squamscott Falls. The reader will consider the importance of the fact that in 1638 and 1639 the expressions above cited were used to designate the Pascataqua River, or a branch of it, as bearing upon the contention of Mr. Jenness (Notes on the First Planting of New Hampshire, etc.) respecting the southern limits of the Hilton Patent. He remarks (pp. 54, 55) : "It may well be doubted whether at the time the Hilton Patent was granted [1629-30], the name *Piscataqua* was ever applied by the English or the Indians to Exeter River." As we have seen, the name was so applied in 1638 and 1639, and it is probable that its application then was in harmony with the popular usage from the time of the first English settlements on the Pascataqua. See note 3, pp. 103, 104, *antea.* — H.

[2] It appears that the original writing, containing the combination adopted in 1639, has been lost; but we have it "for substance" in the new combination adopted in 1640, as given above. Unless this fact is borne in mind, the date, "Mon. 5th d. 4th, 1639," affixed to the paper draughted in 1640, is likely to mislead the reader. For a facsimile of the paper, see Bell's History of Exeter. — H.

John Wheelwright

Augustine Storre

Thomas Wight

William Wentworth

Henry Elkins

his
George X Walton
mark

Samuell Walker

Thomas Pettit

Henry Toby

William Wenbourne

his
Thomas X Crawley
mark

Chr Helme

his
Darby X Feild
mark

his
Robert X Read
mark

Edward Rishworth

his
Francis X Mathews
mark

Ralph Hall

his
Robert X Soward
mark

Richard Bullgar

Christopher Lawton

his
George X Barlow
mark

Richard Moris

Nicholas Needham

his
Thomas X Wilson
mark

his
George X Rawbone
mark

his
William X Coole
mark

his
James X Walles
mark

Thomas Levitt

Edmund Littlefield

his
John X Crame
mark

his
Godfrye X Dearborne
mark

Philemon Pormort

Thomas Wardell

his
Willia X Wardell
mark

his
Robert X Smith
mark

Hilton Patent.

It is probable that the settlers within the territory granted in 1630 to Edward Hilton (see note 3, pages 103 and 104) had some kind of civil government as early as 1633, but there is no record of a formal combination for that purpose prior to the year 1640. The form of local government entered into on the 22d of October, 1640, is usually, but erroneously, spoken of by Hubbard, Belknap, and more modern writers, as the "Dover Combination." The instrument is here reproduced. It will be observed that the name Dover does not occur in it, and that the signers describe themselves as residing on "the River Pascataquack." The Hilton Patent included, so it was claimed, not only a portion of the present town of Dover, but also a portion of the present towns of Newington, Greenland, and Stratham. Among the signers was Captain Francis Champernowne. Champernowne never resided in Dover. His residence in 1640 was in that part of Greenland which was then claimed to be a portion of the Hilton Patent.

The original Hilton Patent Combination is supposed to be lost, but a copy, made for Governor Cranfield, was sent by him to England in 1682, and is now in the Public Record Office. Some of the subscribed names are evidently misspelled. The following copy is taken from Jenness's Abstracts of Original Documents relating to New Hampshire : —

Whereas sundry Mischeifes and inconveniences have befaln us, and more and greater may in regard of want of Civill Government, his Gratious Matie having hitherto Settled no Order for us to our Knowledge —

Wee whose names are underwritten being Inhabitants upon the River Pascataquack have voluntarily agreed to combine ourselves into a Body Politique that wee may the more comfortably enjoy the benefit of his Maj^{ties} Lawes, and do hereby actually engage our Selves to submit to his Royal Maj^{ties} Lawes, together with all such Orders as shalbee concluded by a Major part of the Freemen of our Society, in case they be not repugnant to the Lawes of England and administered in the behalfe of his Majesty.

And this we have mutually promised and concluded to do, and so to continue till his Excellent Maj^{tie} shall give other order concerning us.

In Witness wee have hereto Set our hands the two and twentieth day of October in the Sixteenth yeare of the Reign of our Sovereign Lord Charles by the grace of God King of Great Brittain, France, & Ireland, Defender of the Faith, &c.

Annoq : Dom^i 1640.

John Follett	Hanserd Knowles	Tho. Layton
Robert Nanney	Edward Colcord	Tho. Roberts
William Jones	Henry Lahorn	Edward Starr
Philip Swaddon	Abel Cannmond	James Nute
Richard Pinckhame	Henry Beck	Anthony Emery
Bartholomew Hunt	Robert Huggins	Richard Laham
William Bowden	Thom. Larkham	Bartholomew Smith
John Wastill	Richard Waldern	Samuel Haines
John Heard	William Waldern	John Underhill
John Hall	William Storer	Peter Garland
Fran. Champernoon	William Furbur	John Dam .

Steven Teddar	John Phillips	John Cross
John Ungroufe	Tho. Dunstar	George Webb
Thomas Canning	William Pomfret	James Rawlins

This is a true copy compared with yᵉ Originall by me

EDW. CRANFIELD.

[Endorsed] New England N. Hampshire. The Combination for Government by yᵉ people at Pascatq (1640).

Rᶜᵈ abᵗ 13ᵗʰ Febr. 82–3.

No. 2. Page 122.

FRANCIS CHAMPERNOWNE'S WILL.[1]

IN the Name of God, Amen : I, Francis Champernowne, Gent, Inhabitant of the Island commonly called Champernowne's Island, in the Towneship of Kittery in the Province of Main in New England, being weake in Bodie but of sound and perfect Memory, doe make and ordaine this my Last Will and Testament in manner and forme following, Vizt. :

Imprimis. I commit my soule unto God, hoping by his Mercy through the Merits of Jesus Christ to enjoy Life Eternall, and my Bodie to the Earth to be decently buried in such manner as my Executrix hereafter named shall think fitt, and as for my Temporall Estate and Goods with which it hath pleased God to endue me, after my Just Debts and Funerall Charges are payd, I give and bequeath as followeth :

Item. I make, Ordaine, and Constitute my welbeloved Wife Mary Champernowne full and sole Executrix of this my last Will and Testament.

Item. I give, bequeath, and confirme unto my said Executrix the One half part of yᵉ said Champernowne Island, wᶜʰ I now possesse,

---

[1] The editor is indebted to John S. H. Fogg, M.D., of Boston, for this copy of the Will, made from the original in his possession.

to her my said Executrix for Ever, which I have already given by Deed under my hand and seale to my said Executrix.

Item. I give and bequeath and confirme unto my Son in Law Humphrey Elliot and Elizabeth his now wife and their heirs for Ever the Other part of my said Island, which I have already given by Deed under my hand and seale to the said Humphry and Elizabeth his Wife.

Item. I give and bequeath unto my Son in Law Robert Cutt, my Daughter in Law Bridget Scriven, my Daughter in Law Mary Cutt, and my Daughter in Law Sarah Cutt, and to their heires for Ever, All that part of Three Hundred Acres of Land belonging unto me lying between Crocket's Neck & the Land formerly belonging unto Hugh Gullison on the Eastward side of Spruce Creek, to be equally divided between the said Robert, Bridget, Mary, and Sarah, Except what I have not before the making of this my Last Will and Testament disposed of to any other person, and also excepting Thirty Acres of Land in this my last Will and Testament hereunder given to Elizabeth Small.

Item. I give and bequeath unto Elizabeth Small my Servant Maid, and to her heirs for Ever, in behalfe of what I formerly promised her, Thirty Acres of Land at Spruce Creek, which s⁴ Thirty Acres of Land, part of the aforesaid Three hundred Acres, It is my will shall be first layd out by my Executrix and my Overseers hereunder named. And also I doe give and bequeath unto the said Elizabeth Small Ten Pounds, to be payd to her in Cattle, and ten pounds in goods, which is in Lieu of what I promised her.

Item. I give and bequeath unto my Son in Law Richard Cutt the Summe of Five pounds, to be payd by my said Executrix.

Item. In respect of the great Affection that I beare unto my Granchild Champernowne Elliot, Son of Humphry Elliot, I doe by these presents adopt, declare, and make the said Champernowne Elliot my heir, giving to him, the said Champernowne, all the Lands of right belonging unto me or that may belong unto me either in Old England or in New England not by me already disposed of, and doe by this my last Will and Testament appoint and constitute him, the said Champernowne, my Executor of all my Estate that either is or may of right belong or be due unto me in Old England from any person, and the same to have and enjoy to him the said Champernowne and his Heires for ever.

Item. I doe hereby constitute Robert Mason, Esq!, John Hincks, Esq!, Major John Davies of Yorke, and Robert Elliot of Great Island, Merchant, my loving Friends, to be Overseers of this my Last Will and Testament, and desire they may see the same performed and be Assistant to my said Executrix.

Lastly. I doe declare and Publish this to be my Last Will and Testament, annulling and making void all former and other Wills and Testaments. In witnesse whereof I have hereunto put my hand and Seale this Sixteenth day of November, in the Yeare of our Lord God One thousand Six hundred and Eighty Six, Annoqe R. R⁵ Jacobi secundi 2ᵈᵒ, &c.

FRANC: CHAMPERNOWNE.

Signed, Sealed, declared and published
to be the last Will and Testament of
Francis Champernowne, Gent.
  In the presence of us.

> WILLIAM MILBORNE,
> EDM: GEACH,
> ROBT ELLIOT.

M⁷ William Milborne made oath this 28 : nouember, 1687, before John Hinckes, one of his Majestes Councill for his Teritory and Dominion of New England, that this was the Last will and Testament of Captin Francis Champernown.

JOHN HINCKES.

Edmon Gaege and Rob! Eliot, Esq!, Came before us this 20ᵗʰ day of Sept!., and made oath they weare present and Saw Cap!'t Fransis Champernown Signe, Seale, and declare this Instrument to be his Last will and testament.

W. BAREFOOTE, J. P.,
THO: GRAFFOLD.

At his Majestyes Inferiour Court of Common P[l]eas held at Wells for this Province this 14th

PROVINCE OF MAIN. March, 1687, Mr Robert Ell[i]ott, & Edmund Gage appeared before Joshua Scottow, Esqr, Judge of the Said Court for the Sd Province, & Mr Samuell Wheelright & Capt Francis Hooke, two of his Majestyes Justices of the Peace for the Sayd Province, & made Oath that they Saw the late Capt Francis Champernoon Sign, Seale, & proclaimed the within written Will as on the other Side expressed (he the Sd Champernoon being in full and perfect Understanding), & that they Sett their handes to the Said Instrument as Witnesses,

FRANCIS HOOKE, Just. p, JOSH: SCOTTOW,
  SAMLL WHEELWRIGHT: Jus: Pece. THOMAS SCOTTOW, Clerca.

The within written Will entered in ye Book of Records for Wills, &c., Augst 18th, 1698, Fol. 56.

℗ JOSEPH HAMMOND, *Register.*

No. 3. Page 122.

THE CUTT, ELLIOT, AND ELLIOTT FAMILIES.

THREE brothers, John, Robert, and Richard Cutt (in modern times the name is Cutts), came to New England and settled on the Pascataqua. Savage states that they were natives of Wales, but upon what authority it does not appear. The precise date of their immigration has not been determined. John Cutt was an eminent merchant at Portsmouth, in the Province of New Hampshire, and by appointment of the Crown in 1679 was the first President of the royal government instituted in that Province. He died in 1681, and was spoken of as an aged man. He is usually mentioned as the eldest of the brothers. In the town records his name does not appear until Jan. 30, 1653-4; his brother Richard's name is recorded under date ot April 5, 1652. The last named was at first engaged in the fisheries at the Isles of Shoals; but he finally settled at Portsmouth, and died there in 1676.[1]

Robert Cutt was a shipmaster, and resided for some time at Barbados, where he married his second wife, Mary Hoel. Returning to New England, he settled at Kittery, in the Province of Maine. Here he carried on the business of ship-building. He died in 1674, and his will, dated June 18, 1674, was admitted to probate on the 6th of July next ensuing. His estate was inventoried at £890; a large sum, says Savage, for that neighborhood. Among the chattels enumerated were eight negro slaves.

By his wife Mary, Robert Cutt had one[2] son and four daughters; namely, Mary, Bridget, Sarah, Elizabeth, and Robert. Sometime subsequent to 1675 his widow married Capt. Francis Champernowne. As will be seen by reference to Champernowne's Will (Appendix, No. 2), his wife and her children received by gift or devise the principal part of his estate.

Bridget Cutt married the Rev. William Screven, the first Baptist minister in Kittery. Having suffered persecution for his religious opinions, and being finally expelled, he removed to South Carolina, where he helped to establish his religious denomination on a permanent basis. He appears to have been an able and devoted minister. His descendants are among the most respected people of South Carolina and Georgia.[3]

Elizabeth, the fourth daughter of Robert and Mary Cutt, married Humphrey Elliot, a resident on the Pascataqua. They had two

---

[1] For the Wills of John and Richard Cutt, see Brewster's Rambles about Portsmouth, First Series, No. 5. — H.

[2] Champernowne in his Will mentions his son-in-law, Richard Cutt. Hence it has been inferred that this Richard was also a son of Robert and Mary Cutt; but the inference is not a necessary one. He may have been a son of Robert Cutt by his first wife. Champernowne bequeathed to him £5. — H.

[3] For a notice of Mr. Screven and his labors, see New England Historical and Genealogical Register for October, 1889. — H.

sons, Robert and Champernowne. The latter, who was named heir
and residuary legatee by Captain Champernowne, is supposed to
have died early, as no mention is subsequently made of him in the
records of Maine or in those of South Carolina.

Humphrey Elliot, with his wife and family, and his mother-in-
law, Mrs. Mary Champernowne, accompanied or followed Mr.
Screven to South Carolina, where it is supposed they continued
to reside, and where they died. After the death of Humphrey
Elliot his widow married Robert Witherick, also of South Carolina.
Robert, son of Humphrey Elliot, married Elizabeth Screven, probably a daughter of the Rev. William Screven. The descendants of
the Elliots and Screvens are numerous.

The Elliotts of South Carolina and Georgia are for the most part
descended from Joseph and Elizabeth Elliott, who removed from
Barbados to South Carolina previous to 1697. It is not improbable
that the Elliots of Pascataqua and the Elliotts of Barbados were
originally of the same stock, and nearly related by blood. Persons
bearing this surname have been eminent in every succeeding generation, in Church and State, in arms and in civil life. By intermarriage the family is connected with many of the families in
South Carolina and Georgia, who for more than a century have
been most distinguished and influential.[1]

[1] An extended genealogy of the Elliots and Elliotts of South Carolina and Georgia, communicated to the writer of this note by Langdon Cheves, Esq., of Charleston, S. C., will be found in the New England Historical and Genealogical Register for January, 1890. — H.

No. 4. Page 135.

THE KING'S LETTER TO MASSACHUSETTS, ANNOUNCING
WAR WITH THE UNITED PROVINCES, April 3, 1672.[1]

Charles R.

Trusty and Wellbeloved, Wee greet you well.

Having found Our selfe obliged for the iust vindication of the
antient & undoubted Rights of Our Crowne, and for reparation as
well of the many affronts & indignities done to Our Royall Person
& Dignity, as of the frequent wrongs and iniuries done to Our Subjects by the States Generall of the United Provinces, to declare warr
against them, Wee have thought good hereby to give you Knowledge thereof, willing you forthwith upon receipt hereof in the usual
manner to cause the said warr to bee proclaimed within that Our
Colony according to Our Declaration (Coppies of which Wee have
directed to bee herewith sent you), and that att the same time you
cause seizure to bee made of all Shipps-goods & Marchandises belonging to the said States Generall, or their Subjects. And because Wee have reason to beleeve from the constant evill mind they
have always been known to bear to Our Foreigne Colonies & Plantations, and having likewise understood that a considerable number
of private men of warr are preparing in Holland & Zealand to bee
forthwith sent into the West Indges to infest & annoy our Plantations there, Wee have thought fitt of Our Princely care & regard
to the safety of those remote parts of Our Dominions, and for the
securing Our good Subjects inhabiting there, or trading thither, to
recommend it to you, as Wee do by these very particularly, forth-

[1] Mass. Archives, ccxli. 263, 264.

with to apply your selves jointly to consider of the condition thereof, and by all the speediest & most effectuall means you can, early
to provide for its safety & defense, and for the protection and security of such Shipps & Vessells as shall bee from time to time rideing
in the Roads & Harbo's there from the assaults & attempts of the
Dutch.　And particularly Wee think fitt to repeat Our former
orders to you, That all such Shipps which shall come thence bee
enioined to saile in considerable numbers, for their common security, and that then and ever during their stay there, it will bee fitt,
some of the most experienced Officers have authority given them to
command the rest.　Wee have thought fitt hereby to authorize &
empower you to do therein what according to this or any other
emergencies shall appear to be most for the safety of Our Colony &
Navigation of Our Marchants ; and further, that in all other matters
relating to the Jurisdiction of Our most Dear Brother, the Duke of
York, Our High Admirall, &c., you observe such orders and directions as you shall from time to time receive from him, whom Wee
have commissionated to grant letters of Marque & generall Repri-
salls against the Shipps, goods and Subjects of the States of the
United Provinces : conformable to which Our Will & Pleasure is,
that you take & seize the Shipps, Vessells, & goods belonging to the
said States or any of their Subjects or Inhabitants within any their
Territories, and to bring the same to Judgment and condemnation
according to the course of Admiralty & laws of Nations.　And
these Our letters that you communicate to the rest of our Colonies
your Neighbo's ; Our Pleasure being that with all care and application possible they arme themselves against the dangers which
threaten them in this coniuncture from such an Enemy, and proceed according to these Our directions, and such as they shall
receive from Our said Dear Brother, assuring them and all Our
loving Subjects in those parts that Wee shall not bee wanting on
Our part on all occasions to helpe and succor them to the utmost
of Our power, and to contribute all possible means for the security
and improvement of the trade and Commerce.　And so Wee bid

you farewell. Given att Our Court att Whitehall, the 3ᵈ day of Aprill, in the 24ᵗʰ year of Our Reigne.

By His Majᵗⁱᵉˢ Command. ARLINGTON.

These, for Our trusty & Wellbeloved the Governᵗ. & Council for Our Colony of the Massachusetts, To bee communicated to the other Colonies.

No. 5. Page 137.

ACTION OF THE GOVERNOR AND COUNCIL ON RECEIPT OF THE KING'S LETTER IN REGARD TO THE DUTCH FLEET.[1]

ATT A meeting of the Gournᵗ & Council in Boston, 31ᵗʰ July, 1673, upon Information of a Considerable fleet of Dutch Infesting the Coasts of Virginia, It is Ordered that all masters and Companyˢ of vessells, whither ketches, shallopˢ, or other Coasting boates, that rainge these Coasts & doe belong to this Jurisdiction, doe after publication hereof endeavouᵗ to make a true discovery, & forthwith give notice unto the Governᵗ or any magistrate, or others in Authority of the approach of any fleet of shipps being fower in number or upwards; for which their care & timely intelligence givin, the Council will Order a meet recompense to be Given to them for that service.

By the Councill.

EDWARD RAWSON, *Secret'y.*

It is Furtheᵗ ordered that the Constables in the Port tounes doe Commicat this Order unto the masteᵗs of the Severall vessells belonging to or Coming into such Ports, and Give them Expresse order to be vigilant & circumspect in the prosecution thereof from time to time until the Council shall take further Order.

By the Council.

EDW. RAWSON, *Secret'y.*

[1] Mass. Archives, lxi. 6, 7, 8.

It is ordered that Capt James Oliver of Boston do take special care that there be some meet person or persons appointed to look out by day & night upon Point Allerton, to descry the approach of any fleet of ships, and upon discouery of four or more to fier a beacon, the wch he shall ord^r to be erected on the highest part of ye said Point, as also on Long Island, soe that it may be seene at Castle Island by the Com̄and^r in cheife, who is to act accordingly, & the charges thereof the Treas^r is hereby ordered to sattisfie.

E. R., S.

It is ordered that ye Secretary issue out speedy warrants according to these orders to the scuerall Constables, requiring all the Inhabitants to yeild due & speedy assistance, & to the parties concerned.

At the opening of the Council the Gouern^r declaring wh^t Information he had recieued from Nathaniel Walker & William Masters[1] lately arrived here from Virginia, that seuenteen Dutchmen of war being there, & had engagement wth two of his Majesty's friggots & seuerall other English Shipps & vessells there in the road, who fierd and burnt sixe of the English & took sixe more. What further their intents are or may be towards the Country not fully understood. The Gouern^r & Council Assembled judged it an Incumbent duty on them to improue all opportunity and meanes that God hath put into their hands for the safety and welfare of his Majesty's interests in these partes ; in order whereunto

It is ordered that all masters of ketches & other vessells, shallops Cruising to and againe [going ?] between the Capes, Cape Ann & Cape Cod, on their fishing & other occasions, take notice that they & euery are hereby required in his Majesty's name to make dilligent & exact discouery of the Dutch Cap[tai]n[s] or other vessells, which they shall see to be in Company aboue the number of three on any part of our Coasts, and of their number of men & intents what they can, and to speed such intelligence so obtained to the

---

[1] The last two words may be *Williams, masters.* — H.

first Magistrate, Gouern^r or Assistant in the nearest port, that so all due further meanes may be used for the preservation of the Country.

To the Constable or Constables of Boston or either of them. These require you & every of you in his majestycs name to take speciall notice of the Orders of the Council above written, and that you & every of you forthwith put forth yor utmost dilligence effectually to Accomplish the same in all respects, as you will answer the Contrary at yor utmost perrill. Dated in Boston this first of August, 1673.

By order of ye Council,

EDW. RAWSON, *Secret'y.*

No. 6. Page 141.

LETTERS OF COUNT FRONTENAC.

Count Frontenac to M. Colbert.[1]

MÉMOIRE DE M. LE COMTE DE FRONTENAC AU MINISTRE.

À QUEBEC, le 14 Novembre, 1674.

Quoyque je suis désespoir de n'avoir qu'à vous mander des nouvelles aggréables, je ne puis m'empescher de vous donner avis du malheur arrivé à M. de Chambly, de sa blessure, de sa prison et de la prise de Pentagoüet avec celle de Gemisic dans la Rivière St Jean et du St de Marson, qui y commandoit.

Ce que j'en sçay par une lettre que le dit St de Chambly m'a escrit, est que le 10 Aoust, il fust attaqué par une bastiment de Boucaniers qui venoient de St Domingue, et qui avoient passé à Baston, dans lequel il y avoit cent dix hommes, qu'après avoir mis pied à terre, soustenu pendant une heure leur attaque. Il reçoit un

---

[1] Paris Documents, Mass. Archives, ii. 287–289.

44

coup de mousquet au travers du corps, que le mist hors de combat, et qu'aussy tost son Enseigne et le reste de sa garnison qui n'estoit composée avec les habitans que de trente hommes, mal intentionnez et mal armez, se rendisent à discrétion. Que ces forbans ont pillé le Fort, emporté tout le canon, et qu'ils devoient mener le dit St de Chambly à Baston avec le dit St de Marson, qu'ils envoyèrent prendre dans la Rivière St. Jean par une détachment qu'ils firent, et l'ayant mis à rançon, et luy voulant faire payer mille castors.

Comme je n'ay reçeu cette nouvelle qu'après le fin de Septembre, par des Sauvages que le dit Sieur de Chambly m'a envoyée son enseigne, pour me conjurer de donner ordre à sa rançon, et que ne restant plus qu'un mois de navigation, j'estois dans l'impuissance de pouvoir envoyer à l'Acadie du secours, quand mesme j'aurois eu les choses nécessaires pour cela, je ne suis contenté d'envoyer quelques gens avec canots pour essaier d'avoir de nouvelles de l'estat où il aurent laissé le Fort, et s'il n'aurent rien entrepris contre Port Royal, de leur ordonner de reméner la damoiselle de Marson et ceulx qui sont restez dans la Rivière St Jean, et d'envoyer à un correspondant que le St Formont m'a donné à Baston, les lettres de change pour la rançon de M. de Chambly, que je me suis obligé de faire acquitter par mon marchand à la Rochelle, ne croyant pas qu'il fust de la gloire du Roy, pour laquelle je sacrifiray toujours le peu que j'aurai de biens, de laisser à la vue de nos voisins un Gouverneur entre le mans des Pirates, qui l'auroient amené avec eulx, on peut estre assomé, outre que ce pauvre Gentilhomme est assurément, par son mérite et ses longs services, digne d'une meileure destinée.

J'ay aussy escrit au Gouverneur de Baston une lettre dont je vous envoye la copie pour laquelle je luy tesmoigne l'estonnement où je suis de voir que n'y ayant point de rupture entre sa Majesté et le Roy d'Angleterre, il donne retraite à des forbans qu'ils nous ont faict un pareille insulte et que pour moy je croyois manquer aux ordres que j'ay d'entretenir avec eulx une bonne correspondance si j'en usois de la sorte.

Je suis persuadé que ceulx de Baston se sont servis de ces gens là pour nous cette avanie, leur ayant mesme donné un Pilote Anglois pour les conduire, supportant impatienment nostre voisinage et la contraintre que cela leur donne pour leurs pesches, et pour leur traitte.

Je ne sais sy ceulx que j'ay envoyez pourront estre de retour avant le départ des vaisseaux, et si je pourray vous mander d'aultre nouvelles plus escris présentement, et sur ce que M. de Chambly vous mandera infailliblement par la première voye qu'il trouvera vous pourriez voir les ordres que vous à donner pour la seureté de l'Acadie, et ce que vous voulez que je fasse puisque vous sçavez bien que je suis dans l'impuissance d'y pouvoir manquant de toutes choses, et que vous me deffendez très expressement de faire aulcune dépense extraordinaire, ce que j'observeray avec la dernière exactitude.

Il est à propos, je croy, que je finisse cette lettre qui vous doibt ennuyer il y a desjà longtemps, et que j'y ajouste seulement les protestations que je vous faicts d'estre, jusqu'au dernier soupir de ma vie.

Monseigneur,
Vostre très humble, très obéissant, et très obligé serviteur,
FRONTENAC.

Count Frontenac's Letter of Safe-Conduct to M. Normanville.[1]

The Earle of Frontenac; Counseller of the King In his Counsels, gouernor & generall Lieftenant for his majesty In Canada, Acadie, Isles of newfoundland, and others places of the Northerne french.

To all Lieftenant-generalls, gouernors of Principaltyes; mayors, Consults, Sherifs, Judges & officers of Cittyes, Capⁿˢ of bridges, & Customes, places, passages & Straigh's, Greeting: haueing Commanded mʳ Normanville to goe speedilly to Boston for the express affaires of his majesty & our, wee doe Injoine to all upon whom our authoritty is, & Intreate all others to lett him freely & safly pass with one of

[1] Mass. Archives, ii. 515. The original is missing. -- H.

our Line gard their men, Canoes, & Equipage ; without any trouble or hinderence both in goeing, staying, & Returning, Butt Rather to giue them all helpe & fauor In what they shall haue need, tendreing for the licke Case to Doe the same.   In witnesse whereof wee haue signed these presents, to which wee haue sett our seale & vnder-written by one of our secretairyes.   giuen In Quebec the 24ᵗʰ of May, 1675.

Fʀᴏɴᴛᴇɴᴀᴄ,
By my Lord, vahassem.[1]

Letter of Count Frontenac to the Magistrates at Boston.[2]

A Qᴜᴇʙᴇᴄ, ce 25 May, 1675.

Mᴇssɪᴇᴜʀs, — Si tost que j'eüs appris l'Insulte qu'on avoit fait au Sʳ de Chambly, Gouverneur de l'Acadie, et qu'après la prise du fort de Pentagoüet on l'avoit conduit prisonnier à Baston.   Je vous depé-chay par deux différents endroicts pour vous temoigner la surprize où j'étois que nonobstant la bonne correspondance dans laquelle le Roy mon maistre m'a commandé de vivre avec vous et les ordres que vous avez dû reçevoir du Roy d'Angleterre sur le même sujet, de forbans et gens sans aveu eüssent trouvé une retraite dans vostre ville ;[3] et pour vous conjurer aussi en mesme temps de procurer

---

[1] It is impossible to determine what was the original name which the translator in 1675 transformed into *vahassem*. It may have been Sᵗ Luisson. — H.

[2] Mass. Archives, ii. 517.

[3] It has been seen that Frontenac, in his Memoir, dated Nov. 14, 1674, to the minister, M. Colbert, after giving an account of the capture of Pentagoüet, and the captivity of M. de Chambly and the Sieur de Marson, goes on to say that he had written to the "Governor of Boston" a letter, of which he encloses a copy.   This letter is not now in the Archives of Massachusetts, nor have we any copy of it.   But we may gather the substance of it from a passage in the Memoir above referred to.   A translation of the passage, beginning with the words "Je luy tesmoigne" (p. 346), is as follows : " I expressed to him my astonishment at seeing that, while peace exists between his Majesty and the King of England, he gives shelter to pirates and ruffians without a commission, after they had so grievously insulted us ; and that, for my own part, I should deem myself delinquent in respect to the orders I had received, to cultivate a good understanding with them, if I had behaved toward them in like manner."   He repeats this language, in part, in the foregoing letter to the magistrates at Boston. — H.

auprès deux la liberté du dit Sieur de Chambly ayant mis entre les mains de ces mêmes personnes par qui je vous écrivois des lettres de Change pour payer ia Rançon dont il estoit convenu avec eux. Cependant quoique je leur eusse ordonné devenir me retrouver sur les neiges avec toute la diligence possible je vois l'hiver passé et la saison fort avancée sans que j'aye eue de leurs nouvelles ny que j'aye pû apprendre ce que le Sr de Chambly est devenu.

C'est ce qui m'oblige Messieurs à vous depescher pour la trois fois le Sr de Normanville accompagné d'un de mes gardes pour vous reiterer la mesme prière et vous supplier de lever tous les obstacles qui regarderont la liberté tant du Sr de Chambly que des autres personnes qui sont avec luy. Si par hazard ils estoient encore prisonniers. J'ay même esté bien ayse que cela m'ait fourny une occasion de vous donner de nouvelles assurances de la bonne union & intelligence que je desire entretenir avec vous dans l'ésperance que j'ay que vous y correspondrez avec autant de franchise que vous me l'avez assuré par vos lettres.

Prenez donc s'il vous plaist une entière croyance en tout ce que le Sr de Normanville vous dira de ma part et me croyez tres veritablement,

Messieurs,

Votre très humble & très obeissant Serviteur,

FRONTENAC.

No. 7. Page 145.

COMPLAINT OF JOHN FREAKE.[1]

To the Honble Gouerno^r & the Rest of the Honrd Magistrates Setting in Councill at Boston, Feb. 15, 1674–5. Amen.

The Complaint of John Freake of Boston humbly sheweth, That whereas yo Complainant had a Small Vessell under the command of George Manning bound home on her voyage from the Eastward was

[1] Mass. Archives, lxi. 66.

by accident met with all in the River of St. John by John Roades
& some Dutchmen his complices in a small vessell Sometime in
the Month of December last past ; who overpowering of them with
men pyratically seized my said Vessell & goods on board her, &
haue wounded the Master of her & another of his Company, &
doe still keepe both vessell, goods, & men, as by a letter from the
Master given in to yo' Hono'ˢ

My humble Request therefore to yo' Hono'ˢ is that you would be
pleased to take some speedy Order for the Seizing of the said
Roades & his Complices by Commissioning some meete persons
whom yo' Hono'ˢ shall think fit with such aide as may be requisite
to go out in a small vessell & range along the said Coast, & to seize
& secure the said Roades & all his Complices, & to bring them to
Boston for due tryal, being out upon a pyraticall Account, & having
Seized severall of the goods of the Inhabitants of this Jurisdiction
besides yo' Complainants, & it 's very probable will doe much more
mischief, without yo' Hono'ˢ in yo' Wisdoms finde some speedy
Course to prevent the same. Submitting myselfe to yo' Hono'ˢ
Wisdom & dispose therein, I subscribe

Yo' Hono'ˢ Most humble Servant,

JNO. FREAKE.

No. 8.   Page 146.

ORDER OF THE GOVERNOR AND COUNCIL TO STOP ALL VESSELS GOING EASTWARD FROM BOSTON.[1]

WHEREAS Mᵣ Waldern & others not long since complayned to the
Goūn' & Councill Assembled in Boston 29 December last past, and
Mʳ John Freake of Boston, merchant, complayning to the Honoured
Goūn' & Councill of yᵉ peratical actions of one Jⁿ Roades & others,
Inhabitants of yᵉ Colony joyning wᵗʰ some Dutch & other nations

[1] Mass. Archives, lxi. 67.

in seizing of seuerall of o' vessells, spoiling them both of their vessells & goods to their great losse & damage, and hauing lately taken y° ketch of y° said Jn° Freake, wounding of y° Master of his said ketch, George Manning, & some other, wth seuerall their acts of Piracy on y° seas upon seuerall Inhabitants of y° place their lawfull negotiations, in all which the Council judgeth it meet to order a comission be granted to A. B. C. for y° Apprehending & seizing of y° said Jn° Roades & his Company in order to his & their tryall before any Court of y² jurisdiction that hath cognizance of such cases, and that he & they so Apprehended & seized be brought before y° Goũn' & other Authority of the Colony to be secured in order to his & their tryall ; that so y° said Freake and such others as have suffered may be in a way to get their satisfaction & reparation for such their losses, and that y° trade of this country be y' better secured & damage prevented. Past by y° Councill this 15th Feb. 1874.

E. R[AWSON, *Secretary*].

Cap' Samuel Mosely being proposed to y° Councill by M' Jn° Freake as y° Commander of ye design, the Goũn' & Councill approve thereof. — E. R., *S.*

Also y° Councill ordered that the vessells stopd by y° Goũn' on y° Saturday last, y° Councill ordered y' all vessells going or to go forth into those parts till y° said Capt. Samuel Mosely be gone, till y° Goũn' give further order & that y° secretary issue out warrants to y° seuerall Constables of Boston accordingly. — E. R., *S.*

Instructions for Cap' Samuel Mosely.[1]

1. That you looke to yo' Company y' they keepe Good orde' aboard y° vessell and abroad :

2. that you suffer no Injury to be done to any of His Majesties subjects in these pts or any in Freindship wth his mãjty their Goods or Estates by Sea or land,

[1] Mass. Archives, lxi. 68.

3. that you Labour wth all your Care & skill to seaze & surprize ye said Roades & his Company wthout blood if it may be : & to secure them & bring them forthwith to Boston in order to their tryall.

past by ye Councill,

15 Febr. 1674.   E. R., S.

To ye Constables of Boston.

You & euery of you by virtue of an ord^r of the Goūn' & Councill [are] hereby Required in his Majesty's name forthwith to make stop of all such ships or other vessells that are now in the Harbour bound out to the Eastward till Capt Samuell Mosely begon forth ; and untill further Order be Given by ye Honoured Goūn' hereof you & they are not to fail at yor & their perill.

p^r Edward Rawson, *Secretary,*

By ord^r of the Goūn^r & Councill.

Dated in Boston, the 15th February, 1674[5].

———

No. 9.   Page 146.

DEPOSITION OF GEORGE MANNING.[1]

The Deposition of George Manning, Aged thirty years or there Aboutts, Testiffieth

That Being sent outt By the Latte Mr Jo^n Freke a traideing voyadge to the Eastward in ye Shallopp Called the Philipp, Was on the Fowerth day of Decemb^r last Surprized and taken in Adowake Bay to ye Estward of Mount deZart By Capt Petter Rodrigoe & Capt John Rodes In Maner as·ffollowing : I Being att an Ancor as aboue Said, they Came vpon vs wth theire Duch Cullers fflyn, and Comanded me a board By Capt Petter Rodrigoe, & their vpon I went wth my boatte on board of their vesell ; and being there hee ordered mee to bee their detained, & Went him Selfe, wth seu^{ell} of his Comp^a

———

[1] Mass. Archives, lxi. 117, 118.

on board of my shallop, & their Opened the hatches & tooke all my
peltery & Caried itt on board their owne Vesell, and alsoe Scu^{cll}
Other things, and then they would haue me Sett my hand to a paiper
that they had taken nothing Frome me but w^t. was of the groath of
that Countrey ; butt knowing of itt to bee Fals, I Refused Soe to doe,
butt I deseired him to Showe me his Comition by Vertue of wch hee
was Soe Impowered to acctt as hee did, vpon wch hee said hee would
goe and Fech itt, and then brought a lardg paiper wth Seuer^{cll} sealls,
an Extract, butt nether Read itt nor would sufer me soe to doe, butt
only asked mee what I thought of itt ; to wch I Replyed, nott haueing
opertunity to hearr itt nor to Read itt, I Did not know butt itt might
bee a Lawfull Comition; vpon wch hee Demanded my Invoice of y^e
goods I had. I Replyed againe that his people hauing rumedged my
Chest & Cabin, that some of his Comp^a might haue itt; butt hee asking
of them they all denied itt, whervpon I went on board to Looke for
itt, and their found itt, and then being downe in ye Cabing, James
Debeck handing one of the Small guns that was on the Deck downe,
before I Receud the Other ther was an vproar amongst them, and they
presently Fiared in Seu^{cll} Shott vpon vs, by wch I was wounded in my
hand, and presently Comanded James on board of their vessell and
much abused him in striking him many blowes, wch I heard, and alsoe
heard him Crie for god sake to spaire his Life ; after wch ye Capt
hauing broake his Cuttles aboutt James, he presently went aft and
fetched my Cuttles, & Came Forward to mee saying, wher is this dogg,
Maning, I must talke wth him alsoe ; whervpon I beged them to Spaire
my Life. Sume of them Replyed that if I would Come vpe I should
haue noe harme ; butt Coming vp by ye Scuttell I Receud Seuerall
blows vpon my head, wch soe stuned me that for a good Space of time
was depriued of my Senses, nott knowing where I was, thought [I had
been] throwne ouerboard ; and Caried [me] one board of their vessell
and keept me prisner till the next day, whereupon they Concluded to
Send me away wth my Boatt, and hall my vessell ashoer and burne
here ; I then heareing of theire Sentance, I beged Capt Rodrigoe
that I might nott be sent away ; soe Considering the Condition I Was

45

in, and yᵉ time of yᵉ yeare, & wounded as I am, hee Shaking of his head replied that hee Could nott doe anything in itt wᵗʰout yᵉ Consent of yᵉ Rest of yᵉ Compᵃ, wherevpon I Adresed my Selfe to Capᵗ Roedes; hee then Replyed wᵗʰ an oth, Saying, Dam you! what doe you Come to mee For? Can I Clear you? then I Adresed my Selfe to Randall Jetson, desiering of him yᵉ Like. hee then wᵗʰ yᵉ Like others told me if I had my desarts should bee turned ashoar vpon an Island and there to Eatt the Rootts of the trees, whcre vpon I desiered that I might Rather bee keept as a prisnor amongst them and goe A Long wᵗʰ them then to bee done Soe by, wᵗʰ Could nott bee granted. Then I desiered that I might bee putt outt of my troubles and End my days att yᵉ mast; they then hering of What I Said Withdrew them Selues, Consulting what they should doe wᵗʰ mee, and halling Tho: Michells Vesell on board of me and take outt all my goods and prouision Except a Small Mattᵗ of prouition, pretending itt Was to Cary mee home, and gaue mee my Vessell againe, butt by Capᵗ Roeds & Tho: Michells Doengs was Forced to Condesend to goe along wᵗʰ them; & Further Capᵗ Roads did before my going Frome boston thretne John King that if hee went to the Estward wᵗʰ me hee would be yᵉ death of him; & iff itt had nott ben for yᵉ rest of their Company hee had suffered. The nit before I Sailed Frome boston I demanded of Capᵗ Urrin[1] iff hee did grant any Comision to Capᵗ Roades or any of yᵉ Compᵃ that went wᵗʰ him For to take any Englishmen. I desiered him iff hee did hee must Resolue mee of itt; where vpon hee replyed hee had nott nor would nott grant any, and that I had as much liberty to goe, or any one, as they had, and Wishing mee a good prosperous voyadge, wherevpon hee departed.

After wee Sett Saille Frome Adowaket to Aplaisse Called muspeka Racke, where I Caused ouᵗ boatte to bee histed outt, and went aboard of them, and Desiered that they would looke vpon my hand; Finding My Selfe in much paine, I desiering they would Clear me For I was

---

[1] Capt. Jurriaen Aernouts, commander of the Flying Horse, is probably the person referred to. — H.

afraid of loosing of my hand, and they Replyed itt was a fleshe wond, and their was noe fear of y° Cure, Soe would nott lett me goe home, butt was forced to goe withem ; and further sayeth nott. taken vpon oath in open Court the 17ᵗʰ of June, 1675.

As Attests EDWARD RAWSON, *Secret'y.*

Georg Manniḡ on his forme' oath ouned yᵉ testimony on his forme' oath to yᵉ trueth as to yᵗ pᵗ of Judgmt.

E. R., S.

17 June, 1675.

No. 10. Page 147.

EXAMINATION OF THE PRISONERS CHARGED WITH PIRACY.[1]

2ᵈ Aprill : 1675 : The Examinačon of the severall prisonᵗˢ brought in by Capᵗ Samˡˡ Mosely[2] are as followeth : —

Jnº Rhodes[3] Examined. Sᵗʰ that hee came now from the Eastward wᵗʰ Capᵗ Mosely : being asked whither hee had any comission, hee Answered No ; being asked why hee Fought agᵗ the King's colours, hee answered, because that they with Capᵗ Mosely fought under French colours, dutch colours, & English colours, & they thought they should haue noe quarter & therefore fought.

This was ouned to be the trueth by Jnº Rhoades in open Court 25 May, 1675. — E. R., S.

Peter Rodriego[4] Examined. Sᵗʰ that his name is Peter Rodriego, & that hee sailed from Boston to Nova Scotia with power from Capᵗ Vrin-Arnelson,[5] which power was written at the beare in Boston, & that the sᵈ Arnelson put the Scales to it. — Sᵗʰ that hee hath taken two english vessells, one from George Manning, the other from Walton, & that goeing to the Eastward, stopping at Casco, hee was

---

[1] Mass. Archives, lxi. 72.
[2] Mosley is the correct spelling.
[3] Rhoade.
[4] Roderigo.
[5] Jurriaen Aernouts.

one day asleep in his cabbin, & his men went ashoare & killed four Sheep & brought them aboard. Ouned in Court by Peter Rodriego, 24 May, 1675, this his confession on examination to be the trueth, & in open Court, as Ates's E. R., *S.*

Cornelius Anderson,[1] Examined. S.[th] that hee came now from round pond as neere Muscongus Island, S.[th] that hee hath taken two English Vessells, one from Waldron, the other from Hilliard. Ouned that he had took two vessells vnder his inst.[r]? but deliuered them againe; only took the peltry from them. — E. R., *S.*

Tho: Mitchell Examined. S.[th] that hee lives neere Mauldon, & that hee came last from Penequid, & that hee sailed in a vessell part of her his own, & that the privateers hee carried with him tooke some English Vessells, that hee himselfe was in her, & one Peter Rodriego comanded her; but it was against his s.[d] Mitchell's will they tooke the vessells, & that hee eat of the mutton that the company on board his vessell tooke away from m.[r] Mountjoy, which were in number Four, and that Rodrigo, Grant, Fowler, & Rhodes compelled him to pilot the vessell from Johns unto twelve penny harbour, where they plundered one Lantrimony & killed his cattle.

Randolph Judson — Examined. S.[th] that hee came now from Matchias with Cap.[t] Mosely, & that hee was one of Cap.[t] Rodrigo's company, & was at the taking of George Manning's Vessell, Waldron's Vessell, & Hilliard's Vessell, & that they tooke them by virtue of the comission given to Peter Rodrigo, & that George Manning was wounded in the hand & James Debeck was cut over the arme by Cap.[t] Rodrigo. Ouned in Court 17.th June, 1675. — E. R., *S.*

Edward Youring Examined. S.[th] that hee went out in a vessell with Thomas Mitchell upon a trading Voyage to the Eastward, & that going along the Shoare Cap.[t] Rodrigo & the Company on board theire vessell tooke George Manning's & Waldron's vessells.

Richard Fowler Examined. S.[th] that hee was in company with Peter Rodrigo & sundry others when they tooke George Manning's & George Walton's vessells & goods, & that hee was on shoare at casco

---

[1] Cornelis Andreson.

& Fetcht on board theire vessell some Sheep, from off an Island saide to bee m' Mountjoy's, & that Tho: Mitchell sent him on shoare for them, Saying there was noebody lookt after them. — ye examination was ouned as abuve writt 17th June, 1675. — E. R., S^r.

Peter Grant Examined. Sth that hee was in company with Peter Rodrigo & sundry others when they tooke George Manning's & George Walton's vessells & goods by order of theire Capt Rodrigo, & that hee was ashoare at Casco & did help take the Sheep on board & Fech't wood to make the Fire to dress them with & eat part of them. — Peter Grant ouned the 1st pt of this Confession as to be wth Capt Peter Rodriego, &c. — E. R., S.

John Williams Examined. Sth that hee is a cornish man, sailed out of Jamaica with Capt Morrice, was taken by the dutch & carried to Carrisaw,[1] came hither with Capt Urin-Arnelson, & that hee went from Boston in comp^y with Capt Peter Rodrigo & sundry others, & was in company & acted with the s^d Rodrigo & the rest in the taking of George Manning's Vessell ; but was ashoare at Machias when the rest were taken.

John Tomas Examined. Sth that hee was one of the company that sailed with Capt Peter Rodrigo & sundry others, & was present at the taking of George Manning's & George Walton's Vessells. Being asked whither hee did not kill a Frenchman, hee denyed it ; confessed that hee did shoote at him, but knew not that hee hit him.

Taken and read to the several persons & ouned by them before us

JOHN LEVERETT, *Gov*.

EDWARD TYNG.

The partyes all ouned in Court their seûll Confessions as aboue written, being Read to them in Court of Admiralty.[2]

---

[1] Curaçoa.
[2] The original record of the examination of the prisoners, from which the foregoing paper is copied, is, except the last two sentences and the signatures, in the handwriting of Isaac Addington. The signatures appear to be autographs. — H.

No. 11. Page 149.

INDICTMENT AND SENTENCE OF PETER RODERIGO.[1]

ATT A Court of Assistants held at Boston y⁰ 24ᵗʰ of may, 1675, & called by yᵉ Court for tryall of the prisoners.

Peeter Rodriego [2] Dutchman being presented & Indicted by the Grand Jury, was Indicted by the name of Peeter Rodriego for that he not hauing the feare of God before his eyes, he wᵗh other his Complices sometimes in the mounth' of November, December, & January last by force of Armes did vpon the sea' pyrattically & Felloniously seize & take severall smale English vessells (and theire Companyes) belonging to his Majtys subjects of this Colony & made prize of theire Goods, & in particular the barque Phillip & her goods belonging to the late m' John Freake of Boston, Georg mannig being master then of hir, wounding the said manig & his mate contrary to the peace of our Soueraigne Lord the King his Croune & dignity, the lawes of God & of this Jurisdiction. To wch Indictm' yᵉ prisoner at the barr pleaded not Guilty, put himself on triall by God & the Country, saying he had no exception ag' any of yᵉ Jury: the Case proceeded, and after the Indictment & euidences in the case were Read, Comitted to the Jury & are on file wᵗh the Reccords of this Court the Jury brought in the virdict ; they found him Guilty according to the aboue written Indictment, and Accordingly had sentenc of death pronounc' ag' him by yᵉ Court to be Carryed from hence

present
Jno. Leueret Esq' }
Gou⁰ |
SamSymondEsq' |
dept Go. }
Symon Bradstreet
Symon Willard
Richᵈ Russell
Tho. Danforth Esqʳ
Wᵐ Hathorn
Edw. Tyng
Wᵐ Stoughton

Grand Jurymen
Return'ᵈ to serve at
yᵉ Court & sworne
were :

M, Jn⁰ Sherman
Richᵈ Willington
Richᵈ Baker
Tho. Russell
Jn · Long
Symon Lynd
Jn⁰ Woodmansey
Jnothan Bolston
Habbaccuk Glouer
Jn⁰ Bateman
Jonas Clarke
Fearing Moore
Tho. Hastings
Jn⁰ Bowles
Tho. Weld

Jurymen Return'ᵈ to
serve on the Jury of
tryalls :
m' John Checkly
Jnᵒ Bird
Benj Bale
Benj Moore
Benj Gillam
Samuel Goffe
Tho. Langhorne
Tho. Fanig
Tho. Hastings
Jn⁰ Stone
Edw. Bridge
Daniel Brewer

---

[1] Records of the Court of Assistants.
[2] This name also is variously spelled in the records. Roderigo is the correct spelling. — H.

to the place from whence he came, & thence to the place of Execution, & there to hang till he be dead, and on his petic̄on the Court Gaue him opp'tunity to petic̄on the Geñll Court for his life.

INDICTMENT AND SENTENCE OF JOHN RHOADE.[1]

Att A Court of Assistants on Adjournment held at Boston 17ᵗʰ June, 1675, Jn° Roads was brought to the barr & holding vp his hand was Indicted by the name of John Roads late of Boston, for that he not having the feare of God before his eyes, he wᵗʰ others his Complices sometimes in the months of November, December, & January last, past did by force of Armes vpon the seas Pyrattically & Felloniously seize & take seuerall smale English vessells & theire Companyes belonging to his Majⁱʸ subjects of this Colony, and made prize of their Goods, & in particcular the barque Phillip & her Goods belonging to the late mʳ John Freake of Boston, George Manniḡ being then master of hir, wounding the said Mannig & his mate Contrary to the peace of our Soueraigne Lord the King his Croune & dignity, the lawes of God & of this Jurisdicc̄on, to wch he pleaded not Guilty, put himself on God & the Country for his triall. After yᵉ Indictment & evidences produced agᵗ him were read, Comitted to the Jury & are on file wᵗʰ the Reccords of yᵉ Court, the Jury brought in their virdict; they found him Guilty according to Indictment, and accordingly yᵉ next day had sentenc of Death pronount agᵗ him : yᵗ he should Goe from the barr to yᵉ place from whenc he Came, & thence to the place of executione where hang till he be dead.

present
Jn° Leueret Esqʳ }
        Gouʳ }
Sam Symonds }
  Esqʳ depᵗ Goʳ }
Symon Bradstreet
Daniel Gookin
Daniel Denison
Symon Willard
Richᵈ Russell
Tho. Danforth
Edwᵈ Tyng
Wᵐ Stoughton
Thomas Clarke

Jn° Roads objected agᵗ yᵉ foremⁿ Jn° Checkly, so Benja Gillam was Foreman in the rest. Jurymen Impaneld & Sworne were for yᵉ Triall of these.
Capt Benja Gillam
Jno Bird
Benj Bale
Wᵐ Whitwell
Richᵈ Knight
Sam Goffe
Tho. Longhorne
Edw. Bridge
Daniel Brewer
John Holbrook
Jn° Swett
Jn° Davenport

[1] Records of the Court of Assistants.

No. 12. Page 151.

THE DEFENCE OF RODERIGO, ANDRESON, AND OTHERS CHARGED WITH PIRACY.

Capt. Pette^{r}. Rodrigo, & Cap^{n}. Cornelius Andreson, and theire Asociates, officers & Souldiers belonging to the Prince of Orrange, & as his Subiects Inhabytants In his highneses Terrytories in New Holland, Allias Nova Scotia, And now Prisono^{rs}. in the jurrishdiction of the Massathusetts Collony, in New England, etc. Thier Plea And Answare for theire Defence against what they stand Charged With and Impeached of as Pirates For Acting Pirazie on Severall vessells belonging to the inhabytants of the aforesaid Jurishdiction :

May it Please yor Honno^{rs} The Honno^{ble} Bench : To take notis that wee thankefully acknoledg the Honble Benches Fauou^{r} in a Redy Answareing ou^{r} Petition by vouchsafeing vs to Express our Broaken English by way of Decleration, And that wee might not be to Copiuous therein, shall in shortt p^{r}sent this Hono^{ble} Court as a direct Answare to the Tenor of our jnditement as wee stand Impeached of Pirazie, or being Pirates, we doe Say that wee are not Guiltye, neither in Act nor yet intent, neither are wee Contieous to ou^{r} Selues of anny thing that wee have Done, that is either a breach of anny knowne Law, or may So much as tend either by ou^{r} words or acts jniureous to the Libertyes or Genurall Priveleadges of this yor jurishdiction or Common Wealth ; but if anny of yor inhabytants haue Sustaynced Loss by vs they haue benne only ptickeler psons Private Intrests occationed by them Selues (or there owne Sceeking) and not ours, in theire Presumeing To Intreanch vppon our Great Princes Rights and Priveledges Gained him From His Declared Enemies by the Blood & Swoards of his Leige Subiects, amongst whome wee are nombread. Yett notwithstanding had anny of those yor Inhabytants Found themselues Agreeued, there was a more regular way for theire Releefe wch they might haue had: Naimely, that vppon Makeing theire Complaynt to this Authoritie, We should vppon the Least Summons from the Cheife Authoritye of this Place, in honno.' to our Prince, and vindecation of our Selues, So farr Honnored them (being Desireous of a Continewed amecable vnitye & Commerce of Trayd as Naighbores, and being Subiects to Such Great Princes in Loue, pease, And ametye with each other) as forthwith to a dispatched a shallop away with not only one to Giue acc.ᵒᵘ of our actions, but with Soffitient Effects to a Answared anny Ciuell action in yo.' Law ; and then if by Law wee Could not a warranted our Actions we ware Redy to giue and make the iniuried psons Sattisfaction, wᶜʰ in our Aprehentions would A benn farr better then Such Indirect And hosteele proseeding against vs, that Except by the wisdom of yo.' Authority be not tymely Pevented, will inevetably invoulue the Subiects of a Potent ' Prince, and yo.' Comonwealth whare euer they meete in such Brieles & Discontents (wᶜʰ yet by a Preudentiall Care may be Prevented, but if not) as will hardly Bee Determaned without a Declaritiue warr from ou Great-masters, Which God Forbids that anny of our Blood Should be shead to be omynus as bespeak So Sad a Conclution : for as its ile medling with edg tooles so its as ile intermedleing to vsurp Princes Prerogatiues & Priveledges. . . .

1.ˢᵗ Therefore with Leaue may it please the Honorᵃᵇˡᵉ Court to take Cognizence that wee are parsons whome by our Aleigance are Swoarne Subiects to the Great Prince of Orrange his heires And Suesesers, and as Such ware the Last yeare vndo.' the Comand of Cap.ᵗ Vrine Arnhoutson, Comando.' of the Flying horse Frigott, whome Receued from the Renouned Governo.' our Princes Representatiue at Carrysaw in the west-indias a Generall Comition in our Princes naime, in Genarall tearmes Comprehending to take Plundo.' Spoyle and Poses anny of the Garrisons, Townes, terrytories, Priveleadges, Shipps, Persons, or Estates belonging to anny of his highneses Enemies that are at varyence and in acts of Hostilitye against his highnes & the Great states of Holland. And accompt

46

thereof to take, and the Tenths thereof Secure all Princely Prerogatiues indeauou.^r to mayntayne for the Honno.^r of our Prince according to our Powre and Alleagence jn psueance of wch Comition our Frigatt Arriued at New Yoarke, Dureing wch tyme of our abode theire to recruit with Vituall, Cap^{tt} John Roades Came to vs from Boston, who Gaue ou^r Comando^r Such a Satisfactory accompt of his aquaintence on the Coasts of Nova Scotia and occada, and Rasinall Probabilities of makeing ou'selues Masters thereof to ad to or inlardg our Great Princes terrytories, it being then Mantayned and Possesed by the French, our Masters Implacable and Declared Enemies in open hostillitye, wee did with a vnanimus Consent all conclude to dispatch the Designe as an Honnor^{able} Expedition, to wch end ingaged Cap^{tt} John Roades as our Pilott, haueing Swoarn him to aleagence To our Prince, the Prince of Orrange our master, and then admited him one of vs our Princes Leige Subiects, whare in Due tyme wee Arrived on the Coast of Nova Scotia and Landed at Penobscott, the Enemies Princeple Garrison, the wch in storming, after a shortt Dispute, by Gods Blessing quickly made our Selues Masters thereof; but haueing not Sofitient Strength to Leaue to Garrison the Place, wee demolished the Fort and fired Sume of the houses of the French, bringing away the Artilleryc & Plundo^r. And after we had made oure Selues masters also of St Johns, Mathyas, and Gamshake,[1] & Severall other Places of Fortification And trayding houses of the French and Brought away the Plundo.^r and Princeple Persons Prisono^{rs}, wee did not only Burrye in two Glass Botles at Penobscott & St Johns vnde^r Ground A tru Copia of our Cap^{ts} Comition, and a Breviate of the Manno.^r of takeing the Said Places by the Swoards of the Prince of orringe Subiects for his hignes vse, but also Left both att Penobscot and gamshake sume men of the poorer soart of oure Cap^{ttiues} the formor Inhabytance, whome had Submited to be subiects to our Prince, to whome wee gaue libertye to trayd and order.^d to keepe Possion for his highnes till farther ordo^r or Sum of vs Retorned theither. Wee then Coming a

---

[1] Gemesic or Gemsic. — H.

way in ou' Frigott to Boston, whare after your Authorytie was aquainted with our Comĩsion and Enterprizes, wᶜʰ was So farr Satisfactory to them as manufasted theire Aprobation theireof by Admiting vs to Dispose. & share ouᵗ Plundo⸱ & sell our Marchandize & Plundoʳ to the Inhabytants heere, yea ouᵗ Cannon or Great Gunns being Bought for the Safegaurd & vse of this very Colloñy whare our Capᵗ was Adresed to by Severall trayders to the East-ward belonging to this Jurrishdiction, to grant them Libertye to trayd in those his higneses the Princes of Orranges ꝓsinctes taken by vs, but by our Comãndoʳ in Cheife was Reffused, whome Replyed to them that if there was anny Priveleadg of trayd to be had it did ꝓperly belong to his men, who had with him ventered theire Liues with the Loss of there blood for it. And therefore all Such ꝑsons vppon the Perrell of there being made Prize on was by him forbid Comeing to trayd on those Coasts, withĩn our Masters ꝑsinctes, &c. Yett not withstanding did sum of these ꝑsons in Contempt intrench on our Priveledges as is heere after Expresed. For after our Frigott was Goñ From Boston, and the Cheife Comãndoᵗ had Given Capᵗⁿ Petter Rodrigo & Capᵗⁿ Cornelius Andreson, with 8 more of there Conscarts, an ordoʳ to Retorne to new holland, Alias novascotia & occada, our Princes Lands (wᶜʰ after wee had Gained it by the Swoard Called it as afforesaid, new holland), and ordors from him theire to trayd, keepe posesion, & in what vs Lay mantayne our Princes Prerogatiues theire till farther Ordor, either from our Masters in holland or himselfe, Wee then did with the Assistence of sume Creditt in Boston fitt a Cople of smale vessells out & went to new holland, Alias Novᵃ Scotiᵃ, whare as we ware on our Coasts.

The First English we mett with theire was one hilliard, of Sallem, whome finding him trayding on ouᵗ Coast Comãnded him aboard, whome jmediatly Submiting and Complayning of his bad voyage, And that he was ignorant of our being theire, we Retorned him not only his vessell and Goods againe, but also all there Peltry. And after we had Bought Sume nesesaryes of them, Paying them theire Price for the Same, wee dismissed them with an Admonition And warning to Com̃ no more on there Perrell to trayd theire within those our Masters persinctes.

The Second English vessell wee tooke was William Waldron, whome we had forwarned Severall tymes not to p̃rsume to Com̃ to take away our Priveledges of trayd on therre Perall of being made Prize on by vs ; yet in verry Contempt, as wee may say, he Came to take our trayd from vs, whom when wee found him that he had ben trayding with the jndians and was vppon our owne Coasts, wee tooke him and made Prize of ownly his Peltry, And after A Civell treating them, Dismised them with is vessell and other Goods.

The Third English vessell we tooke was Georg Mañing, whome was forewarned, both by our Com̃andoᵗ of our Frigott & our Selues at Boston, that if Came to trayd theire in ouʳ Princes Persinctes wee would make Prize of him ; but now finding of them that he had ben trayding, wee Com̃anded him aboard And demanded of him weather he had Anny ordoᵗ from the Honnoᵇˡᵉ Governoᵗ or Authoritye of this Place to Com̃ and trayde theire or Anny Lett Pass from anny Authoritye of this Jurishdiction, he tould vs no ; so then finding his Peltry aboard him wee only tooke that from him, and Civerly treating him, we tendread him also a Pass to Goe free from being againe Examined by our other Consoarts, and also A Letter to mʳ John Freake his Marchanᵗ that wee would Secure his Peltrye by it Selfe & Send it to Boston (with others) in the Spring. And if we did not then and there Cleare to be a Leagall Prize would Retorn it to his Imployer againe, and in the mean tyme haue a faire Corry Spondengsye with them ; to which End the Said Mañing went aboard his owne vessell And theire invited Capᵗ Rodrigo aboard, whom (after that Civell vsedg) he had Privately designed to murdor, haueing prepared a Pistell Charged with a Brace of Bullotts vndoʳ his Pillow, And whilst he was a drinkeing in his Cookeroome to a Pis-tolled him, Butt was discovered by the boye aquainting Capᵗ Rodrigo to Looke to him Selfe, informing of his masters designe, wᶜʰ Caused the Said Rodrigo forth with to Com̃ out vppon the Deck, and rann to the Cabbin of Georg Mañing according to the boyse information,

And found the Pistoll theire Loaden as aforesaid, whome after he had in few words sharply Reproued Georg Mañing for his treacherous and Murdorous designe, Cald for his owne Boat and Goes aboard his owne vessell, whare had not ben Long, but vnexspectedly Geo. Mañing, haueing had all his Gunns and Blunderbuss Redy on his decke, at once Presented his Gunns at vs, Leueling them each one at our men vppon our deckes, Desineing at once to Cutt them off, and then to Surprize vs and Cutt off the Rest. And whilst they ware Thus a Fireing at vs, as God in his mercie and wisdom ordered it, there Powde Flashed in there Panns, and there Gunns Did not Goe off (to Admiration by wch Meanes wee may all thanke God theire hath benn no blood shead), the wch oure Men Perceueing at once Leapt Doune for theire Armes, Cryeing, Cap^{n} shall wee be Killed without Fighting for our Liues; at wch word in A Maize euery man of vs hasted vpp his Armes and forthwith Gaue them Such a charge as Comanded him aboard vs; then wee thought that wee had Good Reason to Condemne him whollye for a Prize, but instead thereof wee only tooke his Goods and Gaue him his vessell againe, and would a dismissed; but he so ernestly beged and Besought vs that he might stay with vs, and that wee would take his vessell and men into our Seruis, at whose solicitation wee hired of him his vessell with him selfe & men, and jngaged to Pay him Seauen Pounds p month; it being his first pfer & full demand of vs.

The Fourth and Last English vessell wee tooke was, viz Mai^r Sheapleigh Barque, whome wee Found by Seuerall Papers that they had not only trayded for Peltry, but was Com with pvition from Port Royall to Releue ou^r Enemies at Gamshake, wch Place had Reuoalted From vs, wch actions to vs was Ground Sofitient to make Prize there of; but we only tooke from them ye quantitie of three Beefes and a few Skynes, and after a Civell vseadge of them, Gaue them a dismission, et^c. After wch wee ware betrayed by Georg Mañing to Cap^n Sam: Mosely, whome at the takeing of vs wee ware at one tyme psued And chaced with vessells vndo^r both English, French,

& Dutch Collors, Cap.ᵗ Sam.ˡˡ Mosely Fighting vs vndo.ʳ English Col-
lors, And had Putt Both force and men aboard the French, and
Georg Mañing fircing vppon vs vndo.ʳ dutch Collors; wᶜʰ manor of
disiplyn and actions wee vndoʳstand not, And therefore with Sub-
mision Desiere Cap.ᵗ Moselyes Coñission may be Produced and
Read to the Honn.ᵃᵇˡᵉ Bench, that So it may Appeare weather the
Cuntrey And Authoritye will vindicate not only Such theire actions,
Butt by Force bringing of vs from out of our Princes Countrye
Gained him by the Swoards of his Leige Subiects and also his
Accomadateing of our Princes declared Enemies, with both force,
men, Amonition, & ᵽvition against vs, and thereby to disposes our
Great Prince of his Rights, Priveleadges, & Prerogatiues So Honnor-
ably Gained him.

Thus may it Please yᵉ Hon.ᵃᵇˡᵉ Bench we haue Given A shoart
accompt of our Particuler acts and tranceactions as they are in
truth ; & now with Leaue in the Second place shall shoe by what
Powre or the Reasons of our thus farr ᵽseedings and wherfore wee
haue thus Acted as vizᵗ: —

1.ᵗ Because wee Looke at and beleeue Cap.ᵗ Vrn Arnhoustons
Coñissiō To be Sofitiently Lawfull and warrantable for the takeing
the fore Mentioned Places of Nova Scotia, wᵗʰ the Priveledges and
trayd thereof To Ad to his highnes our Masters Terrytories and also
alike Confirmed Lawfull by this authoretye as by ouʳ Second Con-
seption heereafter Expresed.

2.ˡʸ : A second Reason for ouʳ thus acting is Because wee ware
ᵽswaded and doe judg the ordo.ʳ wee had from Cap.ᵗ vrin Arnhoutson, as our then Cheife Coñandoʳ, had it ben only verbaly, ware
Equivealent with his Coñision vnto vs that was Equally Concearned
in the stormeing & takeing yᵉ Same, Butt more Espeatially for the
keepeing Possesion & mantayneing our Princes Prerogatiues &
Priveleadges wᶜʰ wee had for the Honno.ʳ of our Prince before so
gained by our Swoards with the Loss of our Blood and Perrill of our
Liues.

3.ˡʸ : Because of the Great ᵽvocations of and Insolencies Coñited by the English in theire first abuseing and Plundering ouʳ Subiects, And Conquered Places before euer wee Assumed to medle with anny of yoʳ jnhabytants vessels, wᶜʰ is more Fully Explayned heereafter in the first & Second Recited iniuryes wee haue Sustayned.

4ʸ : we had Sofitient Reason because wee ware not vnsensable that verry Places thus for our Prince Gained him by vs hath in all Changes of Goverment ben a Lowed a distincke Priveledg Place of Trayd; and all ꝑsones Attempting So to trayd without Licence from the then Present ꝑpriatoʳs to be made Lyable to be made Prize on ; & that both vessells and Goods, wᶜʰ Propriatoʳs at pʳsent wee owne our Selues to bee in the behalfe and for the vse of the Prince of Orrange, to whome only we are Legaly accomptable for what we haue doune.

5ˡʸ : Because we ware farther Sensable that the Authoritye of this jurrishdiction hath taken Such Cognizence of our Last foregoing Reasons as hath made it a Ground to Establish a Law, as in Pag: 75, Granting Libertye to anny Private Parson, as an inhabytant, To zeise both vessell and Goods of anny so trading in the persincts of this Jurrishdiction, and Therefore warrantable for vs to mantayne those formar Priveledges, as we mind the vindication and mantayneing of the Honnoʳ Prerogatiue and Priveledges of our Great Prince in this his highneses Territories Gaind him by vs As afforesaid.

6ˡʸ : Because wee being jletterate ouʳ Selues, or at Least the princeples of vs, The Consideration of the Aprobation of the Authoritye of this Place, Aproueing of ouʳ Comandoⁿˢ Comision Manufasted by Admiting vs not only to sell and share our Plundoᵗ heere, but yoʳ Authoritye Byeing our Great Gunns for the vse & Safegaurd of this verry Jurrishdiction, Confirmed our judgmenᵗˢ in the Legality of our ꝑsceedings and actions.

7 : Because those Comandoⁿˢ of the vessells wee did so take & make Prize off ware only such men whome wee had forbiden and Given fore warning not to Com to trayd or ꝑʳsume on our Priveleadges in these our masters ꝑsinctes vppon the Perrill of Being made Price, wᶜʰ we Legaly might according to the Practis of Sum of

the Inhabetants of this Jurisdiction when they had the Powre as ppriato^{rs} of the very Same places ; witnes the Case of Cap Spenser & others ; but wee ware so favorable as tooke only there Peltrye.

8. Because further, what wee haue acted hath not bin out of anny Mallace or Prejudize wee haue to this Cuntrey or ile will to the Authoritie thereof, but out of a tru Souldiers of Fortunes intrest and vallou^r, and an vpright, Honnest heart to Mantaync the Honno^r, Priveleadges, & Prerogatiues of our Prince, wch wee haue Lately Espoused in his highneses jntrest in new holland, Allias Nova Scotia, etc.

And thus haueing Given the Honno^{rable} Court sum Princeple Groundes and reasons wch we make for our defence and vindecation, shall in the Third Place, with Leaue, give the Bench a short acc$_:$ of the jnjuries wee haue Sustayned And Abuisses given vs by yor in-habetents, and then Leaue to yor worships Breasts to Consider weather wee haue not benne Sofitiently pvoaked to a acted with farr Greate^r Seuerritye then as yett wee haue donn.

1^t Gamshake Fort, wch wee Left for a Garrison for those that wee Left behind, in wch wee putt Sum of the Honnestest and Poorer Soart of the Formar Inhabytents that Submited themselues to vs in y^t Possesion theire of, and to keepe the Same for the vse of ou^r Prince vntill Sume of vs Retorned ; but George Hollett, Rich. Suiet, And john Greene, in octobe^r Last, went to Port Royall, & from thence Trance Ported Frenchmen, our Enemies, to the Said Fort, & Setled them theire, Furnishing of them with Arms, Amonition, & Goods ; that when wee Came to St Johns Riuer in ordo^r to Posses the said Fort, The French, so setled by them, maintayned it against vs, and, being winter time, wee Could pseed no farther, but Retreated to Penobscott and the other of our Conquared Places, whare wee found those wee Left there welcoming vs and Redely yealding there obe-dience to vs ; wch thing, when Com to vnderstand, wee thought it straing that yor inhabytants should not only indeauoer to Cerconvent vs of the Priveledges of our trayd with the Indians, the wch they might, one would a thought, haueing taken there share thereof, a benn Contented, and not a medled with states matters in furnishing the French, ou[r] Enemies, and Suporting of them against y[e] Dutch, (with whome you are at Amytie), and that in ou[r] Princes owne Cuntrye. So that how this is Consistant with the Late Articles of Peace made betwext our Great masters, wee Leaue for the wise to judg.

2[ly] : The jnhabytants of Pemequick or quid & severall English Fishermen Came to Penobscott, whare did not only Breake vpp the Plankes of our Demolished Fort and Gott out y[e] Iron worke and Spikes & Carryed them away, but also Robed, pilidged, & Plundered ou[r] Poore Subiects theire, w[ch] wee Left to keepe Possesion for our Prince till we Retvrned of all theire pvition and store w[ch] wee Left them for to Sustayne their Poore Famelyes in the hard winter that nessetated The men to Leaue there wifes and Children to Joyne with the Indians, and with them Runn in the woods a hunting for there Famelyes to Keepe them from starueing, whilst yo[r] English had taken there pvition as aforesaid from them ; soe that when wee Retorned, those our Subiects presently welcoming of vs Gaue vs a ptickeler accompt thereof, & with all declareing to vs that the abuises they so Receved From the English was tenne times worse then when the dutch first Came and tooke there Forts ; and all this was done before euer wee offered to take anny of yo[r] vessels, according to our third Reason, before Recited.

3[ly] : On march the 10th Last Thomas Coole, of Nantaskett, on of yo[r] Inhabytants, Came to maythyas, a place whare wee had built A Trayding howse and Layd in a stocke of Goods. the said Coole Came a shoare with his boat full of men, Armed with Gunns, Pistels, swoards, whare, finding but foure of our men, takes them at a disadvantadge, Surprizes ther psons Prisonors, Riefels and Plundo[rs] ou[r] house, and Carryes away all ou[r] Peltry and other trading Goods, Plucks Downe our Princes Flagg as it was Flying, & Carryes our men Prisoners aboard his vessell, and in pticuler binds Randall judgsons Arms behind him and torned him ashoar for foure nights & foure dayse with out anny shelter or Couering in that Could

47

Season, but in that Condition to be Left as a pray to the mercye of his Enemies, had they found him, and all this without anny Powre or Comision from anny Authoritye ; so that how farr this Lookes like Pirazie, wee Leaue the jmpartiall to judg.

4ly: Geo: Maning, after that Ciuell vsedg shewed to him at our first takeing of him, that he should so Secritly, in a treacherous way, Contriued and Designed to murdor our Cap', & after discouered, and our men all aboard our owne vessell, to Com vp vnexspectedly and Attempt to fire a broad side of smale shott vppon vs, who Could a done Less in there own defence then wee did ? yett wee Rewarded him Good for his Euell, as witnes Geo: manings owne Letters to mr John Freake ; this Likewise wee desire may be Considered, with its Cercomstances.

5ly: vppon Capt Moselyes takeing of vs, this Geo: maning Re-uoalts frō vs, being then vndor both our Comand, jmploy, & hire, both for men and vessell, and with a Lye in his mouth he betrayes vs, and afterwards fires vppon vs or Fights vs vndor dutch our owne Princes Collors ; and how like New England Pirazie or Pirates this may be tearmed, wch Law of Pirazie defines those that Rise vpp in Rebellion against ther Comandors, marchants, ownors, or Imployers, to be, such wee Leaue to the jmpartiall oppinion of this Honnorable Bench to judg, etc.

6ly : whilst wee ware thus taken by Capt Mosely, hee had before Furnished a French man, our Enemie, with both men & force to assist him against vs ; and after wee So Submited, he Plundors vs of all wee had Gotten the whole Winter, not only by our Swoards from our Enemies, but all that wch wee had trayded with the stocke wch wee Carryed out of Boston with vs, and also all our owne Goods & the Remaindor of the Goods wrh wee had on the Credit of those Merchts in Boston to whome wee are still obleiged, and thus Brings vs all away from our Princes Cuntrey, Leaueing it to be Sirprizd by our Enemies, whilst hee by his Consoarts Reapes the Great Benefitt & Advantadg of our Spring trayd, and that with our Goods, And wee kept Close Prisonors all the while, and not Admited neither our owne

nor yet a Copia of our Comͥission or ordoͬ from Capͭ Vrin Arnhouthson, our Cheife Comͣandoͬ and Papers taken from vs By Cappͭ
Mosely, by wᶜʰ wee should better be Capassitated to make our Defence, Although hath ben Requested of Capͭ Mosely Severall times;
and how farr these actions are Consistant with the Maintaynence of
that Amycable Peace made betwext ouͬ Great masters for there
Subiects in these Parts thus to act, wee Leaue to the wisdom of the
Prudent jmpartialy to Judg Whome are the Trancegressers, etᶜ.

Thus may it Please the Honᵃᵇˡᵉ Court, haueing Giuen Sum shoart
accompt of the Princaple Iniuries wee haue sustayned, Craue only
yoͬ Patience to Giue vs Leaue with Submition, in the fourth And
Last Place, to Present you with Sume few Conseptions of ouͬ owne
as an Aditiñall matter for our Defence And Confirmation of our Reasons before Recited, & that Grounded vppon either Precept or
Example of This verry Jurisdiction, vizͭ.

1ˢͭ Wee humbly Conceue if our first Comͥison, Given Capͭ vrin
Arnhouthson, By vertue of wᶜʰ wee tooke the Cuntrye, be warranta-
ble, & by Law Legall, then as we ware pportionably Concearned &
Parties in that Expedition, all that wee haue acted for the Keepeing
Posesion & Mayntayning the Priveledges of the Same for the Honnoͬ
of ouͭ Prince is alike warrantable and by Law Legall; for if the
Cuntry thus Gained becomes thereby pperly the stats of hollands
Land, then all the intrest and Priveledges of trayd in those his high-
neses pSinckes Belongs to the Hollands oͬ likewise.

2ʸ: Wee Humbly Conceue that if the Authorityc of this Place,
when they first saw our Comͣandoͬˢ Comͥision and had a full & tru
accompͭ of our Actions, jn there wisdom had not benne well & fully
Satisfied jn the justis or justness and Legalytie of our Enterprizes,
they would not a Suffered anny Such Goods or Plundoͬ Soe vniustly
taken to a benne Receued or Sould Amongst yoͬ jnhabytants, By
Reason (Receuers And takers in A Sence are termed a like), But
Rather, by a Discountenanceing the Same, would A bear a testymony
against vs as an Enterprize vn Lawfull, and so ile legall, etc. Butt
ouͭ Comͥision and Enterprize, by this Authorityc, was so well Aproued

on & Satisfied in, as boath ouʳ Com̄andoᵗ & men ware Civelly treated and Admited to share and Sell our Plundoᵗ to yoʳ Inhabytent, and our Great Gunns, Bought By yoʳ Authoritye for the farther Safeguard And vse of this verry Collony, and therefore vnto vs Confirmes our Enterprize and Actions to be boath Lawfull, warrantable, and Legall, By wᶜʰ this Authoritye also hath Confirmed our first before Recited Reason, etc., as we humbly Conceue.

3ˡʸ Wee Humbly Conceue that should wee out of zeale for the Honnoʳ of ouʳ Prince through our want of judgmenᵗ as being jleiterrate or misvnderstanding of ouʳ ordoʳˢ Goe beyond our Com̄ision in anny of the acts wee haue donne, Wee are accomptable only to ouʳ Prince For the Same, at whose marcie wee are, who is Sofitiently Respond to make Good anny jnjurie his Subiectes Doth (weather it be Reall or in Pretence), vndoʳ a Colloʳ of his name or Athorietye, he haueing Security given in hollonds from all pravateteers to make good yᵉ same before there Com̄ision is granted.

4ˡʸ: Wee Humbly Conceue that as ouᵗ Accusations toucheth Life, that wee are not Lyable to answare anny such charge heere ; neither doe wee beleeue the Authoritye of this Place is ꝑper for the tryall and determening this our Case (at Least without a joynt consent) by Reason the Fact wee are Charged with was Donne in the Hollandoʳ Cuntrye, Farr Enough out (with Submition) of the Powre of the Chartoʳ of this jurishdiction, the Case and matter indefferrance arriseing there by Sum English of the inhabytants of this Collonys intreanching vppon the Prince of orrange, ouᵗ Great masters tray'd & Priveledges in his owne ꝑSincte ; and that without anny ordoᵗ or Comision from either anny Authoritye or ꝑpriatoᵗ to jmpowre them soe to doe but at the ownly Hazerd of theire owne fortunes of being made Lyable to be made Prise off.

5ˡʸ: Wee Humbly Conceue againe, that the Esentiall Part of this Differrence Lyeth not so much in Meum & tueum of Single ꝑsons Intrest properly, as matters of Genarall Priveledges and Princely Prerogatiues. And therefore none but ouᵗ Great masters or Sume jmediately Authorized from them, is Legally Capable to take Cogni-

zence thereof, So as to Contradict vs or hindo' vs in ou' Dutys as
obleiged by ou' oaths, & in Honno' to mantayn to ou' Powre for
ou' Prince all Formar Priveledges in this ou' Case vntill wee
are Contradicted by ou' Superiours of ou' Great Masters Leige
Subiectes, etc.

6'y: Wee Humbly Conceue if yo' Honno'' Please only to Consult
yo' owne Lawse and Record, and but Exarsize yo' Reflctiue Faculties by Lookeing back on the Practises in yo' Remembrances, you
will find Such Parellell Cases with ours to bee tearmed warrantable
and Legall.

That Putt vs to a startle how wee Can be questioned for ou' Liues
with Pirazie without Breach of yo' owne Law, Page 143, Granting Libertye for straingers to haue Equall Priveledges of justis as
yo' owne inhabytants without Parshallitye, and that wee may Cleare
this ou' Argumen', wee shall indeauoer to Euince the Honno'able
Bench with the truth of ou' Assertion, by Sum pticuler Instances
w'h wee may appeale to the Contienees of Sum of yo' Honno''
Breasts, for the verrytie of a Good Part theireof, viz''.

(1st) Instance Maio' Sedgwicke, that well Knowne Worthy Comando, whome jn his Comision for these parts, Doubtles, by pticuler
instructions was Designed agst new yoarke, the Dutch being then
Declared enimies Although his Comision at Lardg against anny of
the protecto'' Enemies (if sum of vs then ware not mis informed),
but when he Came heere, before he Could Gett Redy, newse of peace
betwext the two states Came that torned his Expedition another
way to these verry French Forts, w'h places after so taken became
the then states of Englands Lands trayd and Priveledges w'h was
by this Authoritye Counted warrantable and Lawfull. A Case
pellell with our first before recited Reason, whare ou' Cap'' Comision
though in Genarall tearmes against ou' Princes Enimies yet pticu-
lerly Expressed to Com to these Parts on the Coasts of vergina
against the English, our Enemies, as the Dutch ware then, but sence
our Coming Into these parts, the welcom newse of Peace Came betwext ou' Great Masters that torned ou' Expedition another way, to

the makeing ou'selues Masters of the selfe same Forts and Places now gained from ou' Declared Enemies ; and therefore those Lands, trayd, And Priveledges of Nova Scotia are now properly becom the staits of Hollands Proprietye, and so with Submision wee humbly Conceue alike Lawfull & warrantable.

(2) Instance, Those officers and Souldiers, maio.' Sedgwicke Left behind to keepe posesion Looked at it as theire Dutye to mantayne those Priveledges of trayde in those parsincts wch they ware actiue in Gaineing by the Swoard, for doeing of wch they ware not Deemed Pirates, but by this Authoritye Such actions then ware accompted iust and Legall ; a Case parclell with ou' Second before recited Reason, Wee being ᵱsons Equally ingaged in the Gaincing the Places with the Loss of ou.' Blood and Perrell of our liues, and thereby obleiged to mantayne the Priveledges thereof, & therefore ou' Actions therein a Like Legall.

(3) Instance Both in Maio.' Sedgwick & Collonall temples tyme, and all other chang of Govermen^ts those vessells that hath Presumed to a traided with the Indians in those ᵱsinctes without Lycence from the Propriato^rs hath Ben Deemed by this Authoritye Law Full Priztis (to ᵱticulerize the Case of Cap! Spencer not out of memory), A Case ᵱelell with ou' 3 before Recited Reason.

Where, we being for ou.' Prince till farther ordor the ᵱsent ᵱpriato^rs, Such vessells Coming not only without ou' Leaue, but in Contempt to vs, after fare warning, to vsurp from vs our trayd and Priveledges, becoṁs Legaly a like Lawfull Prize.

(4) againe ; for anny Private inhabytent in this jurrishdiction to zeise and make Prize both of vessell and Goods of anny So trayding in this Jurishdiction it is by yo' Law, Page 75, warrantable, wch Case is ᵱelell with ou' fourth before recited Reason, whare wee in like nature Acting for the Priveleadges for ou' Prince in his Territories may with Submision to yo' Honno Judgm! be a like warrantable.

So that wee thinke we may say we haue either by Preceipt or Example of the Practises or Lawse of this Cuntry for to justifie the Legallitye of what wee haue donn without being deemed Pirates, the

Cercomstances of wch with submition shall Leaue to the Breasts of the Hon^{able} Court to seriously Consider.

Butt seventhly, and in the last Place, with out troubling yor Honno's farther wee Humbly Conceue that if the Authoritye vppon heereing and Debateing our Case see Ground to acquit vs, as we see no Cause to the Contraye ; yett wee Cannot but pswade ou'Selues that there might be Such a Comodations propossed or found out as Rationaly might Reconsile all psons agreeable or injured on boath sides ; that so ou^r masters might heere only of the Amicable according of theire Leige Subiects in these Parts of ou^r Great masters territoryes. . . . Thus may it please the Hon^{able} Court, having vouch-safed vs yor Patienc, now to beare with our Copiaousnes, Exscuseing ou^r obserdityes, Pardon ou^r Bouldnes and Accept of this ou^r Deffence and decleration as wee are not only in the vindecation of ou^r persons Arraigned for ou^r Liues, but the Honno^r Priveledges and Preroga-tiues of ou^r Prince wch as Swoarn Subiects wee are in Good Contience to ou^r Gods, tru valou^r as Souldiers, and Loyaltye to ou^r Lord and master, obleiged to mantayne to the Last Drop of Blood in ou^r Bodyes. And Surely then wee that hath So oft Hazearded and jeoperded our liues for triefels or things of Nought, wee hope shall not vppon So Honorable accompt be affrieghted at the threating of Death, for its not that wee feare, being Consceous to our selues That it is not imposeble for men by the Subtlety of there Adversaryes to be Cheated out of there sweet liues when in justis they Cannot be taken from them ; but blessed be God that we haue not only Ground to hope, but beleeue ou^r Lott is not Cast in such a place, but amongst mersifull judges, and men so feareing God as we doubt not but will judge for God. And then will before judgment^r Consider That what wee haue Donne and acted against anny of the Inhabytents of this Jurishdiction hath Benne from the Reasons Before Expressed, and not out of anny Piraticall designe, or mallas to the Cuntrye, but in Honno^r and Aleigence to ou^r Prince ; and if we haue Earred therein wee hope the Hono'able Court will impute it Rather to ou^r ignorance then anny mischeife Designed by vs ; and thus Beseaching the

Honble Court with the most favourable Construction of ou^r Lynes to way the varrieous Cercomstances of this our Defence in the Ballance of a tru and jmpartiall judgment To which End that wisdom may be a directorye therein, wee doe Submissiuely Conclude, Subscribing ou^r Selues Loyall 'Subiects To ou^r Great maste^r the Prince of Orrang, And yor Honno^rs Closs Confined Prisono^rs, to Doe with all in justis As wisdom shall Dirrecte.

wee Subscribe fo^r ou^r selues
And our Asociates
or Soldiers

his
PETTER × RODRIGO.
mark

his
CORNELIUS × ANDRESON.
mark

JN° RHOADES
RANDALL JUDSON
RICHARD FOWLER
PETER GRANT
JOHN THOMAS
JN° WILLIAMS.

all these in open Court owned this pap^r or their declaration to be there deffence to ye Court as 17th may, 1675.

E. R., *S.*

No. 13. Page 153.

THE COMMISSION OF JOHN RHOADE.[1]

The Directors of the Privileged General West India Company of the United Netherlands.

To all those who shall see or hear these presents — GREETING :·

Know, that whereas, in the year 1674, Captain JURRIAEN AERNOUTS, Master of the Frigate The Flying Horse, from Curaçoa, and

[1] The originals of the Commissions of John Rhoade and Cornelis Steenwyck, and the other documents included in No. 13 of the Appendix, are in the possession of the New York Historical Society. Translations of the same are printed in General De Peyster's monograph, The Dutch at the North Pole and the Dutch in Maine: New York, 1857. — H.

charged with a Commission of his Highness the Prince of Orange, has conquered and subdued the coasts and countries of Nova Scotia and Acadie, in which expedition was also present and assisted, with advice and force, JOHN RHOADE :

Therefore, we, after consulting the demand of the aforesaid RHOADE, to establish himself in the aforesaid countries, and to remain there, and to maintain himself, have consented and permitted, and do consent and permit hereby, that the aforesaid RHOADE, in the name and by the consent of the General West India Company, shall take possession of the aforesaid coasts and countries of Nova Scotia and Acadie, in whatever place of that district it may please him, to build houses, and to establish, to cultivate, and to keep in repair, plantations ; that he may trade and negotiate with the natives, and all others with whom the State of the United Netherlands and the aforesaid Company is in peace and alliance : in the first place, to send hither and thither his own goods and merchandize, after paying the duties to our Company ; in the second place, to defend and maintain himself against every foreign and domestic power of enemies. Also, we charge and command our Managers, Captains, Ship-Masters, and all other officers in the service of our Company, and we request all persons who do not belong to our Company, not to trouble or disturb the aforesaid RHOADE ; but, after shewing this Commission, to assist him in the execution thereof, and to give him all help, aid, and assistance.

Given at AMSTERDAM, Sept. 11, 1676.

GASPER PELLICORNE.

For Ordinance of the aforesaid Directors.

C. QUINA.

COMMISSION OF CORNELIS STEENWYCK.

The Directors of the Privileged General West India Company of the United Netherlands.

All those who shall see or hear these presents — GREETING :

Know, that we, being convinced that the wealth of this Company would be greatly increased by the cultivation of those lands and places under the jurisdiction of our aforesaid grantees, and that it will be useful that these aforesaid lands and places should not remain uninhabited, but that somebody be duly settled there, and populate the country; and afterwards thinking on expedients by which the navigation, commerce, and traffic of the aforesaid Company, and of all others who belong to it, may after some time be increased and augmented ; so is it that we, wishing to put our useful intention in execution, for the aforesaid and other reasons, by which we are persuaded; following the second article of our aforesaid grant, and by the authority of the high and mighty States-General of the United Netherlands, and upon mature deliberation of the Council, have committed and authorized, and we do commit and authorize COR-NELIS STEENWYCK, in the name of, and for, the High and Mighty and the Privileged General West India Company, to take possession of the coasts and countries of Nova Scotia and Acadie, including the subordinate countries and islands, so far as their limits are extended, to the east and north from the River Pountegouycet ; and that he, STEENWYCK, may establish himself there, and select such places for himself, in order to cultivate, to sow, or to plant, as he shall wish.

Moreover, to trade with the natives of the country, and all others with whom the Republic of these United Netherlands and the aforesaid Company are in peace and alliance, to negotiate and to traffic in the goods and merchandizes belonging to them, send them hither and thither, and fit out ships and vessels for the large and small fisheries, to set the cargo ashore, to dry and afterwards to sell them, so as he shall think it best ; and, generally, to sustain and maintain himself and his family, by no other than honest means.

Moreover, that he, STEENWYCK, in the name of the High and Mighty, and of the General West India Company, will be admitted to make contracts and alliances and engagements with the natives of that country ; also to build some forts and castles, to defend and to protect himself against every foreign and domestic force of enemies or pirates ; and also to admit and to protect all other persons and families who wish to come under obedience to the Company, if they swear due faithfulness to the much esteemed High and Mighty, as their highest Sovereign Magistrate, to his Highness, My Lord the Prince of Orange, as the Governor-Captain and Admiral-General, and to the Directors of the Privileged West India Company.

That, moreover, the aforesaid STEENWYCK, with the title and power of Manager and Captain, will provide, deliver, and execute everything that belongs to the conservation of these countries ; namely, —

The maintenance of good order, police, and justice, as would be required according to the laws and manners of those countries ; and, principally, that the true Christian reformed religion is practised within the limits of his district, after the usual manner ; that STEENWYCK, according to this, may place some one — if he is a free-born subject — in his office ; who, in name and authority, moreover, with the title and a power as aforesaid, may take possession of the aforesaid countries to establish himself there ; and further, to do and execute all those things whereto STEENWYCK himself, in aforesaid manner, is authorized ; all those things, nevertheless, without expenses, charges, or any kind of burdens to the Company ; and with the invariable condition that the aforesaid STEENWYCK, or the person whom he might place in his office, will be obliged to execute the present Commission and authorization within the next eighteen months, or that by negligence or failure thereof it will be in our faculty and power to give such a Commission and authorization to other persons than STEENWYCK, or his Lieutenant, without any reference to this present one.

Moreover, that the aforesaid STEENWYCK, or whom he shall commission, and who establish himself within the limits of that particular, privileged, and conceded district, shall have freedom and immunity of all rights and recognizances for the time of six years successively.

At last, and to conclude, that the aforesaid STEENWYCK, or his Lieutenant, within the limits of the aforesaid district, will have the right to distribute to others such countries and places for Colonies and farms as he shall think best ; and that the managers and principals of those Colonies and farms, for the time of six years, shall be entirely possessed of the aforesaid rights and recognizances.

We command and charge all our Directors, Managers, Captains, Masters of ships, and all our other officers who may belong to them, that they will have to acknowledge, to respect, and to obey, the aforesaid CORNELIS STEENWYCK, or his Lieutenant, as Manager and Captain, within the limits of the aforesaid district ; and to procure, to give, and to afford him every help, aid, and assistance in the execution thereof, — seeing that we find it useful for the service of the Company.

Given in AMSTERDAM, October 27, 1676.

GASPER PELLICORNE.

For Ordinance of the aforesaid Directors.

C. QUINA.

MOST HONORABLE, VALIANT, AND HONEST BELOVED, FAITHFUL:

In answer to the remonstrance of your brother-in-law, Nicolaas, the Governor, we have thought convenient to send your Honor the enclosed Commission and authorization, being the permission to take possession of the coasts and countries of Nova Scotia and Acadie, so far as its limits are extended from the River Pentegoüet, to the east and north, in the name and upon the authority of the High and Mighty States-General of the United Netherlands and the

Privileged West India Company, confirming all such conditions as your Honor will see himself, by reading the aforesaid Commission.

But our intention is not to prejudice a Commission of the 11ᵗʰ Sept'r last, given to JOHN RHOADE, a native of England, was helping to conquer and subdue the aforesaid coasts and countries in the year 1674, under the direction of CAPT. JURRIAEN AERNOUTS. A Copy of that aforesaid Commission is herewith, as witness for you : —

We have commanded the aforesaid RHOADE to give your Honor, from time to time, his advice in regard to the state of affairs, and as to what could be done for them by virtue of our aforesaid Commission, and we hope that it will be observed by him.

Moreover, we ask and desire eagerly, that as soon as your Honor shall have taken possession of the aforesaid lands, or may have sent somebody there in his name, you will tell us the state of affairs there, and also what kind of business could there be practised with gain and advantage ; also to let us know all those things which you may think advantageous for us to know.

If, afterwards, there should be found any minerals in any place there, we wish that your Honor would send us some samples, with, and besides, your opinion and advice in order to decide upon it. Finally, we command your Honor to do all that which may increase the wealth of our Company.

Wherewith finishing, we commend you to the protection of God.

AMSTERDAM, October 27, 1676.

GASPER PELLICORNE.

For Ordinance of the aforesaid Directors.

C. QUINA.

No. 14.　Page 154.

LETTER FROM THE DUTCH AMBASSADOR TO THE KING OF GREAT BRITAIN.

Au Roy de la Grande Bretagne.

LE soubsigné Ambassadeur Extraordinaire de Messeigneurs les Estats des Provinces Unies se trouve obligé par ordre exprès de ses Maistres de representer à sa Maj^te qu'un Capitaine nommé Juriaen Aerents Commendant le vaisseau Le Cheval de poste de Curassao estant party du dit Curassao avec commission du Goûverneur de cett' isle, et s'estant rendu Maistre des Forts Penatscop, et de St Jan appartenants aux Francois, et situez sur la Riviere Pontegouet qui est du Nord de l'Amerique dans Les Pays de la Nouvelle France, et y aiant laissé une partie de ses Gens pour la garde des dites places et pour traffiquer avec les peuples du Pays d'alentour.　Il a plu aux Anglois qui sont à Boston d'attaquer à main armée les gens y laissez en garnison, de les faire prisonniers, et de raser les fortifications y faites dans la seule veue de n'y pas souffrir d'Hollandois. Ce qu'estant une violation ouverte du Traieté de la Paix faite avec Sa Maj^te.　Elle est très humblement priée du faire punir exemplairement les coupables, et d'envoyer les ordres necessaires pour le promt relâchement des dits prisonniers et la restitution des dits Forts avec entier dedommagement.　A WINDSOR ce ^{26 Julij}_{5 Aoust} 1675

C. VAN BEUNINGEN.[1]

[1] Copied from the original in the English State-Paper Office. — H.

No. 15. Page 155.

ORDERS IN COUNCIL.

At WHITEIIALL, February the 11ᵗʰ 1675[-6].
Present the King's Most Excellent Majesty.

THE BOSTONERS IN NEW ENGLAND TO ANSWER THE COMPLAINT OF THE DUTCH AMBR. Upon the Memoriall of the Ambassador Extraordinary of the States General of the United Provinces representing that Capt. Jurian Arensen, Commander of the Shipp Flying Horse of Curasso, having received a Commission from the Governor of that Island, made himself Master of the Forts of Penotscop and Sᵗ John, belonging to the French, situated upon the river of Pentagolt in 'the North of America in New France, and having left part of his men there, for the defense of the said places, and to trade with the inhabitants thereabouts, the English of Boston did by force of armes attack the men left in Garrison in the said places, made them Prisoners, and razed the Fortifications, upon no other consideration but because they would not suffer any Hollander there ; Praying his Majestie to cause exemplary punishment to be inflicted upon the Offenders, and to send requisite Orders for the speedy setting at liberty the Prisoners, and restitucion of the said Forts, with satisfaction for damages. It is this day Ordered that a Copie of the said Memoriall be sent unto the Magistrates of Boston in New England, who are hereby required to return their answer to said Complaint, That so 'his Majestie understanding the nature of the Fact may give such order as is agreeable to justice therein. And the Right Honᵇˡᵉ Mʳ Secretary Williamson is to prepare a letter for his Majesties Signature accordingly. [Charles II., vol. xii. 119.]¹

---

¹ Coll. Mass. Hist. Soc., xxxii. (4th Series), 286, 287. — H.

Here follows the King's letter: —

The King's Letter to the Governor and Council of Massachusetts.

CHARLES R.

Trusty and welbeloved. We greet you well. Whereas the Amb: Extraord: of the States Generalls of the United Provinces hath complained unto Us, that Cap: Juriaen Arenson Comander of the ship Flying Posthorse of Curassao having received a Commission from the Goûvernor of that Island, and made himself master of the Forts Penatscop and St John belonging to the French scituated upon the River Pountegoult in the West of America in New France, and having left part of his men there for the defence of the said places, and to trade with the Inhabitants thereabouts, That some English belonging to Boston did by force of armes attack the men left in Garrison in the said places, made them prisoners and razed the fortifications upon noe other consideration, as is pretended, but because they would not suffer any Hollander there. We having taken the same into Our Royall consideration, have thought fit by the advice of our Privy Councill to send a Copy of the said Memoriall to you, and to require you to returne your speedy answer to the said complaint, that soe We understanding the nature of the Fact may give such order as is agreable to Justice therein, in pursuance of the good correspondence between Us and the said States. And soe We bid you farewell. Given at Our Court at WHITEHALL the 18th day of February 167⅞ in the eight and twentieth yeare of Our Reign.

By His Maj[ty's] Command.

J. WILLIAMSON.

To our Trusty and welbeloved
The Gouvernor and Councill of the
Massachussets Colony in New England.[1]

[1] Copied from the original in English State-Paper Office. — H.

No. 16. Page 156.

ANSWER OF THE GOVERNOR AND COUNCIL OF MASSACHU-SETTS TO THE MEMORIAL OF THE DUTCH AMBASSADOR.[1]

To the King's most Excellent Majesty:

The answer of the Gouerno͞r & Councill of the Mattachusetts Colony to the complaint exhibited against them by the extraordinary Embassado͞r of the Lords States Generall of the United Provinces, January 22ᵒ 167⅝, which came to o͞r hands Sept͞r. 3ᵈ 1676.

That Capt͞t Jurian Aronson, Comand͞r of the Ship Flying Post horse of Curassoa, haveing received Comission from the Gouerno͞r of that Island, made himselfe Master of the Forts Penatskop and S͞t John, belonging to the French and scituate upon the River Pentegoult in the North of America in New France, and having left part of his men there for defence of the s͞d place and to trade with the Inhabitants thereabouts: The English of Boston have thought fit by force of armes to attack the men left in garrison — in the s͞d place making them prison͞rs and raceing theire Fortification made upon no other consideration but because they would not suffer any Holland͞rs there; which being an open violation of the treaty of peace, &c.

That Capt͞n Jurian Aronson Comand͞r of the Ship Flying Post horse of Curassoa came into the harbour, in the Mattachusetts, in the yeare 1674, and applied himselfe to the Gouerno͞r to have liberty to come up to Boston to repaire & revictuall his Ship, hee having been at the River of Pentegoult and there made himselfe Master of the Fort & brought the French Gouerno͞r his prison͞r Shewing his Comission for what hee had done; which Comission was against English as well as French; the Gouerno͞r having the proclamation of the peace agreed between his Majesty and theire Lordships, granted him the s͞d Capt͞n Liberty according to his desire to come up with his Ship; who informed the Gouerno͞r that hee had not left any men to keepe possession of his conquest; but had dismantled

---
[1] Mass. Archives, lxi. 134-136. — H.

the Fort and brought away the gunn's. The Capt. having fitted his Ship and dispatched his buisness, hee came to the Gouerno. to take his Leave and have a permit for his Sayling ; at which time the Gouerno. asked him if hee had given Comission to any to goe and keepe that Country or any part of it, or whither hee had given to any a coppie of his Comission to that end ; hee said hee had given no Comission nor a coppie of his, nor would hee give any, for that hee would not make himselfe liable to answer for others' actions, this was in October 1674. at his departure hee left in Boston severall that had been of his company in the former action — Viz! John Rhodes, a Boston man, and four other English — two of them of Boston — with one Cornelius Andreson, a dutchman, and Peter Rodrigo, a Flanderkin ; The Gouerno. hearing that there were of those men going forth to those parts, sent for John Rhodes, being informed that hee was the principall, and demanded of him whither hee was goeing, hee saide a trading to the Eastward, being asked whither hee nor any of the company did not goe to take vessells that were coasting and trading there, hee answered no, nor had they any Comission so to doe.

In december following William Waldron made his complaint to the Gou. & Councill, that upon the Seas coming homeward, hee was met with by Cornelius Andreson, John Rhodes, and some others in a Vessell, out of which they fired two guns at him, & comanded him to anchor ; they came on board him, and forceably tooke from him beaver, with other peltry & small Furr's to value of about £60 Sterl. & carried himselfe & goods by force on board theire vessell, and there forced him to Set his hand to a writing drawn by John Rhodes that they had taken from him nothing but peltry, and had taken it in New Holland. After, in February 167⅘ John Freake, Merchant, made complaint that hee had a small vessell, under the comand of George Manning, bound homewards on a Voyage from the Eastward, by accident was met withall in the River of S. John by John Rhodes & Some Dutchmen his complices, in a small Vessell sometime in the month of Decemb. last past ; who overpowering them with men, piratically Seized his s. Vessell & goods on board her, had wounded the Master & another of his company, and kept both Vessell, goods, & men ; Severall other of his Maties Subjects complained, some of them being of the Jurisdiction of the Mattachusetts, that the s^d persons had robbed & plundered them ; who prayed that some course might bee taken for theire Security against them. Whereupon the Gou^r. & Council taking the same into theire consideration what might bee requisite to bee done for the securing of the Inhabitants on shore & the navigation by Sea, concluded it necessary to send forth, that they might bee certainly informed by what Comission the s^d persons and theire complices had so acted, and in case of theire resistance to bring them in by force, and for that end comissioned Captn. Sam^ll. Moseley ; who in pursuance of his Comission Seized & tooke John Rhodes, Peter Rodrigo, Peter Grant, Thomas Mitchel, and Edwd. Youring in the vessell that was Tho: Mitchels, whome they hired for a trading voyage as by Charter party appeared ; afterwards hee also tooke the other vessell wherein Cornelius Andreson, John Thomas, & John Williams with others were, and returned to Boston with them the 2^d of april 1675. Captn. Moseley bringing his prisoners before the Gouerno^r. and Magistrates at Boston, who Examined them, whither they had done according to the complaints exhibited against them in Seizing goods & Vessells &c., they owned the Fact, but denied that they had done it piratically ; then it was demanded of them by what comission they had done what was done in taking Vessells & goods from his Maties Subjects in a hostile way, and by wh authority they had robbed & plundered the Inhabitants of this Colony, all which was fully proved against them by honest men upon Oath ; whereupon Peter Rodrigo produced a paper wth three Seales according to the inclosed Coppie. Cornelius Andreson produced another of the like tenor without any Seale, which gave them no power to Seize any Vessell or goods, onely had liberty to trade, keepe the Country, & Saile upon the coast ; for which they were not Seized and imprisoned ; but for piratycally Seizing the Vessells & goods that belonged to his Maties Subjects and so were comitted in order to theire tryall. Peter Rodrigo, John Rhodes, Richard Fowler, Randolph

Judson, Peter Grant, and Cornelius Andreson, by the Grandjury were indicted severally by theire severall bills for such theire pyraticall practices, and after, by the Jury of Tryalls all but Cornelius Andreson found guilty; for which they were Sentenced to death; but after repreived, and upon theire humble petitions to the Generall Court wherein they acknowledge the justness of the Courts proceedings, the s⁴ Court pardoned them for theire lives, but banished them the Colony upon pain of death unless they should obtain from authority leave to return. So that what was done in prosecution of that matter was not done because the English would not suffer any Hollanders to bee nigh them; but to prevent & suppress the pyraticall practices of English, Dutch, or other Nations. Of them that were brought to tryall there was but one Dutchman, Four Englishmen, & one Flanderkin. Wee did not nor do judge it tolerable for any Gouernment, much less for a Gouer'm! deriving theire authority from his Ma^ᵗⁱᵉ to Suffer any under pretence of theire useing the name of any Prince or State from whome they have derived no power, to associate themselves and by wayes of hostility molest peaceable and quiet minded Subjects in theire lawfull occasions; So that had the matter been truly laide before the Lords States Generall, wee doubt not but theire Lordships would have seen the justice of oᵣ proceedings at Boston — both by the law's of God, of all civill Nations, as well as the Law's of oᵣ Colony, & no cause of complaint against the innocent whose principles, profession, & practices are against such proceeding as the complaint imparts: and wee doubt not but by the clemency & Justice of his Ma^ᵗⁱᵉ oᵣ Sovereign to bee justified in these oᵣ just proceedings & have not been any violatoᵣˢ of the treaty of peace between his Ma^ᵗᵉˡ and theire Lordships.

This letter[1] or narrative is past by yᵉ Council to be sent to one of his Maj^ᵗⁱᵉˢ Secretaryˢ of state to be presented to his Maj^ᵗʸ as an Answer to his Maj^ᵗʸˢ Comands. 5^ᵗʰ of October, 1676.

EDWᵈ RAWSON, *Secᵣᵉᵗʸ.*

---

[1] The draught of this letter in the Massachusetts Archives is in the hand-writing of Isaac Addington. — H.

No. 17. Page 159

CORRESPONDENCE BETWEEN THE STATES-GENERAL AND
THE ENGLISH COURT RESPECTING THE ARREST AND
TRIAL OF RHOADE AND OTHERS AS PIRATES, ETC.

The Dutch Ambassador to the Lords of the States-General.[1]

WESTMINSTER, August $\frac{1}{5}$, 1679.

MOST HIGH AND HONORABLE LORDS:

MY LORDS, — The King returned yesterday to Windsor from his
trip to Duyns and Por[t]smouth, having spent only so much time in
these places as was allotted for that purpose. It is my intention to
call this evening on His Majesty at Windsor.

You, the Most High and Honorable, having ordered me to continue the matter commenced by Mr. Beuningen, and which he did not
finish, I have, therefore, at the request of the Directors of the West
India Company, insisted upon the release and the indemnification of
one John Rodes,[2] who, being duly provided with a commission from
the West India Company, had attempted to trade in New Scotland
and Accadie on the Coast of America, and was prevented to do so
by one Capt. Namton,[3] who took away from him his ship and merchandise, and besides detained him as prisoner. In consequence of
a Memorial preceding, I presented myself to Mr. Beuningen on the
21st of May last, and requested indemnification for damages inflicted
upon the citizens (or subjects) of the State by those of Boston in
taking and destroying the two forts Penaskop[4] and St. John, which
the Capt. Juriaan Arentsz[5] with his ship, the Flying Horse, in the

---

[1] This letter, and all the letters in
English that follow, were translated for
this volume from the Dutch by the Rev.
J. W. Warnshuis, A.M., late pastor of
the Holland Reformed Church, New
York, now pastor of the Reformed
Church at Alton, Iowa. — H.

[2] Rhoade is the proper spelling. — H.

[3] Knapton. — H.

[4] Penobscot. This name is variously
spelled in this correspondence. — H.

[5] Capt. Jurriaen Aernouts is the person referred to. — H.

year 1674 had taken from the French, as you, the Most High and Honorable, will please learn from the accompanying Memorial, and would also order that in the future such excesses must not again take place. I was promised that in the near future an answer would be given me with reference to this matter, but by way of anticipation, it was said that the King's orders were little obeyed by those of Boston and the adjacent colonies, that they consequently scarcely dare send goods in exchange or ships to England, since those colonists lived there in a kind of independent republics ; however, they would carefully consider every thing pertaining to the matter.

It appears, etc. —

Since the King is away and the members of the Council, nothing happens here worthy the knowledge of you, the High and Honorable ; wherefore for the present I will close, remaining,

High and Honorable Lords,

Your humble, obedient, and faithful servant,

D. v. Leyden van Leeuwen.

Here follows the Memorial mentioned above : —

Au Roy de la Grande Bretagne :

Le soubsigné Ambass! Ex^{re} de Messeigneurs les Estats Generaux des P^{es} Unies, a ordre de representer à Sa Maj^{té} que, nonobstant qu'il soit sans contredit, qu'en l'année 1674 le capitaine Juriaen Aernouts avec la fregatte le cheval volant, par ordre et commission de L. H. P. aye pris sur les françois, les forteresses de Penatscop et S! Jean, situées sur la rivière de Pointegourt dans l'Amerique, dans la nouvelle Escosse et Arcadie, et qu'aynsi L. H. P. s'estans mis en possession par le droit de la guerre de ces terres appartenantes à leur ennemis. Les sujets de Sa Maj^{té} establis à Boston ont entrepris sans aucune raison de chasser led! cap^{ne} Juriaen Aernouts de ses conquestes et de demolir les d^{es} forteresses, en un temps, que L. H. P. avoient l'honneur d'estre amis et alliés de Sa Ma^{té}, et que depuis ceux du d! Baston ayants pretendu la possession des dites terres ap-

pertenantes à la compagnie Belgique des Indes Occidentales, jusques
là, qu'un certain capitaine Namton se soyt saysi de la personne, du
vaisseau et des marchandises de Jean Rodes, quoy qu'authorisé des
Directeurs de la susd. compagnie Belgique, par commission datée
des $\frac{1}{11}$ Septembre 1676, pour trafficquer avec les peuples de la susdite Acadie et d'autant, que le S.^r van Beuningen cy devant Amb.^r
Ex.^{re} à cette cour, aye au nom de L. H. P. demandé, par une mémoire presenté le $\frac{11}{21}$ Maÿ 1679, reparation et chastiment exem-
plaire dud. exces, et qu'il plaise à Sa Maj.^{té} donner les ordres
necessaires pour relâcher et dedommager le dit Jean Rodes, in-
terdisant à mesme temps ses sujets de ne plus troubler ceux de
L. H. P. dans leur commerce et autres droits dans le susd.^t pais
de l. Acadie et que jusqu'à présent on n'aye eu aucune réponce
sur le susd.^t mémoire.

Le soubsigné Amb.^r 'Ex.^{re} supplie treshumblement Sa Maj.^{té} de vouloir en toute equité et justice terminer sans plus long délay, cette
affaire.

WESTMINSTER, ce $\frac{4}{14}$ d'Aoust, 1679.

Letter from the West India Company to the States-General.

AEN DE HOOGH MOGENDE HEEREN STATEN GENERAEL
DER VEREENIGDE NEDERLANDEN.

HOOGH MOGENDE HEEREN, — Aengesien de Bewinthebberen van
de Generale Geoctr: Westindische Compagnie deser landen, beright
werden, dat seecker capiteyn off commissie vaerder, met name Jur-
rian Aernouts, voerende 't schip genaemt 't Curacaosche vliegende
postpaert, eenigen tydt geleden uyt de haven van Curacao, met be-
hoorlycke commissie van den directeur aldaer is uytgeseylt, omme de
vyanden van desen staet affbreuck te doen, ende dat uyt kraghte van
dien, den voorn: capiteyn vervolgens van de Fransche heeft ingeno-
men ende verovert de forten Penatscop en St. Jan, gelegen op de
riviere Pountegouet alwaer hy eenige van syn volck hebbende gelaten

soo omme de possessie van de voorgedaghte plaetsen te behouden
ende te mainteneren, als wel, omme met de naturellen aldaer te
lande, in rust en vrede te trafficqueren ende te handelen, het gebeurt
is, dat die van Baston, gehoorende onder syne Conincklycke Mayesteyt van Groot Brittannien, hier van jalours synde, sigh niet ontsien
hebben de aldaer geblevene personen, waervan U. Ho. Mog. de
namen des noots gesuppediteert connen werden, vyantlyck aen te
tasten, ende gevanckelyck na Baston voorsz. wegh te voeren, hebbende alvoorens gedestrueert ende ter neder gesmeten de logien ende
seeckere vastigheyt, die de voorn : personen aldaer by provisie opge-
reght ende gemaeckt hadden, contrarie den uytgedruckten text van
het jongste vredens tractact tusschen hoogstgedaghte syne Conincklycke Mayesteyt, ende desen staet gesloten, dicterende, dat naer
expiratie van de respective termynen tusschen de wederzydsche
volckeren ende onderdanen, soo buyten als binnen Europa, in alle
landen, heerschappyen ende plaetsen, van derselver gebiedt aenstonts
sullen comen op te houden, ende verboden syn alle acten van hos-
tiliteyt ende vyantschap ende dat oversulcx ongeoorloft is naer het
sluyten van soo een opreghte vaste en onverbrekelycke vrede directe-
lyck ofte indirectelyck, onder wat prætext het oock soude mogen
wesen, te vernielen, beschadigen, aen te tasten, te bevegten ofte te
spolieren des anders goederen, landen, ofte eenige van de ingesetenen
van dien soo vinden de voorn : Bewinthebberen sigh ampts ende
pligts halven genootdruckt U. Ho. Mo. hiervan by desen kennisse te
geven, ende in aller onderdanigheyt te versoecken, dat het derselver
goede geliefte sy, den heer Ambassadeur extraordinaris van desen
staet by hoogstgedagte syne Conincklycke Mayesteyt, ende aen 't
Hoff van Groot Brittannien voorsz. specialyck aen te schryven ende
te recommanderen, aldaer serieuse instantien ende devoiren aen te
wenden, ten eynde de personen, die in maniere, als vooren naer
Baston gevanckelyck syn weghgevoert, ten alderspoedigsten op vrye
voeten mogen gestelt werden, ende dat voorts meer hoogstgemelte
syne Conincklycke Mayesteyt, die voorsieninge come te doen, ende
alsulcken ordre te beramen, dat van de voors : plaetsen met al den

aencleven van dien, sonder eenigh verhinder ofte empeschement, daer ende sulex behoorlyck is, costeloose en schadeloose restitutie magh geschieden. Twelck doende etc.

Uyt den name van de
Bewinthebberen als boven

C. QUINA.

Letter of the Dutch Ambassador to the Lords of the States-General.

WESTMINSTER, August $\frac{13}{23}$, 1679.

HIGH AND HONORABLE LORDS:

MY LORDS, — Since my last letter I have received the accompanying reply to my memorial, a copy of which was sent to you, the High and Honorable, on the $\frac{1}{13}$th instant, touching the releasing and the indemnification of John Rodes, and also the repairing of the excesses committed by those of the colony of Boston, in taking by force the forts Penatskop and St. John in New Scotland and Acadie, and since I have been informed in person that the position taken in my memorial will need to be proven, as the King has returned it to the Commissioners, to whom it was referred, for the purpose of informing him, and believing that the necessary papers for that purpose are in the hands of the authorized West India Company, I have, therefore, with the permission of you, the High and Honorable, written to them about the matter.

It appears that His Majesty, etc.

High and Honorable

Your humble, obedient, and faithful Servant,

D. V. LEYDEN VAN LEEUWEN.

Here follows the King's reply to the Memorial of the Dutch Ambassador: —

Le roÿ ayant vu un mémoire de son Ex^{ce} Monsieur van Leeuwen Ambassadeur Extra^{re} de Messieurs les Estats Generaux en date du 4me de ce mois contenant une plainte contre la colonie de Boston dans la nouvelle Angleterre, de ce qu'ils ont entrepris de chasser le capitaine Juriaen Aernouts, de ses conquestes, qu'il avoit fait sur les françois en l'année 1674 dans la nouvelle Escosse et l'Accadie, et de demolir les forteresses de Penatscop et S.t Jean situées sur la rivière de Pointegomt, lesquels ledit capitaine avoit aussi pris des françois et de ce que depuis ceux de Boston se sont saisis de la personne, du vaisseau et des marchandises de Jean Rodes, quoy qu' authorisé des Directeurs de la Compagnie Belgique des Indes Occidentales pour traffiquer avec les peuples de la susdite Accadie, et suppliant aussi le Roy de vouloir donner les ordres necessaires pour relâcher ledit Rodes, et interdire à ses sujets de Baston de ne plus molester ceux de Messieurs les Estats dans leur commerce. Sa Maj.té a ordonné de faire cette reponse audit Sieur Ambass.r extra.re qu' elle a desjà donné ordres aux Seigneurs de son conseil députez pour les affaires du commerce et des colonies, de s'informer au plutost de cette affaire, et d'en faire rapport a sa Maj.té afin qu'elle puisse estre terminée selon ce que la justice et la bonne correspondence, que Sa Maj.té veut conserver entre les deux nations, requereront.

Fait au chasteau ROYAL DE WINDSOR, ce 8.me jour d'Aoust, 1679.

SUNDERLAND.

Letter of the Dutch Ambassador to the Lords of the States-General.

WESTMINSTER, October 3, 1679, S. N.

HIGH AND HONORABLE LORDS:

MY LORDS, — In the prosecution which I have been conducting here with reference to the excesses committed against the person of John Rodes, and the ship under his command, and the merchandise, who was provided with a commission from the authorized West India Company, I have at last been informed that as regards this matter and his imprisonment in New York, representation thereof must be made, not to the King, but to His Grace the Duke of York, to whom, in sovereignty, and independent from the crown of England, His Majesty had ceded that country.

I have, therefore, on the occasion when His Royal Highness was present at the Court here, spoken to him about the matter, and I found him favorable disposed to make repairs of excesses committed, with many protestations of good will which said His Royal Highness bore to the State of you, the High and Honorable; and although said Duke assured me that he was entirely ignorant of this matter, and that never any complaint had been made to him about it, yet he agreed to seek all possible information, and after two days he sent his Secretary to me, together with a person who had recently come from New York and was the General Steward of His Highness at that place, who then informed me, and showed me on maps that seemed to be accurately made, that the river St. George was not in Nova Scotia and Accadie but in New England; that consequently the aforesaid John Rodes, nor any other person, could be qualified by the West India Company to trade with the natives on that river; that, therefore, the aforesaid John Rodes, with his ship and goods, although seized upon and brought to New York, had, nevertheless, been released after having been detained only about fourteen days, and the ship and goods, not belonging to the aforesaid John Rodes, but to a certain merchant of New London, had been returned without cost, and that only a fine of ten pounds sterling had been required of him, which was still unpaid; and that with regard to the patents of Sir William Temple, that in these not only the river of St. George was included, but that they also extended to seventy miles along the coast, in which would be included the greatest part of Accadie itself; but that in the year 1670 an agreement had been made with the French, that the river Pontegourt should be the limits, and that so much as lay west of said river should belong to the Duke, and that which is on the East side to the French, in such a manner that the English should manage the said west side of the same river with the natives, and the French the east side, to that extent that His Royal Highnes, as far as it concerned him, would lay no claim to anything East of the river Pontegourt, and could have even witnessed with indifference in case the West India Company had taken Nova Scotia and Accadie from the French, and thereby obtaining certain rights, should have exercised and maintained the same, giving me, furthermore, to understand, that the aforesaid John Rodes did not have the best reputation of being an honest man, but should have committed many dishonest deeds. I have taken a great deal of trouble to get a written statement of what was said, but have been put off until certain papers that were on ship-board at Dover should have been sent hither, and I fear that His Royal Highness shall have left for Brussel before I shall have obtained it [the written statement]. I shall in the meantime not cease to prosecute the claims of repairing the excesses committed by those of Boston in the year 1674, with reference to which the King has appointed commissioners; but these delay the matter, saying that they, by the first chance, will write to Boston for information, and as soon as that arrives they will make report thereof to the King.

I have the treaty, etc.

With which I remain,

High and Honorable Lords.

P. S. I have also sent a copy of this missive to the Directors of the West India Company.

High and Honorable

Your humble, obedient, and faithful servant,

D. V. LEYDEN VAN LEEUWEN.

WESTMINSTER, October 6, 1679, S. N.

HIGH AND HONORABLE LORDS:

MY LORDS, — His Excellency, the Ambassador Jenkins, returning, etc. —

His Royal Highness, the Duke of York, sent to me the day before his departure from here the accompanying answer (see enclosed copy No. 4), in the matter of John Rodes and his ketch, of which matter I gave you, the High and Honorable, an extended account in my last letter of the third instant. I should have been very much pleased if I had seen in the answer the proof that the river Pontegourt was the acknowledged boundary line between what the English and formerly the French had possessed in that quarter of America ; but His Royal Highness has declined to do so, saying that it could not be required of him to make a declaration about the boundary lines, without obtaining further knowledge thereto. I also send copy of this answer to the Directors of the West India Company.

With which I remain,

High and Honorable Lords,

Your, high and honorable, humble, obedient, and faithful servant,

D. v. LEYDEN VAN LEEUWEN.

Copÿ Nº 4.

His Roÿ<u>ll</u> High<u>sse</u> haveing perused a Memoriall from the Extraordinary Ambassadour of the States Gen<u>ll</u> of the United Provinces dated the 19<u>th</u> instant, is pleased to returne this answer thereunto.

That His R<u>ll</u> High<u>sse</u> is informed that St. Georges River, there in mentioned, is unquestionably within the limits of His R<u>ll</u> High<u>sses</u> territoryes, belonging to Pemaquid in America, and is not in Nova Scotia, and hath allwayes beene in the possession of the English.

That ensigne Knapton was command<u>t</u> of the fort at Pemaquid, and its dependancyes, and that he did seise on the person (and ketch) of Jean Rodes, in the s<u>d</u> river of St. George, for presuming to trade there, contrary to act of Parliament, and the lawes of that government, haveing neither passports, cleerings, nor certificates from anÿ English place or port.

That the s<u>d</u> ketch and part of the cargo, being brought to New Yorke, were condemned by due course of law, and in open court, wherein most of the magistrates were Dutchmen originally, though now inhabitants of new Yorke.

Notwithstanding which soe reasonable sentence (the s<u>d</u> Jean Rodes after a very short confinement having allready gotten his libérty) such kindness was used herein, that the s<u>d</u> ketch was restored to the owner and master (John Alden an inhabitant of Boston, from whom the s^d Rodes had hired her, in partnership for a tradeing voyage) and that only ten pounds worth of the cargo was distributed among the souldiers that fetched her from St Georges to Pemaquid, the rest being all returned by inventory, without payment of any Fees or court chardges.

That the truth of this information can plainely be made out, by authenticke papers from New Yorke, for which His R^{ll} High^{sse} (if it be desired) wil give immediate orders, that they may be sent hither by the first opportunity, and if anything farther be necessary for the reasonable satisfaction of the States Generall of the United Provinces or theire extraordinary Ambassad^r touching this matter, His R^{ll} High^{sse} will att all times hereafter readily grant such orders as may most effectually conduce thereunto.

WHITEHALL, 23^d September, 1679.

Letter from the Directors of the West India Company to the Lords of the States-General.

TO THE HIGH AND HONORABLE LORDS STATES-GENERAL OF THE UNITED NETHERLANDS.

HIGH AND HONORABLE LORDS, — The Directors of the general authorized West India Company of these lands did on the 11th of September, 1676, grant to John Rhodes, an Englishman, a commission that he might sail to the coasts and lands of Nova Scotia and Acadia, and furthermore that he might trade with the natives of that country in quietness and peace; yet the Directors aforesaid have learnt by the advises, at least of the aforesaid John Rhodes, that a certain Capt. Napton, being commander of a certain adjacent English fort, had hostilely prevented him from doing so, and had taken him, John Rhodes, prisoner, besides seized his ship and its cargo under pretence that by virtue of the aforesaid commission he had no right to come there, nor to trade, notwithstanding the aforesaid coasts and lands of Nova Scotia and Acadie in the year 1674, by the

Capt. Jurriaan Aernoutsz, commanding the frigate called the Flying Horse of Curaçao, and was provided with a Commission from His Highness, the Prince of Orange, in name of the aforesaid Company, were taken from the French, and consequently, by the right of war, became the property of that Company ; therefore, the aforesaid Directors have felt compelled to inform by these presents you, the High and Honorable, thereof, which we do in all obedience, and humbly pray that His Excellency, the Ambassador Extraordinary, in behalf of this State at the Court of England, may be informed and advised to use all diligence and every obligation with the King, to the end that not only the aforesaid John Rhodes may again be set at liberty, and his ship and goods be released without cost and without damage ; but that also His Royal Highness will please provide and enact such an order, that the aforesaid West India Company may hold quietly and peacefully possession of the aforesaid coasts and lands, so that this Company, or any one who may have been sent there by them, or may be sent, shall not again be troubled or hindered in any manner whatsoever in maintaining the aforesaid possession.

The doing of which, etc.

In behalf of the Directors as above.

C. QUINA.

INDEX.

INDEX.

The names of authors, publications, and other authorities, cited in this volume, are placed alphabetically in the Index under the words *Authorities Cited ;* names of places, towns, and cities, under the word *Places ;* Kings and Queens, under the word *Sovereigns.* Academic degrees are omitted.

406
Index.
Hubbard's Troubles with the Indians, 217.

Hume's England, 80, 91, 94, 95, 127, 128.

Hutchins's Dorset, 90, 96.

Hutchinson Collection, 117, 133, 142, 295, 322.

Hutchinson's Massachusetts, 115, 133, 136, 158, 227, 229.

Independent Chronicle, 263.

Jenness's Isles of Shoals, 85.

Jenness's First Planting of New Hampshire, 111, 178, 332.

Jenness's Original Documents, 117, 119, 183, 193, 291, 292.

Jewitt's Plymouth (Eng.), 92.

Jordan Memorial, 112.

Josselyn's Voyages, 97.

Lansdowne MSS., 106.

London Morning Chronicle, 235.

Longfellow's Poems of Places, 123.

Lower's Family Names, 67, 76.

Lyson's Devon, 70, 93.

Lyson's Magna Britannia, 78, 80, 81, 90.

Markham's Voyages, 87.

Massachusetts Archives, 116, 134, 150, 164, 167, 200, 203–206, 211, 229, 230, 308, 318, 341, 343, 345, 347–352, 355, 385.

Massachusetts Historical Society Collections, 120, 130, 166, 199, 201, 203, 204, 286, 310–312, 383.

Massachusetts Historical Society Proceedings, 17, 35, 46, 50, 52, 163, 170, 178, 181, 197, 200, 217, 256, 271, 277, 288, 290, 291.

Massachusetts Records, 102, 133, 136, 150, 152, 197, 200, 201, 211.

Mather's Magnalia, 164, 171, 204, 218, 219.

Mather's Parentator, 310, 320.

Maine Historical Society Collections, 82, 96, 102, 117, 118.

Memorials English and French Commissaries, 129, 132.

Moore's Devonshire, 70.

Murdoch's Nova Scotia, 130, 139, 200.

Narrative and Critical History of America, 129.

New England Historical and Genealogical Register, 30, 31, 35, 89, 106, 110, 118, 130, 148, 219, 236, 288, 292, 296, 322.

New Hampshire Historical Society Collections, 118, 175, 189, 202, 203, 205, 210–212.

New Hampshire Provincial Papers, 104, 105, 120, 178, 205, 206, 208, 211, 212, 218, 330.

New Hampshire Town Papers, 102.

Newport Gazette, 263.

New York Colonial Documents, 132, 141, 218, 312, 324, 325.

New York, Documentary History of, 170, 200, 206, 231.

Nouvelle Biographie Générale, 74.

Palfrey's New England, 102, 105, 115, 117, 120, 198, 291, 296, 309, 324.

Parsons's Pepperrell, 229.

Perry's Papers relating to the Church in Massachusetts, 322.

Pole's Devon, 70.

Polwhele's Devonshire, 70.

Popham Memorial, 83, 89.

Portsmouth (N. H.) Records, 111.

Prince Collection, 296, 304.

261 ; proceeds to Halifax with the royal forces, 261 ; commissioned Lieutenant-General, 262; displays valor at the capture of Fort Washington, 262 ; becomes Baron Percy, 263; takes part in the capture of Newport, R. I., 263 ; having been accused by Gen. Howe of disobeying orders, he obtains leave of absence and returns to England, 263; tributes to his character and conduct in America, 263 ; his generosity, 263, 264; moves the address in the House of Lords to the King, and defends the officers of the army in America, 264; his speech in moving the address, 264 ; his second marriage, 265; his letter to the Rt. Hon. George Ross, complaining of neglect by the ministry, 265; resigns the colonelcy of his regiment, and becomes commander of the Grenadier Guards, 265; succeeds his father as Duke of Northumberland, 266; made General in the army, and Knight of the Garter, 266; on account of illness withdraws from public view, 266; his last years, 266; organizes and supports a large body of yeomanry as a military force, 266; his annual income, 266; his death and burial, 267 ; his children, 267.

Pettit, Thomas, 333.

Philip's War, 150, 152.

Phillips, John, 335.

Phillipps, Sir Thomas, 321.

Pickering, Charles W., xvi.

Pickering, Capt. John, 183, 208, 211, 212, 214, 330.

Pigot, Col. Sir Robert, Bart., 256.

Pike, Rev. John, 170, 171.

Pike, Major Robert, 200, 201, 204.

Pim (or Pym), Charles, 281.

Pim (or Pym), Mrs. Elizabeth (Randolph), 281, 290.

Pinckhame, Richard, 334.

Places:—

Albany, N. Y., 170, 236.

Amsterdam, Neth., 295, 296, 300, 301, 377, 380, 381.

Annapolis, Md., 320.

Ashton Court, Eng., 96.

Ashton Phillips, Eng., 95.

Athlone, Ire., 245.

Bangor, Eng., 283.

Barbados, 107, 109, 273, 299, 302, 325, 339, 340.

Battcombe, Eng., 106, 107

Beckenham, Eng., 265.

Bermuda, 49, 280.

Berwick, Me., 109, 217.

Betchworth, Eng., 232.

Beverly, Mass., 307.

Biddeford, Me., 110.

Biddenden, Eng., 285.

Boston, Mass., 12, 16, 27, 34, 39, 45, 54, 57, 101, 102, 111, 131, 133, 135, 136, 138, 141-148, 152, 164, 169, 170, 184, 186, 201, 204, 211, 218, 226, 227-234, 237, 238, 241-244, 252-262, 271, 286, 288, 291-293, 296, 300-304, 311, 312, 318-320, 326, 331, 343-358, 363, 364, 370, 382, 386-388.

Bosworth Field, Eng., 91.

Breda, Neth., 128, 129.

Brighton, Mass., 233.

Bristol, Eng., 283.

Bristol, Me., 110.

Brookline, Mass., 54.